Help us Rate this book...
Put your initials on the
Left side and your rating
on the right side.
1 = Didn't care for
2 = It was O.K.
3 = It was great

	1 (2) 3
	(1) 2 3
	1 2 3
	1 2 3
	1 2 3
	1 2 3
	1 2 3
	1 2 3
	1 2 3
	1 2 3
	1 2 3
	1 2 3
	1 2 3
	1 2 3
	1 2 3

DEMCO 38-296

DATE DUE

FEB - 4 2013	NOV 2 8 2018
FEB 2 3 2013	MAR 0 4 2019
MAR 0 6 2013	FEB 1 5 2022
MAR 1 6 2013	
JUN 1 8 2013	
AUG 1 3 2013	
APR 1 1 2014	
JUL 1 0 2014	
JUL 2 8 2015	
JAN - 4 2016	
MAR 2 5 2016	
JUN 2 1 2016	
AUG 1 9 2016	
JAN 3 0 2017	
FEB 1 3 2017	

Published by:
Jamie McGuire, LLC
1016 Saybrook Drive
Enid, OK 73703

FIRST EDITION

Cover design by Justin McGuire

Library of Congress Cataloging-in-Publication Data

Jamie McGuire
Providence
ISBN 0-615-41717-5
ISBN 978-0-615-41717-2 (13 digit)

For Beth, who gave Providence its wings,

And for Mom, who provided the wind for it to fly

Contents

Chapter One
Loss and Found

The average daughter respects her father. She might regard him as her hero, or she may place him so high on a pedestal that no object of her affection could ever compare. To me, my father deserved more than respect, or loyalty, or even love. I had a reverence for him. He was more than Superman; he was God.

One of my earliest memories was of two men cowering in my father's office as he spoke words I didn't understand. His verdict was always final and never argued with. Not even death could touch him.

When I answered my phone on December 14th, that reality came to an end.

"Nina," my mother sighed, "he doesn't have much time. You should come now."

I set the phone beside me on the bed, careful to keep my hands from trembling so much that it tumbled to the floor. The past few weeks had been an alternate universe for me, as I had been faced with one horrible call after another. The first from a nurse at the hospital informing me of my father's car accident. My number was the most recently dialed on his cell phone, leaving me with the horrifying task of being the one to break the news to my mother. In his last days, when reports of no improvement were replaced with gentle suggestions to prepare for the inevitable, I was thankful to be at the receiving end of the phone calls.

It felt strange to walk across the room and grab my coat and keys. The tasks seemed too mundane to begin the journey to say goodbye to my father. I lamented the ordinary life that seemed so long ago as I walked out to my car and turned the ignition.

My father had risen to the top of the shipping industry ruling with an iron fist, but I knew the gentle side of him. The man that left important meetings to take my trivial phone calls, kissed my scrapes, and rewrote fairytales so that the princess always saved the prince. Now he lay helpless in his bed, fading away in the vast bedroom he shared with my mother.

Our housekeeper, Agatha, greeted me at the front door. "Your mother's expecting you, Love. You best get upstairs."

Agatha took my coat, and then I climbed the stairs, feeling the bile rise higher in my throat with every step.

His private nurse brushed past me as I entered the room, and I winced at the sight of him. His face was sallow with a thin sheen of perspiration, and his usually clean shaven jaw was darkened with whiskers that crowded his parched lips. My mother spoke soft, comforting words to him as his chest heaved with every labored breath. The muted beeps and humming of the pumps and monitors were the background music to my worst nightmare.

Like the other times I'd visited my father since his accident, my legs transformed into deep-seeded roots that tunneled through my shoes and plunged into the wooden floor. I couldn't go forward or retreat.

My mother looked up with weary heartbreak in her eyes. "Nina," she called. "Come, dear."

Her hand lifted to summon me forward but my feet wouldn't move. She sighed in understanding and walked toward me, her arm still reaching out in front of her. I couldn't take my eyes off of my father's feeble attempts to breathe as she cupped her fingers around each of my shoulders and eased me forward. After a few reluctant steps, I stopped again.

"I know," she whispered.

Peeling my shoes from the floor, I let her guide me to his bedside. My first instinct was to help him, but the only thing left to do was to wait for his suffering to end.

"Jack, darling," my mother said in a soothing tone. "Nina's here."

After watching him struggle for sufficient breath, I leaned down to whisper in his ear. "I'm here, Daddy."

His breath skipped a bit and he mumbled inaudibly.

"Don't try to talk. Just rest." My shaking fingers reached out to his hand. "I'm going to stay with you."

"Cynthia?" My father's attorney and friend, Thomas Rosen, called to my mother from the back corner of the room. With a pained expression she glanced at my father, clutched me to her chest for a moment, and then quietly walked to Thomas' side. Their voices became a stream of humming no louder than the machines attached to my father.

He sucked in another breath while I tenderly swept his salt and pepper hair away from his moist brow. "Neen...," he swallowed, "Nina."

My eyes wandered to my mother, who was in silent conversation, searching her face one last time for a sign of hope. Seeing the sorrow in her eyes, I looked back to my father and prepared to say goodbye.

"Daddy," I began, but words failed me. My eyes closed as the urge to ease his suffering grew insistent. A faltering breath escaped from my chest and I started again. "I should tell you that it's okay... that you don't have to stay for me, but I can't."

His breathing slowed. He was listening to me.

"I don't want be the one to let you go, Daddy. I want you to get better, but I know that you're tired. So if you want to sleep...I'll be okay." The corners of his mouth shook as they attempted to turn up.

My mouth smiled as my face crumpled around it. "I'll miss you, Daddy. I'm going to miss you so much." I sucked in another breath and he did the same, but his was different this time. He had no more fight left in him.

I glanced back to my mother, who watched me with heavy, wet eyes. He took in another deep breath and slowly exhaled. His life slipped away as the last bit of oxygen left his lungs. The sound reminded me of a tire losing air, slow and level until there was nothing left. His body relaxed, and his eyes became vacant and unfocused.

The nurse silenced the solid tone of the heart monitor while I scanned his peaceful face. The realization that my father was gone washed over me in waves. My insides wrenched, and my arms and legs felt foreign, as if they no longer belonged to me. I nodded and smiled, ignoring the tears that spilled over my cheeks. He trusted my words, and so he let go.

Thomas touched my shoulder and moved to the head of the bed. He reached over to place his hands over my father's eyes and whispered something beautiful in Hebrew. I leaned over my father's chest and hugged him. For the first time in my life, he didn't hug me back.

Looking down into my hands, I scanned the obituary from the funeral. Separated by a dash, the dates of my father's birth and death were displayed in elegant font on the front cover. I grimaced with the recognition that such a short line of ink was meant to signify his life.

The paper fit snugly in the inside pocket of my coat just as the wet sloshing of bus tires approached, slowing to a stop in front of me.

The door opened, but I didn't look up. The sounds of commuters stepping out onto the sidewalk never came. My neighbors had little need for public transportation, specifically so late in the evening. Those that used it at all were the hired service that worked in the colossal residences nearby.

"Miss?"

The bus driver cleared his throat to get my attention, and when I falled to acknowledge him, the door swept shut. The air breaks released, and the bus slowly pulled away from the curb. I tried not to think about the day that had just taken place, but my memory became saturated with it.

Just as I did in childhood, I rocked back and forth to comfort myself. The warm peach hue had long since left my fingers, reminding me of my father's folded hands as he lay in his coffin.

A frigid breath of air flooded my lungs and my chest heaved, giving way to the sob that had been clawing its way to the surface. I had thought moments before that my eyes couldn't cry anymore, and I wondered how much more I would have to endure before my body would finally be too exhausted to continue.

"Cold night, huh?"

I sniffed and shot an annoyed glance to the man settling into the space next to me. I hadn't heard him approach. He breathed on his hands, rubbed them together and then offered a reassuring grin.

"I guess," I answered.

He looked down at his watch and sighed. "Damn it," he muttered under his breath. "Guess we missed the last bus."

He pulled a cell phone from the pocket of his black motorcycle jacket and dialed. He greeted someone and then requested a taxi.

"Did you want to share a cab?" he asked.

I peered over at him, immediately suspicious. His blue-grey eyes narrowed as he raised one eyebrow at my expression. I must have looked like a maniac, and he was reconsidering his offer.

I folded my arms, suddenly feeling the discomfort of winter breaking through my coat, seeping into my skin, piercing through to my bones. I had to get back to school; I still had a paper to write.

"Yes. Thank you," I said with a shaky voice.

After an awkward moment of silence, the man spoke again. "You work around here?"

"No." I hesitated to continue the conversation but found myself curious. "You?"

"Yes."

How odd. He didn't look like hired help. I glanced at his watch out of the corner of my eye. Definitely not help.

"What do you do?"

He didn't answer right away. "I'm...involved in the home security sector," he nodded, seeming to agree with himself.

"I'm a student," I offered, trying to clear the ridiculous quivering in my voice.

He stared at me with an expression I couldn't quite decipher, and then looked forward again. He was older than I, though not by more than five or six years. I wondered if he knew who I was. There was a glimmer of familiarity in his eyes, though I couldn't quite place it.

His cell phone vibrated, and he opened it to read a text message. He attempted to hide an emotion and then snapped the phone closed without replying, and didn't speak again until the cab arrived.

He opened the door for me, and I scooted over to the farthest end of the seat while he slid in behind the driver.

"Where to?" the cabbie asked in a throaty voice.

"Brown University," I instructed. "Please."

"Uh-Huh. One stop?"

"No," my unanticipated companion said.

I noted that he was careful not to mention his address, and that struck me as odd. Maybe it wasn't odd at all; maybe I was more curious about him than I would have liked to admit. I was surprised that I had noticed anything at the moment, and found myself grateful to this stranger for the diversion he'd inadvertently created for me.

"I'm Jared by the way," he grinned, holding his hand out to take mine.

"Nina."

"Wow, your hands are freezing!" he said, clasping his other hand over mine.

I pulled my hand away, noting his exceptionally warm grip. I watched him for a moment, listening to any inner voices that might have sensed danger, but the only feeling that stood out was curiosity.

With the realization of his offense, he apologized with a small smile. I tucked my hair behind my ears and stared out the window. The wind whipped around outside, blowing the collecting flakes across the road like white snakes slithering ahead. I shivered at the image and pulled my coat tighter around me.

"Brown, huh?" Jared asked. His cell phone vibrated in his pocket and he flipped it open once again.

I nodded. "Brown." He continued to look at me so I offered more. "Business major."

The residual frustration from the unwanted caller melted away once our eyes met. It seemed as if he'd just noticed I'd been crying.

"Are you all right?"

I looked down, picking at my nails. "We buried my father today." It occurred to me that I had no idea why I was sharing such personal information with a stranger.

"You were close," Jared said. It was more of a statement than a question.

I waited for the expected pity in his eyes, but there was none. My relief caused me to smile which in turn made a grin turn up one side of his mouth. I noticed then that he had a nice face. It was more than nice, now that it had come to my attention. He was quite attractive, really....

"Where's your place?" The cabbie squawked. I peeled my eyes from Jared and pointed in the direction of my dorm. "East Andrews Hall."

The cab pulled in, and Jared automatically stepped out. As soon as his door had shut, mine opened.

"Thank you," I said.

"It was nice to meet you, Nina." There was an edge to his words. It went beyond politeness or even sincerity. He spoke the words with conviction.

I nodded and sidestepped toward my dorm. He paused before getting into the cab to smile at me once more, and for the first time in weeks I felt something other than hollow. I watched the cab pull away and then turned against the wind to walk toward Andrews.

Once inside my room, I noticed my appearance in the mirror and gasped. Good God, it was no wonder that Jared felt compelled to come to my aide! I looked like a homeless, desperate crack addict overdue for my next fix! My brush ripped through my blonde bob and I pulled my bangs straight back, pinning them away from my face. I went to the sink and scrubbed away the smeared mascara and streaky foundation.

With a frown, I pulled my cell phone from my pocket and pressed the speed dial to call my mother.

"Nina?" she answered.

"Back in my room, Mom."

She sighed. "Good. You know I don't like for you to take the bus. Robert could have driven you. Take two of those pills I gave you today, all right? They'll help you sleep."

I rolled my eyes. My mother: the frequent flier of Providence drug stores.

"I'll probably fall asleep the second my head hits the pillow." Not the pure truth, but it would do to keep my personal pharmacist at bay.

"Okay, Darling. Sleep well."

My dorm room seemed smaller. The white walls were pitifully empty on my side. Feeling I was being watched, I peeked across the room at my roommate. Her side of the room was covered in posters of teddy bears and team colors. My decor consisted of an ornamental frame on my night table displaying a picture of me and my parents at high school graduation just a few months before.

"How's your mom?" Beth asked from under her baby pink comforter.

"She's...sad."

"How are you?"

"The same," I sighed. My conclusive tone seemed to relax Beth, and while I changed into my pajamas I noticed her breathing even out.

I sat on my bed and pulled myself against the pillows. My thoughts effortlessly moved toward the last hour. Jared's grin kept my mind occupied for a while, but before long my thoughts brought me back to the funeral. I rolled onto my side and curled into a ball, trying to cry quietly. Relief finally replaced the crushing grief as I slipped out of consciousness.

I turned to the side and blinked my eyes, noting the large, red numbers on the clock. Five A.M. had come quickly. My eyes felt swollen and scratchy. It was then that I realized my dreams had been cruel. There would be no miracles, and my father was still gone.

The finale of the worst experience of my life hadn't ended with what was supposed to be my closure.

I clambered from my bed and opened my laptop, determined to finish my term paper by eight. The screen lit up, and I peered over at Beth, her head buried under her pillow. My fingers tapped out the next cross-reference and soon began a muted symphony of clicking against the keyboard.

The paragraphs formed swiftly and I finished by a quarter after seven. With a click of the mouse, the printer lurched and buzzed with its new task. I looked over at Beth, knowing a newspaper press wouldn't wake her. I gathered my toiletries to make my daily commute down the hall to the showers.

Red-faced and sufficiently exfoliated, I tightened my robe and walked down the hall. While brushing my teeth over the quaint sink in our room, Beth sat up in bed and stretched out her arms. Her chin-length auburn hair was smashed in some places, and stuck out in others.

"Good morning," she chirped. Then reality set in. "Oh...I mean...."

"It's okay, Beth. It is a nice morning." Glancing out the window, I noticed the sky was looking bleaker from the onset, but I wasn't going to mention that.

Beth smiled and began making her bed, setting her stuffed animals haphazardly in front of her frilly pillow.

"Are you going to the game Saturday?" she asked.

"I don't know. Maybe."

She usually invited me to go, and at times insisted I go, always in her cheery, pleasant voice. Beth hailed from the South. She worked hard and had been awarded numerous scholarships to make her escape from the small Oklahoma town she called home. Her side of the room was covered in trophies, sashes and crowns from the numerous pageants she'd entered and won. She wasn't the typical beauty queen. Although beautiful, she seemed very introverted—a trait she was trying desperately to break away from. She explained to me the day we moved in that the pageants were a necessary evil for tuition.

"Well, I'll give you a break this week if you decide to opt out. I'd understand with finals and...everything else," she conceded without looking in my direction.

"I appreciate it."

I pulled my hair back into a small burst of ponytail at the nape of my neck, looking like a bouquet of wheat shooting out from the back of my head. I sighed at my closet and gave myself a pep talk before dressing in the inevitable layers: one after another; bra, tank top, undershirt, sweater, socks, jeans, boots, coat—and not always in that order.

With my backpack bursting at the seams, I pulled up the handle and angled the bag onto its wheels.

"I'm going early for coffee."

Beth smiled as she booted up her laptop. "Good luck getting that thing across the ice."

I stepped out of the elevator into the hallway wondering if Beth was right about the weather. I held my breath and pushed the door open, waiting for the freezing temperature to sting my face. The wind blew the heavy glass door against me, working against the already pitiful pressure I had managed with one hand. Using my arm and shoulder, I forced the door open and gasped at the frigid burst of air burning my face.

I stumbled into the dining hall the student populace affectionately and appropriately dubbed "The Ratty", and brushed off my coat. Shuffling across the muted tile floor, I made a beeline for the coffee pot. I filled my travel mug almost to the brim and mixed in my favorite hazelnut creamer and two packets of Splenda.

"That stuff is death in a package, you know," Kim said from behind me.

"You sound like my mother," I grumbled.

"I'm surprised you came today. Sucks that your dad died during finals."

Kim was never one for holding back or mincing words. I usually found it very refreshing, but I hadn't had time to brace myself before the words left her lips, and my ribs wrenched in response.

"Yeah."

Kim watched me for a moment, and then shoved a blueberry corn muffin at my face.

"Breakfast?"

I shook my head, uncrossing my eyes from looking at the muffin. "No, thanks. I need to get to class."

"I'll walk with you," she said, pulling the muffin back.

Kim pulled a faded, red plaid hunter's cap complete with ear covers over her short brown hair. If I thought I could laugh, I would have.

"Oh, Kim," I said, attempting to make my voice sound cautious.

"What?" she asked, stopping in her tracks.

"Nothing," I shook my head, deciding to leave it alone.

If any hat could be made for Kim, it was the ridiculous atrocity she'd placed on her head. Kim was above average in height, a head taller than my five feet, seven inches. Her short, caramel-colored hair framed her face in care free waves. Crazy and unpredictable as she was, people were drawn to her. I knew we would be friends the moment I met her in the hallway of Andrews; I couldn't fathom having someone more interesting in my life.

Kim walked with me across campus to class, keeping my mind from more somber thoughts by regaling me with her most recent week of fantastic mishaps and blunders. She never failed to entertain me with her unbridled honesty and lack of brain-to-mouth filter.

Once in class, Kim leaned toward me and kept her voice low. "So, the funeral...."

I squirmed in my seat. "I...don't really want to...."

"Oh, right. Yeah. So...it was yesterday?" Unlike Beth, Kim didn't avoid unpleasantness. At times she seemed to slam face first into it with a smile on her face.

"Yes," I sighed. "It was very nice."

"Very nice," Kim echoed, nodding. "I tried to call you last night. You didn't answer."

"I didn't get in until late. I missed the last bus and ended up taking a cab."

Kim eyed me with disbelief. "The last bus? I didn't know public transportation had a curfew." I considered that for a moment before she continued. "Why didn't you drive? Your mother picked you up, didn't she?"

"I ended up sharing a cab."

"With your mom?"

"No, Kim. Not with my mom," I deadpanned. "I met a man at the bus stop. We both missed the bus." I didn't confess that I'd had a momentary conscious black out and let the bus pull away.

"You shared a cab with some random guy at the bus stop? Interesting."

"Not everyone's stories end with a dramatic punch line like yours. We just shared a cab," I said, trying to make my answer sound final.

"Was he old?"

I rolled my eyes. "No."

"Ugly?"

"No, Kim. He was nice."

"I didn't ask if he was nice. So...he was cute, young...and?"

"Jack's funeral was yesterday, Kim. I was a mess," I said, feeling my eyebrows pull together.

"Why do you do that?"

"Do what?" I asked, exasperated.

"Call your dad 'Jack'? I thought you were close?"

"We are. We were. I don't know...because that's his name?" Kim stared at me, unimpressed with my answer. I began again, "It's always felt weird calling him Dad to other people. Just like I wouldn't call a boyfriend 'Honey' to you. It's just...personal."

"That's weird, Nina."

"Well, you are the authority on weird."

Kim nodded, unaffected by my insult. "So who was the mystery guy? Does he go here?"

"I don't think so. His stop was after mine," I murmured, rolling my pen between my fingers.

Because my stop was first, I was curious if he lived near the university, and if I might run into him again. I cringed at the thought of that prospect. What would I possibly say to him? "Hi, Jared. Remember me? The Alice Cooper look-alike that you shared an awkward cab ride with for twenty minutes?"

"What's with the face?" Kim's expression screwed in a way I could only assume mirrored my own.

"Nothing. I just...," I shrugged, "he probably thought I was nuts."

"That could possibly be the most boring story I've ever heard," Kim said, deflated.

"I tried to spare you the non-details. He did have a cute smile, though," I mused.

Kim looked up at me with renewed interest and opened her mouth to say something, but Professor Hunter walked in the room. I hadn't noticed the numerous empty seats. Some of the students were tossing their papers on his desk and leaving the way they came instead of meandering to their seats as usual.

"What are you still doing here? Turn in your papers and get out. Your grades will be posted on the web site. Happy Holidays," he said to those of us still peppered across the room.

As finals week came to an end, the nightly ritual of curling into a ball to cry seemed to be a permanent fixture in my life. The first week of break, I had a bit more control over the emptiness when it hit. After that, there were a few nights that I escaped the sadness all together. The grief found new strength Christmas night, but to my relief falling asleep without tears became a bit easier after the holidays came to a close.

I found it disconcerting that although time provided some relief, I was also further from when Jack was a part of my life. Each passing day was that much longer since I'd been able to call him or hear his voice. With time, relief and apprehension intertwined.

When the spring semester began, Jared had become a blurred image from a day I wanted to file away, so it was a surprise to see him standing a few feet away from me in line at the Urban Outfitters off campus. I wasn't confident that it was him at first, but when he accepted his receipt from the sales person and turned, I stared at him long enough to be certain. He didn't suffer from the same hesitation that I did.

"Nina?"

I felt my eyebrows rise while I tried to think of something besides 'yes' to reply with. My mouth opened, but nothing came out.

He pointed at his chest like he was speaking to a deaf mute. "I'm Jared. We shared a cab?" He patiently waited for me to recall his face, and I realized I hadn't forgotten an inch of it.

"I thought that was you," I said, trying a polite smile. Something was wrong with my throat. It felt dry, and as if I was drowning in my own saliva at the same time. I swallowed hard and tried to remember how not to be a ridiculous teenaged undergrad.

Jared's expression skipped from relief to elation as a broad smile appeared across his face. A warm feeling bubbled up from my chest into my face, and I felt the heat release from my cheeks.

Oh, God, don't blush! I thought to myself. But it was too late. I had no idea how to recover. "You seem to be having a better day. Made it to the bus on time and all that?"

"Something like that," I mumbled. "How is the security business?"

"Interesting." A glimmer touched his eyes that I wasn't quite sure how to translate.

Our attention was simultaneously drawn to the phone vibrating in his jacket pocket. He smiled apologetically before reaching down to silence the distraction.

"Did you have a pleasant Christmas?" I tried not to cringe once the words left my mouth. Ugh. So unimaginative, I thought.

"Something like that," he quoted.

I smiled at his teasing. He seemed so comfortable around me. I wasn't sure if it was confidence or that he was just one of those people that could carry on a conversation with anyone and make them feel he'd known them for years.

I raised the silver sweater tunic in my hands. "Birthday shopping for my mother."

A man behind me cleared his throat, and I realized that we were holding up the line. Jared smiled and took a step backward toward the register. I realized our conversation wasn't over, and I turned my attention to the red-haired girl behind the counter, trying to conceal my enthusiasm.

She handed me the receipt, and Jared accompanied me outside. He stared down into my eyes, warmly scanning my face. I didn't remember him being quite so tall. He towered over me, at least six feet two inches. How had I not noticed the incredible color of his eyes? They seemed to glow as he watched me fidget.

"Are you from Providence?" I asked.

"I am," he said, seeming amused by my awkwardness.

"Did you go to Brown?"

"No."

If his eyes weren't so animated by the conversation, I would have guessed by his short answers that it was my cue to excuse myself with my tail tucked between my legs.

"Really? I'm trying to place you. It seems like we've met before." Did I just issue him a pick up line? Fantastic, I've now sunk to the level of desperate teenage boys everywhere.

"I don't think so. That's not something I would forget," he said. "I was just going to grab a bite to eat at the end of the block. Would you join me?"

I thought I had said yes, but he continued to stare at me expectantly.

"Nina?"

"Yes? I mean yes. That would be great." I tried to smile through my humiliation and wondered if I was always so articulately clumsy. I couldn't imagine why he was still speaking to me.

We walked to the end of the block to cross the street at the light. Jared guided me forward with his hand on the small of my back, and looked all around us as we crossed. I stifled a giggle; he reminded me of the President's security detail. The only thing missing was a communication device in his ear and standard issue black Ray–Bans.

Jared opened the door for me. I had seen the restaurant several times, with it being close to campus, but I'd never ventured in.

"You'll like it," he assured me. I paused in a thought wondering if I'd said anything out loud.

"Welcome to Blaze," the hostess said, motioning to us that she could seat us immediately. The waitress appeared a few moments later, and Jared waited for me to order.

"I'll have a Dr. Pepper."

"Make that two," Jared said, raising two fingers. His eyes didn't stray from mine.

The waitress nodded and left us to each other. I was curious if he would have ordered a beer had he not asked a toddler to accompany him.

"I don't think I thanked you for getting me home."

"Actually, you did," he said, putting his elbows on the table and crossing his arms.

"Oh. That night is sort of a blur," I grimaced.

"I'm sorry you lost your dad, Nina. I'm glad I was there."

I tucked my hair behind my ears. "I'm glad you were there, too."

"It probably wasn't the safest idea...sitting alone in the dark. Lots of crazies out there," his tone was casual, but underneath I caught a hint of anxiousness.

"I grew up in that neighborhood. It's safe, I assure you."

He laughed and shook his head. "It's always safe until something bad happens."

The waitress brought our drinks and asked if we were ready to order. Once again, Jared waited for me to begin.

"I'll have the Greek salad," I said. I glanced over at Jared, who studied me with raised eyebrows and a wry smile. I wasn't about to be one of those girls, "And the linguine."

The waitress turned her attention to Jared. "For you?"

"I'll have the house salad with blue cheese and the Shrimp Scampi. And would you bring us some of those sweet potato fries, please?" he said, handing the menu to the waitress. Once she left I looked around the restaurant and then peeked over at Jared, who still hadn't taken his eyes off me.

I floundered for conversation under his stare. Jared's eyes were an incredible blue-grey; they almost glowed against his lightly bronzed skin. His thick brown eyebrows sat atop his almond-shaped eyes and were just slightly darker than his strategically messy dark blonde hair. His natural highlights glimmered in the early afternoon sun that broke through the windows. He was clearly more than just attractive. I wondered again why he was still speaking to me.

"Sweet potato fries?" I asked.

"They're famous. Well, they're famous to me. You have to dip them in these little sauces they give you to fully appreciate them. It's an experience."

"Sweet potato fries," I said, still unsure.

He smiled. "Trust me." His cell phone vibrated, and he flipped it open. It was more than a text message this time; he masked an irritated look and pressed it to his ear.

"Ryel," he answered.

Righ–el? I was fairly sure that was his last name, but I couldn't be certain. He lowered his voice and tilted his head away from me. He was unhappy with the caller, but it was only the tone I could understand; he was speaking what I guessed to be Russian. He was devastatingly handsome, kind, and spoke a second language. If the sweet potato fries turned out to be all that he'd promised, I might have fallen out of my chair.

He became impatient with the person on the other end of the line and hung up the phone.

"Sorry about that," he said.

I shook my head, fielding his apology. "No, it's fine. I just inadvertently learned two new things about you."

His eyes were still focused on mine, but they were a bit fogged over as if his attention was divided between me and the problem with the caller.

"Ryel?" I asked.

"My last name."

"And was that....Russian you were speaking?" I raised my eyebrows.

"Yes," he sighed. His shoulders relaxed as he exhaled. "Doesn't everyone speak a second language these days?"

"You only speak two?" I said, feigning dissatisfaction.

He laughed, and a new twinge formed in my chest. I couldn't get over his smile and how remarkable it was, as if he had come straight out of a magazine.

"I took French in high school. It didn't stick," I said, feeling inferior.

"My dad spoke fluently. I learned from him."

"Oh, your family is from Russia?"

"Er...no," Jared said, looking uncomfortable with the question.

"It was beautiful," I said. "You're very popular. Business must be fantastic."

His eyes tightened as he studied my face. "Business is...," his eyes softened and he leaned in a bit towards me, meeting my gaze, "better than it's been in a long time."

I forced myself to breathe. It felt unnatural when he looked at me like that. "So you enjoy what you do?"

"Some days more than others," he shrugged.

"And today?"

He smiled again. Something was amusing him about our conversation, and I wasn't in on the joke. "Today's a good day."

My attention was diverted to the waitress walking up behind him, bringing our sweet potato fries and salads. Jared looked down at the table and then to me with a calculating grin.

"Feeling brave?"

I leaned over to get a better look inside the woven bowl. "You're making me awfully nervous over a basket of fries. These should be some earth shattering potatoes."

"Truly, potatoes that deserve an introduction." We both laughed. He picked up a few and dipped them in a cup of strange looking goo.

"No ketchup?" I asked, eyeing the misshapen spear in my hand.

Jared wrinkled his nose. "Ketchup is for those who don't want to taste their food."

"Ketchup is for suckers." I concentrated on the basket, my eyebrows pressed together.

Laughter erupted from his throat, and I plunged my fry into the sauce. He took a bite and watched me raise my hand to my mouth. His expression grew playfully anxious as I chewed.

"Not...bad. Pretty good, actually," I said, nodding as I swallowed.

His face was triumphant. We joked and laughed as we eliminated the remaining fries, and politely discussed the weather through our salads. After we finished our entrées, he eyed my empty plate and nodded his head in satisfaction.

"I like a girl with an appetite."

"I have a feeling we'll be good friends, then," I laughed. "That's the first non-Ratty meal I've eaten since I've been back to school. Thanks for bringing me here."

Jared beamed. "It was absolutely my pleasure. I'm glad we ran into each other."

The waitress brought the ticket and Jared scooped it up, placed his card in the pouch and handed it back to her. He looked as if he'd just won the lottery. I couldn't believe that my enjoyment of some alternately flavored French fries had made him so cheerful.

He helped me with my coat. I wasn't the type of girl to enjoy gallantry, but the casual way he went about it made me a tad giddy. I picked up my Urban Outfitters bag, and he followed me outside.

"You walked?" Jared asked.

"I walked." I tucked my hair behind my ears and waited for him to be chivalrous again.

"It's getting colder. Do you mind if I drive you?" he asked, shoving his hands in his jeans pockets.

The grin that swept across my face was uncontainable. "Do you remember where I live?"

"Andrews, right?" he said. I nodded, and he seemed pleased that he could give me the correct answer. "I'm this way," he said, directing me down the street.

Jared parked beside the curb next to my dorm, and I subliminally willed him to ask for my number, for another date, anything. I didn't want to have to wait so long this time before I saw him again.

"Thanks again," I said, stalling.

He smiled, but it wasn't as broad as it was during lunch. He seemed to be as disappointed as I was that our brief encounter was over.

"You're welcome. Truly, the pleasure was mine."

He stepped out and less than a second later, opened my door. I stood to face him and after a small pause, began making the walk to my dorm. A sense of urgency overcame my nervousness and I turned on my heels.

He hadn't moved. Standing in front of his black Escalade, he looked exactly like a security guard. The glass was blacked out, and it looked more like a scene in the Middle East than on a quiet Providence street.

"Jared?" I pulled my cell phone from my purse to ask for his number, but the words left me. I gulped as his eyes pierced through mine. I didn't know if the attraction was mutual, but on my end at least, it was intense.

"We'll run into each other again," he said, grinning. I started to argue, but what could I say? If I wondered aloud how soon that would be, I would sound more desperate than I wanted.

"It was good to see you again, Nina," he said, before disappearing behind the dark tint of his windows.

I smiled and waved, then continued my trek to Andrews.

Chapter Two
Invitation(s)

"It's raining again," Kim grumbled. "That's something new and different." She lit her cigarette and jostled her knees back and forth to ward off the cold. I gave her a disapproving look. "What?" she asked.

"That's really disgusting. My father smoked cigars. I just don't get the appeal."

She shrugged. "There is no appeal. I'm a nonconformist."

"You're a masochist," I said, rolling my eyes.

We waited outside for Beth to finish her class, planning to kidnap her to the nearest coffee shop off campus. A group of students emerged in mass exodus, and I scanned each face. I noticed a shaggy-haired boy break away from the river of students and smile at Kim.

"Hey, Josh," Kim said.

"Hey, Kimmie. Did you get the calculus homework finished?"

Kim shrugged. "I'll do it before class."

Josh's friends meandered closer to us and talked among themselves.

"Nina, this is Josh. We went to high school together in Quincy. He wants to be me when he grows up," Kim teased, playfully punching him in the arm.

Josh laughed and shook my hand. "Only if I get to wear a hat like that."

"It's nice to meet you, Josh."

Josh pointed to each of his friends. "Tucker... Chad...Ryan."

Tucker and Chad nodded in typical boy fashion, but Ryan reached his hand out, first to Kim and then to me.

"Hi... hi," he said to each of us. His eyes lingered on me for a moment.

"So, we're going to The Gate later for pizza if you want to come," Josh said.

"We've already made plans with another girlfriend of ours, but maybe next time," Kim said.

Josh nodded and Chad followed him as he left. Ryan stayed for just a moment and then trailed behind them.

Kim looked at me with her eyebrows raised. "Well. Who says there's no such thing as love at first sight?"

"Quit it," I murmured.

Beth joined us a few moments later.

"It's about time! Gah!" Kim said in her typical dramatic fashion.

Beth laughed. "Who's he?" she asked just as Ryan turned to look at us again.

"Ryan. Friend of a friend. Isn't he dreamy?" Kim said as she nestled against Beth's shoulder.

"You're so...weird!" Beth giggled, pushing Kim away.

Beth and I huddled under an umbrella while Kim walked in the rain unaffected. We reached Kim's elderly Sentra and climbed in, Beth taking the back seat. Kim pretended to say a little prayer and turned the ignition. After a few sickly whirring noises, the engine erupted and Beth clapped.

"Thank you. Thank you," Kim said, ducking her head in little bows.

We crowded the counter and Beth and Kim both scanned the menu.

"I'll have a Grande Café Misto, please." I heard Kim sigh beside me. Unlike me, she refused to have the same drink twice.

I settled into my chair, cupping my drink with both hands. The wind and rain had picked up, and was intermittently beating against the large glass window. Just as Beth sat beside me, the bell above the door clanged and I automatically glanced up.

It was him.

Beth noticed me staring past her and she twisted to see Jared walking to the counter. "Are you okay, Nina?" she asked.

Kim sat down and traded glances with Beth, then pivoted in her seat to see what I couldn't peel my eyes from.

The girl behind the counter cooed. "Well, if it isn't Jared Ryel. Long time no see. How have you been?"

"Things are good, Katie. I'll have the usual," he replied, indifferent to her flirting.

By the time Jared casually turned our way all three of us were staring at him. I was expecting an uncomfortable expression at our gawking, but he smiled.

"Who is that?" Beth asked, clearly impressed.

"That's Jared," Kim said, leaning in and grinning from ear to ear.

"Jared. Who's J –?" Beth whispered.

"Sssh!" I hissed.

"Nina?" Jared called. I thought I detected uncertainty in his voice.

When his eyes met mine, I immediately felt lost. As usual, Kim saved me.

"You must be Jared," Kim said with an impish grin.

"I am," he confirmed, slowly walking the few feet to our table.

"I'm Kim," she reached over and took his hand, shaking it vigorously and not at all ladylike.

"It's...nice to meet you," Jared said, glancing at her briefly before returning his eyes to mine. Confusion draped over his face, and he leaned his head a few inches to the side before speaking to me. "Is everything all right here?"

From my peripheral I could see Beth's eyebrows press together and her eyes shift to me, confused by Jared's behavior.

"Everything's great," I murmured, setting my cup on the table. "How have you been?"

"I've been...fine. Am I interrupting?"

Kim's loud voice rose an octave. "Of course not! Would you like to join us?"

Jared looked at me for a moment and I smiled at him, waiting. I felt a strange adrenaline rush; afraid he would say yes and terrified he would say no.

He looked back to Kim and sighed. "I should be going."

"Couldn't you stay? Just for a minute?" I asked, hopeful.

Jared sighed with what sounded like relief. He looked around him and then pulled a chair to our table. I couldn't contain the excitement I felt and my mouth instantly spread into a smile.

"How could I say no to that?" he asked. I felt my ears get hot.

"Yes, she's very persuasive," Kim said flatly, eyeing me.

I ignored her to introduce both of them properly. "Jared, Kim Pollock. Kim...Jared Ryel. And this is my roommate, Bethany Layne."

Jared extended his hand across the table and briefly shook Beth's hand.

She smiled. "It's just Beth."

Jared nodded. "Nice to meet you, Beth."

"So...how do you know each other?" Beth asked.

"I got her a cab," he said, smiling at me.

"He did. The night of Jack's....we shared a cab," I said, trying to keep the conversation on Jared instead of the circumstances.

"Oh," Beth said. I could see the confusion on her face. It occurred to me that I would have quite a bit of explaining to do later.

"And we had lunch," Jared added.

"You did?" Kim asked, turning to me for confirmation.

Jared chuckled. "I can see it was interesting enough to share."

I fingered the lid of my coffee cup. "He introduced me to that Blaze place on Thayer. It was really good."

"I think it was the company more than anything," Jared said, his eyes softening.

"Sounds like you two had a great time," Beth chirped. She had gotten over the fact that I hadn't let her in on the news and had become slightly over-enthusiastic.

"We did," he said, his eyes focused on mine. "It was good to see you again, Nina, but I have to get going." He stood up and returned the chair to its proper place. I stiffened, wanting to ask him when I would see him again but couldn't find the courage. I settled for relaying my feelings with a disappointed frown.

To my relief, he noticed.

"I'll see you soon," he reassured me, amused at my deflated expression.

"Good," I nodded once.

He strode out just as marvelously as he came in, and I crumpled into the back of my chair. My muscles complained, I hadn't noticed I was so tense. I sipped my coffee and took a deep, relaxing breath.

I had gone from never knowing he existed to inexplicably running into him. My life was suddenly full of these little miraculous surprises, moments I was finding so much happiness in that I was already wondering when the next one would come.

My friends' eyes bored into me. I looked up, conscious of their burning curiosity.

"Yes?" I prompted, smiling innocently.

"Oh please, Nigh. Like you're not swimming in your own freakily potent pheromones right now," Kim said.

"He's really cute," Beth added.

"I guess...if you like the type," I mused, trying to keep my cool.

"If...?" Beth cried. "You mean the well-dressed, gorgeous, movie-star type that is polite and interested in you? You mean that type?"

Kim laughed. "You are being ridiculously calm about this, considering while he was here you had the personality of a clam."

"I did not!"

"She could have shot coffee out of her nose and he still would have stayed," Beth giggled.

"He's not cute. He's angelic," I sighed, dwelling on every detail of him.

Kim joined Beth's giggling and all three of us erupted in laughter.

Over the next few days, every time I stepped off campus I watched for him. Beth and I went for coffee more than once, and I was shamefully preoccupied. I would answer when prompted and nod my head in the acceptable places of conversation, but she and I both knew I was anticipating my next moment with Jared.

I couldn't believe how annoying I'd become over a man I barely knew. I was not one of those girls who became wrapped up in such things, and truth be told I lost patience easily with those that did. When I caught myself searching for him in every store, every restaurant and coffee shop I frequented, I scolded myself.

Five days of this ridiculous behavior paid off.

The sun disappeared behind the horizon as Beth and I waited by pump four of Eastside Shell gas station. I yawned out of boredom, listening to the pump clicking with every dollar I put in. Beth wrinkled her nose at the smell and I mirrored her expression.

"What?" she asked.

"Nothing. I just love this smell and you look like you just took a whiff of an Oklahoma pig farm. Bringing back harsh memories?"

"Hilarious." She looked up and a large grin spread across her face.

"And I thought you were going to be a poor sport," I said, surprised at her expression.

"Hi, Jared," Beth said, smug.

I flipped around and there he was, standing on the other side of the pump looking just as stunned and elated as I felt.

"This is getting spooky," Jared said.

"Hi to you, too," I said, letting my delight to see him show.

"How are classes going?" he asked.

"Good. How's business?" I smiled. I'm getting better at this, thank God, I thought. I finally felt somewhat normal around him.

"It's a good day," he said, smiling his incredible smile. It absolutely was. "That's a nice car," he gestured with a nod.

"Thanks."

One of the few grandiose things my father had purchased for me was my white BMW. He had bought it as a graduation present, and aside from the Peridot and diamond ring he had bought for my sixteenth birthday, it was my most prized possession. Normally I didn't put much stock in the ostentatious things my father bought, but this was special; it had been given with the proud-father expression that I relished.

"Going somewhere?" I asked.

"Why?" He cocked his head, confused at my question.

"You look like you're headed to a hot date or something."

He laughed. "No...no date. How about you? Anyone forcing strange cuisine on you this evening?"

"I don't do that for just anyone," I said, raising an eyebrow. I was impressed with how I sounded, so much braver than I felt.

He beamed. "Is that so?"

I pulled my receipt from the gas pump and looked at Beth, who pretended not to watch. He walked over to me, stuffing his hands in his pockets.

"How would you like to put that to the test, then?" he asked.

"Is that a challenge or are you asking me to dinner?" I prompted, looking him square in the eye. I didn't know where my sudden courage and sass came from, but it was less humiliating than the gaucheness I demonstrated the last two times I had seen him.

"Both," he smiled. He leaned his side against my car, just inches from me. I tried to seem relaxed, although my heart was pounding in my chest over his proximity.

My face twisted into a frown as I realized my dilemma. "I have study group tonight."

He didn't look ruffled, to my chagrin. "Maybe next time."

He walked back to his Escalade and left without another word. I flipped around to Beth and she ducked into the passenger side. The door slammed behind me as I sat next to her.

"What was that?" Beth asked.

"I don't know."

Beth's eyes widened in disbelief. "You passed up a date with him for study group? You've wanted to run into him for a week!"

"I can't just break my plans anytime he asks me out. How would that look?" I insisted, frowning at the thought of him thinking I was that accessible.

Beth shrugged. "Who cares?"

I started my car. "Beth! Be serious. He won't give me his number," I shoved my gear shift into drive and pulled forward, "and he just shows up out of nowhere and asks me out."

"You're nuts! You like him. He asks you out. You tell him no? There is something wrong with you, Nina!"

Back at Andrews, I had to deal with it from both sides.

"What is wrong with you?" Kim shrieked.

"Ugh! Not you, too!"

The smugness on Beth's face radiated throughout the room. "I told you."

"I have to study. You two are studying tonight," I reasoned, mostly to myself.

"I wouldn't if I had a date," Beth said, crossing her legs on her bed.

"I bet you would if said date asked you ninety minutes before study group," I rebutted.

"Okay," Kim said, spreading her arms between us. "Nigh's right. Prose before bros."

Beth rolled her eyes as she packed her various study items and I folded my notes and stuffed them in my coat pocket.

Kim snapped her fingers. "Let's go, ladies. I don't want to close The Rock down at 2 A.M. like last time."

We headed to the John D. Rockefeller library, ducking our heads to hide from the bitter wind. Just as we crossed the street, the snow began to fall in large flakes. The dead grass crinkled under our feet as we cut across to save steps. Beth begged us to drive, but Kim insisted we walk so she could smoke.

Beth hooked her arm around mine. "Brown needs to generate some type of small transportation system to get us from here to there more easily. Like a trailer hitched to a four-wheeler."

"Yes, Oklahoma, let's hire a hay rack ride. Brown needs culture," Kim deadpanned.

Beth narrowed her eyes at Kim. "It was just a suggestion. I'm freezing."

"Don't listen to Kim, she's not even wearing a heavy coat," I said, my teeth beginning to chatter.

"You two are babies, gah!" Kim groaned.

"It does sound like a hay ride," Beth giggled.

When we arrived, our study group was already waiting on us. Carrie and Tracey—from the basketball team—sat on one couch. On the adjacent couch sat Kim's friends Justin and Kristi. Lisa, a pre-med student, barely noticed our arrival, and beside her was someone I recognized right away.

Ryan had a head full of dark hair and he was barely taller than I. Because his T-shirt was a bit tight, I noticed his athletic build. His baseball cap was pulled low over his eyes, so I could see only his perfect, white smile, and a deep dimple on his left cheek. The other girls in the group seemed to appreciate his presence.

"Look at you, being all responsible!" Kim said.

"Josh was going to come, but he ended up going on a date," Ryan explained, pulling up his cap to display his bright green eyes.

"Hmmm," Kim hummed, angling her neck so I would get the full effect of her accusing expression.

Beth did the same.

Ryan was suddenly uncomfortable, his eyes darting back and forth between the three of us. "What did I say?" he asked.

"Nothing," I grumbled, shouldering past Beth.

I sat in the chasm between Ryan and Lisa. While everyone discussed their notes and how confused they were, Ryan turned to me.

"Are you taking chemistry? Do you get any of this?" he complained.

"What are you having problems with?" I asked.

He smiled. "You're not having any problems, are you?"

Feeling caught, I smiled and then erased a line toward the top of his paper. I explained his mistake and started writing it down in my own girlie script. "Do you see how I got there?"

Ryan nodded, still unsure. "I see how you got there, getting there on my own is the persistent problem."

As the night wore one, I erased quite a bit on Ryan's paper. We had hundreds of tiny shreds of decimated eraser all over us. His patience and humor made the night go much faster, although I worked on his chemistry and didn't study the notes I had brought.

"I appreciate you helping me," Ryan said, folding his paper into his book.

"I'm not sure how much I helped, but you're welcome. We have study group here twice a week, come anytime."

Ryan's face lit up. "I will. Thanks. Uh...some of us guys are going out for drinks this weekend. It'd be cool if you'd come."

"There are only a handful of places I can get in to."

Ryan winked at me. "That won't be a problem."

It sounded harmless enough. "That sounds fun. I'll see what the girls are doing."

Kim looked at her watch and yawned. "Stick a fork in me. I'm done."

"Nigh, are you ready?" Beth asked.

"Nigh?" Ryan asked with a raised eyebrow.

I grimaced. "It's a nickname they came up with to torture me. Don't call me that."

"Noted," he said.

Kim laughed and shook her head at Ryan's comment. "I've got to go."

Kim and I stood, waiting for Beth to gather her miniature office supply store.

"This is why I don't bring anything," Kim said, gesturing to Beth.

"You borrowed my pen!" Beth objected.

"Oh. Right," Kim said, tossing the pen into Beth's bag. "All packed."

Beth rolled her eyes and looked at me. "Will you put some tape on her mouth?"

"I don't think tape would help," I grinned.

We walked back to Andrews and Kim waved goodbye, continuing to her room. I collapsed on my bed as Beth gathered her things to head to the showers. As I traced the imperfections of the ceiling with my eyes, my mind drifted to Jared. Not only had I gone from never seeing him to running into him regularly; it was as if I was seeing him at will.

"Ryan asked you out for this weekend?" Beth burst in, towel-drying her hair.

"No. He asked us out for this weekend. I guess some of his friends are going for drinks; he asked us to come along."

"What did you say?" she asked, suddenly interested.

"I said it sounded like fun."

"You want to go?" she squealed.

"I guess you do," I chuckled, rolling my eyes.

"Yes! I do! You wanna go? Please say yes!" she dropped to her knees beside me on my bed.

"I want to go," I deadpanned.

Beth tackled me. "Thank you! Thank you, thank you, thank you, thank you!" she cried.

"You're welcome! Now get off!" I laughed.

The next day was warmer, a good day to take a walk off-campus. Providence transformed from a beautiful crystalline city of white into the soiled, wet mess the cars and mud quickly created. The pristine snow had become a grey-brown sludge lining the roadways and sidewalks. I happily slipped on my black and white fleur de lis galoshes and stomped through the slush in hopes of proving my sheer-will theory concerning Jared.

After an hour of walking, the sun no longer kept me warm. I slipped into the first coffee shop I came upon and ordered the largest size they offered, thawing by the window.

It occurred to me how ridiculous I had become; walking around in near-arctic temperatures to see if Jared would materialize. I was the future savvy CEO of Providence's premiere shipping company for the love of all things holy! What kind of crack pot had I turned into? Over a boy? An incredibly attractive, intelligent, courteous, well-dressed, fantastically-smelling boy. But he was just a boy. Man. Boy. They were all boys.

When I felt the blood circulating again in my fingertips, I made my way back to the school. It was closer to sunset than I would have liked so far from campus, so I quickened my pace.

Two blocks from the school, I pressed the button at the light and kept my distance from the corner, fearful of the inevitable splashing of the cars passing by. The light changed and I trotted across, noting that the warmth from my coffee was waning.

Before I made it to the halfway point of the cross walk, a car horn blared beside me. I jumped, and my eyes darted to the light. It was still green. I turned to glare at the offending vehicle, but my eyes widened when a black Escalade came into view. Jared waved, quivering from a barrage of laughter.

I wasn't sure if I was annoyed or euphoric, but the mixture of emotions propelled me to the passenger side of his car. I whipped open his door and climbed in.

"You scared me to death!" I said, slamming the door behind me.

"I'm sorry!" Jared exclaimed, trying to keep the corners of his mouth from turning up.

The light turned green and he looked at me. "You want a ride?"

I stared at him blank-faced. "Seriously? I'm in your car."

He shrugged and pulled forward.

"You look frozen," he said, touching the end of my nose. That one tap sent adrenaline running throughout my body and I felt nothing but warmth. He reached for the knobs under his radio and twisted the heat to its highest setting.

"I went for a walk," I said, unable to subdue the ridiculous grin on my face.

"I see that," he frowned, disapproving.

"Where are you on your way to?"

"To pick up a client," he shifted uncomfortably in his seat.

"Are you always this vague?"

He raised an eyebrow. "You're full of piss and vinegar today."

"May I remind you that you honked at me in the middle of a busy street? I could have been killed."

"Doubtful. The light was on our side." I dwelled on how he said 'our' for a moment.

"Let's not discount the possible rabid motorists flying through the wet intersection. My hesitation caused by your honking could have led to some serious sidewalk chalk drawings."

Jared laughed. "Are you sure you shouldn't apply for law school? You have quite an imagination."

"So I've been told," I grinned.

"What are you doing this weekend?"

"I'm having drinks with some friends. I would invite you, but I assume you'll be there," I watched for a guilty or stunned expression at my comment, but I was quickly disappointed.

"You're not old enough to drink," he grimaced, ignoring my accusation.

I leaned closer to him. "We don't tell the bartender that," I whispered.

Jared's expression twisted into frustration. "Am I going to have to make an appointment with you for dinner?"

"I'm pretty sure that's called a date."

He smiled his amazing smile and I tried not to gasp. It was hard being candid with him when he was so stunning. I felt like I had car-jacked a film star.

"Would you like my number?" I asked without thinking. A wave of embarrassment washed over me as soon as the words left my mouth.

He didn't answer right away; instead he let out a long sigh. I felt the heat rise on my face, starting at my neck and surpassing my eyes until it scorched the roots of my hair.

"I don't have to give you my number, I just meant...."

"Are you all right?" Jared said. He watched me as if he thought I would break down into tears at any moment.

I could only nod as he slowed to a stop behind Andrews. I didn't dare look at him. I fumbled with the handle and then felt his hand on my arm.

"Nina?" He reached around to gently hold my jaw and turned me to face him. "Don't be upset. You didn't do anything wrong."

"I'm sorry. I...I think I misunderstood," I bit my lip, drawing his attention to them.

He leaned in closer; his eyes still focused on my mouth. When he was just a few inches from me, he shook his head and pulled back.

The blood rushed in from every inch of my body and my feet tingled as the adrenaline rushed through them and then disappeared. I had been wrong. What I had taken to be flirtation or attraction must have been more of a fondness for me. He looked at me as a little sister, and I had made my misconception all too clear.

I opened the door, hopping out into a shallow puddle. The motor of the Escalade still hummed behind me as I pressed the door closed and walked to Andrews, too humiliated to look back.

Chapter Three
Suspicion(s)

I didn't leave campus again until Beth, Kim and I met Ryan and his friends for drinks in a pub downtown. When we arrived, I saw that it was less of a pub and more of a dingy hole in the wall, but it would serve our purpose.

Tucker nodded to the bartender. "Hey, Tozzi."

Tozzi eyed our group as he dried the inside of a glass and nodded.

We began with a shot and toasted to our mascot, "TO THE BIG BROWN BEAR!"

I lost count of how many drinks I'd had, it was easy to do that with an open tab at the bar and Tucker ordering round after round. My cheeks were beginning to complain from the constant giggling and smiling, so I made fish faces to stretch them out. Ryan squeezed and pulled at my face as he laughed, having far more to drink than I had.

Ryan spoke as quietly as a drunk person was capable, brushing my bangs from my eyes and laughing as if he should be hiccuping tiny bubbles with every word. "Did I tell you how beautiful you look tonight?" he asked.

"A few times," I replied.

He grabbed each side of my face and pressed his forehead against mine. "I'm glad you came, Nina. I never have this much fun."

Beth had just volunteered to call a cab when the door opened and I saw them. Jared walked in with a platinum-blonde beauty. She was all of five feet four inches and clearly younger than I. Her lips were plush, snowy banks glittering under her icy blue eyes. She moved with the confidence and precision of a runway model, disregarding our table as she strode by. Her hair was board-straight, barely grazing her shoulders, and her thick bangs hung just above her eyes. There was a tiny diamond piercing in the crease of her left nostril. I'd never seen anything like her in real life before. She looked like punk rock Barbie with her heavy eye makeup, skintight clothing and knee-high boots.

Jared ignored us, too, as he followed her to the bar, and I felt something catch in my throat when he sat next to his companion.

Kim grabbed my shoulder. "Does he know you're here?"

"I don't think so," I choked out.

"What's going on?" Ryan asked, seeing our reaction to the fair-haired couple at the bar.

"That is the guy that's been pursuing Nina," Kim said, eyeing Jared with disgust.

Ryan looked at me and nodded in Jared's direction. "You're dating that guy?"

"No." I stood up from the table. The door was just a few steps away, but I couldn't take my eyes off of them.

Tozzi took one look at the blonde Jared was with and shook his head. Jared whispered something in his ear, slid something across the counter and the bartender walked away without further argument. The girl—and she was a girl—looked up at Jared with an annoyed expression. I was instantly angry. He had chosen to be with her and she was bored with him.

Beth stumbled back to the table. "Cab's on its way."

"Let's wait outside," Kim said, pulling me with her.

Just before I looked away, Jared raised his eyes to meet mine. I was glad that he had seen me, then he wouldn't be so surprised at the fury I would unleash on him the next time we happened upon each other. My anger gave me the distraction I needed to turn away. I shook my head in heated disbelief that he'd shown up with such a fake looking sl—

My arm pulled in the wrong direction. "Nina, don't go," Jared said.

"What are you doing here with her?" Beth sneered.

I looked down at my arm and then glared up at Jared. He removed his gentle hold on me so as not to offend me further. "Just...wait a minute. It's not what you think."

"I don't think anything," I snapped.

Jared sighed. "Yes, you do. If you would just give me a moment to explain...."

In the next moment Ryan was standing beside me, eyeing Jared. "She's leaving. You need to step back," Ryan said in a low, hostile voice.

Jared turned his head away from us, laughing off the threat. He turned to look directly at Ryan, and I recoiled as his eyes turned from warm pools to steely blue.

After a few tense moments, Jared looked down at me. His eyes softened again. "Nina, I don't want you to leave upset. Just hear me out."

"I don't think I will," I said, turning away from him. His hand shot out to catch my arm once more. Ryan grabbed Jared's arm and I could see that in seconds the situation was going to escalate.

47

A petite hand shot out and gripped Ryan's wrist, bending it back just enough to incapacitate him. Ryan cried out in pain.

A feminine but firm voice came from behind Jared. "I'm just going to tell you this once. Don't put your hands on my brother."

"Okay! Okay!" Ryan begged.

"All right, Claire, that's enough," Jared murmured, watching me. He sighed at the horror that emanated from my eyes as I watched her draw her hand back from Ryan's.

"This is my little sister, Claire," Jared explained with chagrin.

My eyes shot a confused look at Claire, searching for some sort of offense taken by her, but there was none. He was telling the truth.

"Your sister?" I asked. From my peripheral vision, I could see Ryan rubbing his wrist.

Claire watched Ryan, seeming both irritated and concerned, almost as if she had regretted hurting him. Jared noticed the way she looked at Ryan as well, and they traded a strange glance.

"I didn't want you to think...," Jared trailed off, looking at me, "I'm sorry. About the other day, it's difficult...."

Claire rolled her eyes and made her way to the bar. Jared whispered in her ear as she passed.

"Behave yourself."

"Whatever," she snapped.

Claire made herself comfortable on the bar stool and ordered a water, keeping to herself. After a few moments, her eyes flashed to Ryan and then back down to her drink.

Jared turned to me again, obviously wanting to pick up where we left off. His eyes wandered beside me to where Ryan was still standing.

"It's okay, Ryan," I whispered, touching his arm. I noticed Jared stare at my hand as if it would burst into flames.

"Okay?" Ryan repeated, still rubbing his wrist. I didn't miss the edge of uneasiness in his voice.

"Yeah," I smiled.

Ryan walked with Kim and Beth to the wall beside the door to join the rest of the group we came with. They all made a poor attempt to pretend they were watching for the cab.

"What are you doing here, Jared?" I snapped my head back to meet his eyes. He muttered something under his breath, briefly surveying the room full of people that were staring at us. I cocked my head and leaned so that I was somewhat in his line of sight. "Jared?"

"I didn't want you to think I was with Claire. She insisted on coming in," he said, looking back to me.

"I'm not sure why you're here at all," I crossed my arms and glared at him.

Jared noted the stubborn set of my chin and sighed. "I'm here because of what happened the other day. The look on your face when you walked away...I couldn't just let you think that I didn't....that I wasn't...." He was struggling with the truth, and it was irritating me.

"Just say it!"

He winced at my tone. "I have these...feelings for you. When I saw you over here, with that same look

49

on your face, I was afraid you'd never speak to me again if I didn't explain."

"You have feelings for me?"

His face fell. "I can't get you out of my head."

That simple sentence had my heart pounding through my chest. He lightly cupped my jaw and brushed his thumb against my cheek. His touch sent a jolt of electricity throughout my body from my head to my toes.

A sultry guitar solo played from the jukebox. I knew the song vaguely, but wasn't paying enough attention to it to figure it out. Jared's mouth turned up into a half-smile, and he pulled on both of my hands.

"Come here," he said.

He walked backwards and led me to the small wooden dance floor. Pulling me close to his chest, his eyes never left mine. Everyone in the room must have been staring at us through the smoky haze, but I couldn't disengage my gaze from his, even for a moment. He wrapped his arms around my middle, and I slid my hands up his arms, stopping at his shoulders.

I wasn't sure if we were even dancing, with all of my focus on the fact that our bodies were so close. He broke his stare and leaned down to press his lips to my hair. I pressed my cheek against his chest and closed my eyes.

He tightened his grip, and every inch of me that was in contact with him burned in a wonderful way. I looked up and my eyes stalled on his lips, the bottom a bit fuller than the top. I bit my lip in anticipation, the alcohol dissolving all of my inhibitions.

His body stiffened and I turned to follow his glare to the bar. One of the older men still loitering in the pub had approached Claire.

The man reached for Claire and Jared's grip on me tightened, stepping just slightly in front of me in a protective stance.

The man leaned over and patted Claire on the back. He laughed loudly and attempted to whisper into her ear. Claire was staring ahead, her body rigid; seeing just half of her expression it was obvious that she was about to lose her temper. The man lost his balance and used Claire to right himself.

"Claire—," Jared warned, but it was too late.

In the same second, she knocked the man's legs out from under him with incredible speed and then stood up on the rung of her bar stool, slamming his head, cheek down, to the bar. The wood made a cracking noise with the force of her blow, and the man wailed in pain. He flailed his arms, reaching above him for Claire's face, but she quickly reached around with her other hand and grabbed his fingers, wrenching them back. The bones in his fingers snapped and I recoiled, even though I still hadn't quite processed what was going on. The man's bloodcurdling scream sent the bartender running over to try to separate them.

Claire leaned down and yelled over the music into his ear. "Was that good for you, Baby?" and then slowly licked his cheek. Claire released her grip, and he slithered down to the floor. The entire room seemed frozen in time.

Jared heaved an exasperated sigh. He looked at me with a tired ache in his eyes, and then let me go. He walked over to Claire, grabbed her arm and then ushered her out.

"She broke my damn fingers!" the man howled, cradling his arm to his chest.

Several of the older patrons rushed to his side and helped him up while he moaned in pain. Beth grabbed my hand and pulled me out of the pub. The cab waited for us outside in a cloud of exhaust.

I looked around, but Jared had disappeared.

Beth tugged at my coat frantically. "Get in, Nina, before the cops get here!"

I ducked into the cab and my ears were filled with shrieking and chattering in high tones. I wasn't listening to any of it; I was too confused about what I had seen. Jared wasn't surprised at all that his teenaged-sister had broken the hand of a full grown man as if he was made of glass.

I went over it in my head; the memory seemed more like a kung fu movie than something that had unfolded in front of my eyes. Tiny, delicate Claire seemed to have superhuman strength and speed, and Jared's reaction didn't make sense. He didn't act to protect her, and yet he seemed to know that carnage was on the horizon; he even shielded me from it.

"Nina! Are you listening to me? Wasn't that incredible? The way she just—," Beth set in motion with a series of karate chops and then jerked her hand forward in the same motion Claire used to slam the man's head into the bar, grunting with each move. Beth giggled with delight while I shuddered at the recollection.

"I'd hate to meet her on a dark playground, I'll tell you that," Kim joked.

Ryan shook his head. "She's all of ninety-five pounds and when she grabbed my hand, I couldn't break free. What is she? Sixteen? Seventeen? She isn't normal."

"She has to be in high school, still," Beth said.

"She's old enough to drive, though. Did you see her car?" Kim added.

I perked up, then. "You saw them leave?"

Beth nodded. "She took off down the street in some kind of sports car; Jared was with her. They looked like they were arguing."

"It was a Lotus," Kim said.

"It was a phantom black Lotus Exige S two-sixty. Sweet, sweet, car," Ryan mused. "It costs over twelve-grand just for the paint."

"Doesn't Josh's dad have one?" Kim asked, elbowing Ryan.

Ryan shook his head with raised eyebrows.

Kim looked at me. "It's a good thing she wasn't his date, Nigh. That would have been one short catfight."

"Hey," Beth prodded. Her giggling had tapered off. "What's wrong? You'll see him again, I'm sure of it. You should have seen the way he looked at you when you were dancing together."

I couldn't help but notice Ryan frown at Beth's words.

My attention was drawn to the passing lights outside my window. Seeing him again was exactly what I wanted, but my sense of self-preservation cried foul. The entire situation was one big red flag, but did I believe Jared was dangerous?

Something about Jared's eyes assured me that in the short time I'd known him, he was safe. Every piece of me that had been guided by my father to be reasonable and wary was screaming run, but I knew I would intentionally try to cross paths with him at the earliest moment fate allowed. The moment of sadness in his eyes before he left me played out over and over in my head. I had to see him again.

The next study group session, Ryan collapsed in the chair beside me. He teetered his pencil between his fingers while I went over my notes.

"Nina?" Ryan whispered.

"Yes?"

"Who was that guy the other night?"

I feigned a confused expression. "What guy?"

He smirked at me. "You know who I'm talking about. That Jared guy. Are you dating him?"

I shrugged. "No, not really."

"What does that mean?"

I kept my eyes on my paper. "I've gone to lunch with him once, he's given me a ride home a few times, and I've see him around town...," I was purposefully vague. I didn't know where the conversation was headed.

"So what was that, at the pub? Why did he show up with his sister to tell you he wasn't there with her?"

"I haven't talked to him to get that figured out, yet."

"But you're going to talk to him?" His voice was growing impatient with my answers.

"I don't know, Ryan. Why?" I said, unable to conceal my irritation with his line of questioning.

Ryan squirmed in his seat and then turned to face me. "I wanted to ask you...if...you know... if you wanted to grab dinner sometime."

"Oh," I rubbed my forehead, "I've got a lot on my plate right now."

Ryan nodded indifferently. "I just thought I'd ask. I didn't know if you and that guy were...."

"It's not about Jared," I lied.

"Do you think he came there to check up on you?"

I contemplated that for a moment. "I don't know, maybe. I've been running into him a lot, lately."

"That's creepy."

"I like to think of it as fate stepping in," I mused.

Ryan's face twisted to petulance. "Sounds like stalking to me."

"You should talk, trying to fight over a girl you barely know."

"He had his hands on you," he grumbled.

"Thank you," I smiled, nudging him.

"You're welcome. You know that guy's got to be bad news, right?"

"I don't believe that." Ryan scowled at my words, but I shrugged off his skepticism. "I can't explain it. There's something in his eyes."

Ryan shook his head in disapproval. "I just don't want you to get hurt. His little sister is insane."

"I'm with you on that one."

We both laughed and then Ryan shrugged. "Maybe once you get things all sorted out with your stalker, you'll reconsider."

"He's not a stalker."

"MmmHmm," he said, trying to appear interested in his algebra book.

Beth began gathering her plethora of organizational aides and Kim stood up and stretched. The rest of the group disbanded as Kim, Beth, Ryan and I walked out of the library together.

"I'm starving," Kim said.

"I could eat," Beth chimed in.

Ryan turned to me. "Is an after study snack out of the question?"

They all eyed me expectantly. "Let's eat," I shrugged.

Ryan and Kim went over possible plans for the weekend over pancakes and hash browns while Beth and I discussed our intentions to attend the basketball game. Even with the ever-growing puzzle that was Jared, life was a shade of ordinary again. I felt the unease I'd been feeling for weeks slowly dissipate into the greasy air.

While walking out to the car I noticed a short, squat man walking parallel to us. Ryan veered to the outside of our group, positioning himself between us and the stranger. The man arrived at Kim's Sentra the same moment that we did.

"Are you Nina Grey?" The man asked me in a hoarse voice. I felt my body tense.

"What do you need?" Ryan asked, stepping forward.

The man noted Ryan's presence but spoke only to me. "I was an associate of your father's. My name is Charles Dawson. It's important that I speak with you."

I wasn't sure what to say, the mention of my father created a stabbing sensation in my stomach.

"I would like to speak with you alone, if you don't mind," he said, his squinty eyes shifting from each of my friends and then back to me.

"Nina, do you know this guy?" Ryan asked, jerking his thumb at Mr. Dawson.

I studied his face for a moment. He wore an expensive suit like the hundreds of other men I'd seen in my father's company through the years, but his face wasn't familiar.

I tried to be polite. "I–I don't think I do, sir. I'm not sure I could help you."

Mr. Dawson took a step toward me and Ryan did the same.

"I've been trying to get in touch with your father for some time, now. It's come to my attention that he's passed away."

I worked to separate my lips long enough to form the words. "That's correct."

"Your father had agreed to sign over some property to me, and I was wondering if you were at all familiar with our transaction?"

Kim spoke up. "Nina, this is probably not the appropriate time to—,"

"I think you'd rather speak to my father's attorney, Thomas Rosen," I interrupted. "He is with Rosen and Barnes in Kennedy Plaza. I'm sure he will be able to assist you." I turned to get into the car, but the man took several quick steps to thwart my efforts. He held my door and his face turned grave.

"It's of the utmost importance, Nina. I've exhausted all of my options, and I'm asking for your help." His eyes darted to Ryan and then back to me. Mr. Dawson kept his voice low, "Jack has a safe. Maybe you've seen it? My papers are there in that safe and I need to obtain them right away."

The already uncomfortable feeling that I was experiencing grew as the man inched closer to me. I heard Kim make wide strides to intercede, but Ryan beat her to it, stepping between me and the stranger. I slid into my seat and shut the door while Kim wheeled around, hurrying to start the car. Ryan paused for a moment, eyeing the man, and then joined Beth in the back seat. I saw Ryan's arm slide between my shoulder and the door, reaching to press down the lock.

Mr. Dawson leaned down to peer at me through the glass. "I need those papers, Nina. It would be wise of you to help me." He pulled out a card and held it against the window with his palm. I scanned it quickly and attempted to smile.

No one spoke until we were almost back to the school parking lot.

"Does anyone else think that was completely creepy?" Beth shrieked.

"Beth! You scared the crap outta me!" Kim said.

"What are you going to do?" Ryan asked.

"I'm going to call Mr. Rosen tomorrow, and then I'm going to call my mother," I said, fidgeting.

Beth nodded with wide eyes. "Your mom is gonna freak."

"I know," I grumbled.

Kim waved and set off to Andrews while Beth and I said our goodbyes to Ryan.

Beth patted Ryan's shoulder. "I'm glad you were there, Ryan. That guy was...I don't think he would have let Nina in the car had you not been there."

"Yes, thank you," I said, hugging him.

Ryan pulled back to look at me, still keeping me enveloped in his arms. "I'd do anything for you," he said, brushing my bangs away from my eyes.

I took a step back and glanced at Beth, whose eyes were bouncing back and forth between Ryan and me. He scratched the back of his head nervously. "Yeah, well...guess I better head back to the dorm. I'll see you ladies at our next study group."

"See ya!" Beth chirped.

I smiled and waved to him as he turned to walk away.

Beth grabbed my arm and pulled me along with her as she walked. "Neeenah! What are you going to do about him? He's in love with you!"

"He is not," I said, glowering at her. "He just hasn't accepted our strictly platonic relationship, yet."

"And you think he will?"

"Yes," I said, nodding once.

"Or you hope he will?"

"He will."

"Because you're in love with Jared?" she grinned.

"I barely know Jared!" I said, irritated. "Beth, you have to hear how ridiculous you sound right now. Ryan loves me, I love Jared. I've known them both for about two seconds."

"You are in denial."

I rolled my eyes. "I'm going to see my mother tomorrow. Do you want to come with me?"

"No, I have a meeting."

I raised one eyebrow. "What kind of meeting?"

"I'm not talking about it, you'll laugh at me."

"Tell me, Beth. I won't laugh," I said, hooking my arm around hers.

She pressed her lips together and then sighed in resignation. "We're starting a group for students from Oklahoma."

"How many are there?" My words were involuntarily tinged with disbelief.

"A few!" she said defensively.

I fought a grin. "Are you going to have square dances and fight with the Native American Club?"

"You're not funny."

I chuckled and looked away. "That was pretty funny."

"You know the parking meter was invented in Oklahoma? And the shopping cart...? Invented in Oklahoma, too! The yield sign, the autopilot, voicemail! All because of Oklahomans. Bill Gates was inspired by an article penned by Ed Roberts, an Oklahoman. We have affordable housing, natural gas, Will Rogers, and the Sooners!

"The Oklahoma jokes are getting really old. We're not a bunch of hillbillies...you're friends with me, aren't you?" she said, breathless.

"Yes, Beth! Yes, we're friends! You're right, I'm sorry. I won't say anything else about Oklahoma." I could feel my eyes widen in bewilderment. Beth was upset with me.

"And that goes for Kim, too," she grumbled.

"I can't speak for Kim, but don't hold your breath."

Beth tried not to smile, but giggled, anyway. I smiled apologetically and we hugged just outside of our dorm room.

"You're crazy, but I love you, anyway," I giggled.

"I love you, too. I wouldn't rather be shacked up with any other Yankee," she said in a horrible southern drawl.

The next morning Beth decided to rise early and head out with me for coffee. I felt closer to her after

60

our understanding the night before, and she seemed to be in an uncharacteristically good mood for being up so early.

Classes went by without delay. Before I knew it, I was sitting in my room alone, thinking about Jared and his unexplained appearances in my life. My mind abruptly switched to Mr. Dawson. I picked up my cell phone and dialed Thomas' office. His secretary answered and informed me that he was out for the day. I hung up, frustrated.

I couldn't recall a secret safe or any important real estate deal my father was involved in, which wasn't exactly surprising. I was typically clueless about my father's business dealings and had gratefully remained that way. That was before strange men started following me around, though. At least one person thought I had access to that file. I had to know why it was so important.

I burst through the door of my parents' home and called for Agatha.

"Yes, Nina love! What's the racket about?" she answered, scurrying around the corner.

"Is Mother home?"

"She's at Crestwood, planning something 'er other. You know how busy she keeps these days."

Of course she would be out. Immediately after Jack's funeral, my mother immersed herself into every group, every organization, and every charity she could find. She had several meetings a day and, although it was at times frustrating being unable to reach her, I was appreciative of her time well spent away from my dorm room.

After an hour of thumbing through my mother's mail and snooping in every closet downstairs, I headed to Jack's office. It was the most obvious place to look, so I assumed I wouldn't find anything that would be of help. I took my hand off the knob and had almost convinced myself to look elsewhere, but I wheeled around and shoved myself through the door.

It hadn't changed.

His mahogany desk and swivel chair sat commandingly in the center of the room. Hundreds of books including tax law, encyclopedias, poetry, the classics and Dr. Seuss lined the back wall.

I crossed his plush, imported rug and planted myself in the desk chair. The last papers he had looked over before his accident lay strewn on one side, and unopened envelopes on the other. I started with those. Opening one after another, I sifted through statements, invitations, requests and letters. Seeing nothing of interest, I pitched them into the wastebasket under the desk.

Just as I was about to put the letter opener back inside the drawer, the inscription caught my eye. My mother had bought it for me so I could give it to Jack for his birthday. The inscription read simply, *"To Daddy Love, Nina"*. I ran my finger over the words affectionately and shoved it into my back pocket. My mother wouldn't miss it.

My eyes flitted to a two-inch stack of papers with SIGN HERE stickers poking out in various bright colors. I thumbed through them, but didn't see anything about properties.

I pulled his lower desk drawer open and thumbed through every file, but I saw nothing of importance. Searching the remaining drawers, I rifled through old photos, envelopes, paperwork from the last ten years of tax filings, and a set of car keys. I slammed the last drawer shut and puffed.

My eyes wandered over to the file cabinets along the left wall. I started with the highest drawer in the cabinet closest to the back wall and searched for anything pertaining to properties, commercial or otherwise. I began to feel possessed. Every time I shut a drawer, I stifled a sob. Each drawer was slammed harder and harder. Only one cabinet wouldn't open.

While searching through the last drawer my hands began to shake. Upon finding no suspicious evidence or anything related to Mr. Dawson I kicked the drawer shut, causing the cabinet to rock back and forth.

"AGH!" I stomped, balling my hands into fists at my sides.

I paced in a small circle for a minute, and then made my way to the desk chair and collapsed. A small bronze frame sat to my left. It was of me and Jack when I was about four years old. We had gone on vacation to the Grand Canyon and I had fallen. I looked closer to verify my bandaged knee and smiled. I was sitting on my father's lap; he had just finished cleaning up the dirt and blood and used a colorful bandage from my mother's purse. He kissed my knee and told me that it was all better, and even though the sting remained, I nodded my head in belief.

The colors were all so vivid, as was my memory. My eyes filled with tears and I looked around, horrified that I was in Jack's office and at what I was doing there. Mr. Dawson, a complete stranger, had made me doubt my father. I wiped my face and quickly straightened his desk. The door slammed behind me as I quickly descended the stairs.

"Miss Nina?" Agatha called after me, but I raced past her, too intent on escaping the shame that I felt.

I yanked my BMW into gear and flew down the driveway into the street. Tears streamed down my face and I felt my body shudder in the same sobs I had worked so hard to rid myself of. Too many questions and no answers, everything that had made sense died with my father.

The flickering street lamps flew by as I sped down the road. As I passed the bus stop where I'd first met Jared. I noticed someone sitting on the bench and slammed on my brakes. I jerked the gear into reverse and my car made a grievous whirring noise as I backtracked. My tires screeched to a halt straight across from where Jared sat.

Shoving my way out of the car, I stomped to the middle of the street. "Are you following me?"

"Are you all right?" he asked, concern overshadowing his flawless features.

"What are you doing here, dammit?" I yelled.

He stood up and held his arms out to me, but I shook my head. He stopped and furrowed his brow. "Nina, come here."

"I want answers, Jared. You show up in my life, tell me you have these feelings for me. You won't give me your number, and you all but refused mine." I took a step toward him, and he a step toward me.

"Nina, I know you're upset, but it's going to be okay." His voice was calm and soothing, almost too much so, as if he was trying to talk me down from a ledge.

"I'm standing in the middle of the street bawling my eyes out and yelling at you, Jared! Why aren't you asking me what's wrong? Why don't you ever ask me questions?" Jared thought for a moment, seeming surprised at my observation. He took another step toward me with outstretched arms, begging to hold me.

"Is it feelings you have for me? Or are you just following me around because you feel sorry for me? Is it because I'm some tragic, fatherless basket case that you've decided to make a charity project out of?"

His eyes turned angry and his arms lowered. "You know that's not true."

As he took another step, his face for once didn't try to hide emotion. His eyes ached for me to come to him; I could see that my tears caused him pain. I leaned into his arms and he wrapped them around me without hesitation.

I relaxed in his embrace for a moment, the warmth of his arms provided instant comfort.

He leaned down to press his cheek against my temple. "It's more than just feelings, Nina. You have to know that."

I peered up at him with damp eyes. "Then why haven't you...?"

"What?" he asked. I shook my head at first, but he pulled me closer to him and his eyes begged me to confess my thoughts. "Tell me."

"Why haven't you tried to kiss me?"

He seemed stunned, and then his eyes settled on my lips. I watched as his expression changed from desire, to conflicted, to a decision. I didn't know what it all meant, so I closed my eyes and leaned into him, knowing his lips were just a few inches from mine. I felt his grip tighten and he held me at bay. My eyes popped open, humiliation crashing over me in waves. Adding to my already crippling embarrassment, tears once again spilled over my cheeks.

His eyes closed tight and his face crumpled. "I don't want to lie to you."

The humiliation still flamed my face, but it was now obscured by my anger. I'd grown weary of his vague non-answers. He would offer a tiny bit of truth shrouded in confusing ambiguity and my patience had reached its limit.

Seeing the resentment in my eyes, Jared let out a frustrated sigh. He released me and walked across the street to an impressive black motorcycle parked behind the bench. Without looking back he turned the key, and with a push of the button the engine roared to life. The motor snarled as he revved it a few times before speeding off the sidewalk and down the street.

The weekend came and went. Beth and I attended the basketball game and Kim, Beth and I joined Ryan, Josh, Tucker, and Chad for air hockey and nachos. I refused to talk about Jared, even with Beth. I couldn't even bring myself to explain what had happened that caused me to be so furious anytime they mentioned his name.

Ryan seemed to enjoy my change of heart. One night he called to ask me for help with his chemistry, and we found ourselves sitting on the floor of my dorm room alone.

"No...it's...." I pressed my lips together as I rewrote the last line.

"Chad said he failed this test last year," Ryan grumbled.

"Chad didn't have me for a tutor, now did he?" I threw my pencil at him and it bounced to the floor.

"Tutor or not, this test is gonna suck."

"Have you lost your faith in me?"

"Have you reconsidered my offer, yet?" he grinned.

"I don't know what you're talking about," I shrugged, playing dumb.

"Yes, you do. It's okay if you haven't....you will eventually," he smiled wide.

"I'm fairly certain I won't be interested in dating for a long, long time."

Ryan didn't skip a beat. "I'll wait."

Chapter Four
The Ring

The next weeks proved to be fairly mundane. I hadn't seen Jared or Mr. Dawson, and Ryan's propositions had tapered off. Beth had been noticeably absent from our room. I hadn't even been sequestered for a ballgame.

I didn't leave campus for further theory-testing walks, and I tried not to venture off campus in general. My feelings were conflicted at any given second between being desperate to see Jared again and cringing at thoughts of any chance run-ins. I committed to pushing him from my mind, even if I had to do it a thousand times a day.

At study group, Ryan and I took our normal spots to work together on his latest academic crisis. Kim passed the time by shooting rubber bands at Josh while Beth and the new girl, Nicole, compared notes.

Josh caught one of Kim's rubber missiles in midair and yawned. "So, when are we going out again?"

Kim shrugged. "I don't know. When do you want to go?"

"I don't think Nina's up to it," Beth hinted. The entire group stared at me with a mixture of pitiful and expectant expressions that I was desperate to deflect.

"Of course I'm up for it," I said, aiming for a casual tone.

In truth, going out again with the same people to the same place made me anxious that we were just asking for a repeat, and I wasn't ready to see Jared again. In the same moment, I worried that he wouldn't show.

"Are you sure?" Beth asked, leaning forward in her chair.

"Why don't we go tomorrow?" Josh asked Ryan.

"I'm there," Ryan said, nudging me.

"On a Tuesday? How much fun can a Tuesday night be?" I groaned.

"As fun as we make it," Ryan said.

On our way back to Andrews, I grumbled to Beth about going out on a school night. She didn't seem fazed by the prospect, so I left it alone. When we lumbered into our room, my cell phone buzzed.

"Hi, Mom," I yawned.

"You sound tired, Nina. Are you getting enough sleep?" she asked.

"I am. It's just been a long day," I said, peeling back my comforter.

"Well, I won't keep you long. I just wanted to tell you that Thomas called me today. He wanted to apologize about not returning your call. Did you call him, dear?"

"Er...yes. I did." I hadn't anticipated Thomas calling my mother.

"Well? What did you call him about?"

I decided that sticking as close to the truth as possible would be the best option. "Well, I was in dad's office a few weeks ago and came across some unsigned papers. I didn't want to worry you with it, so I called Mr. Rosen."

"You were in Dad's office? Why?"

"I guess I just miss him."

"Oh," she whispered. "I'm sorry I wasn't there."

"It's okay, Mom. It was something I needed to do on my own."

"You don't worry about those papers, Dear. They're nothing you need to concern yourself with. Thomas has copies of all of your father's papers in his office; they've already been taken care of. I wasn't....ready to move them just yet."

"I understand," I said, thinking of the letter opener I'd taken. She obviously hadn't noticed, yet. I wondered if she went into Jack's office at all. "Did Daddy ever discuss an urgent properties deal with you?"

My mother pondered that for a moment. "A properties deal? Your father didn't deal with properties, Nina."

"Oh. Okay." I tried to make my voice sound idle to end the conversation.

"I'll let Thomas know that I've talked to you." She seemed to accept my explanation, but was obviously unconvinced.

"That's fine, Mom. I'm going to bed, now."

I clicked my phone shut and noticed Beth staring at me. "What?"

"You didn't tell her about the Dawson guy, did you?" Beth said, towel and toiletries in hand.

I shook my head. "I can't put that on her right now."

I clicked my fingernails together, waiting for Beth to return. Mr. Rosen chose to call my mother instead of me. The thought flooded my mind with the disturbing words Mr. Dawson spoke, which in turn morphed into thoughts of my father being swindled posthumously. In that instant, I became angry beyond words and scrambled to my feet. Beth wouldn't return fast enough; I needed an immediate distraction.

I grabbed my keys and bolted out the door.

My BMW weaved in and out of traffic just a bit over the speed limit. I figured if I could somehow get lost, trying to find my way back would be an excellent distraction. I drove until the buildings were less familiar and then I stopped paying attention to the street signs. When I was no longer in Providence, I slowed down to make a U-turn to start the challenge of finding my way home. I veered off a bit to the shoulder before making the turn, and then my car bobbled over an unseen object as I pulled my steering wheel in the opposite direction.

"Dammit!"

I peered into my rearview mirror, searching for what I'd run over to decide whether I should pull over to assess any damages. In the next moment I saw the reflective twisted metal and sighed.

I pulled over to the side of the road and came to an abrupt stop. Realizing the situation I'd gotten myself into, I let my forehead fall hard onto the steering wheel with a thud.

A flat tire on the side of an unknown road in the middle of the night was definitely a distraction.

I shoved open my door and walked around to look at the front passenger-side tire. Seeing the rubber pooled on the ground, I raked my fingers through my hair.

Fog blurred the street lights so my vision was limited. In quick strides I ducked back into my car to call Beth. At the same time that I remembered I had left my purse behind, it dawned on me that I'd also failed to bring my phone.

"Nina! You idiot!"

Logic overrode panic. The sun would rise in a few hours and I could flag someone down to use their phone. I turned the heater on high and let the dry air fill the cab. When it was too hot to breathe I flipped back the ignition and turned off the car. Just moments later, I tugged my coat tighter around me. It was going to be a very long couple of hours before sunrise; it didn't take long at all for the stifling heat in the car to fade to mildly warm and then to an uncomfortable chill soon after.

Three quick raps on my window sent me an inch off my seat. I whipped around to see a man in a puffy blue coat standing just inches away. My hand flew up to the lock as he leaned down to look in.

"It's a little late for that, don't you think? I could have carjacked you by now," Jared said, grimacing at my pitiful efforts.

I couldn't speak, the fear sent adrenaline racing throughout my body and I experienced a dozen different emotions before I settled on relief.

"Open the trunk so I can get your spare," he said.

I reached for the button and the trunk sprung open with a pop. Scrambling out of my car, I watched while he pulled out a jack and quickly assembled it, and then pulled out the spare tire, carrying it to his makeshift workspace. I'd always seen people rolling tires around, but Jared lifted it out of my trunk as if it were a grocery bag.

He worked feverishly—as if he were being timed— pumping the jack, unscrewing the lug nuts and yanking off the flattened carcass of the old tire to immediately replace it with the spare. He repeated the process in reverse, tightening the lug nuts and spinning the tire. Once he finished lowering the car, he lobbed the flattened tire into my trunk, followed by the jack and tire iron.

"Go home, Nina," he growled. He slammed the trunk shut and then wiped the grease from his hands onto his jeans.

"Jared...."

"Just go home," he said, avoiding my eyes. He turned his back on me, disappearing into the fog.

"Thank you," I whispered.

I shook my head and scrambled around the front of my car, staring at the new tire to make sure I hadn't imagined everything I'd just seen. My new, perfectly capable tire was fitted flawlessly to my car. I looked to the fog where Jared had disappeared and puffed. It was no longer an indefinite prospect that Jared was always waiting in the wings. I didn't know why or how he was doing it, but he was watching over me.

During the ride home my mind raced with theories and explanations. There was no way for him to explain it away. Jared had basically admitted to following me. Maybe that was why he was so irritated; I'd managed to get myself in yet another situation that he would have to make clear that he was nearby. I should have been panicking—anyone else would have repeated the word stalker over and over in her head—but I only felt an overwhelming sense of calm. Beyond the calm I was even more shocked to discover that I was flattered.

Something else became clear to me: I had absolutely no common sense concerning Jared Ryel. I had become an irrational, ridiculous, sobbing fool and incredibly, he was still in my life. I didn't care if he was a stalker or a miracle. The thought that he was always near me—that he could have been watching me at that very moment—sent euphoric shivers down my spine.

The next night, a knock at the door prompted Beth to grab her purse. When I swung open the door, Kim, Josh, Ryan, Tucker, Chad, Lisa, and Carrie were all standing in the hall.

"We held hands so they wouldn't get lost," Kim quipped.

"That's nice," I said, turning to grab my keys and wallet. "We're not all going to fit in the Beemer."

"I'm taking my jeep," Chad said.

"Sweet!" Beth chirped.

When I followed Beth through the door of the pub, I felt my body tense. I didn't relax until I finished scanning the room and saw that Jared was nowhere to be found. With my relaxation was also discontent, but Ryan's arm around my shoulders provided an immediate diversion. We took a table and Ryan fed quarters into the jukebox. Within an hour we were all on the wooden floor dancing to disco.

"Next time, I'm bringing a CD!" Kim yelled over the Bee Gees.

When we returned to our table, a slow song crooned from the juke box and Chad asked Beth to dance. She was beaming, and I watched him pull her gently by her hand to the dance floor. I felt the corners of my mouth turn up as I watched them, not being able to keep myself from the bittersweet memory of Jared's arms around me in the same space just a few weeks before.

"C'mon. Dance with me," Ryan asked, pulling at my hand.

I might have said no if he hadn't already had me half way to my feet. It had become a full time job to keep him from getting the wrong idea about our friendship. I followed him to the dance floor and he secured his hands behind my back.

"Oh, cheer up. It's not that bad," Ryan smiled.

"You've been drinking; I'm concentrating on not tripping over your two left feet."

"I'll catch you," he said, too close to my face.

"Great, then we'd both fall," I grinned.

Ryan hugged me to him. "I don't mind falling to catch you."

I relaxed my chin on Ryan's shoulder until the song ended. He seemed to want to keep dancing but the next song was upbeat. He hesitated and then let me go, leading me back to the table by my hand.

We tabbed out after last call, and Lisa and Carrie decided to take a cab to someone's apartment for an after party. Beth decided to ride with Chad again and my heart leapt for her when I saw him lead her by the hand to his Jeep.

We quickly crossed against the light to the parking lot and Kim and Ryan giggled while I fumbled for my keys.

I cursed as my keys tumbled to the ground into a pot hole. I reached down to get them, but a dirty hand beat me there. Kim and Ryan were silent as I slowly stood to face the raggedy man in front of me.

"Thank you," I said, holding my hand out for my keys. I noticed there were three other men with him, emerging from the shadows of the alley.

"You're welcome," he rasped. He had an unkempt brown beard and his black eyes were abnormally deep-set. Upon first glance he appeared homeless, but his fingernails were too clean and his face wasn't nearly worn enough. Even growing up on the East Side, I had seen my share of the destitute on the docks with my father.

"I don't suppose you could spare some change for my trouble?"

"Er....sure," I said, looking at Kim and Ryan before I dug into my wallet. I handed him a ten dollar bill and he glanced over to my BMW.

"I'm sure the key to this car is worth more than that," he insisted.

I reached into my wallet and handed him a twenty. "There. Please give me my keys," I said, holding out my hand.

He stared at me for a long moment, prompting Ryan to walk over to us. "She gave you some money. Give her back her keys."

The man looked Ryan over and then peered back at me. "I don't think that's quite enough."

My eyes narrowed. "How much do you want?"

"How much do you have in your wallet?"

"What?"

"And I'd like that pretty green ring on your finger, too, baby doll," he nodded.

"You're not getting her ring," Ryan said, stepping in between us.

"Benson?" the bearded man called behind him. One of the men behind him nodded and signaled the others to move forward.

"Ryan...." I whispered as he sidestepped to hide me behind him.

"Aw, look, Grahm. She's got a little bodyguard."

"Shut up, Stu," the bearded man growled.

"Give me the ring...and the money. And you can go," he said, spitting on the ground.

"I don't think so, Grahm," Ryan shifted as he assessed the other men.

"Ryan...." I warned, and then looked at the ring leader. "Listen, this is everything I have on me...." I said, shoving at him several large bills and more fives and ones. "This is everything in my wallet. Take it."

"And the ring," Grahm said in an obstinate tone.

I looked at Kim's horrified expression and then back at the thief. "I... I can't give you my ring. My father gave it to me and he passed away recently."

"That's a very sad story," he mocked. "Give me the ring."

I hid my shaking hand behind me, and looked around for someone, anyone that could help. "I won't," I swallowed. "I'm sorry."

Grahm looked away momentarily to follow my line of sight and Ryan took the opportunity to attack.

Kim ran around the car. "NO!"

A scuffle ensued, with the other three jumping on Ryan. They were in a huddle, punching and kicking Ryan mercilessly.

I took a step toward the cluster. "STOP IT!"

Ryan let out a muffled cry and stopped fighting. My hands flew to my mouth as I saw that Stu held a knife dripping with blood.

"STOP IT, PLEASE!" I said.

The men were chuckling to each other; the brutality had ended with one last kick to Ryan's ribs. I stared in horror as he lay broken on the wet pavement. Just as he attempted to pull himself up to all fours, Stu used his boot to press Ryan's cheek back into the pavement.

"Agh!" Ryan groaned.

"I didn't tell you to get up yet, did I?" Stu said.

The attention turned to my hand. I balled it into a fist; I wouldn't give up my father's ring. Grahm seemed to notice my decision and they all took a step forward, preparing to take it from me. Four sets of malevolent eyes shifted in unison as a familiar voice growled from behind me.

"I think it's time you gentlemen moved on."

Jared strolled past me, and the air escaped from my lungs with overwhelming relief.

"Jared," I said.

He shot me a reassuring smile. "It's okay, sweetheart. You don't have to give them your ring."

"The hell she's not. You want some of what this boy got?" Stu warned.

Grahm eyed Jared suspiciously. "You're Ryel's boy, aren't you?"

My blood ran cold as I looked down at Ryan's limp body. He was still breathing, but in small, shallow gasps. I looked at Jared, terrified of what would happen to him.

"Gentlemen, you can either leave now, with the money the lady has offered, or you can stay, without further use of your arms and legs. It's your choice. Either way, the ring won't be leaving her finger tonight." Jared's voice began polite, but as his offer ended it became low and frightening.

Grahm chuckled as he lowered his head. Once his laughter ended, his eyes darted up, peering at Jared from under his brow. "Then I guess we'll just have to cut her hand off."

I froze.

Jared turned to me, his eyes steely blue, and then he looked back at the men as he took a step towards them.

"See?" Jared sighed. "Now you're just pissing me off."

"I'm sick of this," Benson said.

"Benson, wait!" Grahm ordered.

Two of the men rushed Jared and just as a scream grew in my throat, I saw Jared pull one of them off his back and throw him across the lot—an incredible distance, at least thirty yards—against the stone wall of the alley. The man's body flew into some trashcans with a loud crash. Benson flew back after Jared punched him in the face, and I recoiled when blood exploded from his nose. Stu ran at Jared with his knife, but Jared lithely dodged out of the way and caught the man's arm as he jabbed the knife at him. Jared pulled Stu's arm to the side and quickly rammed his fist into his elbow from behind, hyper extending it until it snapped. Jared punched him again, this time in the face, and the man fell to the ground.

Grahm attempted to turn and run, but with amazing speed Jared reached out and grabbed his overcoat, stopping him in his tracks. The man whirled around and pushed Jared back against my car.

My hands flew up to my mouth.

Jared quickly spun to elbow Grahm in the side of his face. The bearded man plummeted to the ground; the blow causing him to thrash about in stifled groans.

When I gawked down at him, I noticed that his jaw appeared askew. He held it against his face with his hands, and moaned in agony.

Jared pulled my car keys from the ground beside him and noticed a worn, black wallet next to them. He picked it up and it unfolded automatically to reveal a large metallic object.

"Agh...this is not good," Jared said, rubbing his forehead.

"What? What is that? Is that his?" I tried to get a better look as Jared stuffed it into his jacket pocket.

Breathing heavily, Jared took a few steps closer to me. "Are you okay?"

"Am I...? Are you okay?"

Jared nodded but I could see blood oozing from a small cut on his cheek bone, just below his eye.

"You're bleeding," I whispered.

Jared wiped the cut and glanced down at the blood smeared across the back of his hand. "It's not bad. I have to get you out of here before the police show up."

"Ryan's going to need a doctor," I said, rushing down to Ryan's side. He was still breathing, but he'd been beaten badly.

"Ryan? Can you hear me?" I asked, but he didn't respond.

Jared nodded, and then effortlessly lifted Ryan into his arms to put him in the back seat of my car. Kim ran around to jump into the back and covered him with her coat.

"He doesn't look good, Nigh," Kim said, cradling him in her arms.

Jared opened the passenger side door. "Get in, Nina, I'll drive."

We flew through the darkness; making every red light a blurry afterthought. I wrapped my arms around my chest, finding it hard to breathe.

Jared rested his hand on my forearm. "Are you hanging in there?"

"I'm just worried about Ryan," I whispered, peeking back momentarily at my friend. Jared's hand gripped tighter.

"Everything's going to be okay, Nina. Ryan's going to pull through."

"You shouldn't have...you could have been killed, Jared."

Jared raised an eyebrow, looking at me as if I were overreacting.

"It was necessary." His hand left my arm and gripped the steering wheel. "They're lucky I spared them their lives after he—," he paused, seeing my expression. "You don't need to worry...I won't let anyone hurt you. Least of all me."

When the scowl didn't leave my face, he shifted uncomfortably in his seat. "Is something wrong?"

"Nothing is wrong with me, Jared. You're bleeding, Ryan is...," I turned around, "Ryan? Can you hear me?" I touched his battered face gently with my finger tips.

I could see Jared in my peripheral vision, his entire body tensed as if I was touching a live grenade.

"We need to get to the hospital!" Kim begged, holding her fingers to his wrist.

"Hang on, Ryan. We're almost there," I said, wincing when he did.

I had to turn back around to wipe my tears; I didn't want him to see me cry. Jared tucked my hair behind my ear, and with his warm thumb wiped the moisture away. I didn't notice that I was turning my ring mindlessly around my finger until Jared gently squeezed my hand.

"You don't have to do that. It's going to be okay, I promise."

Ryan was whisked away to surgery and Kim, Jared and I were directed to the ICU waiting room. Jared sat beside me, brushing my bangs back from my eyes.

Kim sat on the adjacent couch, her knees shaking up and down. She bit her nails, staring straight ahead. "I called Beth half an hour ago! When are they going to get here?"

I couldn't look at her; Ryan's blood was smeared on her shirt and jacket.

Beth, Josh and Chad filed into the waiting room, wide-eyed and breathless. Beth crashed into me, hugging me until I thought my ribs would break.

"Oh my God, Nina! Are you okay? Is Kim okay?"

"We're okay," I whispered.

Beth put her hands to her mouth when she noticed the blood on Kim's clothing and shook her head. "Ryan?"

"He's still in surgery," Kim said. "He has some broken ribs, and they think the knife may have punctured his spleen. They'll remove it if they can't get the bleeding stopped."

My eyes welled up with tears.

"Whoa," Josh sighed, rubbing his forehead in disbelief.

Beth hugged me as we both cried. She walked over to Kim and sat down. When Kim only offered a weak smile, Beth pulled her into her arms.

Jared put his arm around me and led me back to the couch. Kim rehashed the account to the others until Josh interrupted.

"Why didn't you just give him the damn ring, Nina?" he asked in an accusatory tone.

"This isn't Nina's fault," Jared grimaced, squeezing me closer to his side.

"Her father gave her that ring, Josh," Beth added.

"It's just a ring," he murmured.

Jared looked into my eyes with an understanding expression; he didn't want me to feel worse than I already did. I didn't expect anyone to understand my attachment to the ring anymore than I expected them to understand my relationship with my father.

"How did you get away?" Beth asked.

I felt Jared shift uncomfortably beside me when Kim spoke, "Jared took all four of them on. He was amazing. Apparently he's taught his little sister everything she knows."

All eyes darted to Jared, who leaned forward and clasped his hands together. "I'm in the security business."

"Where? In Iraq?" Josh sneered.

"Nah," Jared said, downplaying Kim's explanation.

I knew better. I had just glimpsed into a fraction of Jared's secret.

I jerked against Jared's shoulder when he whispered that Ryan was being wheeled into Intensive Care from recovery. "It's okay, you're safe," he whispered, pressing his lips to the top of my hair.

"Oh," I said, wiping my eyes. "I must have dozed off for a second."

"More like an hour," Kim said with heavy eyes.

Jared squeezed me to him. "You didn't miss anything; you needed to rest."

"What time is it?" I yawned.

"Seven thirty," Beth said, looking as exhausted as I felt.

The nurses pushed the stretcher down the hall with a barely coherent Ryan attached to monitors and tubes. I ran into the hallway and grabbed his hand, walking with them.

"I'm so sorry." My voice broke before I could attempt a braver tone.

Ryan mumbled something inaudible and I felt my face compress. "It's okay, you don't have to talk." I choked at how familiar those words sounded. "We'll be right down the hall, okay?" I kissed his hand and he smiled, reaching his shaky fingers to brush my cheek with the back of his fingertips. I held his hand to my face for a moment, kissed it, then let go as they passed through the double doors.

The doors shut in my face, and I brought my hand to my mouth to stifle the cries. Beth came up behind me and Kim joined us, followed by Josh and Chad. We all huddled in the middle of the hall as we hugged and cried.

I had been nestled in Jared's warm arms for twenty minutes when a nurse came out.

"He's resting now. If you would like to freshen up and come back later, he may be ready for visitors then."

"But...how is he?" I asked.

"It's still early, but he's young and healthy. I'd say he's going to recover quite nicely," she smiled.

We shared a collective sigh as she wheeled around and disappeared behind the double doors.

"I'm going to head home. Call me when he wakes up," Chad said.

"Can I catch a ride with you?" Kim asked. With that, Beth, Kim, Chad and Josh all stood up.

"You're staying?" Beth asked.

I nodded and stood up to hug her.

"I'll stay with her," Jared said.

Beth smiled through her fatigue before Chad led her out by the hand.

"You're exhausted," Jared said. "I should take you home."

I shook my head. "I can't leave him here alone. I almost got him killed."

Jared's faced twisted when he spoke. "He almost got himself killed."

"He tried to keep them from attacking me!" I said, offended.

"Fat lot of good it did him," Jared said dismissively, rolling his eyes.

"I know, Jared. If you hadn't shown up, Ryan would have bled out and I would have been left handed for the rest of my life, however brief."

Anger played out across his face and he stood up, stopping just inches from me. "It's not funny, Nina. You were in serious danger. Ryan should have diffused the situation instead of escalating it. He watches too much television. It's the ones that try to impress the girl who end up...."

"He didn't do that to impress me!"

"His feelings for you clouded his judgment. He tried to be a hero....and here you are, feeling guilty."

"You're jealous?" I said, incredulous.

Jared's rigid posture in the car replayed in my head. I was too worried to think about it at the time, but it made sense. He had mistaken my actions for intimacy. He thought Ryan and I were more than friends.

Jared rolled his eyes. "If I were jealous, it wouldn't be for that. I'm used to seeing you with someone else. It's just a matter of enduring it, now."

My eyes narrowed in suspicion. "What do you mean you're used to it?"

Jared didn't answer right away. He heaved an exasperated sigh and his jaws tensed.

"I just meant from before. I've had to see you with him before."

"With Ryan?"

"Yes. At the pub, remember?" Jared eyes wandered everywhere but into mine.

"I remember," I said, still unconvinced.

He took my hand and worry shadowed his face. "I'm glad you're okay. For a moment I thought I wouldn't get there in time."

"Was your judgment clouded?" I said acerbically, still incensed that he had snubbed Ryan's bravery.

"Something like that," he glowered, looking away from me.

"You're not going to tell me the truth, are you?" I pulled my hand from his and crossed my arms.

Jared's head snapped back, and his eyes glared into mine. "And what truth would that be?"

"You know what I'm talking about. You took down four men—on your own—like they were little girls. The incomparable sense of timing you seem to have, the knowing where I am all the time...."

"I don't know where you are all the time...and my sense of timing tonight was almost nonexistent."

"Are you going to be honest with me or not?" I stood there for a moment, and when Jared seemed to deliberate, I walked back to the couch.

Jared sighed in resignation and then sat beside me. "I wanted to kiss you the other night. I knew that you were upset. I wanted to comfort you and I ended up just hurting you more." He winced. "That wasn't my intention, Nina. I would've given anything to lean into that kiss. It's just...complicated."

"You knew that I was upset?"

He looked down and sighed.

"Jared?" He looked up at me. "What do you want from me?" I asked, exasperated.

He didn't look up. "I want you to be safe. I want you to be happy. I'm figuring out the rest."

I nodded. "Okay."

His head snapped up. "Okay?" he said, searching my eyes.

"Okay," I shrugged.

Jared's face was just a short distance from mine, so close that I could feel his warm breath gently blowing against my cheek. He stared at my lips, but I didn't dare move for fear he would pull back and I would have to suffer humiliation all over again. I took in a breath and he looked into my eyes. He leaned closer to me an infinitesimal amount, and his phone buzzed. We both heaved out a sigh and he leaned back to retrieve his phone.

"Ryel," he snapped. I heard a quick chattering on the line, and then he clicked his phone closed, shaking his head. "I have to go."

"It's okay," I smiled.

He kissed my forehead, and the warmth of his lips blazed into my skin.

"See you around," he said, walking to the doorway.

"Jared?" I blurted out, scrambling to my feet. He turned to face me and I smiled. "Thank you. Thank you so much. For everything."

Jared's eyes grew soft and he took a few steps toward me. The warmth of his hands sunk into my shoulders, and his jaw tensed as a flood of emotion scrolled across his face. His eyebrows pulled in before he gingerly pulled me to him and pressed his soft lips against mine. He ran his hands up my neck to my face where he held my cheeks in each of his hands. My surroundings vanished; the only thing I could focus on was the breathtaking heat against my mouth. An entire lifetime could have passed and still the kiss ended too soon. He pulled me tighter to his chest and then wheeled around, disappearing down the hall.

I walked a few paces backwards and fell against the seat. The gravity of the situation pressed down on me with renewed strength. The danger, my fear, and the confusion about what I'd seen—what Jared was capable of—were swimming around in my mind. I should have been insane with anxiety but I felt the same sense of calm I'd felt on the side of the road the night before last. Ryan was going to be all right, my hand was still firmly attached to my wrist, and Jack's gift was safely around my finger.

I felt a twinge of shame as I realized none of those things were the reason for my frame of mind. My lips still tingled from the warmth of Jared's kiss.

I melted into the sofa, turning my head to press my cheek against the cushion for support. I was so fatigued it felt like work just to breathe.

My heavy eyes rose to the wall of windows along the waiting room. Cynthia's heels were quickly clicking down the hall.

Chapter Five
Disclosure

"Nina! For the love of Christ, why didn't you call me?"

"I'm fine, Mom. I wasn't hurt," I said, swaying as she tugged and pulled on me to look me over.

She clutched me into her arms tightly. "Nina Elizabeth Grey, if anything had happened to you, I swear to God... I swear to God, I would have never forgiven him."

"I'm pretty sure those men wouldn't have cared if you forgave them or not, Mom."

She gave me a wry look and hugged me again. "Well, it doesn't matter now. You're safe, that is what's important."

"Did Beth call you?" I asked, trying to keep my eyes open.

"What do you mean did Beth call me?" Her voice raised an octave. "I'm not allowed to see for myself that my only child is safe after she is...is attacked in the street by some junkie? Nina, you infuriate me sometimes! What were you doing at a bar, anyway? On that side of town, no less, you could have been killed! And you have the audacity to ask—"

"Okay, Mom! Okay! I'm sorry!" I pulled her to me. She was very near hysterics. Usually my mother didn't go to such extremes, but she had enough to agonize over without me being assaulted in dark alleys.

Cynthia pulled away and held me at arm's length. "Well, that's enough of that," she sighed, her typical poker face back into play. "Come, Dear. I'll send someone for your car."

I shook my head. "I'm going to stay here and wait for Ryan to wake up."

"You're exhausted." She argued in vain. We both knew I wouldn't change my mind.

Cynthia patted my knee and stood. "I expect you to be in your bed resting in four hours. No excuses, young lady."

I nodded as she clicked down the hallway. I rubbed my eyes and leaned back against my seat. The television was on a medical channel, something about insurance and prescriptions. It didn't take me long to lose interest.

Three hours later, the ICU nurse stood at my side. "Nina?"

"Yes?" I sat up and blinked my eyes.

"My name is Jenny. I'm Ryan's nurse," she smiled. "He's awake. He's asking for you."

I stood up and walked with her to the double doors. Before we made it through, a disheveled woman scampered down the hall toward us. She wore a brown waitress' uniform and her frizzy black hair failed miserably at staying in the messy bun she'd fashioned.

"I'm looking for Ryan Scott! I was told he's in ICU?" she puffed.

Jenny looked at me and then back to her. "Are you his...?"

"Mother! I'm his mom. He's here? Is he okay?" she said, breathless. "I'm Callie Scott. I'd like to see him, please."

Jenny extended an apologetic smile and then turned to Callie. "He's here, Ms. Scott. I'll show you to his room."

I trudged back to my seat, glancing at my watch. According to Cynthia, I had less than an hour to make my way home to rest. Unable to comply, I pulled my phone from my pocket to call in an explanation.

As I dialed, Jenny poked her head into the waiting room doorway. "Nina?"

"Yes?"

She smiled. "He would still like to see you."

"Oh!" I said, surprised. I followed quickly behind her through the double doors and we stopped three rooms down. When she pulled back the heavy curtain, the rings grated across the metal bar.

She smiled to her left. "I found her. She didn't leave."

I peered into the room and inwardly cringed at the tubes and wires leading from Ryan's body.

"Hey, Nigh," he rasped.

I managed a half grin. "Today is the only day I'll let you get away with that."

Ryan laughed and then winced.

"Take it easy, Baby," Callie said, searching for a place to touch him that wasn't attached to a monitor or IV pump. She settled on brushing back his hair.

"Mom, don't fuss," he whispered, leaning away from her nervous stroking.

"Chad, Beth and Josh were here earlier; they'll be back," I said, touching his foot.

Ryan nodded. "Is Jared still here?"

I shook my head, making the corners of Ryan's mouth turn up. I wasn't sure how much he had seen, or how much he remembered.

"It's a good thing he's stalking you."

I rolled my eyes. "He's not stalking me."

"How else do you explain him showing up out of nowhere?" Ryan pressed.

"Who's stalking you? Is this the man that attacked my son?" Callie's face compressed with concern.

"No, Mom. He's the guy that kept us all from getting killed," Ryan said, watching my face.

Callie looked to me, still wanting answers.

I fidgeted under her stare. "He's a friend of mine that came just in time."

"As usual," Ryan frowned. "You look like hell. Get some sleep."

"I can sleep later," I argued. Of course he would be worried about me while he was lying in a hospital bed.

"You can sleep now. My mom's here, I don't need both of you whining over every little thing."

"I don't whine," I said, feigning insult.

"You can be kinda whiny," he smiled and tapped his cheek. I maneuvered around the tubes and wires to kiss the spot he had indicated. Being this close to someone covered in hospital paraphernalia caused my ribs to wrench in an all too familiar way. I bit my lip with apprehension.

"Hey," he reached up an arm to brush my cheek with the back of his fingers. "I'm going to be fine. I'd do it again if I had to."

My face fell at his words. I knew how he felt about me, and how it would end. I couldn't stand it if I ever hurt Ryan enough for him to hate me.

My hands grabbed his. "You just concentrate on getting well before you start planning more knife fights, all right?"

He grinned. "Sweet dreams, Nina."

I walked into the dark, curtains drawn and all bulbs extinguished. Beth was still cocooned inside her comforter breathing heavily. I peeled off my coat and fell face down onto my bed.

I tried to lay still and relax; I didn't want to let my mind wander. Allowing thoughts would mean envisioning the attack, the blood, the eyes of the man that would cut off my hand to take my ring; the chilling sound of Ryan's cry when he was impaled and Kim's horrified expression in the car. I didn't even want to dwell on Jared's lips. I just wanted to sleep.

My eyes shot open to the sound of the door quietly pulling closed.

"Beth?" I called, listening for any motion from her side of the room. She didn't answer.

I leaned up on my elbows and blinked my eyes several times until I could see clearly that Beth's bed was empty and made. A note was on the back of the door, so I pushed myself slowly from the bed and ambled across the cold floor.

Went with Chad and Josh
to the hospital.
See you there.
~Beth

Ryan wouldn't be at the hospital alone. Of course his mother might still be there, but it was good that he would have his friends around him. Beth would be home late, I assumed. I looked at the clock.

Six o'clock!

Scrambling from the bed, I rushed to change and brush my teeth, pulling my hair back into a ponytail. Just as I grabbed my keys, my stomach growled. Going off campus alone immediately seemed like a bad idea, and hoping for something edible at the hospital was being unnecessarily optimistic. Dinner at the Gate meant a long walk in the bitter cold outside, which would keep my mind off more troubling circumstances. I zipped up my coat and locked the door behind me.

Soon I was within a dozen yards of my destination. I was right; shivering with every step had been the perfect diversion from the night before. I puffed out a steamy breath of relief as my mind concentrated on the warmth and subsequent thaw the doors of The Gate assured me.

As I reached for the door handle, a man stepped in front of me from the shadows.

I jerked to a stop. "Mr. Dawson?"

"Do you have the file?" he asked, his eyes intent.

Still on edge from the attack, my hands balled into fists and I shoved them in my pockets. I glanced at the door handle, seeing that it was just a foot or two from me.

I forced my body to relax. "Mr. Rosen isn't familiar with your transaction, but I could give you his number, if you'd like."

"So you'll help me, then?" his eyes narrowed.

"I'm not sure why you would think this incessant harassment would encourage me to be of assistance to you at all." I was lying, of course. I knew how the intimidation game worked. I'd seen my father win it many times.

"Nina, I've told you what I'm looking for. Your father and I—,"

"Were involved in a property deal. You've said that," I interrupted. "I'm his daughter, not his business partner. Please call Mr. Rosen."

I reached for the door, but Mr. Dawson grabbed my arm. With a quick jerk, he yanked me toward him. I gasped as he whispered in my ear with his guttural, growling voice. "I'm not playing games with you, little girl. Your father has documents and photos that I want. The last time I saw them, they were in a file in his office marked Port of Providence. I want that entire file, do you understand me? Unless you want mommy to have to deal with me later, I suggest you do as I ask."

Threatening my mother sent a courageous voice emanating from my throat, "Stay away from her!"

Mr. Dawson snorted. "Just like Jack...never know when to back down."

"My father didn't back down!"

"And that's what got him killed!" Mr. Dawson snarled, jerking my arm again.

I felt my eyes widen in stunned disbelief. His reply didn't make sense. My father died after his car accident.

Mr. Dawson sighed and loosened his grip. "I'm doin' you a favor, Peach. You don't want caught within a hundred yards of that package. There are more dangerous things than me out there wantin' it worse than I do. Bring it to me, and you and your mother will have a lot less to worry about."

His fingers slipped away from my arm, and he disappeared into the shadows of the neighboring building. I leaned my head against the frosty glass door, trying to gain the courage to move. Once the adrenaline absorbed into my body, I sucked in a gasp of air and slid to the ground.

He didn't come. I was in danger, and Jared didn't come. I was surprised when the correlation hit me, and I wondered if I had just realized it or if I had known all along. The last time Mr. Dawson approached me, Jared was a no-show as well, but I reasoned that Ryan had been there. Ryan had controlled the situation enough so that Jared wasn't needed. This time I was alone. This time I needed him.

Someone pushed the door open against me. "Are you all right?" A short, dark haired boy with glasses came into view, poking his head through the semi-open door.

"Did you want to come in?" the boy asked, confused at his discovery.

I pushed myself off the ground. "No, thank you," I said, my voice quivering. I wheeled around and headed to Andrew's.

I didn't look back to see his inevitable bewildered expression; I was too intent on my mission. I would return to my mother's house and turn it upside down if I had to. I ran down the hall to the open elevator and tapped the button of my floor several times, leaning back against the rail. As the doors finally closed, my mother squeezed by them, causing them to jolt open once more.

"I trust you've slept," she said.

"Is that why you're here?" I asked, surprised.

"Do I need a reason?" She was very nearly offended, but dismissed my question to address more important things. "Nina, honestly. You look frightful. How much sleep did you get?"

"Enough," I stepped out of the elevator and pulled her with me.

"What are you doing?" she asked, reluctant to be dragged along.

"I want to go home. Can I go home with you?"

"Of course." I was sure she was curious what had possessed me to make such an atypical request; I had treated our home like ground zero of a quarantined leper colony since the funeral.

I tugged at her coat to quicken her pace and she abruptly stopped. "What is going on, Nina?"

"What do you mean?" I asked, pulling at her arm again.

"This!" she said, motioning to my hand on her arm. "This is what I mean. What is so urgent?"

I exhaled in a frustrated puff. "Beth is at the hospital and I don't want to be alone. I'm sorry if I'm being overly enthusiastic."

"Enthusiastic? Nina, you haven't tugged on my coat like that since you were five. Is there another reason you want to go home?"

I stared at her blankly. I didn't want to lie to her again.

"All right," she sighed. "Robert is waiting in the car."

En route, Cynthia fiddled with her carefully placed French bun and asked generic questions about school. She was suspicious of my behavior, but as was the norm with my mother, she insisted on overlooking the obvious to obtain a false sense of security. She didn't speak for the rest of the trip home to keep from spoiling the illusion with trivial things like the truth.

Robert slowed down when he entered our long drive. My mother smiled at him when he opened her door, and I followed behind her to the house.

Once inside, I peeled off my scarf, hat, coat, and finally my gloves. I rubbed the residual chill still clinging to my arms, methodically going over my plan in my mind.

"Nina, don't hover in doorways. It's rude."

"I'm going upstairs," I said in passing.

I rushed to my father's office, hoping my eyes would open to something I had missed before. I walked along the outer edges of the room and ran my hand along the surface of the wall, feeling the uneven texture with my fingertips. I tried not to concentrate on any one thing; I wanted to leave my mind open to any clues that I might have overlooked before.

My fingertips grazed the spines of my father's books. I pulled a few of them out and looked behind them, knocking on the wall they stood against. I crawled under his desk and felt for anything abnormal.

When I found nothing, I returned to the walls, the cabinets, and then the bookcase. I went over them all again, trying to see them a different way, to touch them differently, to appraise them for anything that seemed out of place. As my patience waned, so did my objectivity. I began plowing through the cabinets as I had before, slamming them shut and muttering under my breath.

I sat on the floor against the front of Jack's desk and stared across the room with my elbows on my knees. The answers were here; I was missing something.

I lifted my chin in interest when my father's favorite painting caught my eye. I scrambled to my feet and reached under the edges of the large frame. Determined, I reached closer to its center, knelt down and peered under it, and even pulled it a bit from the wall. I didn't see anything remarkable, so I reached up blindly, hoping to find something that didn't belong. There was nothing.

I stomped in anger. "DADDY!"

I looked around the room with my hands defiantly on my hips, blowing my bangs from my face. There were four other paintings in the room. I rushed each one, mimicking the sweep I'd just done with the larger painting. I ripped the fourth one off the wall and searched the backside of the frame. Looking at the now-empty wall, I felt another scream of aggravation coming on.

How could there be nothing in his office? No safes, no secret doorways, no....

Keys. There were keys in Jack's desk. The first time I'd searched his office I assumed they were his car keys. But the car he drove himself—his Jag—was totaled. Scrap metal. What were the keys to?

In my haste to get to the desk, my hip smashed into the corner with a loud crack. I stifled a cry and doubled over, using the desk to steady myself. I attempted to rub the sting away with one hand, and pulled open the drawer containing the keys with the other. I held the keys in my palm, trying to remember if I'd seen a lock that the keys might fit. I slowly turned my head toward the wall of cabinets. The center tower of files was locked.

Surely, he wouldn't be this obvious, I thought.

I hobbled to the cabinets and tugged on the drawer. It was still locked.

I began with the first key. It only went in half way. I tried three more keys; the fourth easily slid in, but wouldn't turn. Two keys later, I found myself cursing my father, Mr. Dawson, even the metal in my hands. I gripped the last key between my thumb and finger and closed my eyes.

The key slid in, and I rotated my wrist. It began to turn, and then caught. None of the keys were to the locked file cabinet.

"DAMN IT!" I said, throwing the keys to the floor. I kicked the cabinet, walked away, and then returned to land another kick, this time denting the bottom.

Limping across the floor, I picked up the keys and tossed them into the desk drawer. I was done.

I walked down the hall with my hand still pressed against my throbbing hip and stopped at the top of the stairs. Cynthia's voice was weary as she spoke on the phone. Idling for a moment before taking the first stair, I heard her speak my name.

"Nina's fine. She's upstairs, resting. What do you expect me to do? Forbid her to...? Honestly, you worry too much! She just didn't want to be alone tonight. I heard some commotion upstairs; I assumed she knocked something over. It mustn't have been as bad as...," she sighed, "yes. I'll check on her. Goodnight."

Cynthia turned to look up at me. I sheepishly waved, cursing under my breath for getting caught eavesdropping.

"Are you all right, Dear?" she called.

"I'm fine. Ran into a desk; bumped my side. Who was that?"

She shrugged. "Was it really necessary to yell out such profanities while I'm on the phone? My friends were under the impression that I had raised a lady."

"I'm sorry. I didn't realize I was being so loud."

Cynthia nodded dismissively. "I've got a beautiful ham in the oven. You'll be staying for dinner, won't you?"

"Er...yes. I was going to stop by the hospital, but it can wait."

Cynthia made her way up the stairs. I followed into her study where she set some unopened envelopes on her desk.

"How is your friend doing?" she asked, I assumed just to be polite.

"I'm not sure, I haven't been back since this morning, but no one's called to tell me otherwise. I'm sure there's been improvement."

"Wonderful news, Dear," she said, preoccupied.

She pulled her pearl drop earrings from her ears, and placed them on the silver tray that sat on a small table near the wall. My eyes wandered to a hutch that matched her table and desk. The fronds of a plant obscured the top cabinet, and I focused on a small silver circle on the top right corner.

"Coming, Nina?" Cynthia asked, pausing at the door.

"I'll be down in a minute. I wanted to check my e-mail, if you don't mind."

"Not at all," she smiled. "Don't be late for dinner."

I watched her walk out the door and waited as she descended the stairs. Once she was deeper into the lower level, I sprinted down the hall to my father's office. Yanking open his desk drawer, I grabbed the small silver ring of keys.

With a sense of excitement, I hurried back to my mother's study and pulled the plant to the floor. It was heavier than it appeared, and I grunted as I worked to set it down without overturning the whole pot onto its side.

After the first five keys failed, I blew my bangs from my face with a puff of air. Only two keys left. The sixth key slid in, and when I turned my wrist and the key continued to turn ninety degrees, I gasped.

Pulling the cabinet door open, I peered behind me for a just a moment, afraid of what my mother would say if she caught me snooping in her things. There were several files, so I pulled all of them out and spread them on the floor. On my knees, I thumbed through contracts, shipping papers, a receipt for the ring my father bought me, insurance claims and filings, and the occasional deposit slip.

I slid one folder to the side to uncover another with Jack's no-nonsense scribble on it.

Port of Providence

My hands shook as I opened the flap of the folder. Did I really want to know? I felt I was opening Pandora's Box.

Sitting on top, I found a thick, wrinkled manila envelope. I pulled the packet from the file and opened it. It contained a stack of black and white photos. Picture after picture featured a dozen or so different men, but those same faces appeared over and over, at times alone, and at other times together. One man that was most often the subject in the pictures stood beside the governor of Rhode Island. Another man was pictured in both casual clothes and some type of uniform; I assumed he was a police officer in formal blues.

I'd seen enough movies to know that these were surveillance photos. I turned each of the pictures over, but they were all unmarked. I had never seen these men before that I could remember, and I couldn't fathom why my father would have them photographed. I looked at the file on the floor, knowing I was about to find out.

A handwritten sheet of paper caught my eye, and I poured over it. I flipped to the next page, and the next. My heart pounded as the words burned into my irises. It wasn't true. It couldn't be.

"Nina? Dinner!"

I rushed to gather the files and shoved them into Cynthia's hutch. I locked the cabinet door and heaved the clay pot back to its shelf. After returning the keys to Jack's desk drawer, I met Cynthia in the dining room.

I sat in my usual chair, across from my mother. A steaming plate of food waited for me on fine china, and I grimaced as the mouthwatering smell invaded my nose. I realized I hadn't eaten since five o'clock the evening before. I was famished, but couldn't eat.

"Aren't you hungry, dear?"

I furrowed my brow and stabbed a carrot with my fork. Her strained politeness would soon be chipped away and all the pleasantries would cease.

"Not really."

"Well, why not?" I waited for the right words to come and she rolled her eyes with impatience. "Really, Nina. You know I don't like it when—,"

"Has Daddy always been a criminal, or was it something he took up just before he died?" I blurted out, unconcerned with the consequences.

Cynthia's fork fell to her plate with a shrill clang. She didn't say anything for a long while. We both held our breath, waiting for the other to speak.

"What...did you say?" she finally whispered.

"You heard me."

"No. I don't believe I did. I'm sure you misspoke," her eyes fluttered as she ended her sentence.

"Port of Providence." I sat slightly forward in my chair, watching her expression change from insult to shock.

"What? Where did you hear th—," Cynthia stopped mid-sentence and shook her head. She was flustered, which she rarely experienced.

"I saw the file, Mother. Was it organized crime, or did he just skim off the top at the docks? You know his payroll was full of dirty cops, right?"

"Nina Elizabeth Grey! You will shut your mouth this instant!!" I could see the wheels in her head turning, and then she stood up to come to my side of the table, sitting beside me. "You saw files. What files?" I could tell her fury was subdued, she would address my disrespect later.

"The files locked in the hutch in your study, Mother. Stop playing dumb."

Her eyes tightened; my rudeness narrowly outweighed her curiosity. "I've never played dumb in my life, Nina. Why on earth would you—,"

"I want the truth." I didn't let my eyes move an inch from her gaze.

"I didn't bother myself with your father's business dealings," she said, turning away.

"But you know what I'm talking about when I say Port of Providence, don't you?" My accusing eyes bored into her.

Cynthia nodded slightly. "That's not something you'd want to admit to having knowledge of, Nina. Forget you saw any of that," she whispered.

"Forget—," I was in shock. My father was a... a....criminal? A thief?" My face twisted into disgust. "He stole from the distributors he shipped for, he sold things on the black market, he smuggled illegal contraband, and he used cops to cover up his dirty work...police officers, Mother! All of which he gathered evidence against to keep them from turning on him!" My eyes glossed over with anger. "Everything we have is from blood money. Jack had people beaten...he's had people killed."

Cynthia wiped a tear and looked down at her lap. This took me off-guard; I had only seen my mother cry a handful of times, all of them following Jack's accident and death.

"Oh, Jack," she whispered, shaking her head slowly. She looked at me with sympathetic eyes, "You were never supposed to see those things, Nina. Your father was always so careful to keep you safe from that part of his life. He hasn't been gone six months and I've failed him." Cynthia rose to her feet and walked slowly to the door.

I pushed myself away from the table and called after her. "Tell me I'm wrong, Mother. I need you to tell me this is a mistake." My voice was closer to begging than the firm tone I'd meant to take.

Cynthia didn't turn around; she wiped another tear and sighed.

I took a deep breath and braced myself. "Charles Dawson wants those files."

"He knew where they were?" she shrieked, flipping around.

Anger surged through me. "You know who he is?"

"He worked for your father," she said, touching her mouth nervously in thought.

I sat up higher in my chair, my muscles rigid. "Why is he harassing me, Mother? Why aren't you upset about that?"

"Nina, Dear," her tone turned soft, "I told you. Your father did everything in his power to keep you removed from his dealings. I understand you were frightened; but you were safe, I promise."

"What does that mean? Why won't anyone give me a straight answer?"

Cynthia tilted her head and raised her eyebrows, the way she did when I was little. "Wouldn't you agree that after tonight, some things are better left unsaid?"

My immediate reaction was to scream at her and demand the truth, but she was right. I had lost my father again tonight, the reverence I'd once felt for him was replaced with debilitating disappointment. It was worse than losing him to death. All perception I'd had of him had been ripped away. He was no longer God in my eyes, he was just a man; a flawed, corrupt man.

I considered Cynthia's suggestion and nodded.

She lifted my chin. "I'm so sorry, Love."

"I've got to get out of here," I blurted, turning away from her touch. Everything I knew was a lie. I left her alone to fetch my coat.

"Where are you going?" she called after me.

"For a walk," I said, bundling myself inside my hat and gloves.

"It's freezing outside, Nina! Be reasonable! Please let Robert drive you!"

I yanked my purse over my shoulder and jerked open the door. "I'll walk to the bus stop and catch a ride to Brown. I'll call you when I get there." I avoided her inevitably pleading eyes as I marched outside, slamming the door behind me.

Winter exploded in my face. The air was too cold to breathe, burning my nose and throat with each gasp of air that I took in. The wind had picked up and the large snowflakes whipped around me. My hair thrashed against my face and I squinted as the icy wind blurred my vision.

I tried to sort the new information, but the freezing air along with my anger blocked any rational thought

I could have. I reached the end of the drive and trudged into the street, walking as fast as my legs could carry me. My home had become a dark, wicked thing where corruption and scandal took place. I couldn't bring myself to look back, even though I had no intentions of returning.

When the painful burn from the wind began to wane to a numbing sensation, I heard a vehicle slow down beside me. I continued to walk; I wasn't in the mood to explain myself or argue with Robert. He was less capable of changing my mind than my mother.

"Nina?"

I knew that voice. It belonged to the one person I wanted to see. When I came to a stop, so did his SUV.

"I'm taking the bus, Jared," I said, looking straight ahead.

"No, you're not. I've come to take you home."

I stood perfectly still except for the occasional weaving when the wind attempted to knock me over.

"Nina, it's freezing outside," he said, impatient.

When I didn't budge, Jared opened his door and walked over to me. He stared at me for a moment and then bent down, sweeping me into his arms. He carried me to the passenger side, pressing his warm lips to my forehead.

He placed me gently into the seat and paused. "What were you thinking?"

I couldn't utter a single word. I felt broken; It was all too much for me to accept in such a short amount of time.

Once in his seat, he turned the heater to its highest setting and pulled forward. Occasionally, Jared would reach over and brush my hair back from my face, or hold his warm hand affectionately to my cheek, but the only sounds were the heated air blowing through the vents and the road under the tires.

The Escalade came to a stop on the street behind Andrews. Jared walked with me to the door in silence, but when I put my hand on the knob, he touched my arm.

"Nina, I know it's a lot to take in, but he loved you."

My eyes focused and I shot a glare at him. "You knew my father?"

Jared's eyes tensed in anguish. "I know everything that he did...he did out of love for you, Nina. You were his world."

"You don't know anything about him," I said through my teeth. "You don't know anything about me, and unless you give me some answers, you can leave. I am sick of being lied to!"

"I've never lied to you," Jared said, angry and shocked that I had dismissed him so easily.

"Why are you so secretive? Why do you always know where I am? How did you save us this morning? How did you do all of that?"

"This morning you were fine with not knowing all the details."

"That was before I found out my entire life was a lie." Angry tears overflowed and rushed down my cheeks. "I just need one thing in my life—just one— that I know is real. I need someone to be honest with me!"

"Nina," Jared whispered, reaching out for me. I pushed him away and he winced. "Don't do that. I've had to stand by and watch you cry so many times...I can't do it anymore."

"What does that mean?" I asked him, keeping him at arm's length. "What do you mean you've watched me cry? Please just tell me the truth!"

Jared hesitated and then sighed. "I can't. Believe me when I say I wish to God that I could, but I can't." His eyes were heavy with a lifetime's worth of frustration.

"I believe you," I said, opening the door. "I don't want to see you anymore. Please leave me alone."

"Nina...." Jared said. I met his eyes one last time before shutting the door behind me. He knocked twice. "Nina," he said in a low, desperate tone.

I pressed my head against the door and let out a weak, muffled cry. I couldn't understand why I wasn't worthy enough for the truth. Anger took hold of me again, and I pushed away from the door, making my way to my room.

Beth sat at her desk, clicking the keyboard on her lap top when I swung the door open. She jumped and turned when the door knob hammered against the wall.

"Where were you? Ryan was waiting for you to come." Her eyes bulged when she saw the expression on my face. "Nina?"

"I went to The Gate to get a bite to eat before heading to the hospital, but I ran into Mr. Dawson," I said, slumping onto my bed.

"Mr. Dawson?" Her voice flew up an octave. "Why was he at The Gate?"

"He grabbed me, told me he wanted me to get the papers for him—"

"He grabbed you? Does Jared know?"

My eyes darted to hers with suspicion. "What makes you ask that?"

She hesitated, picking at her delicate fingers. "He always seems to have the best timing."

"He didn't show up this time."

She leaned her head closer so that I would look at her. "Have you seen him today?"

"He just dropped me off," I sighed.

"I don't understand. He didn't show up, but he brought you home?"

"Can we not talk about this anymore?"

"Oh. Sure. I'm sorry." She dropped her arm from my shoulder and left me to sit on her own bed.

After a few moments, Beth sighed and fidgeted.

"What, Beth?"

"Nina...," I waited for her to gain the courage for whatever it was she was struggling with. She took another breath, but it didn't equip her with the bravery she was hoping for.

"What is it?"

"You love him," she blurted out, quickly bracing for my reaction.

"I don't love him. I don't know anything about him."

"How much is enough to know about someone before you can love them?"

I thought back to the way I felt when I was around him, the way his touch sent electricity through my body; the way his eyes melted me when he looked beyond my irises to something deeper, as if he could see my emotions dance around inside of me. I felt protected and whole in his presence that rivaled even the absolute security and love I felt being near my father. I shuddered when I considered how miserable my life would be if Jared did as I asked and left me alone.

"You love him," Beth confirmed as she watched my expression. "He loves you, too, you know. It's so obvious, almost as if he loved you before you met." I shook my head in denial and Beth's voice raised a tone higher. "Nina. Seriously? After everything that's happened?"

"If he does, it's not enough to trust me with the truth." I winced at my own words. I didn't realize how hurtful it would be to say them out loud.

"He's still not talking, huh?"

"I told him to leave me alone tonight." Beth began to speak but I continued, "I didn't mean it. Well, I meant it, but it's not what I want. All he has to do is be honest with me, and he just...refuses."

"Why do you have to understand it? Can't you just be with him and forget about the rest?"

"Be with him how? I don't even know where he lives. I don't know his phone number, if he's right or left-handed, or his birthday...I don't know anything about him," I said, disgusted with my predicament.

"I've seen you two together. It will all work out," she smiled.

I rolled my eyes at her simple solution. Beth's logic made my feelings more complicated than necessary, and I was glad when she seemed to give up. I was devastated about Jack, furious with Cynthia and found Jared guilty on principle. Other than that I didn't want to think about it. Anger was easier to control than feeling betrayed.

Thursday morning I followed Beth to the table reserved for the coffee pots and various sugars and other creamers. Per her usual, Kim appeared behind

113

us and complained about our additives. I gripped my travel mug with both hands, keeping in line with my friends.

Beth stopped in her tracks, initiating a pileup. I slammed into Kim, and the coffee I held exploded from the slit in the lid, splattering in a vertical line from collar to hem of my coat.

"Beth!" Kim and I both yelped in unison.

I looked down at my coat and used my mittens to brush off the dripping, mocha-colored liquid. Someone abruptly grabbed my arm and yanked me forward. I didn't have time to see which of my girlfriends it was, because Jared's incredible blue-grey eyes caught my attention the second I looked up.

I took quicker steps than I should have to be within conversation distance, but once I stood within a few feet of him, I couldn't speak.

"Running late, aren't you?" Jared said, seeming pleased at my reaction.

"What are you doing here?" I asked, baffled.

He laughed and looked down. I saw from my peripheral that Beth and Kim were just as awestruck as I was. I couldn't imagine what had possessed him to show up here, and I was even more clueless at his carefree manner; as if our conversation from the night before had never taken place.

"Will you have a seat?"

I sat down immediately, in an almost comical fashion. He usually didn't make an appearance unless he had something important he needed to say, or if there was trouble. The scenarios were flashing through my mind. I stared at him in silence, waiting for the answer.

He crossed his arms on the table and leaned toward me. "I know you said to leave you alone, but I did a lot of thinking last night and I had to see you. We need to talk."

My mouth opened a bit in shock, and I shut it just as I looked up at Kim and Beth. Their mouths were in a similar state.

"We'll, er...meet you in class, Nigh," Kim said, raising her eyebrows.

I grimaced as they abandoned me. My shoulders felt so tense they seemed to be hovering around my ears. I took a deep breath, and forced them down to their proper position.

Jared appeared nervous and he swallowed. "Did I cross a line?"

"I want answers, Jared."

The corners of his mouth turned up as he slid a card over to my side of the table.

I pinched the thin paper between my fingers and examined it. It was a generically ivory business card with his name and company name in chocolate brown writing. My heart kicked into high gear upon reading the next line, which contained his phone number.

"You're giving me your number?"

"I am." He waited for a moment with an expectant stare, and then I understood what it was that he wanted.

"Oh!" I said, scrambling to search my backpack for something to write on. I scribbled my name and number on a piece of paper and slid it to him, mimicking his smooth, single movement.

Jared grinned and poked the paper into his inside jacket pocket.

"What if that's not my number?" I asked. "What if it's the number to an anger management clinic for your sister?"

Jared shook his head, laughing once. "Then I'd give it to her. But I hope it's yours. I need it to ask you to dinner properly."

I could hear my heart pounding inside my chest, and when I thought he might be able to hear it, I felt my cheeks flush.

"I told you I needed answers, first," I said, trying to seem calmer than I felt.

"I told you we were going to talk, didn't I?" His eyes were bright with amusement, even seeming a lighter shade of blue. "I'm going to call you this afternoon. Will that be all right?"

"Why don't you just ask me, now?" I said, incinerating any chance of seeming indifferent.

"Is that what you want?" he asked, raising his brow.

I nodded and a broad smile lit up his face. "Would you have dinner with me tomorrow?"

"I'd love to. Thank you."

"I don't want to make you late." Even as he said the words, he seemed in no hurry to say goodbye.

We both stood, and Jared held the door open for me as we walked into the morning air. It felt surreal to be walking next to him on campus. He seemed less like a figment of my imagination surrounded by the scenery of my everyday life.

"I'll pick you up around six thirty?" he asked, lightly grazing my finger tips with his. Electricity immediately shot up my arm, and my heart hammered against my ribs.

"Sounds perfect." I couldn't have chosen words more true.

Kim and Beth were waiting for me just inside the building, and I tried to keep from jumping up and down as I approached.

"What happened?" Beth said, grabbing my arm.

"We're going out tomorrow night. Six-thirty," I beamed.

"Yay!" Beth said, clapping.

Kim and I continued upstairs to our class. She wasn't nearly as animated as Beth.

"Ryan isn't going to be happy," she said.

I angled my neck to emphasize my irritation. "I'm not with Ryan, Kim. He doesn't get to be unhappy about it."

"I know...I just think its poor timing on your part for you to go on a date with Jared when Ryan's still in the hospital for trying to save your life."

"Are you saying it's wrong for me to go out with Jared because I'm obligated to Ryan now, since he was hurt defending me? Is that what you're getting at?" I countered, pausing in front of our classroom.

"No. I am definitely not saying that. That would be very Casablanca of me."

Kim smiled when I rolled my eyes at her, and we walked to our seats together.

Chapter Six
Truth(s)

Patience is a virtue I do not possess. Amusement park lines, doctor's appointments, college acceptance letters—all enough to drive me insane. Waiting for my date with Jared felt very much like torture. Each class failed miserably at holding my interest, and by midmorning I had given up on taking notes. The final class of the day was insufferable. I bounced my knee up and down, tapped my pencil on the desk, shifted in my chair, and sighed at least a dozen times.

Beth touched my arm.

"Don't interrupt my anxiety attack. It's rude," I whispered.

Beth pressed her lips together, trying not to laugh. "Stop freaking out. It's a date. You've had dates before."

"Not with Jared."

She tapped her finger on my forearm for a moment and smiled. "Why don't we visit Ryan after class?"

"I think you're brilliant," I said, peeling off the last bit of my eraser.

By the time Professor Hunter had spoken the word 'dismissed' I had shoved the last of my things in my bag, with the fastest path to the Beamer already plotted out in my mind. Beth struggled to keep up, and growled with frustration when we reached the car.

"You're ridiculous," she puffed.

"You have no excuse. Your legs are longer than mine."

She rolled her eyes as I put the Beamer into gear.

Ryan looked much better—he had more color in his face and the network of tubes and wires that had covered him just days before had all but disappeared.

"Hey there," he said, stretching his torso. "They're moving me to PCCU today."

"That's fantastic!" I smiled. "You're going to be out of here in no time. Do you know what room number you'll be in?"

Ryan shook his head. "I'll call you and let you know, though."

"You'd better. How else are we going to sneak in the illegal contraband?" Beth said.

"Speaking of which...did you happen to bring me another burger?"

Beth shook her head. "Nina was in a hurry to get here."

Ryan didn't enjoy her remark as much as I thought he would. "That's surprising. I figured you'd be rushing to Andrews to get ready for your date." He tried to sound casual, but I heard resentment in his words.

I glanced at Beth and then back at him. My face instantly flushed with anger.

Ryan rolled his eyes. "Calm down, Nina. Josh saw you at the Ratty. It pissed him off seeing Jared there. He doesn't trust him."

"It's ridiculous that he's upset about it at all," I snapped.

"It's not Josh's fault. He just thinks I'm better for you than that double-oh-seven wannabe. I happen to agree," Ryan said, squirming to sit higher in his bed.

"That double-oh-seven wannabe is the reason we're alive," I said through my teeth.

"Come on, you guys. This can wait," Beth sighed.

"You're not really going to go out with him, are you?" Ryan said, disgusted.

"Yes, I am. And I really don't care what you, or Josh, or any of your other buddies think about it."

"Buddies?" Ryan repeated, raising an eyebrow. "Who says buddies, anymore?"

"Shut up," I seethed. "Let's go, Beth. Visiting hours are over."

"Oh, come on, Nigh. Don't leave mad," Ryan chuckled, raising his hand toward me.

"I told you that you could only call me that once. The time limit on that has been exceeded.""Nina, I'm sorry. Don't leave. It's none of my business who you date. I'm sure it's obvious why I have a problem with it." He looked down at his hands with a frown.

I stared at him for a moment. It was hard to hold onto my anger when he was lying in a hospital bed. "I hope they clear up whatever it is that has you acting like this before they release you."

"Oh, I'm not that bad. You're coming back tomorrow, right?"

"I will," I said, ruffling my fingers in his hair.

He swatted my hand away. "I don't want to hear about your date, all right?"

"I'm sure we can find other things to talk about."

"We'd better go, Nigh. We have lots to do," Beth said in a sing-song voice.

I stuck my tongue out at Ryan before following Beth to the car.

In search of the perfect outfit, Beth and I blew up my closet. Clothes were everywhere. Something too dark, too tight, too loose, too short, or not short enough covered every surface. I finally settled on a winter white three-quarter length sleeved sweater dress with my favorite fancy brown belt—it boasted a pearl in the center of the cross buckle—and brown strappy heels. Beth assured me over and over that my curve-hugging dress was the perfect balance of sexy and elegant. I stared into our long mirror and worried my dress was too short; I was all legs.

I passed the time taking a long shower, being extra careful about shaving my legs, plucking my eyebrows, and painting my toenails.

After all of the indulging, I'd still managed to be ready twenty minutes before Jared was due to arrive. My heels clicked against the elevator floor as I stepped in, and I couldn't help but fuss with my hair and dress while I waited for the doors to open to the first floor. Walking down the hall, I checked my watch; I still had fifteen minutes before he would arrive. Just as I peeked out, the door popped open. Jared stood in front of me in a solid black dress shirt and charcoal-grey slacks. His hair had the slightest bit of gel in it, easing the subtle messy waves into each other.

I sucked in a tiny gasp, throwing my hand up to my chest.

"I'm sorry, did I startle you?"

"Yes! I wasn't expecting you, yet," I said, breathless.

Jared handed me a small but beautiful bouquet of pink and white tulips—my favorite—and smiled sheepishly, "I couldn't wait until six-thirty."

I pressed my lips together to keep from uttering the embarrassing truth, but I couldn't stop myself. "I couldn't either," I blurted out.

A triumphant smile broke across his face, and then he helped me with my coat. He gently pulled me against his chest and whispered into my ear. "You are stunning."

My ears burned. I willed the blush in my cheeks away, glad to be stepping out into the brisk air.

"Where are we going?" I asked as he pulled away from the curb.

"You'll see," he said, an excited grin spreading across his face. "I'm glad you agreed to come. After the other night, I wasn't sure you'd say yes."

"Well, after you ambushed me at the Ratty in front of everyone, I hardly had a choice.""Coercion was the plan all along," he said, chuckling. He reached over and lightly traced my fingers.

"So this place we're going to...should I expect more strange cuisine or are you playing it safe this evening?" I casually turned up my palm to intertwine our fingers. Normally I wasn't so forward, but the rules had changed. We both knew that nothing about our time together was ever ordinary.

"It's a surprise."

I wrinkled my nose. "I don't like surprises."

"Yes, you do."

"I know," I huffed. It was maddening that he knew me so well. "Am I going to learn anything about you tonight?"

"That's the plan."

Jared pulled onto a narrow street and parked beside the curb in front of a darkened building. I wasn't sure what restaurant it was, but it didn't look open. He took my hand and led me down an alley, guiding me around the water-filled potholes.

"Your cut has healed nicely," I noticed, "I can barely see it."

Jared simply nodded, leading me further into the darkness.

His hand left mine only to reach into his pocket for his keys. He unlocked the door, and then stretched his arm toward the inside to signal me to walk in.

"We're going up the stairs," he said.

My heels clanged against the iron steps as I slowly climbed to a small landing. At the top, Jared edged past me to use his keys again. He stepped ahead of me this time, holding the door open.

I walked into a spacious Bi-level apartment decorated in grays and blues. It was dimly lit and the blinds were drawn, setting off the glow of the numerous candles lit around the room. Chinese panels and manuscripts from different parts of the world hung on the grey cinderblock walls, illuminated by track lighting. He didn't have enough furniture to fill the space—or maybe it was simply clutter free— everything was in its place. The entire room was immaculate. The air was saturated with different spices and flavors, and the small round table displayed empty wine glasses and white plates.

"This is your apartment?" I asked, looking up the wooden stairs leading to the loft.

Jared stood behind me, sliding my coat from my arms. "Is that okay? I thought it would be the best place to talk," he asked, a bit anxious.

"No, it's great. It's amazing...you're cooking?" I asked, preoccupied with my surroundings.

"Something like that. Try not to get too excited." He tucked my hair behind my ears. "Have a seat, it's almost ready."

He took the flowers from my hands and whisked them to the kitchen, filling a vase with water. He reappeared, vase and flowers in hand, placing them in the middle of the table.

Jared brought a serving dish to the table and forked out a slice of meat.

"Pot Roast?" I asked.

"Well, there are other things—," he gestured back to the kitchen.

"No, no, it's just that...pot roast is my favorite. My father had a close friend that always invited us to dinner when I was little, and his wife made this amazing pot roast. It's been a long time since I've had it, but it smelled a lot like this."

Jared made a strange face as if he didn't know how to react to my little anecdote, and then returned to the kitchen. He brought out a bowl of steamed vegetables, a plate of dinner rolls, and a baked potato...all of them favorites of mine.

"You thought of everything," I said, bewildered at the food sitting on the table.

"There's an Angel Food cake in the oven," he said, sitting across from me.

"I love angel foo—," I cut myself off when I realized how redundant it would be to say the words. "You knew that, didn't you?"

"Yes," Jared said with an uncertain half smile. It sounded more like a question than an answer.

"We're going to talk, right?" I asked, staring down at my plate.

"We are going to talk. But let's get through dinner, first."

"I can do that," I grinned.

I bit into the pot roast and instantly I was seven years old, sitting in a homey kitchen with a million savory smells floating throughout the room. Cynthia was politely chuckling at something Jack's friend Gabe had said, and Gabe's wife circled the table in a light blue apron, spooning out vegetables onto everyone's plate.

"How is it?" Jared asked between bites, bringing me back to the present.

I shook my head, searching for the words that would do the taste I was experiencing justice. "I haven't had a meal like this in a long, long time," I chewed, "since I was a girl. Where did you learn to cook like this?"

Jared shrugged. "It's my mother's recipe."

I smiled at that. It was the first time he'd ever mentioned anything about his life. "Are you close with your mother?" I asked, settling into my chair.

"We're close now. I spent a lot of time away from her when I was young."

I raised my eyebrows with interest, waiting for him to elaborate.

"School was very easy for Claire and me—we finished at a young age—and we went on to train in more special areas."

"Special as in what you can do? Fight, I mean." Although I was prepared for an outlandish explanation, I was surprised that it began in his childhood.

"Right," Jared confirmed. "My father taught us much of what we know; he took us all over the world to round out our training."

"What kind of training?" I asked.

Jared squirmed in his chair. My insides wrenched as I watched him struggle; I wanted to somehow make it easier for him. I reached across the table and slid my fingers between each of his.

"This is why I'm here, right?" I said, offering a reassuring smile. Jared relaxed a bit and gently squeezed my fingers.

"We were trained to defend ourselves, to defend someone else, and received all the training each branch of military receives, including tactical, structure penetration, reconnaissance and patrolling, hand to hand combat, demolitions, weapons, field medicine...you get the idea."

"Why?" I said in a more incredulous tone than I'd intended.

Jared took another bite, considering my question. I couldn't wait for him to decide the best answer.

"Your father was in the security business?" I prompted.

"More along the lines of security detail."

"Bodyguard stuff," I nodded.

Jared chuckled. "Yes, bodyguard stuff."

"So Claire went through the same training?" I imagined tiny Claire training with the Navy Seals and shuddered. I wasn't sure if it was because I feared for her safety, or because she was even more dangerous than I had previously thought.

"We were separated a lot. When she proved to be accelerated in most things we trained together." His face twisted with irritation.

"Accelerated?"

"She could hit a target from fifteen-hundred yards by the time she was eleven. She's probably the best sniper the military has ever seen," he waited for my reaction. After seeing the deliberate smooth features of my face, he continued, "You can imagine how many elite branches of government and private sectors are falling over themselves for her, counting down the days until her eighteenth birthday." He said the words with a hint of the tone a protective father might have when discussing his daughter's first date.

"Are you close?" I asked, remembering the way they had reacted to each other in the pub.

Jared frowned. "I love her. She's my sister." The crease between his eyebrows grew deeper, "She's also very obstinate and, like most teenage girls, she's very self-absorbed. But in a lethal-type of way because of her training." He was suddenly very far away. "Claire's been through a lot. She didn't get to have a normal childhood because of the way we were raised, and she's angry about a lot of things."

"Are you angry about the way you were raised?"

"No," he said the word softly, but with firm conviction. There was no pause between my question and his answer. He scanned my face with such affection that I felt myself fidgeting with unease.

"Why is that?" I bit my lip, still apprehensive about the intensity in his eyes.

"We'll get to that later. Dessert?" he asked, squeezing my hand before letting go.

I noticed the absence of his touch instantly when my hand turned cold. He took my nearly empty plate and returned with the perfect-sized slice of Angel Food cake. No icing, no layers. Just the way I liked it.

I took a bite and closed my eyes as I chewed. "You have more than one talent, Mr. Ryel," I said after swallowing the moist, spongy goodness. "Tell me more about you. I want to hear the little things, too. You know all of my favorites; it's only fair that I know yours."

Jared laughed once. "Okay." He wiped his mouth with his napkin and leaned against his chair. "The little things....I was born in Providence on May ninth. I'm twenty-three," he explained. "Breakfast is my favorite meal. Summer is my favorite season. I don't have a favorite color, but I've always been partial to that crazy green-honey brown color of your eyes. I have this addiction to sweet potato fries."

"Well. There you go. I knew something about you after all," I grinned.

"See? I'm an open book."

I rolled my eyes. "Go on...."

"I think best when on my motorcycle; I don't really have time for hobbies. I have a sister, whom you've met," I nodded, "and a little brother, Bex, who's eleven. They both live with my mother, but Claire spends a lot of time here...sometimes too much," he grimaced.

I giggled. "And you have your own security business?"

The second I'd asked, I wished I hadn't. Jared's eyes instantly clouded over into familiar twin storms.

"I brought you here tonight to be honest with you, Nina."

"I know," I said, trying to sound braver than I felt. Whatever it was I would listen, believe, and figure out a way to live with it. I had no other option versus the alternative. Now that I'd met him my life would never be the same again. It would be something too peculiar for anyone else to accept, but I had seen enough in the past months to know anything was possible. "I want you to tell me everything."

Jared looked away. "You may feel differently before the night is over."

I tilted my head to draw his eyes to mine. "After everything that's happened, you don't think I know there is something abnormal going on? I'm here, aren't I?"

Jared leaned over and touched my cheek with the palm of his hand. I couldn't help but lean into it, his skin was always so warm that it radiated into my bones.

"Okay, then. The truth." He took a deep breath, "My father has been...close to your father for a long time." He watched my expression, but that part I was somewhat prepared for.

He continued, "My father served as protection for your father and, as you can imagine, Jack was a full time job. He made a lot of the wrong people very angry on a regular basis."

I winced. I had come to this conclusion after reading the Port of Providence file, but hearing it from Jared rubbed salt in the wound.

"I'm sorry, Nina. I don't like telling you this; it goes against the very principle I was raised on." Jared reached his hand across the table to mine.

"What do you mean?"

"That's what my family does, Nina. We protect your father. And your mother...and you."

I shook my head. "I don't understand. Your family protects mine? Since when?"

"My father has known Jack since before you were born...before he married your mother."

I felt my eyebrows pull in. "Why haven't we met before?"

Jared squeezed my hand. "We have. One of my earliest memories is of Jack encouraging you to take your first steps. We went on family vacations with you; I watched you blow out the candles on your birthday cakes; I saw you drive your first car; we were always in the background."

I shook my head. "When we had lunch I asked you if we'd met. You said we hadn't." Frustration made my words sharper than I had intended.

"We hadn't met in the way you were inquiring," Jared pointed out. "The moment I sat beside you on that bench I've been very careful not to lie to you, Nina. I promised myself that if the day ever came that I could finally be in your life—in a real way—I would always be honest with you."

I narrowed my eyes at him. "Your father protected mine?"

Jared nodded.

"Who is your father?"

"Gabe Ryel."

"Gabe is your father? But...I don't remember you. I spent time in his home. You weren't there."

"Claire and I were away. We had to start our training early to be ready in time. Bex is eleven and he's already finished school. He's been in training for the last eighteen months. It's just the way it works."

"It's the way what works?"

Jared winced at my irritated tone. He was struggling with each piece of information, now. He spoke as if he expected me to run away with every new fact he revealed.

"I'm getting to that," he shifted nervously.

I pulled my hand from his and lowered it to my lap. "I don't remember any of that."

Jared watched me pull away from him with a pained expression. "You weren't supposed to. Your father did everything he could to keep you from the dark parts of his life. He did love you, Nina."

I shook my head, trying to keep the tears at bay. I couldn't think of any words. Jared stared at me for a moment and spoke again, "Are you sure you want to hear this?"

I blinked, composing myself. "Yes. I'm sure." Knowing something real, even if it was hurtful, was far better than living a lie.

Jared sucked in another breath. "About the time I was ready to work alone, you were becoming more independent. It was eighteen months before there was a need for my training. Up until then, I'd felt like a babysitter."

I cringed at his choice of words.

"Five days before your sixteenth birthday Jack had begun a deal with the cops you saw in the surveillance photos. My father told Jack it was a bad idea, but the bottom line was always the money, and those men—," Jared spoke with disdain, "—were the easiest way to bypass the system.

"Once Jack realized that dirty cops are a different breed of criminal with even less regard for the law, it was too late. Jack was used to being targeted, but he wasn't prepared for them to go after you. No one had ever been stupid enough to push Jack that far."

"After me? We're talking three years ago, and I had no idea? How is that possible?"

"Because I'm good at my job, Nina. I had to be." Jared tensed as he continued, "I'd hoped your father would be honest with you—although at the time I wasn't sure why—but it only made Jack even more determined to keep you from the truth. He didn't want you to live in fear, and I couldn't argue with that logic."

"What made you change your mind?"

Jared's hands locked together on top of the table. "The first time you were targeted, I took a bullet to the shoulder. The training made it automatic for me to stop that bullet, Nina; but in that one instant, my eyes were opened. The moment I saw Tipton's finger press against the trigger I wasn't protecting you because I had to. For the first time, I realized that I could lose you."

"You were almost killed?" I gasped. I imagined him bleeding from a bullet wound while I went on with my life, oblivious. My heart faltered.

Jared crossed his arms on the table and smiled. "Not even close."

"So these feelings you have for me...you had them before I ever knew you existed," I said, more of a statement than a question.

Jared grimaced, incensed at my choice of words.

"Nina," he shook his head. I had obviously offended him somehow. "I was in love with you before you ever knew I existed. It was very difficult to be around you for hours on end and not be able to comfort you, or touch you...even speak to you. I wasn't allowed to let you see me, but it was my job to watch your every move. That included standing by while people lied to you, betrayed you, caused you pain.

"Jack reminded me constantly that it had to be that way. He could see that every day it grew harder for me to be nonexistent...to be invisible to the woman I loved." His eyes were unfocused, mulling over the memories that troubled him.

Jared had now said it twice: He was in love with me.

"You can't imagine the rage I felt seeing some sleaze that didn't appreciate you take you to dinner, take you for granted, kiss you...make you cry. It was my duty to protect you and I wasn't allowed to protect you from that; although, I would have gladly murdered Howard without a second thought the night of your sixteenth birthday."

Adrenaline rushed through my veins, and my mind burned through the memories of that night. Stacy Howard was my first and only boyfriend. He personified the stereotypical supercilious rich boy, complete with rebellious nature and bad attitude. The longer I put-off a physical relationship with him, the more acerbic he became. It didn't take long for me to grow tired of him, but just when I'd decided to end things, Cynthia insisted on it first. Playing the part of the stubborn fifteen year-old daughter to perfection, I grudgingly stayed with him just long enough to show my mother that I would make my own choices.

We had been together for just over a year when he'd chosen my party to break it to me that he was in love with Emma Noble, my then-best friend. His plans were unnecessary when I caught them having sex in the pool house before he had a chance to tell me. I was so relieved I barely noticed.

"You're referring to Stacy," my eyes narrowed.

Jared nodded with an angry expression on his face.

"You knew about that?" I wailed.

Jared shook his head and closed his eyes. "From the moment it began. It was hell watching him go back and forth, not being able to tell you... or kill him. He was just a kid, and I wanted to end his life...so many times," he whispered in a low, intimidating tone.

I buried my face in my hands. Fire exploded across my face and ears. It was worse than anything I could have possibly imagined. Jared hadn't just been hired to protect me since my father had passed away; he'd observed my awkward tween years, my humiliations, and every one of my embarrassing failures.

The degradation was unbearable. I sprang from my seat and headed for the door, but before my first step, I heard Jared's chair grate against the floor. In the next moment he gently grabbed me from behind, wrapping his arms around my waist.

"I know this is humiliating for you," he spoke quietly in my ear. "I wanted to tell you, I begged Jack to let me expose that cheating little maggot so many times, but he wouldn't let us interfere unless it was absolutely necessary. Doing that to you on your birthday," he said, fuming, "it was the breaking point for me. That night was the first time I'd fought Jack on anything."

I flipped around and pushed away from him. "I'm not humiliated about Stacy! That was years ago! I'm humiliated because of this!" I said, gesturing to the space between us. "When you meet someone new, that's the way it's supposed to be! New! You know all of my bad habits...you've seen me do God knows what. You're only supposed to know the best parts about me in the beginning!"

He stood there for a moment, shaking his head with an expression of confusion and awe. "I love everything about you."

It was at that moment that I realized why his eyes seemed so familiar to me. "You were there," I whispered, scanning his face.

Beyond the cocktail dresses, the twinkling lights draped from every tree and light post, and the smell of the freshly cut grass and imported flowers my mother insisted on, his eyes flickered in my memory. I pressed deeper, feeling the light sheen of perspiration on my skin from the exceptionally warm night, the smell of the chlorine from the pool, and the sounds of the crowd humming in happy, flowing conversation.

When I glanced across the lawn at my father, I caught the glowing blue eyes of a stranger standing by the koi pond. His tailored suit and absent tie set him apart from the sea of tuxedos. Our eyes connected for only a second before he reluctantly pulled them away to face my father, who was having a low, serious conversation with him.

My memory replayed in slow motion as the chiffon of my short, white dress waved gently against my legs. Once again his stormy blue eyes singled me out of the crowd, and I shied away from his stare.

I snapped back to the present when Jared called my name.

"You were speaking to my father by the pond. That was you," I said, my eyes wide with realization.

Jared's brows pulled in. "You remember that?"

"It was just before I'd gone to the pool house. Jack was by the pond, talking with that face he made when he was giving orders." I tried to recall every detail I could. "You were throwing rocks in the pond; I only saw you for a moment, but that was you, wasn't it?"

Jared nodded slowly. "I wanted to throw Stacy out, take him somewhere and...I don't know. Punish him, I guess. Jack refused, but he realized how I felt about you, then. He insisted that my family, including me, be kept a secret from you indefinitely. That was a rough night," he sighed, rubbing the back of his neck.

"I am so sorry," I whispered, not knowing what else to say. My heart ached for all the years he'd spent as a ghost.

Jared took my hand in his and pulled it to his chest. It was then that I realized I'd been absently twisting my Peridot ring around my finger.

"I picked up this ring, you know," he said, softly pressing his lips against my fingers. "Cynthia was up to her neck in party details and she'd forgotten to get it," he smiled. "Because you were in my father's presence, I was sent to pick it up for you."

"Great. They used you as a gopher."

"I volunteered. I wanted to," he explained. "I can't describe the way it made me feel to see your smile when you opened the box. You were so pleased with it, and I had a part in that," he said. His smile faded. "Later, it helped a little with the...misery of never being able to console you when I'd see you twist this ring around your finger. I know it sounds ridiculous, but it has always been comforting to see you reach for it when you're upset."

I stared at him, bewildered. I wasn't sure how to feel; even with the suspicions I'd already had, I couldn't have prepared myself for what he was telling me.

"Please don't leave," Jared whispered, still holding my hand to his chest.

I looked down at my feet and then reached down to unbuckle the straps of my shoes from around my ankles. "You'd just follow me if I left, right?" I said, kicking off my shoes.

"Even if it weren't my job," he said with an impish grin. He looked down at my bare feet. "I'm glad you're staying, we still have quite a bit to discuss."

"There's more?"

Jared nodded and led me to his small, grey couch.

"Maybe we should save the rest for another night. It's a lot to take in," he sighed.

I ignored him. "Why did you sit beside me on that bench the night of Jack's funeral?"

"You were crying. Jack was gone. I couldn't think of any more reasons to stay away."

"What about your father? Didn't Gabe care that you were breaking the rules?"

Jared looked to the floor. "He died the morning of your father's funeral." He spoke as if exhaustion had just set in.

I gasped. "Gabe is...?" I couldn't finish.

Jared had comforted me just hours after his own father's death. I gently pulled his chin to face me. His eyes were thick with grief, as if he was experiencing it for the first time.

It dawned on me how it must have felt to Jared, to see me suffering, and the deep need he struggled with to make it go away. I felt the same urgency that very moment. My eyes focused on the thin line between his lips, and I moved a bit closer to him.

Jared rested his soft hands on each side of my face. He leaned in slowly, inches from my mouth. His jaw tensed; he seemed to be struggling with what he had been told was the right thing to do and what he wanted.

He shook his head. "This isn't why I brought you here," he said, pulling away from me.

"I know," I sighed.

Jared stared at the floor, working to even out his breathing.

I touched his arm. "Maybe you're right. Maybe we've had enough truth for one night."

"Do you want to leave?" he asked, concerned.

"No!" I paused to regain my composure. "No. I just meant that maybe we could talk about something else...if you want," I fidgeted. "Your training, what schools you went to, friends...girls," I said, a corner of my mouth turning up.

"Girls?" he repeated, raising an eyebrow.

"You know about my utter failure when choosing a boyfriend, and I'm sure you saw the awkward dates I've been on."

"Those were never a good day at work for me," he said, furrowing his brow.

"It's only fair," I reasoned. "You must have had at least one bad date...."

Jared shook his head dismissively. "I didn't have time to date."

I wasn't sure what expression was on my face, but it made Jared's eyes squint with chagrin. He clearly didn't expect to talk about his love life, or lack thereof.

"I was focused on keeping you alive. Making mistakes in my family means more than having to say you're sorry."

"Never?"

Jared shifted uncomfortably in his seat. "It wasn't that I never had the opportunity, or that I wasn't allowed the time...or even incessantly encouraged,"—his face twisted into a disgusted scowl—"I just had my priorities."

"Should I feel guilty or flattered?"

Jared looked straight into my eyes. "By the time it occurred to me to care about things like that, I already knew you were all I'd ever want."

I controlled my eyes from bulging from their sockets, but I couldn't stop my mouth from turning up into a half surprised, half appreciative grin. My eyes focused on his lips again.

"So...why did you bring me here?"

He shrugged. "You said all I had to do was tell you the truth. That was all I needed to hear."

"When did I say that?" I felt my eyebrows pull in as my mind rewound the night's conversation.

He hesitated. "To Beth...last night."

"In my room? How did you hear that?"

Jared sighed and sat taller in his seat, bracing for round two. "Just hear me out before you leave," he said in a low tone. "It's my duty to protect you. I can't do that without knowing where you are at all times. I couldn't walk around freely in your dorm, so we had to have eyes and ears in place."

"What do you mean eyes and ears?"

"Your father was meticulous." He was stalling.

"Spit it out, Jared."

"When you were accepted into Brown, Jack had cameras installed in Andrews and different places on campus. We tracked the GPS in your car of course, but that had been in place the day Jack bought it. We tracked the GPS in your cell phone as well, and your parents' house has always been wired." Jared spoke casually, but he was braced for another outburst.

"There's a camera... in my room?" I spoke slowly, the anger and shock nearly choking my words.

"No! No, no, no...," Jared chuckled nervously. "There's a camera in the hall. We only placed a mic in your room."

I considered that for a moment, trying to recall if I'd ever done anything embarrassing. Nothing came to mind—I hoped that nothing would.

Jared squirmed. "Just to be clear, I don't enjoy invading your privacy in that way, but it is necessary."

I pouted as a smile spread across his face. "Well, that's not true. I enjoyed it last night."

I tensed, closing my eyes. "What did you hear?"

Jared's warm hand touched mine. "I heard Beth say that you loved me. And I didn't hear you deny it."

My eyes popped open. "You heard wrong, then. I did deny it."

"I heard you try to convince her otherwise. Are you telling me that I'm mistaken?"

I pulled my hand from his in defiance. I didn't like being ambushed.

He smiled at my stubbornness. "The second you walked away from me, my choice was clear." His expression didn't last long when I didn't return his smile. "You're angry."

"I have no secrets," I sulked. "Does my mother know about this?"

Jared nodded. I threw up my hands in frustration, letting them smack loudly into my lap. He kneeled in front of me on the floor, forcing me to look at him.

"It was necessary, Nina," he said, lightly touching my bare knees.

"So that's how you always miraculously appear?" I was aware that he knew my whereabouts, but I had no idea I was being spied on twenty-four-seven.

"That's part of it," he said with the evasive tone I was bitterly becoming accustomed to.

"The other part is?"

"I'm getting to that."

"There's more?" I howled.

"First, since you now know the worst part of it—," I rolled my eyes, "—I owe you an apology," Jared said.

"I'd say so!"

"I'm sorry about Mr. Dawson. Claire was on watch both of those nights, and she made the decision to let it get farther than I would have for Intel purposes. She wanted to know what Mr. Dawson knew."

"Claire watches me, too?" I shrieked.

"Yes. I'm sorry you were scared. I relieved Claire the second I heard the news, which is when I came to take you home."

Initially I was furious, but the anger disappeared when I remembered feeling desperate for Jared to intervene. How could I be angry with him for wanting the same thing that I did?

"I thought you would come," I whispered.

"You what?" he said, surprised.

"When Mr. Dawson threatened me, I expected you to show up at any moment. It made the whole thing... tolerable."

"Tolerable?"

And then he was angry. He didn't speak for several minutes after that. His jaw flitted under his skin, and he occasionally shook his head. I waited for as long as I could, but I finally prompted him.

"What's wrong?" I asked, searching his stormy eyes.

"The first time that you expected me to protect you...I wasn't there." He spoke the last three words as if they were poison in his mouth.

"You can't be there every second, Jared. You're only human." I returned my hands to his. He brought my hand to his lips.

"I'm sorry," he whispered, his face twisting in torment.

"It's okay," I said, surprised. I didn't expect his reaction.

His earlier description of the suffering he had experienced while witnessing my pain materialized. His time with me must have seemed like purgatory. I felt an overpowering urge to comfort him, and I was just inches away.

"It won't happen again," he promised. His eyes were fixed on mine.

"I'm holding you to that." A match had been lit inside me; I was burning from the sudden need to touch him, to alleviate the self-loathing in his eyes.

I leaned forward and rested my fingers against each side of his neck. My thumbs grazed his jaw line, the fear of rejection a faint memory. Pulling him closer, I pressed my lips against his. He cautiously returned my kiss, but when he began to pull away I refused to let go.

After a brief, surprised pause, Jared gave into my insistence, wrapping his arms around me and pressing me against him. A quiet hum of satisfaction escaped my lips, and his mouth grew more urgent against mine. He sat up on his knees to tighten his grip, and his hand clutched the back of my neck. My breath became ragged as his lips parted and his outstandingly warm tongue found its way to mine. My knees parted and I pulled him against me, eliminating the tiny space between us.

He groaned in frustration and then his grip tightened, holding me a few inches away by my shoulders.

"What?" I puffed.

He took a few deep breaths before answering, staring at my lips. "We still have a lot to discuss," he breathed, letting go of my shoulders to press my knees together.

"I'm done talking," I whispered, leaning in again.

Jared gently restrained me, amused at my fortitude. "I can't," he said, taking a deep breath. "I brought you here to tell you the whole truth, not just half of it."

I sighed in resignation, sinking back into the couch cushion.

He smiled at my pouting. "Not that I'm not incredibly tempted." He sat up on his knees again, and brushed his lips against mine, pulling away as quickly as he began.

"Okay. Let's talk," I said, more eager than ever to have everything out in the open. "You haven't been honest with me."

He raised an eyebrow. "Excuse me?"

"You can't tell me that you haven't had time for girls, now. Not when you kiss like that."

Jared's expression was ecstatic, and then he made a poor attempt to disguise it. "I beg to differ. I'm not an idiot...it's not a difficult concept."

"I have kissed boys, some of those boys more than once, that never kissed like that."

Jared closed in and kissed my neck—from collar bone to the line of my jaw—stopping to whisper in my ear. "That's because you kissed boys, sweetheart."

My heart pounded so loudly that I was sure he could hear it. I let out a long sigh. "Okay, you've got to tell me the rest. The suspense is killing me."

Jared shifted to the couch, turning to face me. His face returned to the worried frown he had before.

"Jared, thus far it's my understanding that you've been raised by a family of assassins. You've spied on me, stalked me, installed microphones in my bedroom, and confessed to falling in love with me before I could drive. If I haven't left by now, I don't think I'm going to."

His face screwed into disgust. "We're not assassins."

"Have you ever killed anyone?"

Jared raised his eyebrows, shocked at my pointed question.

"I...er...yeah. But it was to keep you safe," he explained.

"You killed people for me?" I asked, my mood immediately shifting.

"Don't feel a second of guilt for those people, Nina. They wouldn't have lost a single night's sleep over taking your life."

I swallowed. "Do you regret it?"

He didn't hesitate. "Never. It's who I am."

"What does that mean? You're a killer?"

Jared rubbed the back of his neck nervously. "I don't think of it that way. We're protectors. Though there are those that disagree."

"Like who?" I shook my head, thoroughly confused.

"You're getting ahead of me."

"You're getting ahead of yourself."

"I know." He rubbed his temples with his thumb and forefinger and sighed.

"You're making me nervous." I laughed without humor. He looked up at me; the hardness of his eyes didn't relieve my trepidation. "Is it that bad?"

"It's just...implausible. It will be your first inclination to be skeptical, and I don't blame you. But it's the truth."

I nodded and then took his hand in mine. "I'm ready."

"Gabe," Jared paused for a long time and then cringed, "isn't from here. He's known your father since Jack was an infant, but it wasn't until Jack was a bit older that they met.

"When Jack was twenty-one, he worked for a man named Van Buren. While working there, he befriended Van Buren's oldest son, Luke, and because Jack spent so much time with Luke, my father in turn spent quite a bit of time in Luke's home.

"It didn't take long for Luke's younger sister, Lillian, to catch Gabe's attention. Lillian is my mother. Similar to the way I feel about you, he couldn't stay away from her. Eventually he made the choice to reveal himself to her, which is against the rules."

I started to ask about the rules, but Jared held a finger up so that I would let him continue, "Gabe made a huge sacrifice to be with Lillian. He loved her, and so as far as he was concerned, he had no choice. Even though he had given up everything, his existence still depended on Jack."

I shook my head. "Why did it depend on my father?"

"Gabe was assigned to him. For my father, and those like him, he is assigned to someone—his Taleh —from their birth. Because I'm half of what my father was, the draw isn't right away. We have to figure it out on our own, and that's part of why my siblings and I are the bastards of Gabe's world."

"Gabe's world? I'm sorry, Jared, I don't understand," I shook my head in frustration.

Jared's hardened expression smoothed into a warm smile. "I know. You will. I'm trying to explain this in the best way possible. Trust me."

"Sweet potato fries?" I smiled, trying to lighten the mood.

Jared's grin widened. "Sweet potato fries."

He watched me for a moment, and several emotions scrolled across his face. His hands touched my cheeks and then he pressed his lips against mine. It felt like he was saying goodbye.

He reluctantly let me go, and avoided my eyes when he spoke. "We aren't accepted by Gabe's family or his enemies. It makes it very difficult to do our job in some ways, and easier in others."

"You mean as protectors," I determined. Jared confirmed my revelation with an approving nod, but my expression caused his small smile to vanish.

"What?" he spoke in a soft, hesitant tone.

"Are you saying there is a society of protectors out there that all do...what you do?"

"S–Sort of. But it's...providential." He waited anxiously for my mind to catch up to what he was saying.

"Providential?" I repeated, letting the word simmer...providential protectors. He chose his words carefully, specifically attaching divinity to describe the family he referred to. When the comprehension hit, Jared winced. "Are you talking angels, Jared?" I said, indignant.

"I told you it would be your first inclination."

I waited for him to tell me he was joking, but his eyes were far from amused. I stood up and paced between the table and the couch.

He was serious.

He expects me to believe he is a...he's my....guardian angel! I thought. My mind mulled over wings, halos, and harps, and I laughed out loud. Jared watched me pace as if he were afraid he'd sent me over the edge.

"I'm not an angel," he said as if I was totally off-base. "My father is. Was," he corrected.

"You're half...." I trailed off, unable to mouth the word. I felt ridiculous for even considering it.

"Human," he amended, intercepting the alternative.

My thoughts traced to Jared's lobbing the man the impossible distance across the parking lot. "That does explain some things. But...." I shook my head. I wanted to believe him and that made remaining objective more difficult.

Jared walked toward me, but I instinctively took a step back.

He cringed at my reaction. "I would never lie to you. Do you believe that?"

Just a few moments before I was determined to believe anything he had to say. Jared was asking me to believe in fairytales, in the supernatural. His anxious eyes searched my face, begging for me to believe. I was worth his truth and I stood cruelly obstinate. The need to ease his anxiety overwhelmed reason.

I touched his fading scar with my fingers. "It makes sense, really."

I had described him as angelic once, when I hadn't realized it was closer to the truth than I could have ever imagined. His glowing blue-grey eyes, his strength, the flawlessness of his face and the way he moved; it would be the only explanation. It suddenly didn't matter if it were possible. I believed him.

"I still have questions," I said.

Hope touched Jared's eyes, and he led me to the table. I took a bite of my half-eaten slice of cake and giggled.

"Something's funny?" he raised an eyebrow.

"Angel Food." I pressed my lips together, stifling a laugh.

Jared chuckled and sucked in a big breath, seeming relieved.

"Angel Food. Good one." He attempted an annoyed expression, but the relief on his face thwarted his efforts.

"Sorry."

"You're forgiven," he said immediately. "So. Now you know."

"Everything?"

"Pretty much." A fresh energy seemed to surround him. "There is more, but it's the logistics of what I've told you, and part of that...well, it's best that you don't know about them."

"Them?"

"You know the stories, Nina. Where there's light, there's dark. If I go into detail and you become aware, it attracts them. Do you understand what I'm saying?"

My body suddenly felt cold, causing my shoulders to curve in and shudder. I knew exactly what he was talking about: demons. Of course they would exist if angels did.

Jared's eyes sympathized with my reaction, and he pulled my chair closer to him, leaning over to kiss my forehead. "I suppose I didn't think through the consequences of promising absolute truth. I don't want you to be afraid, Nina. I would never let anything happen to you."

I took a deep breath and put on a brave face for him. "I know," I shook my head, "there is so much that I don't understand."

"You have more questions?" he asked, ready for the next barrage of inquiries.

I looked at my watch. It was almost midnight. "I'm not sure I can get them all in tonight."

"You have somewhere to be?"

"No. I assumed you wanted to sleep sometime. You do sleep, don't you?"

Jared smiled. "I do. But I don't require as much... just a few hours to recharge. Claire and I take shifts." He sighed and touched my arm. "I owe you another apology. I hadn't slept long—about twenty minutes when Claire called to inform me that you wandered out of town and were stranded on a dark road. She was prepared to let you wait, but I couldn't just let you sit in the cold. I'm sorry I was so...abrupt."

"Cranky when tired...check," I nodded once.

Relief brightened Jared's face. "This is surreal. I've dreamed about how I would tell you for years, and now it's done."

"And here I sit, in front of my half-angel Hybrid boyfriend eating cake. I think I win."

Three lines appeared on Jared's forehead when his eyebrows shot up. "Oh. It's boyfriend, now, is it?"

I swallowed hard, feeling the heat radiate from my face. I picked up my wine glass and took a large gulp.

"Are you okay?" Jared asked, concerned.

I cleared my throat. "I'm fine. I just...I didn't mean...ugh!" I moaned, covering my eyes with one hand.

"Nina," he chided, "as if I'm not thrilled beyond words at that idea." Jared pulled my hand from my face. "What could you possibly have to be embarrassed about?"

"Just...forget I said anything, okay?" I said sheepishly.

"Absolutely not," he smiled.

I involuntarily yawned, using the back of my fingers to cover my open mouth.

"I should take you home," he said.

"I don't want to go home. I still have questions," I argued, wiping the inevitable tears that followed.

"We have a long, long time for Q and A, sweetheart," he said, tucking my hair behind my ear. I smiled, realizing why he always seemed to pull my hair from my face the moment it crossed my mind.

I yawned again, but stubbornly shook my head. "The cut on your face?"

Jared touched it with two of his fingers. "There are pro's and con's to being what my father's world calls Half-breeds."

I wrinkled my nose at the word. "Sounds derogatory to me."

"It is. Most Archs don't believe we should exist, and the...Others see us as the enemy as well."

"Archs?"

"There are several types of angels: Seraphim, Cherubim, Thrones...there are nine in all. Archangels serve as protectors for humans. They relay messages, fight demons on occasion, and protect their Taleh against harm, from demon and human alike. But all humans have Archs, and even if their Taleh is threatened by another Arch's Taleh, Arch's are forbidden to harm humans. They are strictly protectors, but that protection has limits because of the Laws. Claire, Bex and I are half-human, freeing us from many of those restrictions, just like my father when he chose to live as human."

"So...Gabe...turned human?"

"No. He relinquished the ability to transfer planes...." My expression must have reflected how foreign the words sounded to me, because he stopped to explain. "To be invisible. Falling from grace has a price. Archs are cursed when they choose to stay, and that curse carries on to their offspring; although, it lessens with each generation. As the blood is diluted with the human gene pool, so is the curse."

"What kind of curse?" I asked. His world was much darker than wings and harps.

"Archs are obligated to protect their humans even after they fall, and because their priorities have been compromised, so to speak, the curse keeps that obligation in check. Fallen and their offspring, like Archs, don't get sick and we can't be killed. But unlike Archs, we experience a degree of pain and have a limited life span. Once our Taleh die, we almost immediately fall ill and expire."

"So you lost your father when I lost mine," I whispered.

Jared nodded infinitesimally and wiped a tear from my eye.

I leaned away from his hand. "Please don't do that. Don't comfort me for your father's death."

Jared shook his head. "I can't stand to see you cry. Not when I'm close enough to stop it."

"I'm so sorry, Jared." I couldn't imagine having to experience the constant worry of not only my father's mortality, but someone else's as well, for the sake of my father.

My eyes widened as my thoughts shifted. "I'm you're Taleh?"

"You are." He sat up a bit taller as his sad expression warmed at the thought.

"How do you know?"

"It's a feeling we get. When you're in pain, embarrassed, scared, sick, happy...aroused—," he looked down for a moment, seeming embarrassed —"...we feel it to a lesser extent."
"You can feel it when I feel those things?"

"It's hard to explain. I guess I could liken it to a mosquito buzzing in your ear."

"So, if I...bump my side on my father's desk?"

"I can sense it," he confirmed, amused that I had caught on.

"Was that you on the phone with my mother?" I raised an eyebrow.

"Yes. I just wanted to make sure you were all right. You hit pretty hard. I'd be surprised if you didn't bruise," he said, lightly touching the exact spot where I had collided with Jack's desk.

"I did bruise. I thought you said my parents' house has cameras. Couldn't you see that I was okay?"

"Your father's office is the only room in the house that isn't wired. When you're in there I have to rely on my senses. I'd prefer it if you wouldn't spend so much time there in the future."

I nodded, preoccupied with an errant thought that had popped into my head. "So...if I'm cramping...."

Jared closed his eyes and nodded. He clearly didn't want to dwell on the subject.

I giggled in disbelief. "That hurts you?"

Jared chuckled and rolled his eyes. "I don't get cramps, Nina, no. I'm aware of it."

His answer caused my giggles to erupt in laughter. I was definitely feeling the effects of fatigue.

I tried to remember where we left off before my short bout of hysteria. "When did you know I was yours?" I asked. Jared's eyebrows lifted and I corrected myself. "When did you know that I was your Taleh?"

He nodded in understanding, but a grin lingered on his lips. "Archs are assigned to their humans, but Half-breeds—,"

"Hybrids," I interrupted. I didn't like him using a derogatory term to refer to himself.

He smiled. "Hybrids have to figure it out on their own. Another reason Archs resent us—it leaves our humans vulnerable for a time. They don't agree with that."

"Lots of cons," I sighed.

"There are pros," he assured me. "We have few advantages over the Archs, the most important being that because we're half-human, we can kill other humans to protect our Talehs if necessary. We can see them, even if they remain hidden to humans. We also retain a fraction of their pronounced strength, focus, intelligence, and accelerated healing. Archs are indestructible and they don't bleed; bullets don't bounce off of them, they simply pass through them."

I glanced at his fading scar. "But you bleed."

"Yes, but we heal quickly. Very quickly."

"So, the wings thing...." I yawned as exhaustion set in.

"You don't have to worry about me sprouting feathers, Nina," he chuckled. "Archs don't fly. They simply appear where they wish to go. I've always found the pictures a bit silly, myself."

"I like those pictures," I argued.

"You're disappointed, then?" The corner of his mouth pulled up as he rested his hand on the back of my chair, leaning towards me.

"Not really. I'd rather be sitting across from my angel without wings than looking at a picture of an angel with them." I could feel his breath on my lips, and I leaned closer to him.

Jared fell against his chair. "I knew this conversation was going to be difficult, but it's become difficult for a completely different reason," he sighed, running his fingers through his hair.

"Why is that?" I asked, surprised at his sudden retreat.

He glanced up at me with a smirk. "I thought I'd have to stop you from running out into the street in a panic, instead I have to concentrate on finishing everything I want to say before you get me too flustered to speak at all."

The blood pooled under my cheeks, and Jared touched my face lightly with his thumb, tracing to my lips.

"It's a nice surprise," he said, letting his thumb slide from my chin.

I rolled my eyes. "I'll try to restrain myself."

"Why don't you leave that up to me?"

I raised a dubious eyebrow at him and he chuckled. His demeanor had improved one hundred percent since the beginning of our conversation, and I couldn't help but grin.

He outlined my fingers with his and I yawned, relaxing with his warm touch.

He gave me a disapproving look. "Nina...."

"I still have questions," I said. "You said you don't get sick. Ever?"

Jared shook his head with an amused smile, he was enjoying my interview.

"But the rest, about dying after your Taleh, do you...?"

"Yes."

I gasped. "But that's not fair!"

"Nina, don't forget...I fully intend on growing old with you." He enveloped me in his arms then, pulling me into his lap. "I literally can't live without you. But I wouldn't want to, even if I could."

I struggled for words to reply with, but they never came. Jared's expression tensed as though he might have said too much, and the need to relieve his quandary had me searching for new questions.

"That's very convenient, isn't it? That you and Gabe's Taleh just happened to be father and daughter?" I asked, hoping to take the uncomfortable expression off his face.

"It's great for carpooling."

I tried not to smile. "Seriously."

Jared leaned his forehead against my cheek, taking in the scent of my hair. "It's quite common. Archs are family as well as an army, existing in groups. Those groups are generally assigned humans that are related or connected in some way. It creates stronger bonds with humans."

His candid desire to grow old with me made my heart race, and I was suddenly focused on his mouth. After all, he'd only qualified that we wait until he told me everything.

And we were so close...

"How many like you exist?" I asked to distract myself. I didn't want to give him another reason to point out my embarrassing lack of self-control.

"Not as many as you might think. Like I said, it's taboo to get too involved with humans. It's even worse to fall in love with one—to betray your seraphic family for one."

"So how can they protect us if they despise us?" I asked, incensed.

"It's not that, Nina. They have an almost maternal love for humans. They see you as innocent, naïve children. Falling in love with a human is frowned upon by Archs as humans would an elderly man falling in love with a five year old. It's a social taboo, it's inappropriate. It's not because they are disgusted by humans, though there are those that feel that way. But those types of emotions lead to falling farther than earth."

"Dem—,"

"Don't say it. Don't even think it. Especially in my presence, they tend to hover."

A shiver traveled down my spine, but when Jared pulled me tighter to him I instantly felt more at ease. As I relaxed my cheek against his neck, I yawned again.

"All right, it's morning. Time to take you home." He stood up and in the same movement, lifted me effortlessly in his arms.

"I'm not leaving until you kick me out," I said, feeling slightly intoxicated.

"Then you may never leave," he said, kissing my lips.

He sat beside me on the couch and I leaned against his chest, sliding my arm across his middle and nestling my head under his chin. He didn't speak; the only sound in the room was the buzzing from his ceiling fan and our quiet, rhythmic breaths.

Before I could focus the fuzziness in my brain to form another question, exhaustion engulfed me, and my eyes became too heavy to keep open. I relaxed further into Jared's side, feeling my consciousness slip away. It wasn't an uncomfortable feeling—I felt I was just where I belonged. My last coherent thought was the contentment I felt as Jared's warm arms tightened around me.

Chapter Seven
Caught

The mangled, dark blue sheets underneath me were unfamiliar, but their wonderful scent was one I recognized right away. I lifted my head, peering around to study my surroundings. I was in a king-sized bed that sat against a grey, cinderblock wall. The alarm clock on the night table read nine o'clock in large, red numbers.

My eyes drifted to a metal frame beside the clock, and I blinked to bring it into focus. It was a black and white picture of me. It had been taken from an indefinite distance, zoomed in on my face. It was from a high angle, and it reminded me of the surveillance photos I'd seen in the Port of Providence file.

Rolling over, I hugged the pillow next to me. It smelled like Jared, and I took in a deep breath. His scent was incredible—like line-dried laundry, soap and something else...the way it smells when it's about to rain?—I couldn't put my finger on it.

The only rooms upstairs were his bedroom and a closed door to what was likely the master bath. The far wall beyond the end of the bed wasn't a wall at all, only a metal railing.

I heard Jared's voice speaking to someone else in French downstairs. His company's voice was distinctly female. They argued in hushed tones, and in my limited knowledge of French I thought I heard Jared reprimand the woman for waking me.

This piqued my interest, so I tiptoed to the railing to steal a glance at the woman below. When my fingers met the metal bar, I saw that Jared and Claire were both looking up at me. I waved sheepishly and bit my lip, feeling foolish for trying to sneak up on celestial beings.

"Good morning, sweetheart." Jared said, almost crooning.

Claire's expression was the polar opposite of Jared's. She glared up at me with ice blue eyes, as if she wanted to scale the wall with murder in mind. I recoiled, suddenly feeling out of place.

While avoiding her eyes, I noticed crisply folded bedding at the end of the couch. Jared had slept downstairs.

"If you'd like to shower, fresh clothes are on the dresser. You'll find everything you need," Jared called up to me.

On the dresser sat a neatly folded stack of clothes, and beside them a pair of boots. My eyes darted to the opposite side of the dresser where my toiletries sat. They were all from my dorm room.

"Where did you get these?"

"I had Claire bring them," Jared explained, making his way up the stairs. When he reached the top, he pulled me to him and kissed my neck.

I glanced down to Claire, who hadn't ceased her death stare. It was clearly more than intimidation. If Jared hadn't been near, I would have been afraid for my life.

"Don't worry about her. She won't bother you," he assured me as he pulled me away from the railing. "Did you sleep well?"

His face was positively lit up; I couldn't recall seeing him quite so cheerful.

"I must have. I don't remember anything after we sat on the couch."

I ran my hands over his light blue T-shirt, letting my fingers glide over the perfect highs and lows of his chest and abdomen. He was incredible. I'd seen plenty of physiques like his on posters, commercials for exercise equipment and movies, but never in person; certainly never within my grasp.

Jared tightened his arms around me. "I was careful not to wake you. You're so peaceful when you sleep."

"You slept on the couch?" I said, letting my disappointment show through.

"I reconsidered...several times," he said, his lips brushing my neck when he spoke.

"When did she bring my things?"

"Earlier. She's been in and out a lot," he frowned. "She's not happy about our conversation last night. I assume it has something to do with that." Chuckling at my inevitably worried expression, he kissed my forehead. "Breakfast will be ready soon. I'll wait for you downstairs."

After my shower, I reluctantly crept down the stairs. Claire and Jared watched me approach the table with equal but conflicting focus.

"You're beautiful," Jared whispered before he kissed my cheek and pulled out a chair.

Claire continued to glower as I sat across from her.

"Claire...." Jared warned. Her irritation turned to him, then. I felt a brief moment of relief.

"Thank you for bringing my clothes, Claire," I whispered. As soon as the words left my mouth I thought better of it. Her icy blue eyes shot back at me and I sunk back into my chair.

Jared stared at her until she shifted uncomfortably. "You're welcome," she grumbled, looking down at her plate.

"Ham, mushroom, green pepper and cheese omelet...toast," Jared pointed out each with his butter knife as he spoke, and then shoved a forkful into his mouth.

I stabbed the eggs and took a bite. He was an incredible cook. Everything he had made for me was exactly the way I liked it.

"Mmmm...that's good. I didn't realize how hungry I was," I hummed.

The fork clanged against my plate as I chewed the last bit of egg, and Jared rested his chin on his hand, amused at my shameless appetite.

Claire sighed in irritation. "You should be aware that Cynthia knows Nina spent the night here last night."

With indifference Claire watched Jared's face morph into anger.

"And how does she know that, Claire?" he seethed.

"I told her," Claire admitted.

Jared slammed his fist on the table. I jumped, but Claire didn't react. I watched them stare the other down, wondering if I should distance myself from the line of fire.

Jared noticed my growing unease and placed his hand on mine. "What exactly did you tell her, Claire? More importantly, why?" he spoke through his teeth, working to keep his tone calm.

"You didn't give me a choice, Jared. After what happened at the hospital, and last night, Cynthia needed to know what was going on. That's what Dad would have done."

"Dad's not here." Jared's voice broke as he fought to keep his calm.

Claire crossed her arms. "Obviously, Jared, or you wouldn't be insisting on going through with this. You've gone against everything Dad taught us, hours after he died. I tried to tell you, but you won't listen...."

"You can go, now, Claire," Jared snarled.

Claire's stoic expression faltered at her brother's stern tone. "Fine. Cynthia is waiting at Andrews. Maybe she can stop this before it gets too far." Claire shoved herself away from the table, grabbing her keys and motorcycle helmet. I cringed when she slammed the door behind her as she left.

The force of the door crashing into the door jamb caused the shelves on the walls to tremble. I peered over at Jared, whose jaws worked under his skin.

"So she knows about us, so what?" I said, squeezing his hand.

Jared didn't answer right away, and I could tell that he was trying to calm down before he spoke.

"This...complicates things," he said in a low tone. "We should get you back. The longer she has to wait the more difficult it will be."

I stood and shook my head. "Have I missed something here? This is my mother we're talking about, right? Why are you so nervous?"

Jared took our plates to the sink and then went directly to the coat stand.

He held out my coat and tried to smile, but it resulted in a twisted, pained expression. "Ready?"

Nodding, I twisted into my coat. I was glad when he took my hand and held it until we reached his SUV, and even more pleased that he didn't release it for the entire drive to Brown, but he didn't speak a word until we reached Andrews.

He put the Escalade in park and looked straight ahead, releasing my hand to grip his steering wheel.

"Aren't you coming in?" I asked.

Jared shook his head. "I'm the last person she wants to see."

"O...Okay," I said, unsure of what to make of his behavior. Jared admitted standing up to my father once, but he wouldn't face my mother.

I reached for the door, but Jared grabbed my arm and pulled me to him with worry in his eyes. His hands cupped my face and he pressed his lips against mine with a sense of urgency. When he finally released me from the kiss, he leaned his forehead against mine, closing his eyes.

"You act like you're never going to see me again," I said, suddenly nervous.

"I can't ask you to go against your mother's wishes, Nina."

I laughed once in surprise. "You think she's going to tell me to stay away from you?"

"That's exactly what she's going to do."

I shook my head. "You should know my mother has a poor track record for changing my mind. Even she knows it."

"She seldom fails to get her way. Just...don't listen to her."

"Her tricks work on everyone but me. I'm not going anywhere."

One corner of his mouth turned up, but it seemed contrived.

"I'll call you later, okay?" I ran my fingers through the sides of his hair, and he pressed his forehead against mine again.

"Okay," he whispered.

The Escalade stood motionless until I was inside the building, and then it slowly pull away.

Knowing he would be listening, I hurried to my room. I was anxious to calm the storms in Jared's eyes, even if that meant going toe to toe with Cynthia Grey.

I opened the door and froze. Cynthia stood in the middle of the room, her arms crossed, prepared for confrontation. Beth twisted around in her desk chair, meeting my eyes with a sympathetic expression.

"I think I'm going to grab some coffee. Would either of you like me to bring you something ba—,"

"No thank you," Cynthia interrupted. She must have been far beyond anger; she was never cross enough to be so rude.

"I'll take some, Beth, thanks," I said, making a show of appreciation. Beth nodded and grabbed her coat, rushing out the door.

"Where were you last night?" Cynthia demanded.

"You know perfectly well where I was," I said, mimicking the set of her chin.

This took her off-guard. Cynthia typically relied on the element of surprise.

She recovered quickly. "You can't get involved with Jared, Nina. You don't know anything about him, trust me."

"I know enough, Mother." I sat on Beth's bed and looked to the floor. I would have to choose my words carefully.

Cynthia reared her head and stepped in front of me. "Nina Elizabeth, it's too dangerous. I know you think you know him, but you don't."

I laughed once. "If he's dangerous then why is he being paid to protect me?"

Cynthia's mouth flew open. "That arrangement was between him and your father. You're not listening. He's not dangerous to you. It's dangerous for you to be...to become...involved with him. He has just as many enemies as your father."

"I know what I'm doing."

"Do you?" she asked. "Do you know what you're getting yourself into? I don't think you have the slightest idea of where this could lead or the choices you'll have to make. I don't think he's thought this through, either, or he wouldn't have done this. Maybe not, maybe he's too selfish to care—"

"Selfish?" I shrieked. "How can you say that about him? After what we've put him and his family through, Mother?"

"Is that what this is about? Guilt?" Cynthia paced the room, arms still crossed.

"No!" I gasped. "It's nothing like that," I said, embarrassed that Jared could hear her words.

She closed her eyes and sighed. "Nina...please. I'm begging you. You know that I want you to be happy...

but this—this is not going to end well," her voice was quiet.

I smiled. "Does anything end well?"

Cynthia heaved her usual resigned sigh, but this time it was different. It was the same she used in the seldom event that she lost an argument to Jack.

"I wish this one time, Baby, that you would listen to what I'm trying to tell you. The last few months have been the culmination of every fear I've ever had."

I had been unaffected by my mother's infamous guilt trips since I was thirteen, but now that she'd used Jack's death, I couldn't break free of the blame. She had never wanted me to find out the truth, and I imagined that it was the one thing she wanted to remain unchanged after we lost my father.

When I thought of her dishonesty and how she'd kept secrets about Jack and Gabe and the Ryels from me for years, the guilt turned to anger.

"You can't tell me how to feel," I glowered.

"It's not too late, Nina. You can save yourself," she said, lifting my chin. Her uncharacteristically soft affection caught me off guard, but I was resolved.

I pulled away from her. "I don't need to be saved from Jared."

Cynthia sucked in a sharp breath and pinched her nose with her thumb and finger. "Nina...."

I could see that she was finished. She had pulled every trick from her bag and laid her cards on the table. I felt triumphant as I imagined Jared smiling at my words.

Beth returned, then, sitting beside me on her bed.

"Hazelnut and Splenda," she smiled, handing me a Styrofoam cup.

"Thanks, Beth."

Cynthia looked at me, exasperated. "I'm going home now. Please think about what I said. It's important."

"I will." I tried to conceal my relief at her departure.

Beth closed the door and then turned to me. "Did she just give you the sex talk?"

"What? No!" I twisted my face in disgust. The thought of discussing my sex life with my mother made my stomach turn, and Beth clearly had the wrong idea about several things.

"You stayed with him last night?" The corners of her mouth turned up in an enthusiastic grin.

"Yes, but I fell asleep. It wasn't like that."

"Oh. Well, did you have a good time?" she asked, deflated.

"We went to his loft, he cooked—"

"He cooked?" Beth interrupted.

I nodded. "He brought me flowers and there were candles everywhere. We talked for hours, into the morning."

Beth pulled her knees up to her chest. "Wow. I told you he was in love with you. I have a sixth sense about these things."

"You're amazing," I granted.

"Thanks for noticing," she said. Her eyes narrowed with her grin. "When are you going to see him again?"

"Later today, I hope. Our morning was sort of cut short."

"Cynthia," she said. I nodded my head and she stood up, gathering her things.

"I'm going to the hospital with Chad and Tucker in an hour. Do you have time before you meet back up with Jared?"

"Yes," I said, deciding in the moment.

Beth dialed her cell phone, calling Chad to let him know that I would be tagging along. Quickly after he answered, her voice lowered. She tried to be vague, but I could tell Chad, Tucker, or both, had a problem with me going. Beth won in the end, and she turned to me and winked.

I was relieved to arrive at the hospital; Tucker and Chad didn't seem angry with me, but there was an obvious air of tension in Chad's jeep. I wasn't sure what all the apprehension meant until we arrived at Ryan's new room in PCCU.

Ryan didn't look happy to see me. In fact, he behaved as if my very presence was an insult.

He wasted no time before he pounced. "So how was your date?" he sneered.

"I thought you didn't want to hear about it." My answer was automatic and venomous. I hadn't intended to sound defensive, but his spiteful attitude took me by surprise.

"That was before Beth called everyone looking for you at three in the morning. It went that well, huh?" he bristled.

I looked over at Chad and Tucker; this is what they were worried about.

Beth looked at Chad with an angry glare, and he shot her an apologetic smile.

"It wasn't me, babe!" he shrugged.

"Who was it?" she snarled.

Ryan rolled his eyes. "It was Josh. What does it matter?"

Beth stomped to my side of the room in protest, crossing her arms.

"What business is it of Josh's?" I said. "If everyone's so worried about me upsetting you, why do they keep passing on my business?" I was being entirely too defensive, but I was still raw from my earlier encounter with Cynthia.

"Maybe they want me to talk some sense into you."

"Or is it because you're making everyone think they have to choose sides?" I narrowed my eyes and mimicked Beth's crossed arms. We must have looked ridiculous side by side; the Prom Queen Mafia.

"There are no sides." Ryan's nose wrinkled at my words.

"Really?" I raised an eyebrow. My eyes darted to Chad and Tucker standing on one side of the room, and then at Beth beside me. "It sure seems like it to me."

Ryan ground his teeth and looked out the window, clearly too angry to continue.

I sighed. "If you'd just give him a chance."

Ryan sucked in a sharp breath, readying himself to really let me have it, but he cringed and grabbed his bandaged wound, letting out a muffled grunt instead.

"Ryan..." I groaned, reaching for him. The pain in his face sent guilt burning through me. I took a step closer to his bed.

"Just go, Nina. Just...go," he said with his eyes clinched shut.

I wanted to apologize, but nothing could make it right. I would never be sorry for being with Jared, and that was my only crime in Ryan's eyes.

I trudged to the waiting room without another word. My perfect morning had transformed into an abysmal day.

Beth, Chad and Tucker returned after half an hour, and we walked to the jeep in silence. I tried to find solace in their conversation on the way back to campus, discussing Ryan's improvement, his possible early release, and the funny stories they were trying to cheer him up with, but nothing helped. I was considered the scarlet letter when I had done nothing wrong.

As we pulled into the campus parking lot, my cell phone buzzed. The display lit up and Ryan's name and number scrolled across the screen. I clambered from Chad's jeep and pressed the phone to my ear.

"I'm sorry, Nina," he blurted out apologetically. "You were right; it's no one's business. I just didn't expect...I don't know what I expected."

"It's not what you think. I just fell asleep," I explained.

"We're friends, right, Nina?" he said. My insides wrenched at the exhausted sadness in his voice.

I covered my eyes with my hand. "Of course we are. I hate it that you're mad at me."

"I have no right to be. I just need to know that I didn't ruin everything."

Ruin everything? He was lying in a hospital bed healing from a wound that I could have prevented. The guilt was unbearable.

"I'm sorry," I choked out.

171

"I'm a jealous idiot, Nina. Just...promise me you'll come back. I won't be a jerk again, I swear." His voice bordered on begging, and I was desperate to take away his regret.

"You can't get rid of me that easily."

Beth smiled after watching me stuff my cell phone into my purse. "I'm glad you two got it worked out."

"Me, too," I sighed.

Once in my room, I dialed Jared's number. The tone repeated over and over in my ear and I was caught off-guard when the voicemail prompt beeped in my ear.

"H–hey, Jared," I stuttered. I had fully expected him to answer. "It's Nina. I'm back from the hospital and just thought I'd give you a call. Talk to you soon."

After two hours, I became suspicious when I hadn't heard from him. He had been so anxious about the outcome of my mother's visit that I couldn't imagine why he'd wait so long to return my call. It didn't help when I realized he had probably heard my message in real-time the second I'd left it.

Just as I had lost the fight to keep from calling him a second time, there was a knock at the door.

"Happy Saturday, ladies," Kim said, bursting in.

"Hey Kim," I said, disappointed.

"Well. I love you, too."

"She was expecting Jared," Beth explained.

"I heard the date went well." Kim raised her eyebrows repeatedly.

"I fell asleep. He slept on the couch."

Kim wrinkled her nose. "Bummer." She immediately turned her attention to Beth. "What are we doing tonight?"

"Oh...Chad is taking me out. Sorry," Beth said, not sounding the least bit sorry.

Kim smiled. "Oh well, maybe you can have a more interesting time than Naughty Nina over there."

I stiffened, knowing that Jared or Claire could hear everything. I felt the blush span from collar bone to crown.

"Whoa! Just kidding, Nigh!" Kim said, mistaking my embarrassment for anger.

Kim forced me to rehash the entire evening. It was difficult for me to explain the length of time that I'd spent there and leave out everything that Jared had told me. I kept checking my phone, even though I knew no one had called.

Beth discussed the juicy details of our earlier visit to the hospital, which seemed to intrigue Kim.

"What do you expect? He's crazy about her," Kim said. "I know you really like Jared, Nigh, but Ryan's a good guy, too."

"I know," I said, looking at my phone again.

"Who are you expecting to call? You've been checking your phone like a crack addict waiting on her dealer," Kim chided.

"Kim!" I wailed, my face burning again.

"What is with you, today? I thought you slept last night," Kim asked, confused.

"I did. I just wish you would keep your mouth shut!"

"Nigh, we're in your room. Who's going to hear?" Kim looked at Beth like I'd gone insane.

"No one," I said. "You just...nothing. I have to go." I grabbed my coat, shoved my phone in my purse and headed out the door. I wished that Jared had forgone the microphone part of the truth. I didn't feel comfortable having a normal conversation in my room.

By Monday, I still hadn't heard from Jared. It was heartbreaking that he was somewhere close, yet he refused to speak to me. Even after everything Jared had said, my thoughts continued to return to one horrible prospect: that for some reason after he'd dropped me off, he realized how unworthy I was of the adoration he'd felt for so long.

The week dragged on and I found the only place I felt somewhat normal was at the hospital. I escaped campus day after day, feeling I could finally breathe the moment I sat at Ryan's bedside. We were nearly caught up on all of his homework by the time he finally broached the subject.

"Are you going to tell me what's been going on with you or not?"

"What are you talking about?" I asked with a contrived smile.

"Nina. This is me you're talking to."

I felt my eyes gloss over and I buried my head into Ryan's blanket.

"Nina? What's wrong?" he asked, awkwardly patting my head. When I couldn't speak, Ryan pulled my hair away from my face. "Are you okay?"

I shook my head and peeked up at him. "No. No, I'm not okay."

"Did something happen?" Ryan's face looked as desperate as I felt.

"No. Nothing happened. You don't want to hear about it." I sat up and wiped the moisture from my face.

"Is it about Jared?" he guessed. I nodded and his face twisted into rage. "Did he hurt you?"

"No!" I shook my head, wiping away more tears. "No, he didn't do anything to me. He doesn't...," I sighed, "it's embarrassing."

"Just tell me."

"He doesn't...want me," I said, my face crumbling around my words.

Ryan's expression made it seem as if the sentence I'd put together didn't compute; as if he couldn't imagine that being possible. "I'm sure there's just been some misunderstanding. What makes you think that?"

I was disgusted at myself for making Ryan feel he needed to reassure me about Jared. I was a terrible person.

"Nina. Tell me." He spoke in the tone I provoked in people when they'd had their fill of dragging information out of me.

"I just thought we...I thought he...." I couldn't say half of what I wanted. Certainly not enough to keep me from sounding like a spoiled child.

Ryan laughed once and I looked up at him. "He's an idiot, Nina."

"No, he's not," I said, wiping my eyes with my sleeve.

"If he took you out, spent an entire night with you and can't see how incredible you are—he doesn't deserve for you to be waiting for his call. You're so much better than that. Anyone that makes you feel any less is a fool."

"Thank you, but it's really more complicated than that."

Ryan's face grew serious. "No. No, it's not. If he doesn't realize what he has right in front of him, than to hell with him. And I'm not just saying that because I was hoping for something like this."

I shot a glare at him and he winked at me. I smiled and sighed, letting my frustration escape with my breath. He leaned over to issue a comforting kiss to the top of my head.

"Why are you so good to me?" I asked as he handed me a handful of tissues from his bedside table.

"Because you're worth it." He looked at me as if I should know that already, and I couldn't help but smile.

"I think that's been trademarked by L'Oreal," I said.

"Oh, I meant 'Maybe she's born with it'."

"Maybe it's Maybelline?" I quipped.

He pointed at me. "You're good."

"I take a licking and keep on ticking," I smiled, resting my head against my hand.

He shrugged. "Sometimes you feel like a nut, sometimes you don't."

I giggled again and wiped the residual wetness from my eyes. "You can't top the coppertop."

Ryan sat for a moment, looking stumped, and then an impish grin appeared on his face. "I have good news. I just saved a bunch of money on my car insurance by switching to GEICO."

My eyes narrowed. "Are you in good hands?"

Ryan intertwined his fingers in mine. "Easy, breezy, beautiful, Covergirl."

I bit my lip, not wanting to stop our game. It was such a wonderful distraction.

"Just Do It," he nudged my arm.

"Leggo my Eggo," I countered, playfully pulling my arm back.

He flexed him arm. "Beef. It's what's for dinner."

I pointed to his arm and shook my head. "Tastes great, less filling." I sat up and waited for his riposte.

"WASSSSSUP?" he leaned over into my face and I burst out into a roaring laughter. He bellowed out his own and we covered our mouths to keep the nurses from rushing in to quiet us down.

"Thank you. I needed that," I breathed, holding my stomach.

"You most certainly did," Ryan agreed.

The next morning, I woke up to the ring of my cell phone. I scrambled to my night stand, ripped the charger cord from its port and jerked it to my ear.

"Hello?" I cringed, waiting for the person at the other end of the line to mention the near maniacal tone in my voice.

"Hey Nigh, it's Ryan. You left your Anatomy book here yesterday. I just wanted to let you know before you got to class."

"Oh. Oh! Thanks. I don't think I'll need it today, we're preparing for a lab." I rubbed my eyes, wondering when I had finally fallen asleep. It didn't feel like I'd slept at all.

"Did I wake you?"

"Yeah, but that's okay." I looked at the clock. "The alarm goes off in ten minutes, anyway."

"The nurse said that they may release me today or tomorrow," he said.

"Excellent! Let me know when and I'll rally the troops to spring you."

"Will do," he chirped, sounding extremely enthusiastic for the early hour.

Classes dragged, and I had to force myself to finish out the day. By the time I got to my room, exhaustion had set in, and I decided to cook something quick and then take a nap.

Finishing the mounds of homework scattered on my bed was impossible. I couldn't concentrate knowing that every time I turned a page, every time my spoon scraped the bowl, every time I sighed, Jared was listening.

When that thought crossed my mind, anger pulsed through me. He had told me secrets—which he expected me to keep—he told me that he loved me, made promises, and then he just...left.

"Who does that?" I asked aloud. I shook my head, thinking of the show he'd put on when dropping me off at Andrews. He seemed so terrified of losing me, of my mother talking me into staying away from him. In the end, it was Jared that was evading me.

I dwelled on that for a moment and wondered what had changed from the time he dropped me off until after I'd returned from the hospital. I had only focused on what I could have done wrong; I hadn't stopped to think about other possible reasons for Jared to avoid me like the plague. Like my mother.

My hand flew to my mouth as the revelation sunk in. She had spoken to him. She had told him to stay away from me, and he had listened to her.

Grabbing my coat and keys, I shot out the door as if my room were on fire. I ran to my car and violated every traffic law between Brown University and my parents' home. Once I pulled into the drive my courage had somewhat waivered, but I had to know why Jared had changed his mind. I had to know it wasn't that I didn't live up to his expectations.

I burst into the door, calling for my mother. After the third time that I yelled her name, she came hurrying down the staircase.

"Nina? What are you carrying on about?" She held onto the banister with one hand and clipped on an earring with another.

"What did you say to him?" I demanded.

"What did I say to whom?" A disgusted look immediately clouded her face.

"Mother, stop it!" I yelled.

Cynthia raised an eyebrow and spoke slowly. "You will watch your tone while in my house, young lady."

I shook my head and took another step toward her. "What did you say to Jared?"

Cynthia deliberated for a moment. "I told him what he needed to hear, Nina. Of course you wouldn't listen, so I had no choice."

"Why? Why would you deliberately try to hurt me?"

Cynthia was stunned by my assumption. "Nina, I'm simply trying to save you from yourself. If you won't have the sense to...well, I'm glad that he did."

"Mother, I'm begging you...don't do this. I have been...." I couldn't finish. I sat on the bottom step and covered my face with my hands.

Cynthia descended the remaining steps and sat next to me. "I know you think you understand, Darling, but you don't. Whatever you think you know...you couldn't truly grasp what it was that you were choosing. I'm glad that Jared loves you enough to let you go."

I glared at her. "Do you even hear yourself? He loves me, Mom. He loves me and you...." I shook my head and walked to the door. "Do you even care how I feel?" I asked, standing with my back to her.

She didn't answer.

I returned to my car, choking back a frustrated cry. There was only one way I could talk to him, now.

Chapter Eight
Purgatory

I searched under the desks, running my fingers along each of the twisted wires underneath. Jared would listen to me whether he liked it or not, and in my determination, I left nothing to chance. I meticulously inspected the edges of the mirror, the back of the microwave, the mini-fridge, under both beds and under the dorm's standard-issue cord phone.

An hour had passed, and I found nothing. Jared was a professional. Of course I wouldn't find the mic he'd planted. I tried to recall any spy movies I'd watched when revelation hit. My eyes slowly followed the wall up to the ceiling, and focused on a rectangular vent in the center.

I rolled Beth's desk chair directly underneath. There were two screws, and I had no tools. I rushed to the residential advisor's room and tried to catch my breath while rapping on the door. She opened it with a bored look on her face.

"Yeah?"

"Hey, Dara. Listen, I'm having some trouble with the vent in my room...."

"I'll call maintenance in the morning," she deadpanned, closing the door.

I pushed it open. "I was wondering if you had a screwdriver. One of those cross-ones that I could use?"

"A Phillips?" she asked, bored with the conversation.

My eyes lit up. "Yes! Do you have one?"

"What size do you need?" she asked, turning her back to me.

"I...don't know." I peered up at her vent, and she did the same.

"You need a small one, here." She handed me a tiny screwdriver, and I thanked her before rushing back to my room.

The screwdriver was smaller than I needed, so I had to press on one side to get the screw to rotate at all. Once the first screw became loose enough to use my thumb and finger to make more progress, it didn't take long for it to drop into my hand. I began working on the other screw, and after two laborious turns my right hand slipped. Trying to catch myself, my palm grated against the edge of the vent, and the ragged edge of metal sliced through my skin.

I pulled my hand back with a gasp, watching the blood ooze from the cut and drip down my forearm toward my elbow in a thick red line.

"Ow! Sssshhhhoooot!" I cried, bending at the waist.

I climbed down to grab a wad of tissue and held it tightly in my hand, unwilling to give up.

Tissues in hand, I tried to fit the screwdriver into the tiny slot at the best angle possible for traction. When I pressed against the side of the screw, I leaned into the movement and the wheels of the chair shifted. Before I could right myself, the chair jerked from under me and I tumbled down, smacking my elbow on the floor.

It took a moment for the pain to register, and once the sharp stabbing sensation shot up my arm, I closed my eyes. "Ow," I whimpered. Once I could think about something other than the pain, I hobbled back onto the chair.

Tugging the vent loose, I inched up on my tip toes to peer inside. My heart skipped a beat when I saw a tiny black object nestled in the decades of dust. I reached inside the vent and pinched the small piece of plastic, tugging on it once before it gave way. I pulled it toward me and brought it into view; Jared's miniature microphone.

Overwhelmed by the undeniable truth I held in my hand, I pulled the mic down with me as I slumped to the chair. Jared could hear me and was aware of what I had done. Coupled with the pain in my arm, the fact that he was just on the other side of this device made my eyes well over with tears.

"Jared?" I breathed, trying to keep my voice from shaking. "I know you can hear me." I sighed, closing my eyes. "I don't know what she said to you. I don't care, I just...," I trailed off as my voice broke, "I miss you," I whispered. "What are you doing? All that talk about growing old together and being honest? Now you're going to listen to her and walk away?

"Will you please just...." I struggled to form the words. "Will you please just talk to me? Please?"

I watched my cell phone, praying, willing it to light up and ring. An eternity passed, but it lay on my nightstand, still and dark.

I wiped the moisture from my eyes, looking up at the wire spiraling down from the ceiling. Anger surged through my veins and I stood up, yanking on the wire over and over until it finally ripped from its source. I noticed the frayed edge of the end of the wire and wiped my face once more, satisfied. It wasn't fair that he could hear me when I was alone.

A buzzing noise came from the night table and I stiffened. It buzzed again and I threw the wire down, nearly tripping over it to reach the phone before I missed the call.

"Jared?" I breathed.

"It's uh...it's Ryan. Sorry."

"No! Don't be sorry," I sniffed.

"Are you okay? You sound like you've been crying."

"Was there a reason you called?" I wasn't in the mood to discuss my latest moment of insanity.

"Yes," he hesitated, "I'm being released in the morning."

"Oh. Oh yeah, okay. I'll come in the morning, then. Did you let everyone else know or should I call them?" I asked, hoping he would catch the meaning.

"I just started making the calls."

He'd called me first. I wasn't sure how to feel about that.

"Nina?"

"Mmmhmm?" I said, distracted by the wire curled and arched beside my bed.

"Tell me why you're upset. Is it Jared?" My silence was all the answer he needed. "I could kill him for doing this to you," he growled.

"It's not his fault, Ryan. I've told you, it's complicated."

Ryan sighed, accepting my vague reply. "I'll see you in the morning."

Friday was easier than I thought it would be, with the six of us choreographing Ryan's on-the-fly homecoming party. We caravanned to the hospital; balloons and shoe polish decorated our cars. The windows of Josh's truck vibrated to the beat of "Paradise City" as Tucker wheeled Ryan out of the double doors of the hospital. We all whistled and clapped as Ryan lumbered into Josh's passenger side. "C'mon, Nina," Ryan smiled, gesturing for me to accompany him. When I scooted in next to him, Ryan weakly lifted his arm to the top of the seat behind me. We giggled and joked all the way to Brown, and the seven of us made our way to Ryan's room.

"It looks like a parade threw up in here," Ryan said, beaming. He hobbled over to his desk chair and fell into it, visibly spent.

We sat and talked, and then Beth, Chad and Tucker left for class. Thirty minutes later, Kim and Josh had classes of their own to go to.

"What did you do to your hand?" Ryan asked, staring at my haphazardly bandaged palm.

"I sliced it on the air vent in my room," I shrugged.

"Ouch. Are you all caught up on your tetanus shots?"

I nodded. "I'll come by later, okay? We have a lot of work to do."

"You have class?" he asked, disappointed.

"I've had class for the last two hours, Ryan," I grinned.

"Thanks for today. Maybe we could do this every month."

"Okay, but I'm not volunteering to get stabbed next time. Or ever." I hugged him and an awkward pause followed when I pulled away. "You take it easy. I'll come over later and we can study."

Ryan watched me with a soft expression as I walked to the door. "See you later, Nigh."

I pulled his door closed and let out a gust of air. I couldn't be sure if it was guilt or the look in Ryan's eyes after I'd hugged him, but everything felt different when we were alone. I forgot about angels and demons and feeling unwanted. In Ryan's presence, life was normal.

Soon after class began, my thoughts zeroed in on Jared. I clenched my eyes shut when I thought about the night before. I had probably relieved him of any regret he might have felt after my antics. The professor's voice blurred into the background, and I took shallow breaths to keep the tears from forming; it was embarrassing enough that everyone peered over their shoulders at me every day as if I'd gone crazy, the last thing I needed was to break down in class.

In the solitude of my room, I let the tears flow. I was glad that Jared couldn't hear me. I had become a blubbering, pathetic mess. My eyes drifted to the vent to see that the cover was securely fastened to the ceiling. My eyebrows pressed inward. I was too exhausted the night before to replace it.

Scrambling to the floor, I lifted my comforter to peer under the bed where I had hidden the frayed carcass of the wire. I gritted my teeth seeing that the only thing under my bed was a lone sock surrounded by a herd of dust bunnies.

Jared or Claire had come into my room while I was gone and replaced the mic. I looked to the ceiling, balling my hands into fists at my sides. "Stay out of my room!"

The screwdriver was missing from the top drawer of my dresser as well. I had left it there for safe keeping until I could replace the vent cover. I burst into the hallway, letting the door crack against the wall. Anger fueled my march to the RA's room and I pounded on her door.

She opened it with the same impassive look on her face as before. "Yeah?"

I sighed. "Dara! Oh good, you're here. Um, I seemed to have lost your screwdriver. Do you think I could borrow another one? And, I need a bigger one this time."

"You lost one of my screwdrivers and you want to borrow another one?"

"Yes," I said, more of a question than an answer.

"Hold on," she sighed, leaving for a moment. She returned with a larger screwdriver in hand.

Running back to my room, I pushed Beth's chair under the vent. The new screwdriver was a better fit, and I had the screws out in record time. I reached up again and stood on my tip toes, finding the familiar small plastic object without effort. An exact replica of the first mic came down in the first tug.

I climbed down and pulled on the wire until it quivered with tension. With one swift yank, the wire dislodged from the vent and dropped to the floor. A strange sense of accomplishment came over me; I had perfected the art of ripping out surveillance wires.

With a smug smile, I looped the thin, mangled wire into a tight circle. "I'm not a zoo animal," I whispered.

The door pulsed as someone banged on it from the other side. I twisted the knob, hoping for a scolding from Jared, but instead I found Claire standing in front of me with a murderous expression.

A lump lodged in my throat as she shouldered past me. In one lithe movement, she climbed onto Beth's chair and reached up into the duct. It took her longer to get the new wire installed than it had taken me to rip the old one out, but she replaced the vent quicker than I had removed it.

She walked to the door and stopped to look at the wire in my hands. Her hand blurred as she snatched it from me.

"If you do it again," she eyed the vent and then whispered in my ear, "I'll rip out your tongue."

My tongue curled up inside my mouth as I tried to swallow. Claire leaned back to offer a disturbing sweet smile, and then left. I shut my door behind her and locked it, wrapping my arms around my middle. She terrified me.

The thought of Jared hearing my every movement made tears trickle from my eyes and down my cheeks. "I can't do this," I whispered. The sudden need to distance myself from that microphone became urgent, and I grabbed my coat and keys. If I was going to have any type of normalcy again, I would have to convince Cynthia.

"Mom?" I called, walking into the dining room.

"In the kitchen, Dear," Cynthia called.

I watched her expression change to concern when she saw my puffy, wet eyes.

"What happened to your hand, Nina?" she said, noticing the makeshift wrap around my palm.

"I want you to talk to Jared, Mother."

Her concern vanished and she returned to preparing her lunch. "I'm sorry, Nina. I can't do that."

"Then let me have my privacy."

Cynthia seemed a bit uncomfortable with the topic, but she was never one to be intimidated. "That is between Jared and your father."

"Daddy's not here."

She ignored me. "Jared and I talked for a very long time. If it helps, he argued with me at first. He was quite determined. When I reminded him how hard it is for his mother, and how hard it will be for you, he couldn't deny doing what is best for you. This is the easy part. You can't begin to imagine how hard your life will be if you continue this ridiculous—"

"You have to try. You owe it to me to try," I begged.

She clicked her tongue. "He won't listen to me now, Nina. There are some things that you just can't take back. Once you've made your case, you can't argue the other side."

"Mother...." I pursed my lips, but it was no use. The tears fell from my eyes.

"I warned him that if he continued a relationship with you, I would be forced to fire him."

"You what?"

"Carrying on a relationship with him could get In the way of—"

"You know he's the only one that can keep me safe! You're willing to risk my life to prove a point?"

"Of course not! Your father insisted that Jared stay away from you, Nina. You're just going to have to forget him!"

"Mother, I love him!"

Cynthia's eyes widened at my words. After a short pause, she shook her head dismissively. "You don't know what you're saying."

I could barely form a whisper. "Look at me." I let my shoulders hang in defeat. "Does this look like just a crush to you? I'm in love with him."

"Then stop. This is not what your father wanted for you. Did Jared tell you that? That he was forbidden to get involved with you? I won't help you go against your father's wishes."

"That had nothing to do with me or with Jared, Mother! Daddy didn't want me to know the truth about him!"

"Nina," she breathed, "you don't believe that."

I could see my efforts were in vain; Cynthia wouldn't help me. I escaped her apathetic eyes and fled to my Beemer. The rain poured relentlessly, and I was soaked by the time I entered the car. I sped down the street, the tires creating a wake behind them.

The farther I drove, the less I wanted to return to my dorm. Walking into Andrews would be admitting defeat. Worse, something deep inside of me knew that the second I stepped inside my room, I would begin a life without Jared.

When the street lights began to flicker, the rain tapped against my windshield in tiny crystals. Some of the roads had been blocked off by the flooding, and I was soon corralled onto a dead end road. Through the gush of windblown rain, a bridge came into view just ahead of my car, arching high into the night sky.

I turned off my car and sat, mulling over the last week. My feeble attempt to gain any control over the situation had ended dismally. I hadn't truly considered giving up until that very moment.

I pulled my hat and gloves off and threw them on the seat beside me, deciding that the only option I truly had was to leave. But Jared would follow, he would have to, and I would take him away from his sister, his brother, and Lillian. I gripped the steering wheel as the realization sunk in; I was trapped.

One of my gloves fell to the floorboard, drawing my attention to my purse. Barely peeking out, the sharp end of Jack's letter opener glinted under the light of a lone street lamp. Without another thought, I grabbed it from my purse and shoved my way out of the car. The rain immediately blasted against me, but I planted my feet on the ground, determined to get Jared's attention this time. I grabbed the handle of the letter opener as tightly as my freezing hands could manage and held it above me.

"He'll come," I whispered.

With a loud cry, I shoved the golden spear into my back tire. It pierced the thick rubber, but not deep enough to do any damage. I used my foot to shove it in the rest of the way, and to my relief it made a loud hissing sound.

Icy rain soaked every inch of me, and my body began to tremble as the biting wind blew against my skin. After a few minutes, I shed my coat and threw it into the seat. My body shook uncontrollably as rain pelted against me.

I waited.

When my sweater was soaked through, I yanked it over my head and threw it on top of my coat. Down to a long-sleeved cotton shirt, the rain felt like ice splinters driving into my bones. My teeth were chattering with such force that I opened my mouth to keep them from breaking. A puff of air escaped my mouth as a wind gust sent stinging rain tearing into my skin.

Still, I waited.

Just when I thought I would collapse, a pair of headlights broke through the curtain of rain and came to an abrupt stop behind my car.

"Nina! What the hell are you doing?" Jared yelled over the rain. He took off his coat and stepped toward me, but I backed away. "Do you know what hypothermia is? You're going to freeze to death!" he said, shoving his coat toward me.

"I l-l-love you," I said as my entire body shuddered.

"I heard," Jared said, pressing his eyebrows together. "Let me take you home." He held out his coat again, but I took another step back.

"Y-you I-listened t-t-to her!"

"I didn't listen to her! If she fired me it would make it harder for me to protect you. Keeping you safe is my first priority. Now, please get in the car!"

"H-How would it make it h-h-harder if you're with me?"

"We can talk about this when you're out of the rain!"

I took another step back.

"Cynthia controls our funding!" Jared said in a desperate tone. "She funds our surveillance, our weapons...everything. I could still protect you, but not as well. I couldn't risk it!"

"So you're j–just going to leave me, we're g–going b–back to the way things were so you c–can buy more microphones and b–bullets?"

Jared sighed. "That's not what I meant. You're too important not to use the best means available, Nina. I thought if I figured out a way for us...I was trying to figure something out."

"You're j–just s–saying that to g–g–get me to go back there!"

"I wouldn't do that," Jared said. He lifted his coat and I took another step back. His jaws tensed. "I made a mistake! I didn't want to hurt you! I just needed some time to fix the mess I've made!"

I tried to turn the corners of my mouth up into somewhat of a smile. "I th–thought you didn't make m–mistakes."

With a desperate expression, Jared took a step toward me, groaning when I took another step back. "Don't make me do this, Nina. Don't make me force you. Please get in the car!"

"I'm not going b–back there," I sputtered.

The rain poured down Jared's face and streamed from his chin. "I wasn't going to take you...," he sighed, "I want you home with me!"

I watched him for a moment, trying to read his eyes.

"I wouldn't lie to you," he said, reaching for me. "I want to take you home."

I sucked in a breath and nodded. Jared wasted no time wrapping me in his coat, but it was already soaked through. He lifted me into his arms and in the next second I was in his car.

Jumping behind the wheel, Jared cranked up the heater and then rubbed my arms with both hands. "Jesus, Nina, your lips are blue."

He raced down streets that seemed more like rivers. I had just closed my eyes when he pulled to the curb in front of the loft.

"Stay awake, Nina. Don't go to sleep."

Jared took the steps three at a time, unlocked his door and skipped more steps to the loft. He held me in one arm while he turned on the shower, and the steam immediately filled the room.

He lifted my stiff body into the shower and held me against him. I cried out as the water burned my icy skin. After a while, the quivering turned less violent. Once I was able to stand alone, Jared adjusted the temperature to a hotter setting.

I looked up at him. "I'm sorry. I didn't know what else to do."

Jared grimaced, his eyes glowing steel blue. "Let's just get your temp up."

He pulled the gauze from my hand and inspected my wound, wincing before glaring down at me. I watched as he gently scrubbed the festering cut with a washcloth.

"You should have gotten stitches for this," he grumbled. His jaw tensed as he rinsed the soap away.

"What's wrong?" I asked, worried that it was resentment in his eyes instead of concern.

"Everything, Nina. I leave you alone for a week and you've got a deep, infected cut in your hand, you nearly broke your arm when you fell off the chair, and

194

you almost froze to death...or drowned, I'm not sure what would have happened first."

"I know. You have every right to be mad."

"Mad? I've made myself believe that when the time came, I would be better at making you happy than anyone else...and look at you. I've made your life worse. You're worried I'm angry with you? You should hate me for what I've done."

I ran my aching fingers through his wavy, wet hair. He closed his eyes and sighed.

"I've missed you," I whispered.

His expression crumbled at my words. "I've been going crazy. When you found the mic, Claire had to restrain me. It's one thing to know you're hurting; it's another to know I'm causing it."

I offered a weak grin. "You're going to have to find a new place to hide the microphone. It didn't take me long to figure it out. I totally outsmarted you. Twice."

"Outsmarted me? You don't even have the sense to get in out of the rain."

"At least I have enough sense to know that we shouldn't be apart."

Jared's eyes tightened in anguish.

I leaned up and pulled his face close, pressing my lips to his cheek. The water poured over us as he pulled me to him, my light kiss making his blue eyes burn with intensity. He kissed me as if I was the air he'd gone without for five days. Neither of us held back, the agony we had experienced apart fueled every movement. Our lips parted, and he pressed me against the tile wall of the shower. I clutched the back of his shirt in each of my fists and pulled him against me, but I couldn't get close enough. Jared's hands gripped each side of my face as he tasted the inside of my mouth.

I reached down and pulled his shirt over his head, exposing the perfection of his bare chest. His wet shirt fell to the shower floor with a slap. I slid my hands down his back and he moaned in response. His mouth grew impatient, then, and he reached down to grab my knee. He lifted my leg and pulled me against him, and I pressed my fingers into the flesh of his back. I braced myself as the intensity in the small space soared to a new level; but his lips slowed down, became gentle, and then he pulled away from me after a few soft kisses.

"It's been a long night, Nina. You need to rest."

"I don't think I can," I said, pressing my forehead against his chest.

Jared kissed my wet hair. "Try."

When he was satisfied that I was warm enough, he pulled me from the shower and wrapped me in a towel. I nestled against him as he carried me to his bed.

"You're still shaking," he frowned.

"I'm feeling much better, really," I assured him.

The front door slammed below and Jared kissed my cheek. "Claire fixed your tire and drove your car here. She's going to help you get into some dry clothes."

My entire body felt like it had been sandblasted, steamrolled and smashed in a garbage truck. I was too exhausted to argue.

Jared left us, and Claire peeled off my wet clothes, sliding a long sleeve T-shirt that read NAVY over my head.

"Thank you," I whispered.

She raised an eyebrow. "I thought I was crazy."

I sighed to form some sort of laugh and my eyes slowly closed and opened again.

Claire pulled a hairdryer out of a hot pink duffle bag and began to dry and brush my hair. I braced myself for her to do her best to rip my hair out, but she was very gentle; almost maternal.

The high-pitched whine of the dryer silenced, and Claire crouched in front of me. "Okay. You're done."

As Jared passed Claire on the stairs, he offered an appreciative smile. He was shirtless, his only article of clothing a light blue pair of pajama pants. In the shower was the first time I'd seen his bare physique, and even through my exhaustion I was impressed. Every muscle in his body sleek and toned, he kneeled in front of me holding a small white box.

"Give me your hand."

The skin around the jagged cut was opaque and wrinkled from the long shower. Jared spread antibiotic along the fissure spanning the width of my palm, from the outside of my wrist to the bottom of my index finger. It didn't hurt, but because of residual trembling I had a hard time holding still.

I raised my hand to inspect it and Jared rolled his eyes. "Is it okay?"

"Nicely done," I nodded in approval.

I leaned against the pillow while Jared walked to the other side of the bed. When he crawled in beside me, it occurred to me that my heart should have been pounding out of my chest, but I only felt exhaustion.

Jared pulled me to him and folded his arms around me. I sighed as I relaxed against his chest; he was warmer than the shower. I was still cold enough that his skin was slightly painful against mine, but I leaned in closer, welcoming the burn.

"Promise me you won't do anything like that again," Jared whispered, kissing my forehead.

I buried my face into the concave of his neck and shivered. In reaction, Jared wrapped his arms tighter around me.

Chapter Nine
Healing

"Nina?"

I raised my eyebrows, but my eyes wouldn't open.

Jared brushed the hair away from my face and kissed the exposed patch of skin on my cheek.

I blinked to focus, and Jared's blurry form came into view.

"It's six thirty, sweetheart. You have an eight o'clock class."

I sat up, immediately grabbing Jared's arm. "Whoa."

"Dizzy?" he asked.

"As if you didn't know."

He smiled, leaving my side to grab a stack of folded clothes and place them on the end of the bed. "Claire brought some more of your things."

With my eyes half-closed, I stood up and stretched, and then inched up the hem of my shirt to change.

"Er...Nina?" Jared said, grabbing my hands. "I've always thought you were the most beautiful in the morning. Seeing you standing here in my T-shirt is nearly driving me mad. Would you please stop trying to send me over the edge?"

I grimaced at his infuriating insistence on putting off the inevitable. I'd always been the one to procrastinate when dealing with the intimacy issue. Now that I'd felt strong enough about someone to want to press the boundaries, he insisted on dragging his feet.

Sensing my aggravation, he kissed my nose and jogged down the stairs, allowing me the privacy to change.

"I'll drive you to school, if that's okay," Jared said after breakfast.

"That would be great. Thank you."

The roads were slick with ice, and the trees and grass were frozen in time under the inch-thick frost. Jared effortlessly navigated the Escalade to Brown's campus, keeping my hand in his until we pulled into the parking lot.

"I'll meet you here, then?"

"Er...yeah?" I said, caught off guard.

"I thought it would be best if you stayed with me for a few days," he shrugged, "until your hand heals. You'll need a fresh dressing every night."

I pressed my lips together, trying not to let myself get too excited. I didn't want to tip him off.

"Or not...I can call you later," he backpedaled.

I slid my arms around his middle. "I would love for you to pick me up."

Jared's eyes relaxed. "I will be right here, one-thirty."

Initially, the excitement of staying with Jared propelled me through the first half-hour of class, but as the hour wore on I had a hard time concentrating. Doubt seeped into my every thought, and I found myself watching the clock, anxiously counting down the minutes.

He had left me on a day much like this one, including the perfect morning of smiles and kisses goodbye. Victory suddenly seemed too easy, and I felt sick with worry that he had appeased me long enough to disappear again.

Beth and Kim met me outside, eager to hear the story behind my bandaged hand. The prospect of enduring lunch and another class added to the stress of constructing a detailed lie of the night before had me nearly in tears. I couldn't shake the feeling that I would go to meet him at the designated time and he wouldn't be there.

Beth noticed my mood immediately. "What's wrong, Nina?"

"Nothing. Why?" I asked, trying to keep my tone light. It was hard to seem casual when my chest felt full of concrete.

"Nina?"

I let out a sigh of relief. "Jared!" I said, grabbing onto his coat and hugging him. I was too relieved to care how ridiculous I looked.

He wrapped his arms around me without hesitation. "What is it?" he whispered into my ear.

"What's going on with you, Nigh?" Kim asked.

I buried my face in Jared's chest, and I was glad when he hugged me tighter.

"Nina," he whispered in my ear again. "Did something happen?"

I peeked over to Beth and Kim, who watched me with confused frowns. I tried to smooth my face before looking at them. "I'll meet you guys at The Ratty, okay?"

"Are you sure?" Beth asked, staring suspiciously at Jared.

"I'll be right there," I smiled.

My friends reluctantly left me behind, and I buried my face in Jared's chest, tightening my arms around him.

"Nina, please tell me," he pleaded. "You've been freaking out all morning."

"I'm sorry."

He pulled up my chin and scanned my face for a clue. He sighed in frustration when I didn't speak. "Nina, I need to know."

"I was afraid you wouldn't come." I looked down to my boots; I couldn't look him in the eye while sounding so pathetic.

Jared took my face in his hands and kissed me tenderly. "I will never leave you again. Not like that."

"Not like what?" I asked, concerned there might be more behind his words.

"I won't make that mistake again. I'm yours for as long as you'll have me."

"You promise?"

Jared smiled. "I love you more than I could ever promise."

I rested my cheek against his chest and closed my eyes, indescribably happy. The euphoria faded when I realized I would have to make it through lunch and another class before I would see him again.

"Nina?"

"I'm never going to get used to that, you know," I said, frowning.

"Get used to what?"

"You sensing how I'm feeling. It's...." I trailed off, wrinkling my nose.

Jared chuckled. "Weird?"

I looked at him sheepishly and shrugged. "Why don't you come to lunch with me?"

"Here?"

"You can't go to class with me, but you can come to lunch. It would help."

"Help with what?" he asked, still stumped.

"With the...." I hesitated. Being honest meant casting blame in his direction, which I had no desire to do.

"Anxiety," Jared finished for me. As I predicted, he was visibly upset that I felt that way.

"I don't mean that it's your fault, I just meant...."

He held out his hand. "Come on."

I felt the corners of my mouth turn up, and I let his warm hand surround mine as we walked into The Ratty. Every face at the table seating my friends seemed to look over at us in unison as we walked to the buffet.

"They're just curious." I said as we walked through the line. Jared simply nodded.

"Everything all right, Nigh?" Beth asked once we were seated.

"Everything is great," I said.

"You didn't look so great when we left you," Kim said. Her eyes narrowed in Jared's direction for a moment, and then returned to me.

Jared seemed amused by my friends' incredulous expressions.

I picked up the spoon from my tray and muttered under my breath; I'd meant to grab a fork. Before I could get up, Jared sat a fork on my tray. I looked up to thank him, but before I could form the words, Ryan puffed a disgusted laugh.

"Is he going to feed you, too?" Ryan said.

"Shut up," I sneered. If I hadn't been so angry I might have feared for Ryan's safety. Jared could have easily reached over the table and snapped his neck. He watched Ryan, but seemed outwardly unaffected.

"What are we doing this weekend, Ryan?" Josh asked.

"I don't know," Ryan answered. His eyes were focused on Jared, full of hate.

Kim spoke, "I say we go to our regular spot. We're making that place a ton of money. The geriatrics love the entertainment we're providing."

"You just like older men," Josh teased.

"Only the ones that carry around a bottle of Viagra," she said offhandedly. Everyone at the table paused for moment, waiting for her to crack a smile. When she didn't, they continued discussing plans.

Ryan looked away from Jared after Kim's comment, and she winked at me after the moment had passed. The girl was a genius.

"I'm in," Tucker said.

Beth turned to face me. "Nina?"

"Oh," I said, quickly glancing at Jared from the corner of my eye. "I don't know what I'm doing, yet."

"Come on!" Kim groaned.

"Why don't you bring Jared? It'll be fun," Beth chirped.

Ryan slowly turned to her with angry disbelief. Beth sank back in her chair.

Noticing Ryan's reaction, Jared hugged me gently to him and smiled. "Sounds good to me. Do you want to go?" he asked, turning to me.

"Uh...sure."

"Sweet!" Kim said with a mouth full of food.

"Spring Break is in two weeks," Carrie chimed in. "Lisa and I are going to Tahoe. Does anyone else want to go skiing?"

"That sounds amazing! Do you want to go?" Beth said, looking at Chad.

Chad shrugged. "I haven't been skiing in a couple of years. How many spots do you have open?"

"My mom has a place there. We can all fit if you guys want to come," Lisa said.

"How much fun is this going to be?" Beth clapped. "Do you want to go skiing, Nigh?" she asked, turning to me.

"I don't know. I usually go on vacation with my parents. I'm sure Cynthia has something planned, already," I looked to Jared who nodded infinitesimally, confirming my assumption.

"You can't get out of it?" Kim asked.

I shook my head. "Not this year. I don't want to make her go alone." Kim and Beth nodded in understanding.

"I've gotta get back," Ryan said, rising. He peered up at me a few times while gathering his things, and then walked away without saying goodbye. Josh followed closely behind.

"What his problem?" Lisa asked.

Kim shrugged, but I caught her glance in my direction.

Jared walked me to my next class. I was glad that he decided to do that on his own; it saved me the humiliation of asking. Suddenly the task of sitting through the next hour was less daunting.

205

"I'll see you after class?" he asked, kissing my cheek.

"I'm sorry you had to come all the way here," I said, leaning my cheek into his lips and closing my eyes.

"Nina," he scanned my face, exasperated. His was the tone he used when I had misunderstood something he thought was obvious. "Don't apologize. I was here, anyway. How would I protect you from the loft?"

"So...you just hang around campus every day?"

"Unless you leave. That is my job."

"So...when I saw you all of those times before, off campus? When I first started running into you?"

Jared nodded, looking caught. "Shamelessly stalking you."

I felt my face brighten. "Good to know."

Class seemed to fly by. Before I knew it, I was on my way to Jared's loft again, riding happily in the passenger seat.

He held the door open with one hand, and held my bag in the other. I put my things in the downstairs bathroom, finding a deep whirlpool tub.

I will definitely be trying that out, later, I thought to myself.

I walked to the couch and sank into the cushions. I was home.

"Nina?" Jared whispered in my ear.

I blinked a few times, trying to focus as I looked around the room. The sun no longer filtered through the windows and a blanket was draped over me. "What time is it?" I asked, stretching.

"It's after six. Did you want to go out for dinner or stay in?" Jared asked.

"Definitely stay in. I'll cook this time," I offered.

"You're still tired, how about we order in?"

"You don't think I can cook?" I looked at him with accusing eyes.

"I didn't say that. I can't say I've ever tasted your cooking. Jack has mentioned it, though."

"He loved my cooking," I said defensively.

"Jack adored you. You could have served him sludge from a toxic waste plant and he would have asked for seconds," Jared teased.

"I'm going to prove it to you." I walked over to the refrigerator and opened the door.

Jared was instantly behind me. "Nina, you've had a long week, a rough night last night, and you went to school today. You don't have to prove anything tonight."

"I'm fine," I said, surveying the contents of his fridge.

Just then, Claire burst through the door, kicking it closed.

"You're going to have to buy me another door—again—if you keep that up," Jared growled, turning to face her.

Claire held two large, plastic bags. "Dinner."

A smug smile immediately appeared on Jared's face.

"I guess that settles it," I said, defeated.

Claire brought the sacks to the table. "I was over by Thai Star. I got you the Green Curry, Nina. Jared... your usual. There are egg rolls and Satay, too."

"Thanks, Claire," Jared said, digging through the sacks and sticking an egg roll in his mouth. After a moment he looked up at me. "What?"

It was surreal enough to have my new boyfriend know all of my favorites, all of my idiosyncrasies, and sense my feelings. With his sister—who I'd seen all of three times— bringing my favorite dish from a restaurant I frequented, I couldn't help but feel a bit dazed.

"I'm sorry. We're going to have to do a better job of easing you into this," Jared said.

Claire realized what he meant, rolled her eyes and spoke in a disgusted tone, "It's dinner, Nina. I've been around you my entire life, so naturally I would know your food preferences. You were less disturbed about us being Half-breeds."

"I know. It just took me off guard," I whispered.

"Don't be embarrassed," Jared said, glaring at Claire then looking back at me with concern. "It's going to take some getting used to. We know it's going to be awkward for you for awhile."

"Speak for yourself. It's annoying how you coddle her all the time," Claire fumed.

"Don't take your daddy issues out on her," Jared snarled.

Claire narrowed her eyes and put her fists on the table, leaning closer to him. Jared automatically angled his body protectively in front of me.

"Wow! I am starving!" I said, a bit too loudly.

Jared and Claire both looked at me with their typical polar-opposite reactions. Jared was amused at my attempt to avoid bloodshed, and Claire appeared to be contemplating a way to choke me to death before Jared could stop her. I sat down and opened the flip-top box Jared had placed in front of me.

I watched him rummage through the other sack, pulling out boxes of appetizers, and I tried to mimic his casual demeanor. Claire stood there for a moment, glaring at both of us, and then sat down to her meal.

After a few minutes of silence, Jared and Claire began discussing their day. I caught on after a while that they were being vague. I didn't press the issue, from the path of the conversation I assumed it was about Claire. At least they weren't speaking a foreign language.

"It looks like I'll be leaving in a couple of weeks," Claire grumbled.

"Spring Break?" Jared asked.

Claire nodded. "Ich hasse diesen See," she said, leaning back in her chair.

That was when my patience faded. "I'm going to have to learn German," I grimaced.

"I'm sorry," Jared said, "we're not trying to exclude you. We were just discussing Claire's training."

"I gathered that," I said, picking at my food.

Jared smiled at me with adoration and then leaned over to kiss my cheek.

Claire rolled her eyes. "Sie bilden einen Dummkopf von selbst."

"I'm not making a fool of myself. She's right, we're being rude."

I smiled at Jared's complimentary translation. He leaned over again to quickly kiss my forehead before going upstairs.

Claire rolled her eyes again and then took her plate to the sink. "I've lost my appetite."

I had to look twice when Jared returned downstairs. He was shirtless, wearing only a pair of red soccer shorts and well-worn running shoes. He stood behind me as I rinsed dishes at the sink, and then wrapped his arms around my waist.

"You don't have to do that. I'll get to it, later," he said, pressing his cheek against mine.

"Don't start," I said, trying to sound tough.

Jared left me to retreat to the corner where he kept his home gym. I loaded the few dirty dishes in his sink into the dishwasher while Claire walked into the downstairs bathroom and closed the door behind her. Suddenly the door opened again and my suitcase was hurled with incredible precision from the bathroom, landing directly beside me.

"This is my bathroom," Claire warned.

I swallowed nervously, staring at the suitcase that sat an inch from my foot. I offered a meek smile. "Nice tub."

Jared puffed from the corner. "They're both my bathrooms, and you're welcome to either."

Claire glared at him and slammed the door, making my shoulders shoot up to my ears.

"Don't let her push you around. She's all bark and no bite," he puffed, pushing an absurd amount of weight.

I eyed the bathroom door. "She bites, Jared. She'd chew me up and spit me out."

"She can't hurt you. She just loves to see you squirm," he chuckled.

"I thought you said you weren't like the Archs, that you could hurt humans if necessary?" I looked back at him, trying to concentrate on the subject at hand instead of his perfect form.

"She could, but she won't. Claire knows better than anyone what you mean to me. Besides the fact that she would have to come to blows with me to even come close to you—and she would never cross that line—she wouldn't make me choose between you and my family. She's just rattling your cage," he said, repositioning himself on the bench.

"I wouldn't let you choose between me and your family," I murmured, knowing he would hear.

"Nina," he said in that familiar frustrated tone, "you're not listening to me. She knows how I feel about you, so you can stop worrying about Claire."

I raised an eyebrow. "She might know how you feel about me, but one of these days she might over look it."

"You're the love of my life, Nina. There's no overlooking that." Jared spoke the words casually, but my legs disappeared. I had to steady myself against the counter to keep from hitting the floor.

"You okay?" he asked, continuing his workout.

"Me? Er...yeah. I'm just fine. Perfectly fine. Why?" I sighed at my utter failure to fool him. Jared simply smiled with a knowing look, never slowing his repetitions.

Claire emerged from the bathroom in a hooded sweatshirt and sweat pants, her hair pulled back into a wiry bun. She looked like a seventeen year old girl, for once. She fell into the couch, feet hanging over the arm, flipping through channels of the flat screen.

Once the dishes were finished I lingered in the kitchen, wiping down the counters over and over again. I decided to take my suitcase upstairs to organize my things as best I could, hanging my clothes in Jared's closet and finding a place for my shampoo and toothbrush. It was fun playing house for the week, but it only took so long.

I stood in the middle of the room, feeling lost. Jared was still deep in his workout, and with Claire on the couch I saw no point in enticing him upstairs. I decided to try Jared's incredible tub to pass the time.

The steam danced above the surface of the water as I let my robe fall to the floor. I stepped in with both feet, stifling a moan. Once I was submerged to my neck, my body instantly relaxed. I loathed the communal showers of Andrews; I would miss more than just the tub when I returned.

"Nina? Did you grab a towel?" Jared said, his voice muffled through the door.

"No, I didn't," I said in a sing-song tone.

"I'll grab you one."

Within moments, Jared's arm poked through as he cracked open the door, extending a thick navy blue towel. I frowned.

"I can't reach it," I teased.

I heard Jared sigh before he opened the door just wide enough to get through, turning his head to the opposite direction. He was still only in shorts and running shoes, dripping with sweat.

He took a few more steps in my direction, holding out the towel. The water sloshed as I raised my steaming arm to grab it, setting the towel beside me on the ledge.

"Thank you."

Jared sighed and left the way he came, making sure not to open the door any wider than absolutely necessary.

I slid under the surface of the water to suppress the laughter. He was working as hard to preserve my chastity as I was to rid myself of it.

I remained in the tub until my feet and hands were sufficiently pruned. Wrapped in my robe, I climbed the wooden stairs, noticing Claire was no longer on the couch. When I reached the top, I heard the shower running.

I rifled through my things and chose a pink silk pajama set, and just when I buttoned the top of my shirt, Jared walked out of the bathroom in a pair of black cotton pajama pants.

"Where's Claire?" I asked.

"She had to go out...training," Jared explained, pulling the first aid box out from under his bed.

I sat down and held my hand palm up for him to work with. "I thought you were finished with your training. What else could she possibly learn? And from whom?"

"You're full of questions tonight," he said, working quickly to disinfect and redress my wound.

"And you're evading them."

"We have to acuminate our skills when we...." he trailed off, his eyes darkening the way they had during our first date.

"What is it?" I asked, watching him place the last strip of tape on my hand.

"Can I ask you to do something for me?" he asked, closing his eyes.

"Anything. Except leave."

Jared's eyes popped open. "I don't want you to leave. I'm asking you to wait."

"Wait for what?"I grimaced. Jared had a knack for confusing me.

"Leave this one alone. For now."

"What's going on, Jared?"

"I promise to explain everything to you soon. I'm just not ready to—," he squirmed uncomfortably, "— can you wait?"

"If that's what you want."

Jared's face instantly relaxed. "Thank you."

"Can I ask just one thing?" I whispered, peeking up at the clouds reforming in Jared's eyes. "I just...was wondering...will you ever have to leave me? For training, I mean."

Jared smiled again, obviously relieved at my question. "No. I'm finished with my training. I'm afraid you're stuck with me."

"Poor me," I teased.

I pulled myself back to lean against the headboard and Jared lay on his stomach beside me. He hugged my legs to him and rested his head on my lap, and I happily ran my fingers through his damp hair.

"Are you running a fever?" I asked.

Jared looked up at me, puzzled. "I don't get sick, Nina, remember?"

"I know, but you...you're burning up," I said, feeling his forehead.

"I run a little hotter than everyone else. It's a constant thing."

"How much hotter?" I asked, skeptical.

"Around one-oh-four usually. I just got out of the shower, so I'm probably a little higher than that at the moment."

I stared at him blankly; I had nothing else to say.

Jared chuckled at my speechlessness and let his head rest against my leg again. "It's really not a big deal. Claire runs about the same. It has to do with how our bodies handle the extra...abilities."

"Abilities...." I repeated. Most of the time I had a handle on Jared being half-angel, but only when I tried not to think about it. The details made my head spin.

"I can't imagine how it must be for you," he said. "It's hard enough getting to know someone when you start dating, and then you have to deal with your boyfriend spouting off unbelievable particulars all the time."

"Oh, it's boyfriend, now, is it?"

Jared laughed and sat up, readying himself to pounce.

My mouth hung open, feigning shock. "Don't you dare!"

He grabbed my legs and pulled, sliding me underneath him. He playfully pinched my sides, tickling me as my laughter chimed through the loft.

"Okay! Okay. Boyfriend it is," I giggled again.

Jared sighed in contentment at my words. "Everything I've ever wanted is right here in my arms."

I couldn't imagine why he looked at me that way. Six billion people in the world, and a man so perfect he was also half divine had chosen me. That fact alone was more than I deserved, but for him to say something so beautiful with that look in his eyes, I couldn't help myself.

"I love you, Jared." It didn't seem like enough, but once the words tumbled from my mouth, his smile turned into pure elation, as if I'd given him the one thing he'd wanted his entire life. Before I could think to say anything else, his lips were on mine.

He kissed me differently this time; it was gentle, almost cautious. I wrapped both of my arms around his neck as he continued to work his warm lips softly against mine. He put so much emotion in these small, slow, tender kisses that I found myself fighting tears. He kissed me like a happy ending.

And then he stopped.

In one smooth movement, he moved me to my proper place in the bed. He crawled over me carefully, lying directly behind me, tracing my body with his. I took a deep breath and let out a satisfied humming sound that compelled Jared to pull me closer.

Just before I drifted off to sleep, I said the first prayer I'd uttered since I was girl. I wasn't sure what I'd done to deserve such a wonderful gift, and I wasn't sure if it was insolent, but I thanked God for fallen angels.

Chapter Ten
Fate

Over the next few days, we settled into a comfortable routine. Jared took me to school, returned to sit with me at lunch, and then waited outside my last class. At night, I studied while he worked out, and I became quite accustomed to falling asleep in his arms. Each time he dressed my wound a sense of dread came over me; the healing cut meant that our nights together were numbered.

The girls at our regular lunch table became quite taken with Jared, while the boys tried their best to ignore him. The lines were clearly drawn. Lisa even invited Jared to a tentative girls' night out, to which Jared only replied with a raised eyebrow, causing those who were paying attention to laugh.

I noticed Ryan being careful to speak only to me, making a point to ignore anything Jared contributed to the conversation. By Thursday, the tension at the table had elevated.

"Are you coming to study group tonight or not?" Ryan asked, clearly in a bad mood.

"I'm not sure what the plans are tonight."

Jared looked at me and began to speak, but Ryan cut him off. "What? You need permission?" he snapped.

I glared at him. "It's called being courteous. You should try it."

I felt Jared lightly touch my knee, I assumed to keep me calm. It wasn't working; Ryan couldn't be more proficient at getting under my skin.

"Just because I'm not happy about how weird you've been, doesn't mean I'm being a jerk," he said, his eyes narrowing.

"You said it, not me."

"You've moved in with this guy," he motioned to Jared, "you don't talk to your friends anymore, you're skipping out on study group...I'm doing what friends do, Nina. I'm making sure you're okay."

"She called me last night," Beth said defensively. Ryan ignored her.

I could feel the heat radiating from my face. "You're not being a friend. You're being aggressively nosy."

Ryan rolled his eyes. "Are you coming to study group or not?"

"I'm coming," I growled.

Ryan's demeanor immediately changed. "So, you wanna grab something to eat after?"

I felt Jared's hand tense around my knee.

"Not funny, Ryan," Kim scolded.

Ryan continued to look at me expectantly. Everyone at the table watched for my—and Jared's—reaction.

"Jared is picking me up afterward. We have dinner plans," I said, glaring at him.

"I thought you said you didn't know what your plans were," Ryan goaded.

I leaned forward in my chair, taking in a sufficient breath to unleash my temper across the table.

Jared finally spoke, "We have dinner plans every night, Ryan. You're welcome to join us." I shot Jared a surprised look and noticed that his face was free of any sarcasm.

Ryan's eyebrows furrowed, taken off guard by Jared's sincere invitation. "I think I'll pass."

I smiled smugly at him, turning my attention to Jared. "Are you ready?"

"I am," he said, leaning over to kiss my forehead.

Lisa and Carrie swooned.

At the door of my classroom, Jared set my bag on the floor beside me, pulling up the handle.

"Thank you," I said, giving him a quick peck.

"I assume you'll be hanging around here until study group."

"You assume correctly," I nodded.

"Call me when you're finishing up, I'll pick you up at the Rock."

I grimaced. "It's ridiculous that you have to sit outside and wait on me. Why don't you just come?"

"Nina, it's what I've done for the last three years. You need to spend time with your friends or they're going to start worrying about you."

"Ryan is the only one that's worried, and he's just being difficult," I said, running my hand over the sleeve of his jacket.

"He's jealous."

I wrinkled my nose. "We're just friends."

Jared smiled and kissed the top of my hair. "I'll see you later, then."

As soon as class was over, I headed directly for Andrews. The sun was shining, and I was just beginning to enjoy my walk when Ryan appeared beside me.

"Hey," he said.

"Hi," I said, less than enthusiastic about his company.

"Oh, c'mon. You're not that mad," he teased, throwing his arm over my shoulder and squeezing.

I squirmed from his embrace. "You tried to humiliate me in front of everyone, Ryan. What was the point in that?"

"I told you what the point was. I'm worried about you."

I breathed out a sarcastic laugh. I was never safer than when I was with Jared.

"Nina...," he said, slowing down. Before I could get too far ahead of him, he jerked me back by my coat sleeve to where he stood. "Nina!"

"What?" I growled, trying not to trip over my bag. I jerked my arm from his grip and smoothed out my sleeve.

"You have to admit you've been MIA this week. What's going on with you? You barely know this guy."

I fidgeted as I tried to think of a believable answer. I knew it appeared that way to him—and everyone else—but I couldn't defend myself with the truth.

"I didn't move in with him. My hand is infected, so he's changing the dressing every night. When it heals I'll be back at Andrews." I couldn't help but frown at the thought.

"He could do that at Andrews," Ryan argued.

Of course he was right, but Jared and I both knew it had been a flimsy excuse all along. I didn't like the thought of him spending the night in his Escalade outside Andrews, and Jared was more than ready to make the present living arrangement permanent. Neither of which I could explain to Ryan.

"What is your problem?" I asked, continuing to the dorm.

Ryan shoved his hands in his pockets, following close behind. "I just think you're getting in way too deep, way too fast. You need to take a step back. Slow down. You just met this guy and you're acting like an old married couple. You have other friends."

Feeling slighted, my mouth flew open. "I am not! I know I have other friends. I've talked to Beth and Kim every night since I've been at Jared's."

"You haven't talked to me," he said, looking hurt.

I rolled my eyes, glad that we had finally reached Andrews. "You want me to start calling you at night? Will that make you feel better?"

"Maybe it would. Will your husband mind?"

I rolled my eyes, pulling my keys from my pocket. "I don't have time for this."

"Mind if I come up?"

"I guess not, since you're already following me in."

I shoved the door open and rolled my bag into the closet. Ryan sat on Beth's bed and watched me, seemingly amused.

"What?" I asked, waiting for a sarcastic remark.

He shrugged, dropping his backpack to the floor. "Nothing. You're just so ridiculous."

"How so?" I asked, peeling off my coat.

"You spend so much time pretending to be mad at me when you know why I say the things I do. I don't get it. You like spending time with me; you like spending time with him; the only difference is that you decided to play house with him this week."

I raised my eyebrows, anticipating a fight. "Are you insinuating what I think you're insinuating?" I asked, pulling off my boots.

"It depends. Are you going to throw your boots at me?" he asked, pulling one side of his mouth up into a grin.

221

"You think I'm leading you on?" I yelled, gripping one boot in my hand.

"Well...," he trailed off long enough to see my temper flare. "Just kidding!" He held his hands up, expecting a boot to fly across the room. When he felt he was safe, he continued, "I didn't say that. I just think you should leave your options open, is all. You're getting all wrapped up in this guy you barely know. You might miss something that's right under your nose."

I knew what he meant, but I refused to gratify it with a reply. I plugged in my laptop, watching the screen as it came to life. "What time are you heading over there?"

"Whenever you do," Ryan shrugged, sprawling out on Beth's bed.

"I probably won't leave until seven thirty," I said, crisscrossing my legs on the desk chair.

"Okay."

I looked over at him in disbelief. "What do you plan on doing here for four hours?"

"Hanging out with you. It's my turn," he sniffed.

"Ugh. You talk like you're sharing me," I groaned, disgusted.

"I am," he said, utterly naive of any offense.

"Quit it."

Ryan bellowed out a laugh and interlocked his fingers behind his head. I watched him for a moment as he stared at the ceiling. Surely being in Ryan's position was nothing to be so chipper about, and I was getting impatient for him to get over this ridiculous crush so we could go back to being friends.

The next four hours passed relatively quickly. Ryan and I caught up on the last week, although I was careful to leave out much of what went on in Jared's loft. We talked like we used to, and it was refreshing. I had missed him.

He was right, I did enjoy spending time with him, not less than I did with Jared, but it was exceedingly different. I always felt at ease with Ryan, but the urgency wasn't there. I didn't feel like the oxygen was missing from the room when he wasn't in it. Ryan was always in the back of my mind, and it hurt me when he was hurting, but he was wrong. There were more differences than just playing house.

We were the last ones to arrive at the Rock. Ryan wanted to grab something to eat on the way, so our detour cost us the prime seats.

Beth smiled at me when we walked in. "Hey!"

"Hey yourself. Where were you?" I asked.

"At Chad's," she smiled. I looked to Chad, who appeared very frustrated with his laptop.

Ryan and I brought a stack of notes to occupy our time, so we went right to work. After an hour, I decided to take a break and call Jared.

"Hey," Jared answered in a tender tone, picking up on the first ring.

"I just thought I'd call and see how you're doing. Did you want me to bring you some coffee or something?"

"No, sweetheart. Just pretend I'm not here."

"I just don't like the idea of you having to sit outside in the cold."

"This is what I do, remember? I'm ready to see you, though," he added.

"Me too." I cringed at how utterly ignoble my words sounded. I was glad that he could sense differently.

I walked back to the group and Ryan grimaced.

"Don't start," I warned.

Ryan shook his head and returned to his book. He fidgeted in his seat for a while, and then finally heaved a big sigh. "Are you staying there again tonight?" he blurted out.

"That's some more of your business," I said, distracted by a particularly tricky equation.

"I thought he said you had dinner plans. Since you missed dinner, I thought maybe you'd just stay here tonight."

"Still none of your business," I murmured, scanning the words on the pages. Any divulging of my sleeping arrangements would only end in another argument that I wasn't in the mood for.

Beginning the third subject, I looked up at the clock.

"Is that clock right?" I asked the group. Everyone looked in unison at the large round clock on the wall, and then peered at their watches or cell phones. In different tones, they all murmured confirmations.

"What?" Ryan asked, stretching as he watched me shove my things into my bag.

"It's late, I have to go."

I pulled out my phone and pressed the speed dial for Jared's cell. He didn't answer, so I rushed out the door. I stood there a moment, looking around, and then hurried down the stairs, banging the rollers of my bag against every step. The Escalade wasn't there.

I tried not to panic, convincing myself that he was just in a well secluded spot. After ten minutes, I walked down the sidewalk a little over a block each way. My search was futile. Jared wouldn't let me walk around in the dark; he wasn't there.

My bag barely touched the ground as I sprinted across campus, glad that Claire had parked my car in the middle lot to be spiteful. I thought of all the possibilities for his sudden disappearance, but my mind kept returning to the hell I'd gone through just a week before. Jared didn't have a history of warning me that he was going to end our relationship.

By the time I reached my car my lungs were frozen and aching. I fumbled with my keys and ripped the door open, heaving my bag to the passenger side. The tires squealed as I pulled out into the street, cursing every stoplight that cost me precious time.

I pulled up to Jared's loft and took a deep breath. His Escalade wasn't parked in front, but I tried the door, anyway. I kept my eyes on the doorknob as I waited, willing it to twist open. Dogs barked down the dark street and I suddenly felt uneasy. Until that moment, I hadn't realized how safe I felt with Jared; the alley had never seemed frightening before.

I walked back to the Beemer, defeated. He would have called if it was anything other than the worst scenario. He had either broken his promise not to leave me, or he was in danger. After twenty minutes and still no call from Jared, my lungs began to feel less satisfied with every breath and my eyes welled over with tears.

A knock resounded on my window and I jumped. Claire's flawless face was on the other side.

She rolled her eyes. "Oh, stop. Something came up. I'm here to let you in."

I stared at her for a moment, dumbfounded. Her explanation didn't make sense, but the knowledge that he had sent her to let me in the loft extinguished half of my fears.

"Is he okay?" I asked, following her down the alley.

"Uh...yeah. You worry too much," she said, her annoyed expression obvious even in the dark.

She led me up the iron stairs of the entry way, and then opened the door to let me inside. I ran up the stairs to the loft and collapsed into the bed. An overwhelming feeling of relief tore through me, and I did my best to weep quietly to avoid further ridicule from Claire.

I dried my eyes as I heard her light footsteps climb the stairs and stop beside the bed.

"Wow," she deadpanned, chomping on a wad of gum too big for her petite mouth. "Why don't you take a shower?" she asked.

I ignored her.

Claire sighed and sat down on Jared's side of the bed.

I froze for a moment, bracing for an obnoxious comment from her. She sat quietly.

I shot a confused glance her way. "W...What are you doing?" I asked, sniffing.

"I'm supposed to sit with you," she said, sounding bored.

"Sit with me? Why?"

"I just am. Go take a shower, will you? You're a mess."

I sniffed again and ambled to the shower, too baffled to argue. Claire never missed an opportunity to make me feel like an idiot, but surely she could understand my tears. I hurried through my nightly routine, anxious that every noise outside the bathroom was Jared returning home.

When I finished, Claire was downstairs. I slipped on one of Jared's T-shirts. It was a poor substitute, but it would have to do until he came home. With impeccable timing, she returned as I slipped under the covers.

She looked away from me, suddenly uncomfortable. "That's Jared's favorite shirt."

I looked down and noticed the dead giveaway: It was ratty and worn. The dark grey heather cotton was thin, and I smiled as I made out the faded words across the front; it was from a Red Hot Chili Peppers concert four years ago. I looked up at Claire who showed signs of a slight grin.

"My dad took him to that concert," she mused, sitting on the bed beside me.

"You look like him," I said. Gabe had light blonde hair as well, and Claire had inherited his ice blue eyes.

Those eyes instantly glazed over with anger. "Don't talk about him. You...," she stopped herself, "just go to sleep, Nina."

Falling asleep with Claire sitting over me like a prison guard wasn't likely, so I turned my back to her, focusing on Jared. I wondered what it was that he was doing, and wondered why he hadn't called. I opened my mouth to ask Claire, but given her mood I thought better of it.

The clock switched from P.M. to A.M. as the numbers switched to midnight. Jared still hadn't called, and I was almost worried enough to ask Claire to call him. At that moment, Claire stood up and walked over to the railing. The outside door slammed, footsteps echoed up the iron steps, and then the front door opened and closed quietly. Claire's eyes followed the footsteps up the stairs until Jared came into view.

The sight of him shocked me. His face was smudged with dirt and blood, along with his shirt, jacket and jeans. His knuckles were swollen and bloody. I noticed that on a few of them the hide had ripped away and hung by just a few centimeters of skin.

"Jared?" I said, ripping the covers off to run to him.

"I'm okay," he said, holding me away. "I'm dirty. Let me jump in the shower."

Without a word, Claire retreated downstairs.

I paced the room, chewing on my nails until he reappeared. He was dressed and clean shaven, the only remnants of his earlier disheveled appearance was his already healing knuckles.

"What happened?" I asked in firm tone.

"I'm sorry I wasn't there. Something came up," he said, eyeing my bandage free hand.

"Obviously," I said, crossing my arms. "Are you okay?"

"I'm fine. Dawson stopped by The Rock to pay you a visit. I had to act quickly." He walked by me to pull the first aid kit from under the bed.

"Mr. Dawson?" I asked, shocked.

"He was armed, and he also had...," Jared's jaw tensed, "he had paraphernalia."

"What kind of paraphernalia?" I said, sitting on the bed.

"The kind you use to tie someone up and torture them. He was planning to get his hands on that package tonight."

I swallowed loudly. If Jared hadn't been there to protect me, I didn't want to think where I would be.

He didn't look up when he spoke, "He won't bother you again."

"You...."

I watched as he worked silently, dabbing antibiotic ointment across my hand. The cut was now the beginning of a bright pink scar, the infection had dissipated days ago.

After a long pause Jared answered me. "I didn't kill him. Not that I didn't have to exercise restraint. He gave up information, but not nearly enough. I let my emotions get in the way," he sighed and shook his head, "he was never conscious long enough to tell me everything I needed."

"You tortured him," I said, watching Jared fasten the last piece of tape on the flawlessly wrapped gauze. I braced for his answer; the Jared I knew couldn't be capable of the horror that I imagined.

"I wanted to snap his spine and throw him in the Narragansett to drown, Nina. He's lucky he ended up with his life."

His job was to protect me by any means necessary; I just hadn't stopped to think what that would be. "What did you find out?"

"We'll discuss it tomorrow. You need to rest," he whispered. He placed me gingerly on the bed, kissing the palm of my bandaged hand.

When he tried to pull away, I squeezed his fingers with mine. "I was worried. I drove here prepared to beg you back."

He laughed once. "In what alternate universe would you ever have to beg me back?"

"I've had to rip out two microphones and nearly freeze to death in the pouring rain to get you back before. Driving to your apartment and knocking on your door isn't the most extreme measure I've taken."

Jared's expression was pained. "I noticed your car out front. I'm sorry I had to leave without an explanation. I didn't have a choice."

"It was better than the alternative," I said, my grin fading as I considered the possibilities.

Jared touched the side of my face, and then left me to walk toward the stairs. I sat up to protest, but Jared paused. "I'll be right back," he assured me.

Relaxing against the bed, I listened to his footsteps jog down the steps, silence when he reached the couch, and in the next moment climb the stairs again.

He sat beside me and held a small red box in the palm of his hand. "Don't get too excited. It's nothing major."

I smiled and took the box from his hands, pulling on the small silver loop on the top. I looked at him, raising my eyebrows in surprise.

"It's to make up for tonight. So? What do you think?"

Hanging from the lid was a shiny silver key.

"To the loft," he explained. "Next time something comes up, you won't have to wait outside in the cold."

"When did you have time to do this?" I asked, still processing the shiny object spinning around from a thin red ribbon.

Jared shrugged. "I had it made a few days ago. I've been meaning to give it to you, but you haven't needed it until now."

"You're giving me a key?" My eyebrows lifted in disbelief.

Jared nodded and then his brows pulled together. "I promised you I would never leave you. I meant it. If something like this happens again, come here. Wait for me." He touched his hand gently to my cheek. "I'll earn your trust back."

"I trust you," I said, mimicking his expression.

Jared leaned over and pressed his lips to mine. "And I trust you. Nice work in your room today."

I cringed. "You heard that, did you?"

Jared chuckled. "All of it. I think it's going to take me by surprise every time I hear you say my name in perfunctory conversation. It's a good thing Ryan...."

"It's a good thing Ryan what?" I asked, leaning over to bring his eyes to mine.

"It's a good thing I have patience," Jared said, looking everywhere but my eyes.

"You have a lot of patience, but that's not what you were going to say."

Jared's eyes bounced from me to the floor to other things in the room, uncomfortable with where the conversation was headed. "It has to do with what I told you we would discuss later."

"Claire's training has to do with Ryan?"

Jared sighed. "You're not going to wait now, are you?"

I shook my head slowly, not sure what to expect. The two names seemed to be on different sides of the universe.

Jared leaned his head down, looking at me from under his eyebrows. "The night at the pub, when you first met Claire, Ryan put his hands on me." I nodded and Jared continued, "When she grabbed his hand, she felt something. She felt his pain." Jared patiently waited for me to comprehend.

"Ryan is Claire's Taleh?" I whispered, knowing she could hear me, anyway. I couldn't believe it, and at the same time I felt excited, like I'd just heard a juicy bit of gossip. "But, when we were mugged...," Claire was talented, even among her kind. She wouldn't have let Ryan be hurt in that way.

"That's why the situation went farther than I normally allow. Claire had them targeted. It would have just taken a second to take them out, but when Ryan jumped in, Claire couldn't get a clear shot. She couldn't risk it. That's when I decided to intercede." Jared's eyes began to cloud over. The worst was coming.

"Why didn't you want to tell me?"

Jared leaned over and kissed me. It was urgent and deep, the way he kissed me before I left him to speak with my mother; as if he were kissing me goodbye forever.

He reluctantly pulled away to look at me. "It was for purely selfish reasons. I wanted to wait so you and I could...so you could get to know me better."

"You lost me."

"Remember when I was explaining the Taleh, you mentioned how convenient it was that Gabe protected Jack, and I protected you?"

I nodded. "Yes, you said that angel groups tend to stay in families or those that are connected somehow." Now that he'd brought it to my attention, it made more sense. "Claire is Ryan's protector because he's a friend?"

Jared sighed and shifted nervously beside me. "Claire being Ryan's protector means he is supposed to be in your life. Permanently."

I smiled and shook my head. "So what are you saying? That Ryan's going to be family somehow?" Jared waited and my eyes widened in disbelief. "You think I'm supposed to marry him? Oh, c'mon! That's ridiculous!"

"That would be the only explanation," Jared said, his expression grave.

"You're not serious. There's no way for you to know that. It could be any number of things."

"I thought that if you didn't get to know me first, then you'd want to be with him. He is supposed to be your husband one of these days. I would understand why, armed with that knowledge, you might feel differently. He's a good friend to you. And he's... persistent," Jared said, his face twisting into an annoyed expression.

I held his face in my hands and looked directly into his eyes. "Quit it. I'm in love with you, Jared. There is no me without you."

He watched me for a moment. "I'm sorry I kept it from you."

"You don't have a single thing to worry about. I promise," I said.

Jared switched off the lamp and crawled over to his side, pulling me to him.

"I missed you," I said, settling into his arms. "It's going to be hard to go back to the way it was when my hand heals. I could probably start staying at Andrews this weekend."

"You don't have to leave," Jared whispered in the dim light.

I buried my head into his chest. I had never wanted anything more, but Ryan's words about moving too fast came to the forefront of my mind.

"I would love that...someday," I said, hoping to preserve his feelings.

"Someday," he repeated, sighing. "I understand. It's too fast."

"Maybe just a little," I smiled, kissing his chest.

The next morning, I woke up in Jared's arms. He was awake, patiently holding me against him. My smile faded when I realized it would be our last morning together for a while.

"What is it?" Jared asked, sensing my disappointment.

I sucked in a deep, disheartening breath. "It's Friday," I breathed. "I'm going back to Andrews tonight."

"You have a key. You can use it whenever you'd like."

"That's right," I said, looking up at him with a smile. "That's comforting."

Jared brushed my bangs from my face. "I'm going to miss seeing you like this in the morning... especially in my shirt. It would have had a whole new significance had I known that one day you would be lying in my arms with it on. An interesting choice, I might add. That's my favorite one."

"I heard," I smiled.

"Take it with you. I want you to have it."

"But it's your favorite shirt!" I argued, pulling away to look at him.

"My mornings won't be quite as disappointing from now on if I know you're waking up in that shirt," he countered.

"Good point. I'm taking it. But it's only on loan."

"Oh, there's no doubt in my mind that one of these days it will be a permanent fixture in my closet again. You can't live in Andrews forever."

I bit my lip and pressed my cheek against his bare chest. It seemed a little silly, lying here with him, knowing we both would rather I just stay. I would never hear the end of it from my friends, and my mother would be an entirely different set of problems.

"I could stay here on the weekends," I said.

"You will?" he asked, his eyes brightening.

"If that's okay, I don't want to impose."

Jared kissed me until I could feel a tingling in my toes. Just as I needed to take a breath, he pulled away. "I would have everything you own here by the time you finished your classes today if you'd let me. You staying here on weekends is absolutely okay."

A smile spanned the width of my face and I wrapped my arms around his neck. When he said things like that, it was hard for me to remember why I couldn't just give in to what he wanted—to what I wanted. I immediately felt better knowing that I had a few more days with him.

"You're going to be late. I'll make coffee," he said, jogging downstairs.

I hurried through my shower and Jared handed me a pink travel mug as I put my coat on. I raised an eyebrow at the color and then looked back at him.

"It's Claire's," he shrugged.

"Um, I thought I would take my car today. Do you mind picking me up, later?"

Jared didn't hide his disappointment. "Sure. Just give me a call when you're ready."

I leaned up on my toes to kiss him. "Okay. I'll see you later."

The professor began lecture just as I slid into my seat. Kim leaned over to whisper in my ear.

"Beth and I are going for coffee after class. You coming?"

"Sure. I'll drive," I offered.

I felt like I hadn't spent enough time with Kim and Beth lately. An afternoon at the café would give us time to catch up. At least I would get caught up on their lives; my news included almost getting kidnapped and tortured, and my boyfriend nearly beating the man to death who had tried.

The three of us huddled at the table of the coffee shop, waiting to thaw. The temperature had dropped significantly after lunch, and the wind was brutal. I was glad that I would be lying on a beach somewhere in just over a week.

I sipped my coffee as Beth chattered about Chad. Things between them were progressing, and she mentioned she wasn't homesick for the first time since she'd come to Brown. She was even considering getting an apartment in the summer instead of returning to Oklahoma.

I tried to concentrate on the conversation, but I found myself focusing on the new information Jared had forced out of Dawson. I wanted to know what it was that Jared was keeping from me; it couldn't be good news.

"Nigh. Nigh! Where are you? You look like you're a million miles away," Kim said. She and Beth were both staring at me with matching expressions.

"Ugh, I'm sorry. I just have a lot going on," I said, blinking.

Beth's cell phone hummed. By her tone I knew that it was Chad. Apparently he was out and about, and she invited him to join us.

"I hope that's okay," Beth said to us after disconnecting the line.

Kim shrugged. "Fine with me."

"Ryan is with him," Beth added, eyeing me.

I made sure my face was smooth. I hadn't seen Ryan since Jared had told me that Ryan and I were meant to be together. I wasn't sure how to act around him with that knowledge.

Ten minutes later, the door chimed as Chad and Ryan strolled through it. They were both in gym clothes, sweaty and tired.

Ryan had his white hat pulled down over his eyes and didn't speak when he sat across from me at the table. He leaned back in his chair and crossed his arms.

"What have you two been up to?" Beth asked, standing up to sit on Chad's lap.

"We just finished a basketball game. We lost," Chad said in an embittered tone.

"They cheated. Repeatedly," Ryan chuckled, only his smile visible.

"What? You can't handle prison rules?" Kim elbowed him, making him sway for a moment.

Ryan pulled his hat up and over to the side, his eyes finally in view. "I can handle prison rules, it's the cheating when there is supposed to be rules that bothers me. I lost twenty bucks!"

"Oh no!" Beth said, laughing. "Did you lose money, Baby?" Chad pursed his lips and nodded, still brooding. "Aw!" she said, rubbing his back.

We sat at the table, discussing the game. Our laughter saturated the room, causing the other patrons to stare. After a while, Ryan leaned over and pulled my chair closer to him, the legs grating against the floor. He stretched his arm around the back of my chair and smiled, flashing the deep dimple in his cheek.

Ryan's destiny to be my future husband popped into my head, and a strange ache overwhelmed me. Ryan's future was forever changed the second Jared sat on that bench. I would never take that moment back, but I cared about Ryan. I wanted him to be happy, and that was impossible if I stayed in the picture. One of these days I would have to remove myself completely from his life, and because of that, either Claire or Jared would be separated from their family.

Ryan gripped my shoulder and pulled me to his side. "Hey. What's wrong?"

"Hmmm?" I said, distracted.

"She's been like that the whole time she's been here," Kim complained.

Ryan hugged me to him again and I turned, throwing my arms around him. He tensed, obviously not expecting my sudden display of affection. After his initial shock wore off, he rested his chin on my shoulder and enveloped me in his arms.

He puffed a short laugh. "What's going on, Nigh?" he whispered into my neck.

I shook my head. I couldn't tell him, and even if I did, I didn't want him to know.

"We're, uh...we're going to take off," Chad said.

"Is it all right if I catch a ride with you?" Kim asked.

I pulled away from Ryan and looked up at my friends. "It's Friday. Did you want to go out later?"

Kim shot a look at Ryan and then back at me. "I already have plans. Tomorrow night?"

I nodded. "Okay."

"I'll catch a ride with Nina," Ryan said.

Beth and I both looked at Chad, who shrugged. "Cool. See ya." He lifted his hand to wave and they filed out of the coffee shop.

I looked at Ryan, embarrassed. "It's official. I'm a freak."

"You're not a freak. Chad was planning to take Beth back with him, anyway. They have dinner plans."

"I cleared the table in less than two minutes. I'm a freak."

"You want to grab some dinner?"

I tried to think of a delicate way to turn him down, but he spoke before anything came to mind.

"We'll just grab something quick...go through a drive thru. Me and Josh are going to grab a few beers later, anyway," he explained.

"Oh. Yeah, okay," I said, standing up.

We sat in the parking lot closest to Andrews devouring our fast food. The slogan game had kept us entertained since we left the coffee shop. Ryan countered my feeble attempts to stump him so quickly that I couldn't help but double over with laughter.

"Have you been practicing?" I giggled, exhausted from laughing so hard.

"I'm not gonna lie. I've had a lot of time on my hands, waiting to heal," he chuckled, throwing up a piece of chicken and catching it in his mouth. "What are you doing tonight?" he asked.

"I'm probably going to get some laundry together, take it over to Jared's," I said without thinking.

"You're staying over there again? I thought you said you weren't moving in," he said, this time without his usual attitude.

"I'm not," I snapped, waiting for him to come back with something spiteful.

Ryan sighed and took my hand. "I don't want to argue about it anymore, Nigh. I've said everything I needed to say on the subject."

"I don't want us to fight, either. I want us to be able to hang out and be friends like we used to. I miss you," I said, suddenly hopeful that we could get beyond all the infatuation nonsense.

"I miss you, too. I'll quit being a jerk," he said, brushing my bangs out of my eyes. "When you hugged me tonight, I realized how ridiculous I've been. I don't want to lose you, Nina. It doesn't matter if you're with him, or me, or anyone else. What matters is that we're friends, and that you can count on me being here when you need me."

I pulled in a shallow breath through my nose, trying to keep my eyes from glossing over with tears. He didn't know that we would have to lose each other if he wanted to be happy. I just smiled and nodded my head, and Ryan hugged me once more.

"Truce?"

"Truce," I smiled.

He walked to his dormitory and I headed to Andrews, feeling morose. I pulled out my cell phone and called Jared, who picked up on the first ring.

"Hey," he answered, sounding a bit sad himself.

"I'm just going to grab a few things from my room and then I'll be ready."

As I rounded the corner, Jared came into view, his cell phone to his ear. He pulled up one corner of his mouth into a contrived half-smile. I put my cell phone away and wrapped my arms around him, burying my face in his chest. He could sense my feelings for Ryan, and I was ashamed for feeling the way I did. It wasn't fair to either of them.

An awkward silence festered in the Escalade until we pulled up to the curb in front of his apartment.

"Nina...,"

"It's okay," I interrupted him. I wasn't sure what he was going to say, but I didn't want to waste time discussing my feelings for Ryan. Jared felt he was getting in the way of fate, but I knew what I wanted. There would be no compromise.

We walked hand in hand to the loft, and I could feel the worry radiating from him. I hung my coat on the rack and immediately went to the kitchen, praying there were dishes to be done or to put away; anything to keep me busy.

Jared went to his extravagant stereo system and tinkered with the multitude of buttons. While I put away dishes in various cabinets, a familiar song permeated the room. I felt Jared's arms surround me, the heat of his skin sinking into my back. His cheek touched mine as he pulled me into his chest, and I closed my eyes when he whispered into my ear.

"Do you recognize this song?"

I simply nodded, listening to the music. It was the song we danced to at the pub. I remembered that moment as if it were just hours before, and yet it felt like a lifetime ago.

"What is it?" I asked.

"It's called 'Little Heaven'." His lips peppered my neck with soft, tiny kisses, working his way up to my ear.

I smiled. "That's appropriate."

Jared turned me slowly to face him and I watched the clouds roll in, darkening his eyes. His jaw tensed as he scanned my face.

"I could step aside, Nina. I could step aside and let you be with who you're supposed to be with. If I was any less selfish...I would. Even after all my stupid mistakes, I still think I can make you happy.

"If it's what you want, I'll step aside," he shook his head, "but if it's not...I'll fight fate. I'll fight Heaven, and Hell, and everything in between to keep you."

I stood there, stunned. Anything I said would pale in comparison. The storms in his eyes raged stronger than I'd ever seen them.

"Jared...," I struggled with what I wanted to say. Jared swallowed, sensing the turmoil within me. I shook my head and he let go of my waist, bracing himself for my next words. But there would be none.

I inched up on the balls of my feet and paused. My eyes moved from his eyes to his mouth. Jared stood motionless, waiting for judgment.

I pressed my lips to his, and he cautiously kissed me back. My hands held each side of his face, and I worked my lips against his, sliding my fingers through the back of his hair. Jared's hands returned to my waist as the kiss intensified. My lips parted and he pulled me to him without hesitation. His doubt melted away, he knew my decision.

Against his body I let out an involuntary moan, causing a chain reaction. Almost simultaneously, I lifted Jared's shirt as he finished the task by yanking it over his head, my knee inched up and Jared firmly grabbed it, pulling it higher up his side, and then he eagerly lifted me on top of the counter.

I wrapped my legs around him, digging my fingers into the bare flesh of his back to draw him closer. His hands gripped my thighs, impatiently pulling me to the edge of the counter. Jared's lips were urgent, but in a new way. His wasn't the kiss that he used to tell me he loved me, or to tell me goodbye. He was giving in.

Jared lifted my sweater over my head and I let out a satisfied sigh when he pressed his bare chest against mine. I pressed my lips harder against his; we still weren't close enough. My breath grew ragged and uneven as he impatiently pulled me from the counter and walked across the room—my legs still wrapped around him—to climb the stairs. As he held me, he never took his lips from mine.

With one hand on my back, and the other on the mattress, he gently lowered me to his bed. His lips caressed every inch of my neck, and my body shivered in anticipation. I slid my hand down the perfect ripples of his chest and stomach, and pulled his belt free of the loops, fumbling with the buckle. A low moan emanated from his lips when I finally unfastened it and his mouth readily returned to mine.

He pulled away with a quick jerk, his eyes unfocused.

"What?" I asked, pushing myself up on my elbows.

His jaw tensed and he closed his eyes in frustration. "Claire."

In the next moment, Claire unlocked the door and opened it without knocking. Jared stood at the top of the stairs and glared down at his sister.

"Busy?" Claire asked.

I covered my mouth to stifle a laugh, thinking of the view from Claire's perspective. It wouldn't take much for her to imagine what we'd been up to.

"I'm going to take that key back if you don't start calling ahead of time," Jared growled.

"You say that as if I can't pick your lock in three seconds."

"I'm serious, Claire," Jared said so quietly that I barely heard him.

Well, I'm sorry," she said, not sounding sorry at all. "Bex left for training an hour ago and mom is all weepy. Ryan is in bed asleep and lucky me, my Taleh doesn't have half the police force and various criminals after him."

Jared turned to face me and his expression morphed from anger to an apologetic expression.

"She's here for the night," he explained, going to his closet and pulling a T-shirt off the hanger. He seemed to have thought better of it, putting the shirt back and walking across the room to search through my suitcase for a pair of pajamas.

"I don't think I'll be able to control myself if you put one of my t-shirts on," he said quietly, handing me the pajamas. I smiled at him, amused.

Claire groaned in disgust downstairs. "Gross."

Clothes shot up and over the railing, landing at Jared's feet. It was the shirts we had left behind on the kitchen floor. The refrigerator door opened, and the sounds of Claire rummaging for food made Jared roll his eyes.

"I'm going to take a quick shower," he said, rubbing the back of his neck.

I smiled. "A cold one?"

"Yeah," he said, turning toward the bathroom.

"I could keep you company."

Jared froze in mid-step, pausing for just a moment before closing the bathroom door behind him.

I changed while he was in the shower, feeling a bit guilty for teasing him. I understood his frustration all too well. I leaned back on the bed, chewing on my thumb nail and smiling at what had almost happened.

Chapter Eleven
The Hunt

"I'll be good," I promised.

Jared came out of the bathroom in only a pair of shorts. He stood several feet from me, hesitating to come to bed. "Maybe you should take a cold shower, too. I don't think it I can concentrate with you...."

"Aroused?" I said, quickly pressing my lips together to stifle a laugh.

His mouth fell open in shock and I cackled, too pleased with the reaction to help myself.

Jared smiled and nodded, complaisant to my playful badgering. He crawled into bed and propped his head up with his hand.

I sat against the headboard and sighed. "She wasn't serious, right? About the half-the-police-force thing?"

His face fell. "I won't let anything happen to you," he said, sliding his fingers between mine.

"Why are they after me?"

Jared cursed in Spanish under his breath resulting in Claire giggling from somewhere downstairs.

"They're not after you, sweetheart. They're after something of Jack's. They just think you know where it is."

"They're after the Port of Providence file?"

"Dawson said they want to dispose of the evidence Jack compiled that proves they're dirty, but they're looking for something else—something that's contained within the file."

"So, we go to my parents' house, figure it out and get rid of it. Toss it off of a bridge or something."

"That wouldn't help us, Nina," Jared said, shaking his head.

"Why not?" I grimaced.

"Whatever it is, it was worth going after Jack Grey. No one does that unless it's...it's something big, Nina. Something we don't want to be caught without."

"What are you talking about?" I was frustrated with the circles we seemed to be talking in.

"I shouldn't tell you this." He pinched the bridge of his nose between his thumb and index finger.

"Do it, anyway," I snapped.

A heavy expression settled on his face. "Jack didn't die from the car accident. He died of complications from a gunshot wound to the chest."

It took a moment for my brain to wrap around what he'd said, but once I processed the words, I was instantly angry. "What?"

Jared put his hand on mine. "Gabe did everything in his power to try to save him, but Jack was in over his head."

"I thought Gabe was indestructible. Wasn't he one-hundred percent angel?"

"They threatened the only thing more important to him than Jack."

"More important than his own life?" I asked, skeptical.

Jared nodded; the severity in his face was a bit frightening. "My mother. They were in my home the day Jack was shot. Claire and I had taken Bex to the airport, so Gabe had no choice but to leave him. My father knew what would happen if he left Jack alone, but his life meant nothing without my mother. Jack was shot en route to his office downtown. He did crash into a guard rail, but it was the bullet that led to his death."

"You're saying the men that want this package murdered my father?" Jared confirmed with a nod and I felt heat burn from every pore in my face. "I don't care what it is. We're getting rid of it. They will never get their hands on it."

"Nina, I know you're upset, but we need to think about this. They want something in that file so badly they went up against Jack and my father, and they knew what Gabe was capable of. I'd rather have it in our possession so we have something to barter with if need be."

Tears filled my eyes and Jared wrapped his arms around me. I mourned yet again for my father. I kept losing him over and over, with one horrible truth after another.

I cried myself asleep, and when I awoke, Jared comforted me once again when the news from the night before replayed in my memory.

"I need to do something. I can't just sit here," I said, rushing over to my suitcase.

"I'm going to figure this out, Nina. Just give me a day or two to decide our next move."

"I can't wait another second," I said, my mind racing to form a plan. When the idea struck, I paused. "I'm going back to my parents'. The answers are there." I yanked a T-shirt over my head and the first pair of jeans I touched.

"We don't have to go now," he argued.

"Yes we do," I said, pulling on my shoes while hopping to the stairs.

Jared scrambled from the bed. The hangers in his closet clanged against each other, and within seconds he was behind me, fully dressed. "Not exactly how I wanted to spend the weekend," he said, frowning.

"C'mon. Let's go. Vaminos!" I said, rushing him out the door.

In my parents' home, Jared followed me up the stairs to Jack's office. He watched me locate the keys to Cynthia's safe, followed me to her study, and then pulled the plant to the floor without effort. I used the key to gain access to the papers and files inside, placing them in somewhat organized piles.

For two hours we searched the documents, separating what we thought would be useful. One photo caught my eye. I held it out in front of me, staring at it, hoping I would recognize what it was that drew me in.

"He looks familiar to you?" Jared prompted.

"Something about his eyes...I can't put my finger on it."

Jared pulled a black wallet from his jacket pocket and tossed it into my lap; it was the one he had taken the night Ryan was stabbed. I took a closer look at the metal object embedded into the black leather. It was a badge.

I gasped, pointing at the picture. "This is the man that wanted my ring. This is Grahm."

Jared nodded.

"They were all cops?" I said, shaking my head in disbelief. "Why would they...?" My eyes wandered to my hand.

Jared stared at it as well. "The ring must be the key to something."

"It doesn't make any sense," I whispered. I looked at the papers for a moment and then rifled through them.

"What is it?" Jared asked.

"There's a receipt in here for the purchase of my ring. I didn't think about it before, but there has to be a connection," I said, impatient with the endless stacks. "Why else would it be here with important business documents?"

My eyes widened with excitement when I found the thin carbon copy. Jared leaned over my shoulder to take a look for himself.

"There's an engraving charge," he pointed out. "Is your ring engraved?"

"No. I don't...Jack never said anything, I've never noticed," I said, looking at my ring.

Slowly pulling it off my finger, I held it up, rotated it, and narrowed my eyes, looking for any words. "There's nothing,"

Jared held out his hand, and I handed it to him. My finger felt naked in its absence. Jared lifted it up, looked at it from every angle, and then returned it to my finger.

"There's nothing," he confirmed. He eyed the receipt again. "I say we go to the designer. Maybe they have a copy of this receipt."

I nodded, prompting Jared to gather the information and return it to the safe.

Jared and I drove to the address on the receipt, and I nervously twisted the ring around my finger as we pulled to a stop beside the curb. At first glance it appeared to be a typical jewelry store, not the underground, surreptitious establishment I had expected.

The bell on the door announced our arrival and a short, pudgy, elderly man with round glasses greeted us. Jared took my hand as we walked toward the glass display cases the man stood behind.

"Good morning. I am Vincent! You like diamonds? Sapphires? Rubies? Emeralds? Semi-precious stones? I have them all," he gushed with a thick accent.

Jared squeezed my hand and introduced himself. "This is Nina...I'm Jared."

Vincent didn't skip a beat. "I'd be happy to help you with anything you need." He paused to look at our hands intertwined and smiled. "Could I interest you in our exquisite line of engagement diamonds? I designed most of these," he said, pointing out a long row of extravagant rings. "I can design one customary, if you wish."

Jared looked at me with a soft expression, and then reluctantly turned his attention back to Vincent. "Not yet."

Vincent smiled at me, and I felt the blood rise to the surface of my cheeks. "Ah, well, then. Another time."

"You are the owner?" Jared asked.

Vincent chuckled, patting his protruding belly. "I am. Thirty-six years, now."

Jared raised my hand, resting it on the surface of the glass encasement. "Do you recognize this ring?"

Vincent leaned down to get a better look. "Yes... yes...," he hummed, elongating the words. "It has been awhile, has it not?" he asked, looking to me.

"My father purchased this from you three years ago," I reminded him.

Vincent lifted my hand and angled it several different ways, proudly watching it sparkle in the bright lights above.

"Your father was a man of vision," he said, smiling in approval.

Jared slid the receipt in front of Vincent. "This paper includes an engraving fee."

"Yes, yes. I remember," he said, pinching his bottom lip with his thumb and forefinger. "I don't ask questions, you know. I just make the customer happy."

"But...there is no engraving on the ring," I said.

He bellowed out a cheerful laugh. "There is, kisa. But it's hidden, you see." Vincent opened his hand, prompting me to give him my ring.

I sighed and looked to Jared, who offered a comforting smile. He took my hand and slowly pulled the ring off of my finger. Once Jared placed it in his hand, Vincent turned the ring upside down.

"He had it marked into the pavilion of the stone. The underbelly," he explained, "very tiny...I had to send it away to a gentleman I know with a laser. I don't have one of those here, of course," he chuckled, shaking his head.

"The engraving order has been covered. Do you have the original receipt?" Jared asked.

"No, no. I would have total in my books, only. If I remember correctly, it was letters and numbers. Gibberish that only made sense to your father, I assume."

It seemed to be too easy. I felt I was in the middle of a cloak and dagger movie, happening upon the perfect clues at the perfect time, watching it come together in front of my eyes.

Jared tucked my hair behind my ear with an apologetic expression. "Vincent?" His eyes were hesitant to leave mine. "Can you remove the stone from the setting?"

I jerked my ring from Vincent's open hand. "No!"

Jared pulled me out of ear shot. "Nina, if you want to see what Jack had put on this ring—and what Grahm wanted—we have to remove it from the setting to read it. He can reset it as if it were never touched."

I pressed my lips together in frustration. We would have to see what was etched into the stone to make progress, and there was only one way to do it.

"There's no other way?" I asked, knowing the answer.

Jared shook his head and opened his hand. I placed my ring in his palm and chewed on my lip.

"Can you do it?" he asked, setting the ring on the glass.

Vincent's eyes moved from Jared to me, unsure of how to proceed. "I could remove the stone, but there is no guarantee we will be able to read what is there, you see what I say?"

Jared nodded. "Remove the stone."

Vincent seemed suddenly disinclined. "It will be a few days before I can get to it. Write down your number and I will call you when—"

"I realize you're busy, forgive me," Jared said, pulling out his wallet. He set a small stack of hundred dollar bills on the glass, and Vincent's eyes widened, jerking his head back up to Jared. "That is in addition to your fee, of course," Jared added.

"You wait here...I'll be just a moment." Vincent gestured for us to sit on a short couch by the door, and then hurried to the back.

We waited together on the couch. A strange calm came over me, and I sighed when Jared began lightly caressing the top of my hand.

My eyebrows pulled in and my smile faded. "Jared?"

"Yes?" he said, playing with the strands of hair that had escaped my ponytail.

"Vincent called me kisa. It doesn't mean 'stupid' or anything, does it?"

Jared burst into laughter. "No, sweetheart. I would never let anyone insult you that way."

"What does it mean?"

Jared kissed my forehead. "It's Russian for kitten."

"Oh. That's a relief."

The minutes ticked by and I became increasingly anxious. I began pacing, and Jared watched me walk the length of the floor. A door shut behind me, and I flipped around. Vincent cupped the remnants of my ring in his plump hand.

Jared stood up and joined me at the display case. "Did you find anything?" he asked.

Vincent flattened a piece of paper in front of us with letters and numbers scribbled across it. He handed Jared a loupe and held out his hand for Jared to take the stone from his palm. Jared looked through the loupe at the stone, but pulled it away from his eyes, shaking his head.

"I can't see anything," he said, holding the peridot in front of him. Jared periodically looked down to the paper and back at the gem, placing it back into Vincent's palm.

"You could see that without the loupe, eh?" Vincent chuckled. "These old eyes aren't what they used to be."

Jared took the paper and handed it to me. "What he has written is what is inscribed in the stone." He looked to Vincent, then. "I'll need that reset immediately, please."

Vincent nodded and returned to the back, taking the pieces of the ring with him.

"Now what?" I asked, looking down at the paper.

825 2TR2TL223TRO5

"Does it mean anything to you?" Jared asked, grimacing in thought.

"Eight twenty-five is my birthday...August twenty-fifth, but other than that...no."

Within ten minutes, Vincent had returned. I sighed as I slid it back to its rightful place on my finger, looking exactly the same as it did before.

We returned to Jared's loft for lunch. I sat on the counter staring at the piece of paper, hoping the answer would spontaneously pop into my mind.

"It's going to catch fire if you keep staring at it like that," Jared teased, pushing the stir fry around in the wok.

"He put it on something he knew would be safe, the last place anyone would look, that he always knew where it would be...."

"He hid it in plain sight," Jared nodded. "The question is how did Grahm figure it out?"

I scanned the floor in deep thought. "I don't know. Maybe an old associate of my father's?"

Jared shook his head. "Jack engraved a code to something that everyone wants and put it on his only daughter's finger. He wouldn't risk telling anyone about it."

I sighed in frustration. "The eight twenty-five is separate from the other numbers. Think that means something?"

Jared shrugged. "It could. It could just be meant to signify your birthday. It could be an area code, or a flight number...some type of location?"

I thought about the safe in my mother's office, the files it contained, the photos...I couldn't make a connection with anything we'd looked over to the number. Shoving myself off the counter, I slammed the paper on the table and walked to the couch, falling over the arm onto my back with a frustrated cry.

"Nina," Jared said, his voice beside me, "we'll figure this out. Try not to make yourself sick over it."

"There's nothing in the safe; I've already poured over my father's office and searched all of his cabinets, there's nothing!" I covered my face with my hands.

Jared kneeled beside me and pulled my hands away from my eyes. "We'll go back tomorrow, look in Jack's office and take another look at the files in the safe. Why don't we rent a movie, hang out on the couch... spend some time together?"

"Ugh," I said, sitting up. "Did I put Jack's keys in his drawer? I don't think I did. What did I do with them?" I asked, patting my pants pockets.

Jared grinned. "They're in my jacket pocket. We can take them back tomorrow."

I sat for a moment, my eyes unfocused, deep in thought.

Jared touched my shoulder. "Nina?"

I scrambled to the coat rack and shoved my hands in his jacket pockets. "They're not here!" Jared eyed me warily. "They're in the inside pocket. What's going on?"

"Eight twenty-five!" I yanked the ring of keys from his jacket and thumbed through them. When I found what I was looking for, I held it away from the rest, showing it to Jared. "See? Eight twenty-five!"

Jared looked at the key and then back at me, his eyes animated. "What does it open?"

"I don't know," I said, looking at the key, "but it can't be a coincidence, right?"

"I doubt it," Jared said, his face twisting into a frown.

"What?"

Jared took the keys from me. "I want you to let me take care of this. I've humored you. You're upset about the way Jack died, I get it. The situation could go downhill quickly if we find what they're looking for. I don't want you anywhere near me when they figure out what we've done."

"You've humored me?" I asked, insulted. "I'm not going to get in your way, I almost have this figured out, I...."

"Did you listen to a thing I've said?" he snapped. After a brief moment, Jared closed his eyes and took a deep breath. "I know you need this to be over. You just don't understand what we're dealing with, here. I can't let my emotions get in the way of my job, Nina. I've already let this go too far. God knows the last thing I want is for you to be angry with me, but you've got to let me handle this."

"But—,"

"No, Nina. It's too dangerous," he said firmly.

My eyes narrowed. "I wasn't asking permission."

"This isn't about me telling you what to do. This is about your safety." He hugged me to him and I reached for the keys, pulling them from his grip. I knew that if he hadn't allowed me to do it, I would never have gotten the keys from his hand. I hoped that meant a part of him wanted my help.

"I'm going to take another look at Jack's office."

I turned to open the door, but I was frozen. Jared held me by my waist. Before I could protest, he exhaled a long, resigned sigh.

"Give me a minute. I'll go with you," he said, obviously annoyed.

I waited at the door until Jared finished packing our lunch, and then he grabbed my hand on the way out.

Halfway to my parents' home he still hadn't spoken.

"I'm sorry," I said, placing my hand on his. "I don't want you to be mad, but this is something I need to do."

Jared sighed. "I don't want you to get hurt. I'm beginning to regret telling you anything."

Those words stung me. "I don't want to get hurt, either. We won't have to keep looking over our shoulders if we end this. We can just live our lives normally. Together."

Jared squeezed my hand as he pulled into the drive.

On a rug in Cynthia's office I thumbed through papers, looking for anything with numbers. I highlighted anything with an eight, two, or five anywhere near each other.

Two and a half hours later, I had several piles of papers, and nothing that included the numbers we were looking for. I sat up straight to stretch my aching back.

"Let's take a break," Jared said. He pulled the highlighter from my fingers and handed me the plastic container with my lunch sealed inside.

I stretched my legs over Jared's lap and chewed happily on his amazing stir fry, marveling at what an exceptional cook he was. Jared pulled off my boot and began rubbing my foot, and I leaned my head back.

"This is taking forever," I groaned.

"We could call it a day. I could take you out to dinner," he offered.

I frowned. "You're not taking this very seriously."

Jared let out one shocked puff of air. "On the contrary, I think I'm taking this more seriously than you are. You don't seem to understand how dangerous this is for you."

"What could happen to me? My boyfriend also happens to be my guardian angel," I said, leaning over to kiss him.

"What in the hell is going on here?"

I looked over to the door where Cynthia stood, her hands on her hips.

"Hello, Mother," I said. "I thought you weren't coming back until tomorrow."

"So is this search and seizure or burglary?" she said, crossing her arms.

"It's good to see you, too," I said, rolling my eyes in response. "We're trying to find something with an eight twenty-five on it."

"Eight twenty-five?" Cynthia asked, looking at Jared, who stopped chewing for a moment under her glare.

He swallowed the lump of food in his mouth before giving report. "I intercepted Dawson. They're finished with the pleasantries, Mrs. Grey. They want the evidence Jack collected on them and they think Nina knows where it is."

"I wonder why that is, Jared? It couldn't be because they've seen you two together."

"It's possible," Jared replied, impervious.

"What does Charles Dawson have to do with the number?" Cynthia asked, closing in on the mess on the floor.

"He doesn't," Jared said dismissively, looking over the papers again. I was a little surprised by his impassive attitude at Cynthia's presence when just over a week ago he balked at just the mention of being in the same room with her.

Cynthia seemed to accept his ambiguity, probably because she was used to being left in the dark by my father. "I trust you'll take care of Mr. Dawson, Jared. That simply won't do."

"It's already been taken care of, Mrs. Grey."

Cynthia nodded in approval. I was shocked that she spoke so candidly of violence.

"Keep me updated," she said, walking out the door.

"That was weird," I said, shaking my head.

Jared looked up from the paper. "What, sweetheart?"

"She threatened to fire you a few days ago if you didn't stay away from me. You quit speaking to me because of it. Just now you nearly ignored her."

Jared shrugged. "My mother discussed it with her. She's had a change of heart."

"How so?" I asked, suspicious.

"Lillian's very persuasive," Jared smiled.

"Nina?" I turned to see my mother round the corner again.

"Yes?"

"We're leaving for Nicaragua a week from Sunday. I need you to meet me here early so we can be at the airport by nine. Jared?"

"I'll have everything ready," Jared said, distracted by the paper in his hand.

My heart began to pound, causing Jared to look up. I realized that I was going to spend the entire week of Spring Break on a beach with him, and the thought made my cheeks flush red.

Jared smiled, guessing what made my heart flutter. "This might be your first vacation with me, but it's not my first vacation with you."

"It's the first time you'll sit with me on the plane," I said a bit too eager, grinning from ear to ear. Jared chuckled at my enthusiasm.

Cynthia's reaction differed. "He's there to work, Nina. Please keep that in mind. Jared, make sure she is here on time."

"Yes, ma'm," he said, his soft eyes never leaving mine.

With that, Cynthia disappeared once again.

I couldn't help but think about lying in a hammock with Jared. It already seemed like heaven.

"I am suddenly looking forward to vacation," I grinned.

Jared leaned over to touch my cheek. "Lying with you on a Caribbean beach at sunset? I'll have to remind myself that it's real."

"What will you have ready?" I asked.

Jared's attention turned to the paper he was holding once more, and his eyes narrowed. He didn't make eye contact when he spoke. "Uh...all of my surveillance supplies. We typically bring about fifteen hundred pounds of tech with us, but with Claire going to Tahoe, I'll be carrying light. I'll set up a perimeter around the premises...."

"What is it?" I leaned over to see what he was so absorbed in and recognized it was a bank statement. I'd seen it several times before during my search, but set it aside in the scrap pile.

Jared pointed to a section of the statement and I gasped. It was a monthly charge for a safety deposit box. Box eight twenty-five.

"Jared!" I cried, grabbing his arm.

Jared looked at his watch. "The bank is closed."

I sighed, deflated. "We'll go first thing Monday morning."

"I'll go. You have class."

I grimaced. "I'm going, Jared. We're doing this together."

He sighed as we gathered the piles of papers and photos and replaced them. Jared lifted the plant as if it were an empty cardboard box and returned it to its proper place.

My cell phone buzzed in my coat pocket. The display lit up with Kim's name scrolling across the screen, and I closed my eyes. "I bet she's calling about the pub tonight. I forgot all about it."

"Hey Kim."

"You're not backing out, Nigh. Don't even try," she said.

"I wasn't going to, I...."

"Sure you weren't."

"I'm sorry, Kim. I forgot," I said, rubbing my forehead with my fingers, feeling a stress headache coming on. "I'll be there."

Jared walked with me to the Escalade and held the door open as I climbed inside. By his expression I knew he was aware of the dull pain in my head.

"You're not going to stand us up again, are you?" she scolded.

"No! No, I'll meet you there around nine."

"Good. See you then." Kim said, disconnecting the line.

I put my cell phone back in my pocket and took Jared's hand. "I'm sorry," I groaned. "I think I unwittingly double booked myself."

My head began to throb. It was difficult skipping back and forth between the two lives I was leading. I was the typical college student when I was with Kim, Ryan and Beth, and when I was with Jared, my life turned into this fantastical dream world with angels and demons and secret safety deposit boxes.

We parked in front of the loft, and Jared sighed. Claire's Lotus was sparkling beside the curb.

"It doesn't look like we'd have much time alone, anyway."

Claire was lounging on the couch in stilettos boots and a leather jacket, flipping through channels on the flat screen. "Ryan's taking a nap. That guy sleeps like a hibernating bear," she said, rolling her eyes. "Every branch of the military wants me on a special ops team, and God sticks me with the most boring Taleh in the history of mankind."

I smiled at her observation, and Jared led me upstairs by the hand.

"Ryan is going to the pub tonight?" Jared called back to his sister.

"Yep," Claire said. "I'll see you there."

"You're keeping Claire company tonight?" I asked, collapsing onto his bed.

"I think I'll hang back tonight, let you spend time with your friends," he said, lying on the mattress beside me.

"You don't want to come?"

Jared brushed his thumb across my sullen lip. "I always want to be where you are."

I smiled. "Because you have to."

"You know that's not true," he said, trying his best to seem annoyed.

I leaned over to kiss his cheek. "How do you expect me to have fun when you're right outside and I'm hoping that any minute you'll just break down and come in?"

Jared grinned. "How can I say no to that?"

"You'll come, then?" I asked, raising my eyebrows expectantly.

"If that's what you want," Jared shrugged. He tried to seem casual, but beyond the cool blue of his eyes was an edge of hopefulness.

"It's what I'll always want," I whispered, touching his cheek with my fingertips.

Jared's expression beamed with adoration. "I knew that if I ever got my chance to be with you, all the waiting would be worth it. It's as if we've cheated the curse, somehow. I've never understood how something could be considered a curse that requires me to spend every moment with you, and that grants me the mercy of leaving a world that doesn't have you in it."

"There's nothing for me to say after that."

"It's just the truth, sweetheart. You don't have to try to outdo me," Jared said, amused.

"I love you...and I will love you forever. That's the truth."

Jared's expression turned intense, as if he was moved beyond words by my simple honesty. He pressed his lips to mine in the same slow, meaningful way he had only once before. It was the sweetest moment of my life.

It occurred to me that the stars had all but lined up for us: Gabe assigned to my father, falling in love with Lillian, and then Jared coming along four years before I did, just in time to be assigned to me—the daughter of a criminal—a girl that would need constant supervision.

I traced the planes of Jared's torso and pondered how perfectly everything had been laid out for us to be together, and then my mind drifted to Claire and Ryan. If I was going to believe in fate, I had to take into account who Jared said I was meant to be with. I closed my eyes, pushing the thought from my mind. Ryan would find someone else that he would be happy with, and Jared could keep me.

Jared's voice pulled me out of my daydream. "You were determined today. I'm impressed."

"Anything's possible with an angel and a little ingenuity," I said, settling in beside him.

Jared let me sleep for an hour, and then we left early to grab a bite to eat before meeting my friends. I descended the stairs in a black satin corset and jeans, with a pair of ruffle-toed pewter pumps. To my extreme pleasure, Jared stood frozen by the door, dropping his keys and then catching them before they hit the floor.

"Wow," he whispered.

"Thank you," I smiled, letting him help me with my coat.

By the end of dinner, I'd already had three glasses of wine. We arrived at the pub at nine sharp, and the various vehicles of my friends were already in the parking lot. I noticed Claire's Lotus parked beside the curb down the street.

When Jared and I walked in, my friends cheered and whistled at our arrival.

Kim yelled over the music. "I brought a CD! We're going to be dancing queens for the night!"

"Okay!" I yelled over the upbeat song blaring over the speakers.

Tucker brought over shots—all of them different colors—and the group howled. Everyone held up their shot glasses and Chad pushed one full of something green in my direction.

We all yelled in unison, "TO THE BIG BROWN BEAR!"

With that, we all tipped our heads back, killed our shots, and glasses slammed to the table at different intervals. Tucker yelled for Tozzi to bring another round, and everyone cheered.

Thirty minutes later, most of us were on the dance floor jumping around like maniacs. My head felt a bit heavy, already feeling the effects of the wine and whiskey. Ryan and Jared watched us from the table and I waved to both of them as I bounced up and down.

I returned to the table and sat on Jared's lap. He pulled me toward him to talk in my ear.

"I love you, but there is no puking in the Escalade."

I laughed and planted a kiss on his mouth. "I'm fine! I'm Irish, remember?"

Jared nodded and leaned into my ear again. "Even the Irish throw up, Nina."

It seemed like the night had just begun when Tozzi announced last call. I lost count of the drinks I'd had, and my eyes struggled to focus.

Jared supported most of my weight as he escorted me to his SUV. He lifted me effortlessly into the passenger seat, and I leaned my elbow against the console, resting my head against my fist.

By the time we arrived at the loft, my head felt too heavy to hold up. Jared pulled open my door and I slipped in and out of awareness as he carried me up the stairs.

"I'm going to take a shower," I said, stumbling to the bathroom.

Jared followed me. "Are you sure that's a good idea? I don't want you passing out in there."

"Why don't you join me, then you can make sure I don't?" I said, steadying myself against the door jamb.

Jared raised an eyebrow, and I frowned at him before grabbing a towel and shutting the door behind me.

I fought with my clothes in slow motion. My eyes wouldn't stay open, and I was incessantly giggling for no good reason, which made me giggle more. I turned on the shower and stepped under the water, letting it rush over me, plastering my hair onto my face. Every movement I made felt like it was at a snail's pace, but I managed to exit the shower before my palms pruned.

I ran a comb through my hair and clumsily brushed my teeth. I giggled again at my blundering of the most mundane of tasks and I heard Jared chuckle outside the door in response.

"Everything all right in there?" he asked, knocking on the door.

I giggled again and spit loudly in the sink. "Everything's fantastic!"

Jared laughed again, and I opened the door and stumbled to the bed.

"I'm going to hop in the shower. Don't try to go downstairs or look over the railing or anything like that, okay? Just stay put until I get out." I understood his words, but they seemed to blur together.

I fell onto the bed face down and moaned into the comforter at how perfectly wonderful it felt. "I'm not going anywhere," I said, my eyes sealing shut.

Jared reappeared in less than five minutes. "Did you plan on sleeping in your towel?"

"Maybe," I said, feeling melted to the bed.

Jared walked over to his closet and pulled a T-shirt off its hanger. "Okay," he said, sitting me up, "raise your arms."

I complied, and he slid the oversized T-shirt over my head. I buzzed my lips as the neck line went over my mouth making Jared erupt in laughter.

"You are something else," he said, covering my legs with the blanket. He stepped away for a moment and then returned, throwing a piece of light blue fabric onto my lap. It took me a moment to realize that it was a pair of my panties.

"I'll let you...take care of that." He started down the stairs, and I spoke up.

"Jared?"

He turned around, immediately catching the panties I clumsily shot at him. I burst into a delighted cackle, knowing if he had been merely human I would have caught him square in the face.

Jared smiled with inexhaustible patience. "These are for you, not me," he said, tossing them back. They landed perfectly in my lap.

I giggled again as he descended the stairs, feeling exhausted and wide awake at the same time. I could hear every step and movement Jared made downstairs, yet the fog in my head kept the sounds blurred together.

I was already settled on my side of the bed when Jared returned, and he wasted no time nestling himself next to me. Though the rest of my senses were lacking, my skin was aware of the heat created when his skin touched mine. Every part of me felt content and peaceful in his arms, as if I was meant to be there. I kissed his chest, but my lips didn't want to stop there. I continued until I reached his neck, and Jared took a deep breath, wasting no time to hold my shoulders far enough away to look into my prurient eyes.

"Nina...." Jared warned, but I put my mouth on his to stop any further protesting.

I skipped over our usual cautious beginnings and let go of all my inhibitions. I leaned over him, lifting my knee at the same time to straddle his hips. Jared's lips were not as urgent as mine, but I persisted.

I felt Jared's torso rise against my lips as they left his chest to slowly kiss my way up the midline of his throat. When my lips reached his lips again, his mouth was less cautious. He turned, rolling over me, positioning me on my back. I smiled at my imminent victory.

Jared pulled away from me, his breath disparate from just moments before. "Nina, we can't do this tonight."

I let out a gush of air I'd been holding in anticipation of my triumph. "Why not?"

Jared kissed my nose and smiled. "Well—although I'm incredibly tempted by the slurring and stumbling—I'd like for you to remember our first time."

I relaxed my legs, letting them fall to the bed. "Why do you have to be so freaking noble?" I complained, pounding the mattress with my arms for emphasis.

Jared chuckled and curled up beside me. "Yes, I'm so noble that I struggle with it every second I'm alone with you. Don't give me too much credit."

"I'm sorry...." I sighed, knowing I would feel guilty in a clearer state of mind.

"Don't apologize. I can't say I don't enjoy it," he chuckled. "...Nina?" he said, whispering my name.

I could hear him, but I couldn't respond. I realized just how fast I was sinking when my mind wanted to answer him but my mouth refused to form the words. He kissed my exposed shoulder and relaxed his head on the pillow behind me. As I was floating into unconsciousness, I felt his arm tighten around me again, blanketing me with the warmth of his skin. I thought I heard him whisper something else, but I was too deep inside the darkness to make out the words.

Chapter Twelve
Eli

My chest hurt. My eyes hurt. My head felt like a railroad spike had been driven through it. I wanted to scream, but that would only make it more excruciating. The only part of the moment that offered a grain of comfort was that I was still in Jared's bed. I felt colder than I usually felt when waking up in his apartment, and I knew at once he wasn't with me.

"Jared?" I rasped, unable to speak louder than a whisper.

I felt the bed indent beside me and I winced at the nausea the movement induced. The fissure I managed between my eyelids let in an infinitesimal amount of light and I cowered from it, bringing my hands over my eyes.

"I'll get the light," Jared spoke in a hushed voice.

The assaulting brightness that seeped through my eyelids faded and I tried again.

"Much better, thank you," I whispered, pulling myself up on my elbows.

"I brought you breakfast." Jared nodded to the bedside table. Two aspirin, a large glass of water and a triangle of toast sat on a plate beside my picture.

I forced a smile and immediately reached for the aspirin. Jared handed me the water and I tossed the pills to the back of my tongue, gulping down the cool liquid. It felt uncomfortable against my parched throat, as if my body wanted to reject any further fluids that might cause more anguish.

"I feel awful," I groaned.

"I know."

"I don't usually get a hangover. I must have been absurdly drunk," I said, rubbing my face with the tips of my fingers.

"You were," he said flatly.

I sank into the mattress. "I'm sorry you had to babysit me. As if you don't have to do it, anyway. I'm so embarrassed."

Jared attempted a smile. "Don't apologize for having a good time with your friends. It's just... uncomfortable." His eyes unfocused and his eyebrows pulled in.

"What's uncomfortable?"

Jared rubbed the back of his neck. "This hazy, painful, tired, irritable heaviness you're feeling."

"Oh," I breathed, still not understanding. I hadn't considered that Jared would be sensing the same symptoms. I sank deeper into the mattress, feeling very selfish. "Do you have a headache?"

Jared laughed with a puff of air. "I don't know. I've never had one before. I'm sure it's a lesser version of what you're feeling."

I raised an eyebrow. "I thought it was faint, like a mosquito buzzing in your ear?"

Jared looked away from me, clearly troubled. "It's getting stronger."

"How?"

"I'm not sure. My father never mentioned our senses increasing more than what I've always experienced."

"I'm sorry, Jared. I didn't know or I wouldn't have—"

"Hey," he interrupted, "don't worry about me. I just need to figure out what this is. It bothers me that I don't feel one hundred percent."

"Oh."

"What?" Jared asked, as if I'd pulled him out of a deep thought.

"The no-drinking policy. You feel off balance this morning and you like feeling in control all the time."

"You say it like it's a bad thing," he said defensively.

"You don't have to be perfect all the time, Jared. It's okay to let your guard down."

I leaned in to hug him but he pulled away just enough to make me hesitate. When he realized what he'd done, he seemed to regret it, which made him even angrier.

"You sound like Claire," he snapped.

"Claire and I agree on this one, then. You are half-human. It's okay to make mistakes," I said, my words more rigid than I'd meant them to be.

"Not for someone like me. Certainly not for someone that has the daughter of Jack Grey for a Taleh. It's like you have no sense of danger, Nina. After everything you've been through lately, I don't understand it."

He mentioned my father to get a reaction, so I kept my temper in check. I raised an eyebrow at his mini-tirade. "Did I strike a nerve?"

Jared's unending patience from the night before had run out. "If I let my guard down you die. Do you understand that?"

I took a drink of water and nodded. "We die."

Jared took the glass from me and slammed it on the table. "Do you think I care about that? I would die for you a thousand times if I could. You're the only thing that matters."

I crossed my arms, incensed with his tender words mixed with their biting tone. "What is wrong with you? Why are you so upset?"

Jared leaned his elbows on his knees, looking to the floor. "I had company this morning."

"I didn't hear anyone come in," I said, surprised.

"It's because he doesn't use doors. It was Samuel. He was a friend of my father's. He's concerned about the situation I've put you in."

I held up a hand. "Back up. What do you mean he doesn't use doors?"

"He's an Arch."

"An Archangel was here this morning?" I asked, mystified. "Do they look like Gabe? Do they look human?"

"Yes," he answered.

"So if they look human, how do you know?"

"Archs have the same light hair, flawless skin, and the bright blue eyes, although Samuel and his family are the exception. They are nobility among the Archs, and are a contrast to the rest of them."

"Contrast?" I had hoped I would learn to decipher Jared's cryptic explanations, but I still failed consistently.

"He's a Cimmerian, a line of dark angels. They are the strongest of Archs, they're sovereigns and they're warriors. They are assigned to those that are marked by Hell—the humans who are born to be stalked and tormented. They go toe to toe with demons quite frequently."

"Oh," I said, thinking about what kind of creature had been just a few feet from me while I slept. Anything built to wrestle demons had to be a frightening sight to behold.

Jared continued, "In addition to that, I can smell them a mile away. It's very difficult for them to sneak up on us. Or each other."

"Like fresh laundry, soap and a thunderstorm?" I asked, the corners of my mouth turning up.

Jared frowned for a minute in thought and then his mouth mimicked mine. "I hadn't thought about it. To me it's those things times ten. I would describe them as smelling like the cleanest air I've ever experienced." After a short pause, he looked at me with curiosity. "What made you say that?"

I smiled, grabbing his hand. "That's how you smell."

"I do? Hmmm. Good to know," he said, nodding his head in thought.

"So...Samuel...?"

Jared nodded, his eyes darkening again. "He's noticed an increase in activity in the area."

"What kind of activity?"

Jared swallowed and shifted closer to me on the bed, holding my hand tighter. "The Others don't understand my draw to you...even with me being half-human. It's interesting to them. So their visits here have increased."

"But I haven't...they haven't bothered me."

"They don't engage us unless they have to."

I swallowed. "So you're saying when you're near, they won't hurt me?"

Jared's eyes clouded over. "They don't want to cross that line, trust me. They know better than to get too close to you when I'm near."

"That's why you had Claire sit with me the night you were with Mr. Dawson."

He nodded. "I don't want you to be afraid. It's only an issue in my apartment; they're drawn to the dwellings of Hybrids. Remember I told you that they're attracted to those that are aware of them?" I nodded. "Claire, Bex and I, and those like us, are very aware of them. Our lineage enables us to see them even when you can't. I've noticed more of their kind coming and going. They're curious about you."

I held his hand tight. "Should I be worried?"

Jared offered a comforting smile. "You let me do the worrying."

I took a deep breath and nodded. "What did Samuel tell you?"

"They've noticed...," Jared rubbed the back of his neck, "they've noticed that we're spending more time together. Both sides. The Archs are unhappy about it. It's unusual—and heavily frowned upon—to become involved with one's Taleh. It's considered more of a taboo than falling in love with a human. Even though I'm half-human, they find it irresponsible. Samuel is concerned that the Archs won't be inclined to help if things get messy."

"Why would we need their help? I thought you said they wouldn't come near me when you're around?"

"I'm not talking about a dozen or so Others, Nina. Samuel wouldn't be concerned if it wasn't serious."

"How serious is it?"

Jared sighed. All of his energy seemed to have been sucked from him. "Hell is familiar with our fathers. Being their children, along with our unique circumstance, we've become people of interest, so to speak. The Others made a game of trying to catch my father off-guard. With me having a stronger reason to protect you...," he choked off. He swallowed and then began again, "Samuel came to warn me."

"Warn you," I repeated. My head was swimming with confusion and the whiskey still saturating my system.

"Our relationship could unintentionally provoke Hell." Jared rubbed his temples. He was having trouble focusing as well. "Samuel informed me that the curiosity they already have, coupled with Jack's death...we could have bigger problems than just the increasing visits."

I shook my head. "What does Jack have to do with it?"

"The men that killed your father knew how to bypass Gabe because of who they work for. Those cops, and a few other enemies of your father's, are employed by a man named Shax. Except...he's not a...he's not exactly a man."

"He's Other?"

Jared attempted a smile, but the tension on his face twisted it into something that resembled pain.

"Shax is a Duke of Hell. He is also a renowned thief and takes great pride in his spoils. Somehow Jack made an enemy of Shax, and I'm going to guess that he took something that Shax felt belonged to him. Not something you want to do to an aristocrat of Hell."

I nodded, unable to speak in a calm voice.

"Samuel advised that we...see less of each other."

"What? No! You're not...you're not going to listen to him, are you?"

Jared took my face in his hands. "I promised I wouldn't leave you again, didn't I?"

I nodded. "You did. You promised," I said, more to myself than to him.

Jared returned his elbows to his knees and lowered his face in his hands. "I have made a mess of everything, Nina," he groaned. "You're in more danger than you've ever been. I see now why Jack forbade me to see you."

I positioned myself behind him, wrapping my arms around his middle and pressing my cheek against his back. "So we have to jump through some hoops to be together. Who doesn't?"

Jared twisted, looking at me with an incredulous expression.

I sighed. "For us to be together...it's a miracle isn't it? A Hybrid and his human, in love when everyone from Heaven to Hell says we shouldn't be. The starvation of a multitude turned into miraculous fish, the enslaving of a nation brought on the parting of the sea, blind men to see, lepers healed, a mother's grief brought back the dead...it takes a nightmare to earn a miracle."

He laughed once. "In this scenario I'm the nightmare—you're the miracle."

"Jared?" I asked, pausing for a moment while I reconsidered broaching the subject again.

He sensed my trepidation and touched my cheek. "What, sweetheart?"

"What do you plan on doing with the information Samuel gave you?" I braced for his eyes to cloud over but to my surprise he smiled. His eyes even brightened a bit.

"We're going to fight through the nightmare to earn the miracle, right?"

I smiled back. "Right."

He kissed my cheek. "I'll let you get dressed."

"Are we going somewhere?"

"To see a friend," Jared said, jogging downstairs.

I thought about that for a moment. "A human friend?"

"Negative," I heard him say from the kitchen.

After my shower, I descended the stairs still feeling a bit woozy. I felt even worse for Jared, who didn't even enjoy the debauchery before feeling the consequences of it.

Jared kept the accelerator to the floor, making the buildings of Providence blur by. I fidgeted with the temperature until finally resorting to the air conditioner. The stream of air blew against my face, and I closed my eyes.

Jared touched my knee.

"It's helping with the nausea," I said, knowing he would be just as relieved to have a small fraction of my symptoms alleviated.

The Escalade slowed to a stop beside the fence of an abandoned warehouse. We were just outside of town, no more than ten miles from Jared's loft. I immediately felt a bit skittish, but the fear disappeared with Jared's warm touch. He took my hand and didn't let go as we hiked along an aging, gravel walkway and stopped at a gate harnessed with

281

rusting chains. He pulled a key from his pocket and twisted it in the large vintage lock.

Jared pressed open the heavy gates and led me around to a side entrance, where he pressed a button on a small grey box. No one answered, but we were buzzed in.

Jared led me by the hand across the vast concrete. Pane after pane of glass lined the walls, shooting beams of sunshine to the floor through the decades of dust. He stopped in the center and smiled at me before calling out into the huge, empty space.

"Eli?"

We waited for almost half an hour. I wanted to ask Jared if he was sure his friend was there, but as long as he was being patient, I would play along.

"Oh, c'mon. She knows," Jared said suddenly, rolling his eyes.

I watched him, the corners of my mouth turning up. It was amusing to see him talking to himself.

"Eli, we need to talk. You know she's important." He looked at me and then impatiently peered up to the extensive ceiling. "You're being ridiculous!" he shouted into the air.

I stifled a giggle.

Jared turned to me. "What?"

"Nothing," I said, forcing the corners of my mouth straight.

"Great. Now she thinks I'm nuts," Jared called out to the massive room.

A tiny giggle escaped my throat, and Jared angled his neck to face me, attempting an insulted expression. He failed miserably when a wide grin stretched across his face.

"Admit it. It was funny," a voice came from behind us.

I flipped around, instinctively hiding behind Jared.

A platinum-haired man stood in front of us with an amused smile. He was taller than Jared, though not by more than a few inches. I was surprised at the way he was dressed. I was expecting the crisp, white, buttoned-down dress shirt, but I hadn't anticipated it un-tucked and the sleeves rolled up to his elbows, or the holes in his jeans, or the light brown leather sandals. I was certainly not expecting the faux hawk.

He surpassed attractive, and his physique was as incredible as Jared's, noticeable even under his clothes. Even though he was fair, warmth emanated from his skin, almost a muted, dewy glow. His ice blue eyes appraised me, and then looked to Jared, who pulled me to his side.

"Eli," Jared said, nodding.

"Yeah. There will be none of that nodding crap, Jared," Eli said, pulling us both in for a hug. "How have you been? I assume the moping has ceased since you've found a way to finally introduce yourself?"

Jared nervously laughed, looking at me from the corner of his eye. "I've been fine, and you?"

"Heavenly," Eli said, with a wide, dramatic gesturing of his arms.

Jared rolled his eyes. "Quit it."

"Hello, Nina. I've heard...," his eyes widened for a moment, "oodles about you. It's nice to finally meet you...formally."

"It's nice to meet you, too."

I extended my hand and Eli took it, appearing pleased with my bravery. His hand felt normal, a little on the cool side. Not at all like Jared's feverish temperature.

"We don't have to run a fever to keep up with what we can do," Eli smiled.

"Oh," I said, nodding.

I looked to Jared, who watched me with an expression as amused as Eli's.

"You were expecting a toga and a harp?" Eli asked, winking at me.

"Leave her alone, Eli," Jared warned.

"I'm just having a little fun, Jay. You know I don't get to do this often," the angel said, letting go of my hand.

Jared turned to me. "Eli isn't an Arch. He is the Angel of the Divine Plan. He watches over spiritual evolution, and when called upon by humans, he assists Him in helping humans to find the correct path."

"Him? As in...your boss is...?"

Eli seemed bored with Jared's explanation. "I am a traffic cop for the Archs and a glorified guidance counselor, Nina. Don't let the title intimidate you."

I tried to stifle a laugh, but the best I could do was to cover my mouth when I giggled. I had expected somewhat of a formal meeting, and Eli had gone from an ominous being to a pleasant surprise.

"I've started experiencing some changes in my senses, Eli. Do you know what that's about?" Jared asked, impatient with the pleasantries.

"I do. Have you become physical with your Taleh?" Eli asked matter-of-factly.

"In what respect? If you're meaning sex, then no," Jared said, impervious to such a forward way of asking a delicate question.

I began to feel a bit dizzy by the sudden turn of conversation. I wasn't sure how many times I could be taken off guard in my condition. Jared pulled me to his side, supporting some of my weight.

Eli eyed us speculatively. "In any respect, Jared. When you revealed yourself to her, the connection became stronger. As you spend time with her, it becomes stronger. Every time you touch her, it grows stronger. As your feelings for her deepen, so does the link between you. If you're with her in an intimate way, the connection becomes a solid, permanent bond. There will be a noticeable difference in how you'll sense her presence, her pain and her emotions when a physical commitment is made. You should keep that in mind. It could hinder your duties as her protector."

Jared nodded, immediately taking Eli at his word.

"You mean he'll be more susceptible to sickness and pain?" I asked.

"It's certainly a possibility. Of course, those things would always be in connection with you, Nina, but only in theory. We don't have much experience with this type of thing. The two of you are only our seventh case since the dawn of humans' time on earth. You would be the first half-breed/human case."

"Hybrid," I corrected.

Both Jared and Eli looked at me with a strange expression.

Eli smiled, clearly amused. "Hybrid, then. You're right, that wasn't very polite, was it?" he said, winking at Jared, who looked away, trying not to smile.

Jared cleared his throat, getting back to business. "I'm told we could have some legions to worry about."

Eli looked up for a moment and then back to Jared. "So far it's just the humans."

"Is there something I can do to get them to back off of her?" Jared said with a noticeable change in his tone. There was a distinct edge of desperation to it.

"I'm afraid the damage has already been done, Jared. You were warned," Eli said without judgment.

Jared glanced at me and then let go of my hand, walking away with his hands on his hips. He kept his back to us, looking down at his feet and then up to the ceiling.

Eli nodded at me with a patient smile. I forced the corners of my mouth to turn up.

Only Jared's profile was visible. His jaws worked just beneath the skin. After several moments he began speaking in a language I didn't understand. It was more beautiful than French or Hebrew; it was the most beautiful language I'd ever heard. The words came out of Jared's mouth like a symphony.

Eli answered him in the same language, and then I understood. They were speaking the language of Heaven. After Eli's lengthy response, Jared turned around with tears in his eyes.

"Can I do this alone?" Jared asked.

"None of us can do anything alone, Jared. That is why we exist in families." Eli's expression was calm, the opposite of Jared's. I felt an overwhelming urge to go to Jared and hold him in my arms until the tortured look left his eyes.

Jared seemed to understand what I did not. He pulled me to him, kissing the top of my hair. I wrapped my arms around him.

"It's going to be okay. Whatever it is, we'll figure it out," I assured him.

He smiled, but his face crumpled around it. "I've put you in serious danger, Nina. You're father was right, I should have stayed away. I'm so sorry."

I shook my head. "I'm not," I said softly.

Eli sighed with satisfaction. "She's a keeper, Jared. She has faith. Maybe it will rub off on you."

Jared's eyes softened. "Maybe."

In the same moment, we were alone. We made our way back to the SUV, and then Jared opened my door, lifting me to the seat.

"I don't think it's a good idea for you to move back to Andrews right now," he said with an apologetic expression.

I touched his cheek, worried about his reaction. "Jared, I can't keep staying with you. What will people think?"

He laughed once, but he was perturbed at my question. "I don't give a damn what anyone thinks. I'm more concerned with keeping you alive."

I smiled patiently and kissed his cheek. "I'm staying with you on the weekends, remember?"

"It's not enough, Nina. I need you with me at all times."

I raised my eyebrows in protest. "Well, you can't. I have class...and friends. I have a life outside of this craziness. Jack didn't move in with you, and he had more enemies than I do."

"If my mother was Gabe's Taleh, he would have moved her in. If Gabe had created a fun new game for a legion of demons to play, he would have moved her in," Jared said, rubbing his forehead with his fingers.

"Do you have a headache?" I asked.

Anger exploded across Jared's face and he walked away from me, paused a few feet away, and then walked back, still furious.

"Nina! For God's sake, your life is in danger! And it's my fault! Quit worrying about me!"

I sat there, stunned. Jared walked away, picked up a baseball-sized rock and hurled it at the warehouse. I lost the rock with my human eyes before it crashed through a window.

"Impressive," I said.

Jared flipped around and seemed to contemplate yelling some more before wrapping his arms around my waist and burying his head in my lap. "Will you please take this seriously? Before I'm consumed with guilt?"

"Do you want me to be afraid?" I asked. Jared looked up at me with a pained look on his face. "Do you want me to be angry with you? Do you want me to scream at you and hate you for coming into my life?" I shook my head and cupped his cheeks with my hands. "I can't do that. I know one way or another, everything will work out. It will."

My optimism didn't help Jared's agony. His face fell, and he let his head fall to my lap again, pulling me to him, grasping at my back. I hugged him and touched my cheek to his hair. I didn't know what else to do for him, but I refused to let my emotions betray me.

When the sun began to set, Jared's head hadn't moved.

"Jared, it's getting dark. We should go," I said, running my fingers through his hair.

After a few minutes, he stood up and slowly walked to the other side of the SUV, in no hurry to get back to town.

"I'm taking you to Brown," Jared said, pulling away from Eli's warehouse. "We'll get the rest of your things, I'll get you a dresser, make you some closet space...."

"Jared...no."

His eyes darted to mine. "Nina, I'm sorry but this isn't up for negotiation. I have to fix this, and then you can go back to Andrews."

I kept my voice calm. "I'm not going to hide, Jared."

Despite my quiet tone, Jared became increasingly angry. "I realize you haven't a clue with what we're dealing with here, but I'm telling you now: You're packing, and you're coming home with me. I don't know for how long."

I shook my head slowly.

His jaws tensed. "Nina, don't be stubborn. Please trust me."

"I do trust you. That's why I'm not going to hide," I said again.

He jerked the Escalade onto the shoulder of the road and shoved the gear in park. "I'm not asking, Nina. I am telling you. It's that serious."

I narrowed my eyes at him and he sighed, hitting his steering wheel with the heel of his hand.

"Don't do this to me! It's bad enough knowing I've put you in this situation without you refusing to let me keep you safe!"

"Jack didn't want you to tell me the truth because he didn't want this. He didn't want me to live in fear or in hiding. If you lock me up you're giving them what they want."

His knuckles were white as they gripped the steering wheel. "What makes you think you know what they want?" His voice was low and deliberate.

"Because Jack wanted the opposite," I whispered.

Jared stared at me, considering my words. "Jack wanted you safe. These things don't show mercy, Nina. They don't care that you're an innocent teenage girl."

I swallowed. "Eli said we were only dealing with humans for now. Let's concentrate on that."

Jared thought for a moment and relaxed a bit. "Okay. We'll do this your way. While we're still dealing with humans, you can stay at Andrews. The second Shax calls out even a fraction of one of his legions, you're coming with me. I don't want to hear a single word about it."

I nodded. "Fair enough." I pulled my arms around me, bracing myself. My curiosity outweighed my need to remain oblivious. "What are Legions?"

Jared grimaced, obviously wishing I hadn't asked. "Shax has thirty legions under his command. Don't ask me how many demons that is. You don't want to know."

I nodded again, swallowing the bile rising in my throat.

"Nina?" Jared asked, feeling my forehead.

"I don't feel well," I said, reaching for the door handle.

I ran to the grass, hearing both car doors shut simultaneously. When my feet touched the soil, Jared was beside me, pulling my hair away from my face. It didn't take long for the dry heaving to commence; I hadn't eaten anything since breakfast.

After my stomach relaxed and the gagging ceased, Jared lifted me into his arms and returned me to my seat.

"I'm taking you to the loft," he warned, putting the gear in drive.

I was too exhausted and sick to argue.

Jared carried me up the two flights of stairs and gently placed me on my side of the bed. I let my body melt into the mattress while I listened to the water run in the bathroom. Moments later a cool, folded wash cloth was laid it across my forehead.

"Déjà vu," I said.

"I wasn't considering your condition when I drug you out to see Eli, and I should have gotten you something to eat. I'm sorry."

"Quit apologizing. You didn't force me to drink too much last night. How are you feeling? Like me?"

"I'm not sick, just uncomfortable. I'll make you a deal. I'll quit apologizing if you quit worrying about me," he said, brushing my hair back from my face. I smiled but didn't make any promises. Jared kissed my cheek. "I'm going downstairs to get you some crackers and soda to settle your stomach. Try to rest."

"I'm really fine. You don't have to fuss," I said, pushing myself up against the pillows.

"I'm just trying to make you comfortable." He had a strange expression on his face, almost sullen.

"Your bed is a thousand times more comfy than my bed at Andrews, and even my bed at home. Neither of them smell like you."

Jared fidgeted before speaking. "So...why is it that you're so against staying here? Is it me?"

My eyebrows immediately pulled in, hurt that he would ever come to that conclusion. "No! I'm not against staying here. I love staying here. I just need to go back to Andrews."

Jared raised an eyebrow. "Why is that? I thought staying alive would be a good enough reason for you to want to stay here with me. You didn't mind when I needed to dress your hand every night."

"It's not about that. It's about being forced into hiding, it's about my friends, and it's about keeping some degree of normalcy in my life. I know you want me here where you know that I'm safe," I explained, resting my hand on his leg.

"Not just to keep you safe. I just want you here," he said, tenderly tracing my jaw line with his fingertip.

I smiled at his words, my jaw radiating with the heat from his touch. "We have plenty of time for that, right?"

Jared's eyes immediately clouded over and I finally understood the urgency. He wanted to spend every second of the time we had left together. I looked away from him; I had to have faith that we would make it through this. My eyes felt heavy and I turned onto my side, pressing my cheek into my pillow.

"I have faith in you, Jared. More than you have in yourself. I'm not afraid," I said, closing my eyes.

The door slammed and I jerked, looking around the room. It was morning.

"Can you close the door like a normal person?" Jared snapped.

"This is a terrible idea, Jared. Maybe the worst one you've had, yet," Claire complained. Small footsteps stomped up the stairs. "You have to talk him out of this, Nina. He won't listen to me. Not in the mood he's in."

"Stay out of it, Claire," Jared said from downstairs.

Claire made a face and then jumped from the railing, landing on her feet. "I can't stay out of it, because you keep making it my business!" she hissed.

I quickly dressed and met them downstairs. Jared was dressed in a buttoned-down shirt and slacks, holding a motorcycle helmet. He shoved it toward me without a word.

"What's this?" I asked, staring at the helmet.

"I think better on my bike," Jared said.

I looked up at him. "What's going on?"

His expression didn't change. "Are you coming or not?"

I looked at Claire and then to Jared. I pressed my lips together and then took the helmet from him. Claire sighed and stormed out.

I followed Jared outside and eyed the slick, black beauty parked on the curb. "What is that?"

Jared sighed. "It's a Vulcan."

"Weird. I thought it was a motorcycle." I smiled, but Jared didn't find humor in my words. I put up my hand and separated my fingers into a 'V'. "Live long

293

and...no?" I shook my head, seeing that Jared was in no mood for jokes.

I shoved the helmet on and fastened the chin strap. My father had a motorcycle and, although I'd never been brave enough to drive one, I was well-versed in being a passenger. Jared revved the engine and I climbed on behind him, glad that it was another fair weather day.

He raced down the street, taking various turns. It wasn't until we pulled onto the sidewalk in front of Sovereign Bank that I understood the reason behind Jared's mood. He lifted me off the seat as if I weighed nothing, placing me on my feet.

"Is there a reason you're not speaking to me?" I asked, shoving his helmet at him.

"It's not you that I'm angry with. It's Jack," he growled.

"Why?"

"Because he's making it impossible for me to keep you distanced from this. They need both of our signatures. The box is in a special area. We need the key, our signatures and our fingerprints to get in," he said, glaring at the door of the bank.

"They don't have my fingerprints."

"I've never given them mine, either, but they have it on file," Jared said, distant and cold.

"You tried to come here without me? Is that why Claire was at the loft?" I crossed my arms. "Let me guess, it just burns you that you needed my help after all?"

Jared's eyes jerked to mine. "Is that what you think?" I stood with my arms still tightly intertwined across my ribs. Jared shook his head at me and held out his arm. "After you."

We walked into the bank and a man in a stuffy and notably hideous light grey suit approached us.

"Mr. Stephens, this is Nina Grey," Jared said.

The man held out his lanky hand and I took it. "It's a pleasure to meet you Miss Grey. Right this way." He ushered us across the lobby to an elevator. Once inside, he used a small key to gain access to a lower floor that wasn't on the button display.

The elevator opened into a cavernous room with an enormous bronze vault. Mr. Stephens briskly walked ahead of us, taking his place behind a tall desk with a computer. As we approached, he was tapping the keyboard.

"Miss Grey, I'll need to see two forms of identification, please," Mr. Stephens said, looking up from the monitor.

I shot an irritated look at Jared, realizing I'd left my purse at the loft. Jared reached into his jacket pocket and pulled out my wallet. I snatched it from his hand and then put my driver's license and student ID on the small space in front of the computer monitor. Mr. Stephens' eyes darted twice between my face and each of the cards and then nodded. I put the cards back into my wallet as he repeated the process with Jared.

"Miss Grey, there is a red pad in front of you. I'll need you to press and hold your thumb there until you see a flash, and then I'll need you to do the same, Mr. Ryel," he said, watching us both follow his directions. "Now sign here and approve the date with the green button when you're finished."

I hastily signed and clicked the button with the pen, handing it to Jared, who signed his name under mine.

"You have the key?"

"We do," Jared said in a low voice.

"Right this way," Mr. Stephens said, the vault automatically opening.

The room was filled with various sized boxes, all plated in the same bronze color as the door. Our steps echoed against the marble floor.

Mr. Stephens turned to us, pointing to a shiny golden square on the wall with a small black button in the center. "Press this button to let me know you're finished. It was a pleasure doing business with you. Miss Grey...Mr. Ryel," he nodded, leaving us alone. The vault door sealed shut behind him, and Jared's eyes drifted to mine.

"Okay, he was creepy," I whispered, half-expecting Jared to offer comfort.

Without a word, he walked ahead, pulling the key from his pocket. I scanned the boxes on the wall and noticed that the numbers were out of order.

"This is going to take forever!" I complained. Jared still didn't respond, so I rolled my eyes and looked for box eight twenty-five.

Ten minutes later, Jared called to me. "Nina?"

I rushed toward his voice and found him in the back corner, looking at a bronze square the size of a shoebox. "Well, we should have looked back here, first. This is just like Jack, isn't it?"

Jared still didn't speak; he simply shoved the key in the lock and opened it, exposing a tan safe with a large black combination lock and handle on the front. He placed the safe on the floor at my feet as if it were a shoe box. I was sure it must have been at least fifty pounds, if not more, but Jared didn't brace himself against the weight. The muscles of his arms didn't even strain.

"The code is a combination," I said.

Jared nodded, pulling out the wrinkled piece of paper from his inside jacket pocket. He read the code aloud and then looked up at me.

"Does that make sense to you?" he asked, holding out the paper for me to take.

825 2R2TL223TRO5

"The eight twenty-five is the box number, and the rest is the key to the combination. But, combinations are just three numbers, one or two digits, right?" I didn't look up, and Jared didn't speak, so I wasn't sure if he agreed with me or not. "So we need to figure out which of these numbers are the numbers of the combination. And the others are...what? Red herrings?" I shook my head. "No. Jack didn't play games, these are all important."

I concentrated on the dial of the combination lock, looking at the numbers and thinking about turning the dial to each number in the different ways they appeared in the code. I burst into laughter and looked at Jared with excitement.

"I've got it!" I smiled.

Jared masked an emotion, which in turn curbed my enthusiasm. It seemed we were back to square one of our relationship.

"You've got what?" he asked, his voice flat.

"The letters, the R T L letters, they mean right turn and left turn. Turn it twice to the right, stopping on two. Turn left twice, stopping on twenty-two. Three turns right, stopping on five."

Jared shrugged. "Try it."

My first inclination was to wad up the paper, throw it at him, and tell him to try it. My temper cooled as reason crept into my mind. I wanted to see what was in the safe, and he would catch the paper, anyway, even if I did manage to aim well enough to hit him.

I kneeled down and twisted the combination. I followed the directions, but when I stopped on the last number, it didn't catch the way combination locks should.

My anger at Jared coupled with my frustration with the lock made my eyes water. When I tried to inconspicuously wipe my cheek with my shoulder, he sighed.

"Are you crying?" Jared asked.

I sniffed. "No. Leave me alone."

"Try it again," he said, indifferent.

I cleared the dial and paid close attention to each turn and stop, but when I reached the five, I passed by it once more. I had only passed it twice instead of three times. The lock caught and I gasped.

"It worked," I whispered, staring in shock at the safe.

Jared pulled me off the floor and kneeled down to open the safe. He slumped over and pinched the bridge of his nose. "Dammit, Jack. What have you done?"

Chapter Thirteen
Guilty

"What is it?" I asked, leaning over his shoulder.

He turned to face me holding a brown, leather-bound book. It surpassed antique in appearance; well-worn on the edges, with a strange branded seal on the front cover.

"It's the Naissance de Demoniac. The Bible of Hell," he said in a whisper.

"Why is the Bible of Hell in Jack's safe?" I said, stunned.

"Each of the patricians of the hierarchy of Hell has one. This one belongs to Shax," he said, eyeing the black brand in the center. "I don't want to know how Jack got his hands on it, but the fact that both of our names are on the account here tells me that he knew I would go against his wishes, and once I did, we would need this."

"Need it for what?"

"To barter for the only thing Jack would be willing to hand this over for: Your life." His expression was tortured, as if the guilt was crushing him.

"Jared...." I said, reaching out to him.

He pulled away and emotion disappeared from his face.

His rejection fueled my irritation. "Are we going to leave it here or take it with us?" I asked.

"It's staying here. I don't want this anywhere near you. Let's hope Shax is the one demon in Hell that won't hold a grudge."

I reached my hand out to the book. "What's in it?"

Jared jerked it away and kneeled down to thrust it back into the safe. He slammed the door shut, locked it and pushed the safe into the safety deposit box with a loud bang. He threw the paper bearing the code in with it and locked the door, shoving the key into his pocket.

Grabbing my arm, he rushed down the aisle toward the door. A short, low buzzer sounded when Jared pressed the button, and he fidgeted until Mr. Stephens answered.

"We're ready," Jared growled.

When the vault opened, I was pulled forward again. His long strides had me trotting alongside him to keep up. The elevator doors slid open, revealing Mr. Stephens' lanky frame. Jared stood rigid as the elevator climbed, and when the doors opened again he burst out, keeping a firm grip on my arm.

At his motorcycle, Jared wasted no time handing me his helmet. I fumbled with the chin strap, and with one movement he snapped his firmly across my neck and swung his leg over the seat, simultaneously pulling me on the seat behind him with one arm.

He wrapped my arms tightly against his chest. "Hang on," he demanded.

We raced down the road, weaving through traffic, blowing through red lights and stops signs until we reached his building.

My feet barely touched the steps, and once we were inside the loft, he released me. Without a word he climbed the stairs and disappeared beyond the railing. I stood at the bottom of the steps and listened as his footsteps stopped in the center of his bedroom. I waited, listening for a clue what he was up to, and then he walked into the bathroom. Seconds later I heard the shower turn on, so I waited.

Ten minutes passed. I sat on the couch, staring at the dark television screen. Nothing about Jared's behavior made sense, and I assumed he would explain it in his own time, as he always did.

After half an hour, I began to doubt my own reasoning. I climbed the stairs and made my way to the bathroom door, pressing my ear against the wood. The shower was still running so I tried to be patient, but after the fourth time of glancing at the clock I couldn't let him avoid me anymore.

I lifted my fist to knock on the door but held back, turning the knob instead. The steam bellowed out around me and dissipated, revealing Jared slumped on the floor. His knees up, his back against the tile wall, his head down; he looked hopeless.

I sat on my knees in front of him. "Jared?"

He looked up at me, his eyes a midnight blue. "The night I sat on that bench, Nina, I signed your death warrant."

"What are you talking about?" The sight of him frightened me. "Please tell me what's going on!"

"We had more company last night," Jared said, with the same tortured look from before.

"Who was it this time?" I asked.

"Gabriel," he choked out.

"You're not talking about your father, are you? You mean The Gabriel?"

"Yes...The Gabriel." Jared said, rolling his eyes at his own words. "He's one of the most vocal advocates for eliminating fallen Archs before they have a chance to procreate. My existence insults him," he said, an indignant look flitting across his face. "Gabriel's a messenger...he also serves as the angel of death."

I swallowed. "What did he say to you?"

Jared leaned his head back against the wall. "He said that he'll see me soon."

My mouth opened as I gasped. "What did you say to that?"

"That he always says that," he said with a contrived smile.

I thought for a moment. "Eli doesn't mind Hybrids. Maybe he can talk to Gabriel?"

Jared breathed out through his nose, trying to be patient with my suggestion. "Nina, no one but the Almighty tells Gabriel anything."

My shoulders sunk. "So now we're fighting demons and angels? How did we sink into this mess?"

"I shouldn't have sat on that bench."

I touched his face. "You sitting on that bench is the best thing that's ever happened to me."

Jared recoiled from my touch. "You don't know what you're saying. You have no idea what I've caused. Shax won't stop until he has the book, and even then there's a good chance he'll retaliate. Hell wants us dead and Heaven won't help us, Nina. I don't know what to do."

"This isn't your fault. If Jack hadn't taken the book, none of this would have happened."

Jared laughed once. "Including us."

I frowned. "Didn't we agree we had to get through the nightmare to get our miracle?"

Jared smiled infinitesimally. "Yeah." He parted his knees and pulled me to him, hugging me to his chest.

"What are we going to do about what we saw today?" I whispered into his neck.

"Right now we're just dealing with humans. We have to make sure it stays that way."Jared shifted and stood up, bringing me along with him. He brought me to the middle of his room and took in a deep cleansing breath, pressing his forehead against mine.

"I'm sorry I've been so...." He shook his head, clearly in full self-loathing mode.

I inched up on the balls of my feet and touched my lips to his. He cautiously kissed me back, and then sighed again.

"You're under a lot of pressure right now," I said, running my fingers through the sides of his hair.

"The last person I should be taking that out on is you. The way I treated you this morning is unforgivable," he frowned.

"It was unforgivable," I said. "But I forgive you."

"We know what they want; we're just not sure how far they'll go to get it. Claire and I can handle the humans. The hardest part will be waiting for their next move."

I nodded and wrapped my arms around him. "Can we start this day over?"

Jared kissed the top of my head. "Why don't we start with getting you to class? You have a test today, don't you?"

I shook my head. "I have a paper to turn in at ten thirty."

Jared released me, disappearing to the bathroom. He emerged in a light grey T-shirt and black soccer shorts, with his ratty running shoes. He looked dramatically different from the more professional attire he wore to the bank.

I stood by the door and waited while he pulled a hooded sweatshirt over his head.

"Get your stuff together and I'll take you to school. I need to finish setting up for next week, so I'll meet you later, okay? Claire will be close," he said, almost in passing.

"Jared?" My fists gripped the fabric of his shirt, holding him tightly to me just as he began to walk away. He looked down at me and tucked my hair behind my ear.

"Yes?" he smiled, the softness finally returning to his eyes.

"Can we just pretend it's a normal vacation and forget about everything here?"

"Absolutely," he said, hugging me to him.

At Brown, Jared seemed to be back to his old self, which helped the unease surrounding me. Bibles from Hell, demons with criminals-for-hire, antagonistic angels—trying to make sense of it all only created more questions.

I snapped out of my daze when I saw Jared's expression. "See you at one thirty?" I asked.

Ryan passed us as he walked into the classroom, nodding to Jared. I noticed Jared watch him for a long moment, and then he looked into my eyes.

"Nina," he said, a bit nervous. "I'm sorry about earlier. It won't happen again."

"You've already said that," I said, pulling up one corner of my mouth.

Guilt displayed across Jared's face. "I know. I just don't think that I was clear."

"You were clear. Consider it forgotten."

His face seemed to relax, then, and he kissed me again. "I'll have your things back in your room. I'll meet you there when you get back."

I nodded and watched him walk down the hall. Before he turned the corner, he looked back at me and smiled. I waved and extended the handle of my bag, continuing to my seat.

"I came by your room about nine last night. You weren't there," Ryan said in a hushed voice, tapping his pen on my desk.

"I was sick last night. I stayed with Jared."

Ryan's face turned concerned. "You could have stayed here. I could have kept an eye on you."

I smiled, knowing he was sincere. I appreciated his attempt to repair our friendship. The bitterness from before was absent from his face, and sitting beside him felt right again.

"I'm fine, now. It was just a bad hangover. I didn't feel well all day."

"Yeah, I didn't feel the greatest, either," he said, shaking his head.

"Yet you offer to take care of me? That would be a sad sight, both of us lying around, puking our guts out," I laughed, shaking my head.

Ryan chuckled, taking my paperwhen the professor instructed the class to pass them to the end of the row. During lecture, a small square of paper landed on my desk. I smiled and pulled open the folds.

It was in Ryan's chicken scratch.

Will you go to lunch w/me? (circle one)
1. I'll lose my appetite if I have to sit across from you.
2. I already have lunch plans w/my husband.
3. Of course, I need to practice my slogans.

I wanted to roll my eyes at his childish note, but when I saw the expectant grin on his face, I couldn't say no. I circled 'C', folded it, and tossed it back. Ryan always came up with the silliest things, and I adored that about him. Unbeknownst to him, he was a safe harbor from my other life, the one that had become full of shadows and uncertainty.

I watched him unfold the paper and read my answer. He didn't look up at me; he folded back the small torn page and stuffed it in his pocket, a wide grin across his face.

After class, Ryan and I walked to The Gate. He was his usual amusing self, and I laughed every step of the way. A few times I noticed he would hug me to him, nudge me, and a few times he led me by the small of my back through the doors he held open. I had the distinct feeling we were on a date, even though that wasn't the case. The only thing that bothered me was that Ryan's touch didn't bother me. It wasn't the electricity I felt with Jared, but it felt expected, almost comfortable.

I didn't realize when Ryan asked me to lunch that the entire study group was coming, but I smiled at the friends that filtered in and surrounded us. Over the next hour, we sat hunched over our paper plates of pizza that we balanced on our laps, the boys trying their best to keep their towering stacks of slices from falling to the floor. Ryan and Kim were inexplicably engaged in a contest to see who could take the bigger bite. Our ordinary moment was a welcomed break and I smiled at the laughter saturating the air around me, absorbing the sweet chaos I hadn't realized I'd missed.

Ryan walked out with me and smiled. "You're staying here, tonight, huh?"

"I am," I grinned.

He prolonged our walk with a leisurely pace. "Are you going to study group tonight?"

"Are you?"

He shrugged. "I need to. I was going to ask for your help."

"You need more help than I can give you, but I'll do my best."

Ryan kept his hands in his pockets, angling his face towards the sunshine. He looked truly happy, and I felt a warm tinge in my chest. I was hopeful that we could remain in each other's lives, after all.

"It's a beautiful day. I could grab a blanket and we could hang out on the greens," he said, purposefully bumping into me.

Jared waiting for me came to the forefront of my mind, but I didn't want to spoil Ryan's buoyant mood. We walked a few more steps as I decided how I should explain to him why I wouldn't. I had experienced normal, the normal I had been desperate for, and yet I found myself giddy at the thought of seeing Jared again.

"It's okay if you can't. I'll see you tonight." Ryan said, squinting as he looked to the sky again. I was thankful that his radiant grin hadn't faded.

I smiled in response and he pulled me into his side, kissing my forehead.

"Later, Nigh," he said before turning toward his dorm.

I pulled in a big, cleansing breath of air. I felt renewed and rejuvenated. Even with the frightening things that lurked in the shadows, something had made it all disappear. I quickened my pace, eager to see Jared again. He was the only thing that could make my afternoon better.

The door was cracked when I arrived, and I pushed it open to find Jared looking out of the opened slits of the window blind. A smile immediately streaked across my face.

"Did you have a good time?" he asked, not turning around.

I walked up behind him, wrapped my arms tightly around his middle and squeezed. He folded his arms over mine.

"As if you have to ask. You should have joined us," I said, closing my eyes and taking in his wonderful scent. When he didn't respond, I released my grip on him and walked around to see the perfection of his features. His eyes were bright and cloudless like the sky outside, but they seemed sad.

"I didn't want to interrupt."

I smoothed the barely noticeable wrinkle between his eyebrows. "It would have been better had you shown up."

He looked away for a moment. "You don't need me with you every second, Nina. You seem happier sometimes when I'm not."

"You think because you sensed that I was happy this afternoon it was because you weren't there? Don't be ridiculous," I scolded.

"I think it's good for you to spend time with your friends. I loved watching you laugh with them. You haven't laughed like that in a long time," he said as a small smile materialized on his face. It looked unnatural against the worried set of his eyes.

I hopped on one foot to pull off one boot and then repeated the process with the other. My feet felt as if I'd been trudging through a swamp from the uncharacteristically warm weather outside.

"Jared, what is it? Did I do something wrong?"

"No," he shifted. "Can we not talk about this?"

"I want to know," I said, keeping myself in his line of sight.

Jared sighed and cringed at the words he was about to speak. "I'm glad that you're happy you and Ryan are friends again. Believe me when I say that as long as it makes you happy, I want that for you. But I'm in love with you, Nina. I can't help but be a little worried knowing what I know."

"I don't feel that way about him, Jared. You have to sense that," I said, touching his arm.

"I know," he pinched the bridge of his nose and closed his eyes tight. "I don't think it will ever become easier to watch him make you laugh, though." He relaxed his face and tried another reassuring smile, but it fell short.

I raised one eyebrow. "Jared Ryel, are you jealous?"

Jared raked his hair with his fingers and let them slide to his neck, rubbing it nervously. "You asked, Nina. I told you the truth."

I narrowed my eyes. "You're jealous."

He shook his head no. "I'm...," he pressed his lips together and shook his head yes with a few quick jerks, "a little jealous, yeah."

"Oh."

Jared positioned himself in front of me and cupped my shoulders. "I don't want to lose you. Especially after the morning we had compared to your afternoon with him. It wouldn't take much more of that for you to question why you chose me."

My feelings had betrayed me. Jared's connection to me had become stronger, and he could feel my relief to be around Ryan. He sensed the contentment I'd experienced at lunch. My stomach reeled with guilt for indulging in such emotions. Nothing could compensate for the love and safety I felt with Jared.

My eyes fell to the floor when I realized how it must have hurt him. I was bathing in my temporary liberation from the madness that had exploded around me, and he must have thought I was glad to be free of him.

He could sense my feelings, but he didn't know the motivation behind them.

I continued to look down, picking at my nails as an excuse. "It was nice to have a little normal today, Jared. I do enjoy spending time with Ryan...with all of my friends," I looked to his face to gauge his reaction. "But do you honestly think I would trade being with you for one silly afternoon?"

Jared didn't speak for a long while. I watched as several emotions scrolled over his face; he seemed to appreciate what I was trying to say, but I could see the turmoil in his eyes.

Jared shook his head and tensed his arms around me. "When I'm with you, Nina...you're the only thing that gives me peace. It seems like I'm the opposite for you."

"It doesn't always seem like you're all that happy and peaceful with me," I pointed out.

Jared's face crumpled. "I don't want you to think that. I said this morning that I should have never sat on that bench...I didn't mean it. That was the beginning of the best moments of my life."

I pressed my cheek against his chest and relaxed into the heat that blazed through his T-shirt.

"Everything around us is crazy," I said. "Being with you is the only thing that makes sense. You were so worried about the way I felt when I was with Ryan that you obviously missed the way I felt when I realized I was going to see you soon."

That caught his attention. "When was that?"

"On my way here."

"So that was about me? It wasn't because you were with him?" Jared's eyebrows pushed up and then pressed together, looking somewhat disconcerted and touched at the same time. Realization hit him and the tension melted from his eyes. A few seconds later, a wide grin flashed across his face.

"That makes me happy," I said, matching his smile.

I leaned up on the balls of my feet and kissed him. He tightened his grip around me and my feet slowly came off the floor. My lips were slow and deliberate. I wrapped my arms around his neck, happy that it was my turn to demonstrate my feelings with a kiss.

After a moment, he returned me to the floor. I pressed my forehead against his chest and sighed at the silly misunderstanding. Jared was obviously more worried about my fate with Ryan than I thought.

I looked up at him. "If I'm happy when you're not around, it's because I'm thinking of you."

"I thought you said you couldn't say things the way I can?" he beamed.

"It's just the truth," I said in earnest. I was beyond pleased that he compared his always elegant articulation with my stunted, debilitated speech.

Jared kissed me again, this time scooping me into his arms and lowering me onto my bed. His lips traveled over to my ear, and then slowly made their way down my neck.

I slipped my hands under his shirt and ran my fingers up his back, marveling at the incredible muscles of his torso and his baby-soft skin. Jared pulled his shirt over his head with one hand and tossed it onto the floor. As he did so, his muscles stretched and flexed under his skin, and the butterflies in my stomach erupted into a frenzy.

"Is it hot in here?" I teased.

"Getting pretty toasty," he smiled, leaning down to kiss me again.

I pulled away from his mouth, sucking in a deep breath of air. His kisses were not the cautious kind. The electricity from his lips pulsated all the way to my toes. His mouth moved the way it did in his kitchen the night Claire made an unexpected a visit.

"It's definitely hot in here," I breathed. With that, I reached down and pulled my sweater over my head. Jared pressed his torso against me and I moaned as the feverish temperature of his skin burned against mine. I took another deep breath between Jared's amazing kisses and pressed my fingers into his chest, pushing him away. Jared leaned back, surprised.

"Is something wrong?" he asked, his breath quick and shallow.

My breathing matched his. "You've told me the truth. We love each other, and I'm sure it's been established that we're spending the rest of our lives together."

"Yeah?" he breathed, clearly impatient.

"Please don't stop," I begged, staring at his lips.

Jared's eyes radiated a sky blue as he pressed his mouth against mine. His fingers traced my collar bone, catching the strap of my bra and slowly sliding it off my shoulder. Every inch of me felt tingly, and the nerves under my skin screamed in anticipation. I pulled him against me as his lips touched the cusp of my bare shoulder. His mouth parted against my skin and his tongue tasted my flesh, giving rise to goose bumps when the air cooled the heat left behind. I wrapped my legs around him and my thighs automatically tensed with an overwhelming sensation.

Jared pulled in a ragged deep breath and firmly worked his mouth against mine. It had less caution than before, eager, a prelude to what we both knew was coming.

He leaned his cheek against mine to whisper in my ear. "Are you sure?"

I wrapped my arms around him, my body aching with a desire I had never felt before in my life. I was more than ready. "Don't stop," I whispered, the need for him becoming almost painful.

I felt his hand slowly and deliberately glide down my side, over my bare ribs, past my hips to settle on the button of my jeans. Effortlessly he pulled it open and the butterflies that had been in my stomach escaped to more southern regions. He steadied himself with one hand on the mattress as he slid his fingers down my hip, in between my skin and the denim. I let a sigh escape my lips, waiting for him to remove any clothing impudent enough to come between us.

"Well, we can just get it at the...." Beth said, pulling her key out of the door as she walked through with Chad. "OH!" she squealed as Jared pulled his shirt over me.

I cowered behind Jared's body, covering my face with one hand. "Hey, Beth," I said, still trying to catch my breath and peeking at her through my fingers.

"Hey! What's up? I mean...how are you guys? I'm... we're...." Beth looked at Chad, mortified.

"We were just leaving," Chad said, pulling Beth's arm with one hand and shutting the door with the other.

Jared playfully collapsed on top of me, and groaned with frustration.

I kept my hand over my eyes, too embarrassed and frustrated to speak.

Jared eased onto his side and pulled my hand from my face. "You're blushing."

"I know."

Jared kissed my hand. "I'm starting to think there is a reason for all the interruptions."

I grimaced. "What is that supposed to mean?"

He chuckled. "Here," he said, holding my sweater.

I pulled the thin lime green fabric from his hand and sat up.

"The only thing the constant interruptions mean is that one of us needs to change the locks," I grumbled, jerking my sweater over my head and buttoning my jeans. I smiled as an errant thought crossed my mind. "We have an entire week in Nicaragua."

"With Cynthia," Jared pointed out. "I'm there to work, you forget."

I felt the crease between my eyebrows deepen. "You promised it was going to be a real vacation."

Jared took my hand and held it between his, sitting higher on his elbow. "It will be. For you and Cynthia."

I rolled my eyes and reached for my phone, sitting up to through the numbers. I sent Beth a text message, giving her the all clear and to let her know I would be at study group later.

Jared slipped his shirt over his head and then pulled me onto his lap. My phone buzzed and I smiled at Beth's apology-ridden reply. I tried to send her back my unconditional forgiveness, but my attention was drawn to the nibbling at my neck.

"I thought you said it was a good thing we were interrupted," I smiled, tilting my head against his tickling breath.

Jared's head jerked up to face me. "I never said that. I said I was beginning to think there was a reason for it."

"By that you mean...?" I prompted.

"I was thinking about what Eli said. Surpassing a certain point of intimacy could hinder my ability to protect you."

"He also said they weren't sure because we're different."

"I'm not sure we should chance it," he frowned.

"What are you saying? That we can never...?"

He pressed his forehead to my cheek. "I'm saying that it might not be a good idea to test Eli's theory while we're in the middle of a war."

"War," I grumbled.

"Nina...."

I stood up and walked to the other side of the room, crossing my arms. "No, I get it. Abstinence it is, then. I don't want you upset that I'm not taking things seriously, again."

"Nina," he said, patient, "I'm not happy about it, either. But I have to put your safety first."

"You sound like a Planned Parenthood commercial," I snapped.

Jared burst into laughter. "That's not the safe I was referring to."

"I know," I said, narrowing my eyes at his infuriating amusement.

"I've never seen a woman so beautiful when angry... especially when you're angry about this. It's very endearing."

"I'm glad this is so entertaining for you," I said with thick sarcasm.

Jared shook his head, trying not to smile. He held out his arms. "Come here."

I stood there a moment, arms crossed, eying him suspiciously. The plan that he would change his mind from my protesting had backfired. He was maddeningly resolved.

I didn't want to give in, but his arms looked so inviting I couldn't help myself. Before I knew what I was doing, I curled up in his lap.

"You're making me crazy, you know. I don't know why you're being so stubborn," I grumbled.

Jared's shoulders shrugged around me. "I'm being cautious. Beth and Chad walked in on us."

I looked up at him with a dubious expression. "Since when do you care what other people think?"

"I didn't hear them. They caught me off guard," he said in a low voice.

I felt one corner of my mouth turn up. "Obviously."

"That's never happened before. I should have been able to hear them exit the elevator. I should have heard her pull out her keys. I heard nothing until they walked through the door. If that had been one of Shax's men, you would have been dead."

My grin faded quickly, and I struggled to push away any worry. "What does that mean?"

"That means Eli was right. When I'm with you like that, I can't focus. I'm not only fighting my feelings, Nina. When we're alone and things get intense, I struggle with your...desires as well. Can you imagine what you were feeling doubled? It's impossible to think about anything else."

"Doubled? I don't think that's possible." As soon as the words stumbled from my mouth, I felt my face flush with crimson. "I just meant that I wouldn't complain about it."

"I'm not complaining," he said, kissing my forehead. "I'm saying we're going to have to wait until I can afford to be distracted. If anything happened to you...I've already put you in danger from my selfishness, Nina. I have to keep my priorities straight."

I grudgingly nodded. By keeping me safe, he was safe. I couldn't argue with that.

Jared stood up, taking me with him. "Let's get out of here. Get some fresh air," he said.

I smiled. "We'd better."

Jared chuckled and held the door open for me. He had the quilt his father had bought me when I received my acceptance letter from Brown. It had the school colors in different scraps of fabric that somehow formed the Brown University crest.

"What is that for?" I asked, stopping in the doorway.

Jared shrugged, the blanket folded tightly under his arm. "I thought we could hang out in the sunshine for a few hours."

I fingered the blanket with sentiment. "I haven't used that blanket, yet. I've been sort of saving it as a keepsake."

Jared's mouth turned up into a half smile. "Why?"

I shrugged. "I don't know. Gabe bought it for me."

"Is that what he told you?" he asked, raising an eyebrow.

"Yes. Why?"

"I had my mother make it for you when you were accepted into Brown. It makes sense, I suppose. He couldn't tell you it was from me."

"This blanket was a gift from you?" I said, my eyes wide with disbelief. "Lillian made this?" I touched the blanket as if it were gold.

"Yes. So you don't have to keep it preserved. We can use it for the first time together," he smiled.

I knew the touched look on my face was pathetic, but I couldn't help it. His first present to me had been sitting in my closet and I had no idea. "Aw!"

Jared flinched. "Don't say 'aw'."

I couldn't change my ridiculous expression. "It's sweet, though."

"You say 'aw' when your boyfriends give you junk," he said, his face twisting into disgust.

The wheels of my mind thrust into high gear, and I scanned over everything Stacy had ever given me, trying to remember if I was ever insincerely appreciative. I came up with nothing.

"I've only had two boyfriends, and neither of them gave me junk."

Jared's face scrunched into a doubtful grimace. "You said 'aw' when Chuck Nagel gave you that crappy mixed tape."

My mouth fell open. "It was sweet! Do you know what lengths he must have gone to? Where would you get a cassette tape these days? And he wasn't my boyfriend," I argued, shuddering at the thought. "And I can't believe you remember that!"

Jared rolled his eyes. "I had to watch that simpleton pine for you for months. You may not have noticed him, but I did."

I pressed my lips together in an amused smile. "I love the blanket. Thank you."

"You're welcome," he beamed, kissing me.

What I thought would be a peck turned into a longer kiss, and with his free arm Jared pulled me to him, pressing his fingers into my back. I found myself hoping he would pull me back into the room.

He leaned back with a jerk, keeping his eyes closed. "We'd better go."

"Laying on a blanket with me in public isn't so tempting?"

"Right," he said, nodding once.

We walked to the Main Green hand in hand, weaving through the sea of students. On the few warm days during the school year, the campus lawn went from being desolate to bustling with movement in every direction.

The clusters moved in a distinct way. A game of touch football was in full swing, guitars were being lazily strummed under the shade trees, and the more studious coeds were hunched over a book. Blankets peppered the grass in vivid colors, creating a patchwork of chatter and laughter. It was a celebration without anything to celebrate, which made it more innocent, more enjoyable.

We settled on a spot by a tree near the center. With a flick of his wrists, the blanket under his arm unrolled and slowly fell to the ground, perfectly flat.

I shook my head in disbelief.

"What?" Jared asked, smiling cautiously. He sat on the edge of the blanket with his back against the trunk of a budding Tulip tree.

"Nothing," I said, standing in place while he clinched his jaw at my impertinence.

"You're going to have to quit doing that. I'd gotten used to knowing how you were feeling without the narrative, but now that I can ask you, when you don't tell me it nearly drives me insane."

I smiled at that. "Then we're even."

Jared rolled his eyes as I sat on the blanket. After a moment he smiled and pulled me to his chest. I leaned back against him to rest my elbows on his thighs, letting the sunshine drape over me. I remembered what Jared had said about feeling happy with him, so I let the bliss I was feeling swell into unbridled ecstasy. I opened all of my senses, the warmth of the sunshine above me, the heat of Jared's skin below me, his amazing scent floating around us, the laughter in the background, and the convivial atmosphere.

It didn't take long for Jared to react. "This is amazing, isn't it?"

I took the chance to make up for the rejection he'd felt earlier. "It's a beautiful day and I'm lying in the sunshine with the man I love. This is better than amazing. This is heaven," I smiled, closing my eyes to the sun.

Jared took a deep, satisfied breath and intertwined his fingers with mine.

We remained that way for a long time, listening to the laughter and babbling voices, their words blurring—to me, at least—around us. Jared jostled me a bit when his arm darted out and jerked. He had caught a football inches from my face.

"Whoa! Nice catch! You wanna play?" A winded male voice said from the foot of our blanket.

I lifted my hand to block out the sun to see the person standing above me. I didn't recognize him. He was tall and slender, had shoulder-length brown hair, and was wearing only a pair of long khaki cargo shorts and running shoes. His hand was outstretched for the football Jared had caught.

"He looks kinda busy to me, Zack."

I recognized the voice right away; it was Ryan. His chest heaved as he struggled for breath, and his bare chest revealed the scar from where he'd been stabbed. I felt a twinge in the pit of my stomach.

"I can't say I blame him," Zack said, smiling down at me.

"Did you throw that at me?" I asked Ryan, knowing I wouldn't be surprised either way. It was his idea to come to the Main Green with a blanket, and I turned him down only to come here with Jared.

"No! I can't believe you'd think that!" Ryan scoffed.

"That was me, sorry about that," Zack said to Jared, breathless, resting his hands on his hips. "Can we have our ball back?"

Jared showed no signs of surrendering the ball. "I think you owe her the apology, not me."

Ryan rolled his eyes and looked at me, and then to Jared. "It was an accident, Jared. Give him the ball."

Jared waited.

"You're right," Zack said. "I'm sorry. I should have been more careful."

"It's okay," I said, uncomfortable that Jared had forced him to apologize.

Zack eyed the football in Jared's hand. "Did you want to play? We're short one player."

"He's not going to play. He doesn't want Nina to see him trip over his feet," Ryan snorted.

Jared stood up, towering over me and both of the other boys. He looked past Zack to the other team. Tucker and Josh stood among them, waiting on the opposite side of their mini-field. Jared reared back his arm and launched the football across the greens like a missile. It soared through the various tree branches, straight into Josh's chest. Josh caught the ball, but it still made an audible thud that caused him to double over. He immediately stood up, although looking somewhat like a hunchback, trying to mask the fact that the wind had been knocked out of him.

Zack and Ryan had matching shocked expressions. I smiled at their surprise.

"I am busy. My feet have nothing to do with it," Jared said, reaching for my hand to pull me up to stand beside him. He leaned over to kiss my forehead.

Ryan reacted with disgust.

My heart fluttered in my chest at the testosterone in the air, and Jared looked down at me. "Unless you don't mind."

A wide smile spread across my face. "Absolutely not. Go get 'em tiger."

He grabbed each side of my face and planted a quick kiss on my lips. His eyes narrowed as he looked across the grass to the other team. "I assume we're skins."

Zack nodded and Jared pulled off his shirt, handing it to me. I was supposed to be good, but it was hard seeing him so animated, not to mention half-naked.

Jared pressed his cheek against mine. "You're going to have to tone that down or I'm going to get pummeled," he whispered in my ear.

I couldn't help but laugh. "Like it would hurt you."

He jogged out with Ryan and Zack, and the other team met them in the center of the grass.

I watched them over the next hour. The skins team quickly realized that with Jared they had the clear advantage. Zack assigned Jared the quarterback position, and I laughed and cheered as his team ran in one touchdown after another. Before long, they had drawn quite the crowd. A small group of girls were soon drowning out my feeble cheering each time Jared made a play.

Jared's face was exultant, and I wondered when the last time was that he was free to let loose. He'd always had to keep an eye on me from afar, and now that I was just yards away he had more time for himself. I realized that it was like that at night as well, and guilt swept over me for making him spend the night in his car instead of beside me in his warm bed.

Jared fired the ball in a perfect spiral, and Ryan caught it flawlessly for the winning touchdown. The crowd cheered, and Josh's team ambled around their side of the makeshift field, notably less enthusiastic.

Jared jogged over to me, glistening with sweat and grinning from ear to ear. He lifted me and then twirled me around, kissing me with boyish enthusiasm.

"You were amazing!" I squealed.

Jared lowered me to my feet. "Agh...I'm sorry honey, I'm all sweaty."

"I don't care!" I said, flinging my arms around his middle.

"You ready to go?" he asked. When I nodded, he cleared the crowd from our blanket.

As Jared shook off grass and folded, Ryan approached us. "Good game, Jared," he said, sounding only half-sincere.

I heard Jared mumble a thank you as he tried not to watch us converse.

"You were great!" I said, waiting as others agreed with me. "It's safe to say you're fully recovered." I held up my hand for a high-five and Ryan smacked it. His fingers intertwined in mine.

I instinctually pulled my hand back, tucking my hair behind my ear to avoid drawing any more attention to the situation.

Ryan smiled. "Thanks. I'll see you in a couple of hours, okay? You want me to swing by?"

"I'll meet you there. I have a few things to do, first." I said.

Ryan stared at me as if he was debating something, and then he leaned over to kiss my cheek, his lips soft against my skin. I gave him an awkward, polite smile and then he walked away. The excited chatter around us died down dramatically, and I felt everyone's eyes on me.

Jared glared at Ryan as he walked away. I met him in the middle of the dispersing crowd and took the blanket from his hands.

"Ready?" I asked, trying to sound unconcerned.

Jared's eyes hadn't left Ryan's back; he looked as if he wanted to punch a hole through it. "Yeah," he said through his teeth.

Jared took my hand and led me through the stragglers that still meandered around us. He stopped at the door of Andrews as he opened it for me. "Claire is close. I'm going to run home...get a shower. I'll catch up with you later."

I eyed him suspiciously. "You're sure you're going home?"

Jared smoothed his features and chuckled. "Yeah, why?"

"You're not going to go find Ryan or anything, are you?"

His jaw tensed. "No. But if Claire wasn't his...he gets under my skin."

I leaned in to kiss him. "I'll talk to him."

Jared nodded and gave me an anxious look. "You're staying at Andrews tonight?"

I fidgeted, trying to decide if my unwanted independence was really more important than Jared spending the night in his vehicle to watch me.

Jared's eyes were suddenly bright and hopeful. "Second thoughts?"

"No. I mean...I don't know," I said, unable to focus with the encouraged look on his face.

I couldn't deny that I would rather stay with him, and he was more than willing for me to change my mind. When I slept at Andrews, Jared was stuck outside in his SUV listening for trouble. I cringed at the thought. On the other hand, it was what he was used to, and by his own words he didn't mind.

Beth expected me home. When I stayed with Jared, she stayed with Chad, which is where everyone knew that was where she would rather be.

When my mind drifted to Ryan, I winced. I had already told him that staying with Jared was temporary. The thought of his reaction to my new living arrangements made my stomach twist with a sick feeling. I wasn't sure why I worried about Ryan's opinion so much. Something about hurting him just didn't feel right.

"Wow, you're all over the place," Jared said, visibly confused.

"Call me later?" I asked. It wasn't exactly a subtle evasive tactic, but it would serve its purpose.

Jared was resigned. "Of course."

"I'm looking forward to more games. I'm sure Josh will want a rematch." I smiled and leaned toward him, staring at his lips.

Jared wrapped his arms around me, smiling at the thought. "It was fun. I'm not sure about more games, though. I didn't mean to cause a scene."

"When you play like a professional football player, Jared, you're going to draw a crowd."

Jared shrugged. "I couldn't help myself. Every time I heard you cheering, I stepped it up a little more."

I raised a dubious eyebrow. "You could hear me over your groupies?"

Jared smiled, pecking me on the lips. "Besides the fact that I could feel how proud you were,"—he kissed me again—"I could hear your voice from the stands in a stadium...at the Super Bowl."

He kissed me again, but this time his lips parted and he caressed my tongue with his. I tasted the combination of sweet and salty on his mouth, and when he pulled back, I licked my lips before pressing them together.

"Please don't do that," he pleaded, staring at my lips.

"How do you expect us to live together if you can't handle me licking my lips?" I teased, watching him scan my face with the same hunger in his eyes from before.

"I'll find a way. I'll sleep on the floor if I have to."

"If you sleep on the floor, I'm sleeping on the floor with you. I want to wake up where you are."

Jared smiled. "I wish that were true."

My mouth fell open. "It is true! You think me staying here during the week means I don't want to stay with you at all?"

Jared grimaced, shaking his head. "No, I don't think that. I shouldn't have said that, that's not what I meant."

"What did you mean?" I said, bracing myself for what he might say.

"It's going to be hard getting used to the way things used to be, that's all."

"You meant more than that."

Jared looked straight into my eyes. "Let me move your things, then. I'll have you moved in by the time you finish up at the Rock."

I looked down at my feet. "I don't know, Jared. I need some more time to think."

The answer should have been simple. I wanted to be there, he wanted me there, and we loved each other. But normal was here. I wasn't ready to give that up, yet.

Jared smiled halfheartedly. "That's what I meant."

I narrowed my eyes, irritated that he had proved his point in that way. "That's not fair."

He leaned his forehead against mine. "I'd better go. I'll see you soon."

"Sooner than I'll see you," I grimaced.

"You could change that if you weren't so worried about what everyone else thinks," he said, trying to keep the disappointment from his eyes.

"I told you that isn't the case. Well, not entirely."

"I know. I understand," he said. He kissed my forehead again before he left me to walk to my room alone.

I felt wretched. We'd had a horrible morning, a heated afternoon, and then I'd ruined it with my stupid, selfish, stubborn theories on normal. There were other reasons, but I couldn't pin point what they were. I just wasn't ready.

I walked into my empty room and sighed. I had a few hours yet before study group. Both Jared and Ryan's sweat were on me, a scent mixed between Ryan's salty boy smell and Jared's salty angel smell. It only confused me more, so I made a bee line for the showers.

Under the steaming water, I couldn't help but think of Jared's shower. The water pressure was better, the smell was certainly better, and I didn't have to wear flip flops to walk around in it. I sighed again, knowing nothing would make me happier than to call Jared and give him the green light to move my things. I couldn't help but smile at the sound of his voice when I broke the news to him, and how I would feel walking into the loft, knowing I was home.

As I walked down the hallway in my robe, I tried to come up with more pros than cons for staying at Andrews. I focused on what my father would want; at first I reasoned that he would want me to stay, but then my thoughts drifted to the fact that Jack would want me to be where I was the safest. I was definitely safer in Jared's arms. Loft...I meant the loft.

I closed the door behind me and pulled off my robe. There was a knock on the door and I automatically tightened my towel around me, anticipating Jared's smiling face at the other side of the door.

When I pulled on the knob, Ryan stood before me, clean and dressed. He gave me a once-over as I stood in front of him shocked and still dripping.

"Well, hello," Ryan said, his eyebrows shooting up in surprise.

I slammed the door in his face.

I pulled on a pair of jeans and slipped on a random pink T-shirt before hearing a knock on the door again.

"Nina?" he said in a muffled voice.

"Just a minute!" I called, feeling the blood rush to my cheeks. I opened the door once again, "Sorry," I breathed. "I wasn't expecting you."

"I see that. Can I come in?"

"I needed to talk to you anyway," I said, stepping to the side.

"Uh-oh. Hubby's jealous?" he smiled, strolling past me with his hands in his pockets.

I closed the door behind him and picked up a brush, raking it through my hair. "This isn't about him, it's about me. You can't kiss me like that, especially with Jared right there. Did you honestly think that was okay?"

"No, I just wanted to do it."

I threw my brush onto my desk and glared at him. "But you can't just do it. It makes things more difficult."

"For Jared?"

"For us," I sighed. "It makes it more difficult for us to be friends."

"I said I wasn't going to fight with you about Jared anymore, I never said I wasn't going to fight for you."

"What?"

Ryan rolled his eyes and then smiled. "I love you."

I heard the words, but I was still processing what he'd said before. I shook my head. "What?"

Ryan took a few steps closer to me and cinched his hands around my hips. "You heard me. I'm not stupid; I can see what's going on with you and Jared. I also see the way you look at me. And don't give me that crap about how you care about me because we're friends, either. It's something else and you know it."

I felt my cheeks flush. "I know you're delusional."

Ryan shook his head. "No. I've waited. I've watched. Today I'm sure. For whatever reasons you're refusing to acknowledge it, but you know it's there, same as I do. The only reason we're not together right now is because you met Jared first. That's not a good enough reason for me to walk away."

My stomach felt sick. I hadn't prepared for this conversation, and the fact that my boyfriend was listening didn't help. Jared was waiting for me to deny it. As much as I wanted to scream at Ryan to get out, I also knew that I couldn't eject him for the truth. That...and I wanted to him to stay. I couldn't tell him he was wrong when we both knew he was right.

Ryan took a step closer and grabbed the crests of my hips gently with each hand, grasping them a bit tighter as he inched closer. He closed his eyes, and I pressed my lips together, praying he wouldn't try to kiss me. I wouldn't kiss him back, but I couldn't tell him no. Either way I would hurt him.

He leaned in for a moment, waiting patiently.

I breathed out from my nose, letting my chest cave in. Something kept me where I stood, so it was the most I could move. Tears glossed over my eyes and I felt them burn, unable to close them or look away.

Ryan released my hips and took a few steps back, sitting on Beth's bed. "Don't worry, Nigh. I'm not going to make you choose. I'll let you decide."

I couldn't look at him. I found a spot on the door and stared at it, a tear finally escaping down my cheek. In that moment it seemed fate had made the choice for me.

"Would you say something already?" he begged.

I thought my eyes might bore a hole into the door when I heard three consecutive knocks. I wiped my face quickly, terrified of who might be on the other side.

Ryan stood up and put his hand on the knob.

Chapter Fourteen
Five Days

"What have you two been doing in here?" Kim teased, walking through the door. She looked at me and made a face. "Have you been crying?" She glared at Ryan, then. "Are you being a jerk?"

"She's okay...I think," he said, staring at me with a blank expression.

"I'm fine," I said. I turned to the sink and splashed water over my reddened face. I twisted around to face them, drying my cheeks with a towel.

"You didn't," she said, turning to Ryan.

Ryan nodded and shrugged. "I had to tell her sometime."

Kim looked at me. "And?"

"Don't," I said, glowering at her. There would be hours of explaining, but it wouldn't be to Kim.

Kim's eyes widened with innocent surprise. "Don't what?"

"I'm not having this conversation right now."

"Nina...," Ryan began.

"Don't Nina me. You show up here, unannounced, and then...say all this stuff that I'm not prepared for. Dammit, Ryan! You're making this impossible!" I was so grateful for the anger that I didn't stop to think if my words were making sense.

"I didn't say anything you don't already know," he said, standing up.

I stomped over to the door and yanked it open. "I want both of you to leave."

Kim tried not to laugh at my temper tantrum, and Ryan shoved his hands in his pockets.

"I'll see you at study group," he murmured.

I slammed the door behind them and stood in place, trying to slow my pulse. Adrenaline pumped through me like I'd been in a physical altercation. I breathed in and out slowly and covered my face. That was it. Any chance we might have had to be friends was over.

My phone buzzed and I jumped. I hesitated before picking it up, and then peered at the lighted display.

It was Jared.

With each ring, I willed myself to answer it but couldn't. The only explanation was the truth, and the truth would devastate him. The phone buzzed again, and I pressed the button, knowing if I didn't answer he would end up outside my door. I wiped my face and tucked my hair behind my ear.

"Hello?" I waited for a moment and my heart pounded through the silence.

"Are you okay?" he finally asked, the pain evident in his voice.

I pressed my lips together and clinched my eyes shut, trying not to cry. "I'm ready."

There was a pause, and then Jared's strained voice came across the receiver. "You're ready for what?"

"I'm ready to move my stuff...I'm not going to study group, so I can help you. We can have my things moved by ten and we can go to bed and forget this ever happened. I won't talk to him, I won't go near him. I swear I won't." I tried to sound optimistic, but my voice broke over and over.

I heard a frustrated sigh. "Nina, you can't do that. He's your friend."

"Yes, I can. I will," I promised.

I waited for him to tell me that he didn't want a weak, faithless coward like me living with him, but he kept silent.

"You don't want me now, do you?" I asked, struggling to keep calm.

He sighed. "I want you. I'll always want you. I want you here because you want to be, not because you want to prove something...to me or to yourself. I don't want you to come here because you don't trust yourself there."

I dropped the phone, covering my face with my hands. Why would he want me after what I had done? It was pathetic at best, and at worst it was dangerously close to being unfaithful.

I sat on my bed and rested my head on the pillow, trying to cry quietly. I didn't want Jared to hear and feel worse than he already did. Ten minutes later I heard a knock at the door. When I didn't answer, it slowly opened. Jared stood at the door, looking as devastated as I felt.

"I love you," he said.

I sat up and wiped my face, trying to look him in the eyes. He walked over to me and pulled me to my feet, wrapping his arms around me.

"I want you to come home with me," he said against my hair.

I nodded. It was the only thing I was capable of.

We kept pace with one another in silence down the hall. Jared didn't reach for my hand; he simply walked beside me, opening the various doors for me as we walked to the Escalade. When he pulled away from the curb I struggled to keep the tears at bay.

Jared reached over and gently placed his hand on mine. "Don't cry," he whispered.

I shut my eyes, praying he wouldn't offer further comfort.

He drove to the loft and parked. Neither of us moved after he switched off the ignition.

"I can have Claire grab some of your things if you decide to stay," he said, looking ahead.

"Do you want me to stay?" I looked down at our hands, afraid of his answer.

Jared's eyes darted over to me. "Do you even have to ask?"

"You shouldn't want me. I'm a horrible person. You must be so angry."

"I'm not angry. You feel bad enough for both of us," he paused for a moment, and then continued. "This isn't your fault. It's not even his fault...I did this. You're supposed to be with him," he said, his voice breaking at the end.

"Don't I have a say in who I want? Don't I have a choice? I don't feel that I do. Even you act as if I don't. No matter what I do, I lose."

"You don't know that, Nina. I could just be in the way."

I shook my head, refusing to even consider that.

Jared gently pulled my chin to face him. "He said he wouldn't make you choose. But if you don't have a choice, I'm the one that loses. So I'm going to make you choose, Nina. Choose me. Please....choose me." He shook his head. "I can't live without you."

I held his face and kissed him tenderly, pulling back to look into his eyes. "I've already made my choice, Jared. I'll make it a thousand times if I have to."

Jared buried his face into my chest and I held him to me, knowing he was as close to despair as I was. He had promised to fight fate for me, but I could see he was terrified that the fight wasn't his at all—it was mine.

The next morning I felt marginally better. The fact that Jared's arms were around me made the world seem right again.

"How did you sleep?" he whispered.

I turned over and pressed my cheek into his chest. "Like a rock. I don't remember falling asleep. How about you?"

Jared shrugged. "All right, I guess. For me."

"Did you get more than an hour?"

"No, not really."

"You didn't sleep at all, did you?" I grimaced.

"I had a lot to think about," he justified.

When he noted my expression, he leaned down to kiss the top of my head and hugged me to him. "There are many things for me to think about right now."

"Like what?"

"How about you get in the shower, and I'll get us breakfast. Waffles sound good?

"Waffles sound great. Don't change the subject."

He chuckled. "I don't want to start out the morning rehashing the chaos. Let's just have a normal morning, okay? You have a test in a couple of hours and I'm just about ready for Little Corn. Once we get those out of the way, we can talk the whole thing to death to your heart's content."

I ignored his dig. "Little Corn. Mmmmm. Hammocks, sun, beach, ocean...that sounds even better than waffles."

I left the bed, pulling off his shirt on the way to the bathroom. I tossed the crumpled fabric into the hamper as I passed. Jared's footsteps stopped abruptly and I smiled as I heard him continue down the stairs with a loud, flustered sigh.

The next days passed quickly. Before I knew it, the tests were over, the papers were turned in, and school had been dismissed for Spring Break. I spent Friday night with Jared, but even in his warm arms I was too excited to sleep. Saturday was spent packing, and I teased Jared with the dozens of bikinis I'd bought for the trip.

Sunday finally arrived. I could barely contain my enthusiasm when I stepped out onto the tarmac. Cynthia had chartered a jet for our trip, as my father had always done. I had never understood before, but seeing the crates being wheeled in and loaded, I knew that flying commercially wouldn't be possible. I tried to remember earlier vacations, scanning my mind for similar memories of Jared or Gabe directing traffic and giving orders as I boarded the plane. There was none. My only memories were of the smiling faces of our flight attendants as I was led into the fuselage by the large hand of my father.

I followed Cynthia up the stairs and tried not to stare at Jared as he handed our luggage to a man wearing a blue jumpsuit. I wasn't sure how many people worked in the background when we left the country, but it seemed to be a full blown tactical operation. Even knowing the truth, the activity around the plane seemed like needless fuss.

Jared was all business. He seemed at ease giving orders and organizing the details of our flight, arrival and return. The men loading the plane worked fervently on each of his specific instructions, seeming to be afraid to make a mistake. When Jared spoke to one or a few, they listened with nervous obedience. He exuded control and leadership, and my heart raced in my chest.

Jared turned around once to look at me, and I waved. His mouth turned up into a warm smile before turning away from me with the no-nonsense expression he used with the crew.

I counted one large crate and three smaller crates. The luggage had been loaded, including an entire set belonging to Cynthia. My mother had never been one to pack light.

I tried to suppress my excitement when Jared finished and began to board the plane. He trotted up the stairs in a crisp white button down shirt and jeans and walked down the aisle, breezing right past me. Bex

My expression compressed into a disappointed frown. Jared was going to insist on just being my protector during this trip. My first inclination was to cross my arms and pout, but I restrained myself so I wouldn't have to listen to Cynthia lecture me on Jared's priorities.

Jared plopped down in the empty seat beside me and fastened his seat belt. He let out an exhausted sigh and leaned over to kiss me on the forehead.

"It's a lot more work when I'm by myself. I should have brought Bex," he chuckled.

I stared at him for a moment, concentrating on keeping my heart rate at a normal pace and my smile polite. I didn't want him privy to the fact that I was giddy about him being as much my boyfriend on this trip as protector.

"I'm impressed," I smiled.

"Is that what it was? I wondered why you were so keyed up. I thought you had developed a sudden phobia of flying."

I felt the blood rush to my face when the realization came why he had turned around and grinned at me from the tarmac. He could sense what I felt as I watched him.

I feigned insult. "I've never been afraid to fly."

Jared's expression turned dubious. "Impressed with what, exactly?"

I shrugged. "Just watching you give orders and how they reacted to you. I haven't seen that side of you. It was very...appealing."

"That's what impresses you? Interesting," Jared said, considering that for a moment.

"Oh, it's more than that. You impress me all the time," I said, scanning his face.

Jared leaned his head against the seat, staring into my eyes. He was clearly amused by the conversation. "Really? And here I thought I needed to work harder," he smiled, leaning toward me.

I leaned in for a kiss, but he took each piece of my seat belt and fastened it snuggly across my waist.

I smiled and sighed, gazing out the window at the various crew members on the run way. I could feel

Jared's warm breath on my neck; he was looking out the window over my shoulder. The exhilaration I always felt before a trip mixed with the elation of being virtually alone with Jared for five days made it almost impossible to sit still.

"Are you all right? Your heart is going to take off before the plane," Jared whispered into my ear.

"I'm just happy," I said, still looking out the window.

The pilot came over the intercom and spoke directly to my mother, telling her our position in line for takeoff, the expected flight time and the current weather in Nicaragua.

The plane pulled forward and we taxied to the runway. Jared grabbed my hand and interlaced his fingers with mine. He leaned his head against the seat and watched me with his light blue-grey irises, a content grin spanning across his face. I smiled and closed my eyes as the plane suddenly gained momentum. The fuselage shuddered and then transformed into a weightless, graceful vessel the second we left the ground.

Jared informed me that from the big island, there would be a water taxi that transports guests to Little Corn, but the small boat wouldn't be possible with the crates of expensive surveillance equipment. He'd contracted a larger water craft to take us over and arranged for a car to take us to Casa Iguana, where we would be staying.

"Just a head's up, you won't see me for several hours when we first get there. I'll be setting up a perimeter and situating the equipment. Cynthia's reserved three cabins. She has the grand casita..."

"Of course."

"...and you and I have deluxe casitas. They're not bad for little cabins nestled in the side of a cliff."

"A cliff? Where's the beach?"

Jared smiled his patient smile. "Close. Just a two minute walk. The cliff cabins are more private. There's nothing to worry about."

"My guardian angel is with me. What could I possibly be worried about?" I grinned, kissing the corner of his mouth.

He smiled at my words and continued. "It will take some time for me to get set up, so that should give you time to get unpacked and settled into your room."

"Three cabins seem wasteful to me. Why don't I get settled at your place while you set up?"

Jared shook his head, amused by my idea. "My place will be full of monitors and computer equipment. Not exactly a romantic setting."

"Aw," I lilted, my voice sickeningly sweet. "You're going to be romantic?"

He wrinkled his nose. "Don't say 'aw'."

I giggled and leaned my head on his shoulder, settling in for the rest of the flight.

We arrived on Corn Island in the early afternoon, and I began peeling layers. Two men, one shorter than I and the other as tall as Jared and twice as wide, met us just yards from the plane. Several other locals stood behind them, ready to work and a bit intimidated. I looked at Jared and couldn't fathom why they would regard him in such a way. I had seen him look far more menacing than he did now.

I quickly discerned that the two men standing in the front of the others were our drivers, and beyond them and the small workforce were their two waiting vehicles. A car that might have doubled as a taxi cab sat with open doors and a rusty, white moving truck waited for the crates.

I waited for Jared to demonstrate his fluent Spanish, but to my surprise he and the driver conversed in the only language I understood.

Once again Jared took charge, issuing orders and getting the crates and our things secured in the vehicles. I stood next to him this time, and I was more than pleased when he took my hand.

"We're ready, Mr. Ryel," the short man said with a thick Spanish accent and a discolored smile.

"The boat is waiting, correct?" Jared asked in a commanding, dispassionate tone he'd never used with me.

"Yes, yes. The boat crew will take you to the Little Island and has been given instruction. You will be quite satisfied, Mr. Ryel. You and the wife will have a happy time."

I felt the blood rush to my cheeks as the small man nodded to both of us with a grin so wide it made his eyes close. Jared squeezed my hand, pulled it up to his mouth and pressed his lips to my fingers, keeping my hand against his chest. His eyes turned a bit softer as he thanked the man and handed him several American bills.

When we went on holiday during my formative years, I loved to pretend. I felt I could be whoever I wanted when we left Providence, and of course Jack encouraged my fantasies. Mostly I was a princess; a few times I posed as a famous ice skater, and once I was even an up and coming young actress. With my father keeping drivers and assistants, it was easy to appear as someone important. Letting the locals think I was Mrs. Jared Ryel was by far the best role I'd ever played on vacation. I righted my posture; I was flattered by what was being assumed and wanted to portray my part to perfection.

Forty-five minutes after we left the wharf, our boat pulled next to another dock, and the fresh hands of the boat crew went into action. Instead of pacing back and forth, they walked down the sand-covered pier to a trail, continuing around a corner past the thick, lazily bent trunks of native palm trees.

We followed the same path the crew had taken to another set of aging vehicles. Jared informed me these were two of just a handful of automobiles on the island. That fact became known when I noticed some of the inhabitants straddling their bicycles and staring at our caravan with minor curiosity.

The morning had disappeared and evening quickly approached by the time I had settled into my room. At first glance, I was wary of what I would find inside, but once I climbed the steps of my whimsically painted bungalow, the inside was spacious and clean. Palm trees surrounded my temporary home, and I noticed Cynthia's casita peaking out of the trees to one side of me, and Jared's on the other.

I splashed my face with water and changed into the turquoise maxi dress I had bought a week before just for the trip. I tied the halter around my neck and chose a pair of sandals from my newly organized closet.

I plodded over the dirt trail to Cynthia's cabin and found her already on her spacious veranda reading one of the many books she'd packed. She wore a large brimmed hat and square shaped sunglasses, her legs stretched across an adjacent chair, properly crossed. Even in her remote casita, she remained a lady.

"Hello, Dear," she said, laying her book pages-down in her lap.

"Hi, Mom. How's your cabin?" I asked, taking a seat beside her.

She leaned toward me and smiled. "It's beautiful. And yours? What do you think about the island?"

"My room is great. I'm not sure about the island, yet, but I'm sure it's going to be... interesting. No cars, no jet skis, no phones, no Wi-Fi, collected rain for water...not exactly what I imagined when you said you wanted to vacation in the Caribbean."

"I'm sure you and Jared will find something entertaining to do. There's snorkeling, fishing, and so on. Take care not to burn," she said, returning to her book.

I took that as my cue to let her be. I strolled back to my cabin and decided to continue my walk, following a trail that led me to the beach in minutes. I gasped at the sight of it. The fishing boats on the horizon, the clear water and the Technicolor clouds were beginning to glow blues and yellows from the descending sun; it all would have been the perfect shot for a postcard.

"Incredible, isn't it?" Jared said from behind me, folding his arms around my waist.

I leaned my head against his chest and stared out onto the ocean. "I think it's the company more than anything," I said, relaxing into his arms.

He pressed his lips against the bare skin of my shoulder and I smiled at the warmth left behind. "You are absolutely beautiful."

I turned around and slipped my arms under his and tightened them around his middle. He was still in his crisp white shirt and jeans, but his sleeves were rolled up and he had changed into a pair of casual sandals.

"Why didn't you correct the driver when he called me your wife?"

He grinned. "I guess I just liked the sound of it so much I couldn't tell him he was wrong. Did it offend you?"

I shook my head. "Not at all. I've always liked to pretend on vacation."

Jared raised one eyebrow, amused. "Are you royalty this time or an award winning actress?"

"Neither," I laughed. "Apparently this trip I'm Mrs. Jared Ryel." The words rolled off my tongue like I had spoken a beautiful foreign language. It felt strange to say the words together, yet it was familiar somehow.

Jared's eyes brightened. "Well...pretend if you like. There's only so much longer you can do that."

I frowned. "Don't remind me. Only five days left and we haven't even started, yet."

"I didn't mean for the remainder of our trip, sweetheart. You can't pretend to be Mrs. Jared Ryel when you are Mrs. Jared Ryel."

"Oh," I said, processing his last sentence.

He looked down at me with the softness in his eyes that he reserved only for our sweetest moments. I took in a deep breath and let a broad grin spread across my face. As talented as I had become over the years at false impersonation during vacations, I couldn't pretend not to be overwhelmingly besotted by his sentiment.

"What do you say we walk down to the village?" Jared suggested. Sliding his hands down my arms, he took a few steps backward and pulled me along with him.

"I say yes," I chirped, still high from the euphoria I had felt just moments before.

At a leisurely pace, Jared and I walked hand in hand down a dirt road—it wasn't even a road, really, more like a double path that had been worn by bicycles, scooters, and the occasional vehicle.

We approached a fork in the path that bore a sign directing us to the nearby village.

It wasn't long before the small huts and aluminum buildings of the village came into view. There were clusters of locals at each one conversing and watching us walk past. Some were smiling at us and some were eyeing us indifferently before returning to their various conversations.

I didn't see a single tourist shop, although there were craftsmen selling various items.

We entered a hut that appeared to be a combined blacksmith and jewelry stand. Jared watched me look over the rings, necklaces and ear rings, some with shells, some with gems, although roughly cut and not one of them held with prongs or soldered. One ring in particular caught my eye. The band was silver, and at first glance there seemed to be tiny shells fastened to it in decoration, but when I looked more closely, I could see the two dozen or so minuscule gems appeared to be rough, uncut diamonds fastened to the ring with a tiny wire.

"You like that one?" Jared asked.

"It's very unique," I said, still staring at the indentations of the band.

The man held it closer for me to see. "This is real silver," he boasted proudly. "We hammer it...see here?" He pointed to the indentions in the band. "Polished by hand and hardened in the tumbler. The diamonds are hand-fastened with the wire. Ten gauge wire, see...?" He made a show of rotating the ring to show how secure the diamonds were. "Made right here," he beamed. "Very beautiful. You try on?"

Jared smiled patiently to the vendor and held out his hand. The man placed the ring into Jared's palm and he lifted my hand, sliding it on my left ring finger.

"It's a little big, but it fits," he approved, looking up at me from under his brow.

"It's beautiful...." I trailed off, eyeing it for a brief moment before taking it off. "Thank you. Have a nice day," I said, nodding.

I wasn't sure what expression was on my face, but Jared chuckled and shook his head. His arm hooked over my shoulder and he pulled me affectionately to him, kissing my cheek. He was remarkably different in this place than in Providence. The clouds in his eyes had been noticeably absent since we'd boarded the plane in Rhode Island, even while he dealt with organizing the crews and getting us and our things to each point in the journey. It was a nice change from the turmoil and angst he usually dealt with concerning our relationship. If it were even possible, I had fallen in love with him all over again.

We meandered to the end of the road, which consisted of four more brightly colored sheet-metal huts, two on each side. Some of the locals had congregated on one side playing their various instruments. The music was a lively blend of Latin and Caribbean, and it seemed to float in the air perfectly with the heat and humidity. Jared led me to where they were gathered and we watched them clap and play. They smiled at us as we approached, and then the man strumming the guitar gestured with a nod behind us. We turned to see an older couple from the other side of the street march to the beat until they were in the middle, and then they danced together.

Another couple joined them and then the guitar player cleared his throat to draw our attention. He nodded again to the street and spoke again, this time to Jared.

"You dance? Take your wife to dance!" he urged with a smile, gesturing again with a nod out to the other couples.

Jared smiled and looked down at me. "Would you like to dance?"

A sudden feeling of nervousness came over me, but the eager expression on Jared's face made it impossible to say no. He pulled me to the center of the dirt street and twirled me around to the beat of the music. We danced for several songs, laughing as the people around us clapped and cheered. Jared effortlessly spun me around the improvised dance floor. My dress fanned out with every turn and my sandals kicked dirt against my legs. Soon I was breathless, but Jared didn't seem to be remotely tired.

As the sun set the music slowed, and Jared pulled me close. My mind flashed back to the first time we danced at the pub, and I remembered what it felt like to be that close to him when he was all but a stranger to me. Just a couple of months later, we were in a foreign country, on a tiny island in the Caribbean Sea, dancing together in the middle of a dirt laden street among strangers, posing as husband and wife. Although both instances would be moments I would forever regard as precious, Corn Island was magical.

Once the song was over and the beat picked up again, Jared pulled away from me with an apologetic smile. "It's going to be dark soon and you've had a long day. We should head back."

I heaved a resigned sigh, pulling my mouth to the side in disappointment.

"We'll come back," he assured me, lacing his fingers in mine as we waved goodbye to our new friends.

"Yes! You come back! We'll play more music for you!" the guitarist said.

Jared walked over to him, shook his hand and pressed a twenty in his palm.

"Thank you. We had a wonderful time."

"No problem! You come back anytime!" The man smiled, even more animated than before.

We waved again before returning the way we came. Once we passed the fork in the road, Jared scooped me up in his arms.

"You don't have to carry me," I said.

"New shoes?" he asked.

"How did you know?"

"They're rubbing against your toes. You don't want to get blisters your first day here. We have a lot to see, yet."

I shook my head. "You sense my feelings and you can pin point exactly where I'm uncomfortable?"

"I've told you that already. But it is getting stronger."

"I know, but I still haven't gotten used to the feelings-thing. It's...." I wrinkled my nose trying to think of an adequate word.

"Weird," he finished for me. "You've mentioned that."

I kissed his cheek enthusiastically. "It's already been an incredible vacation, and we've only been here a few hours."

"I want this to be the best vacation you've had...so far."

"Mission accomplished," I whispered, running my nose along his cheek.

"I'm going to trip over something if you don't stay away from my ear," he chuckled.

"I doubt that," I said, lightly biting his earlobe. I'd only meant to tease him, but a quiet moan escaped with his sigh.

"Nina, please don't."

"Does someone have an ear fetish?" I taunted, grazing the edge of his ear with the tip of my tongue.

He abruptly set me on my feet. I pressed my lips together and tried not to burst out in laughter.

"Well. That's something you didn't tell me on our first date," I giggled.

Jared tried his best to be annoyed with my teasing, but his face twitched until a grin broke out across his face. "That's probably because I didn't know, then."

I grimaced, knowing he would add this to the list of rules. "One more thing I'm not allowed to do."

He scooped me up into his arms. "I'm already fighting with myself every second I'm alone with you, Nina. You...in this dress...as beautiful as you are. Not to mention feeling how happy you are with me, in this place."

He sat me on my feet again and I realized we were already at my casita. I looked over to see Cynthia note our return. Satisfied, she blew me a kiss and retreated inside for the night.

It was only then that I realized my mistake. "You're going to make me sleep alone, aren't you?"

Jared tenderly touched my face. "If I had my way, you'd sleep in my arms every night for the rest of our lives."

"Be careful what you wish for," I said, unable to hide my relief at his answer.

"I'm going to take a quick shower. I'll see you in ten minutes."

I had to work to keep the bounce out of my step as I pranced up the stairs into my room. Jared watched me until I turned to wave at him from the inside of my screen door and then he disappeared behind the foliage.

The next morning, I woke up with a thin sheath of perspiration covering my body. Jared was lying next to me but, much to my chagrin, his arms were nowhere near me.

"What's wrong?" he immediately asked, handing me a large glass of ice water.

"Why are you over there?" I pouted, taking a large gulp.

Jared smiled. "No air conditioning. I had to track down a fan," he said, nodding to the corner. A fan sat beside the futon, oscillating slowly.

I frowned. "You left?"

"I keep it cool in the loft to compensate for you having to sleep with an electric blanket. Even on the particularly cold nights, I kept the heater off until morning so you wouldn't overheat. With the heat and humidity here...," he trailed off, frowning.

"You were worried I'd get too hot," I finished for him, trying to say it in the most diplomatic way possible.

"You did get too hot, so I had to improvise...and you're still sweating," he said, clearly dismayed at the situation.

I looked around to see that all the windows were open. "You didn't sleep last night."

Jared sighed, frustrated. "You could have suffered heatstroke from sleeping beside your boyfriend and you're worried if I got my hour in."

"You need more than an hour," I pointed out.

"I slept."

"Good," I said, gulping more water down before setting the glass on the bedside table. "I'm going to take another shower, I'm sticky."

Jared nodded with a guilty expression and then retreated to his hut.

I showered and then dug through my pile of bathing suits. I held up a small piece of fabric, finding what I hoped would render him speechless. Interestingly enough, it was a one piece. It was blush pink, with a dramatic cut out so revealing it might as well have been a bikini. Small gold circles lined the missing piece and a single strap came over one shoulder, leaving the other bare. I stood brazenly at the screen door; hand on hip, waiting for Jared's reaction.

Jared kept his back turned. "Do I want to know what you're up to?" he asked, sensing my impish disposition.

"Why don't you turn around and find out for yourself?"

Jared slowly turned. The second I came into his line of sight his eyebrows shot upward and his mouth parted infinitesimally. He struggled with words for a moment, and I beamed with satisfaction.

"Feel like trying out the beach today?" I asked, smiling innocently.

"Wow," he said, his eyes scanning over every part of me.

"Jared?"

"Yeah?"

"Beach?"

"I'll get my trunks," he said, wheeling around to his cabin.

I giggled as I watched him swiftly vanish behind the palms and return within moments. He walked over to me in light blue board shorts and it was definitely my turn to be impressed.

We spent the morning playing in the water, diving through the waves and splashing each other. After an hour, Cynthia strolled out of the trees and parked in a lounge chair, laying her book beside her on the sand. She had brought her camera with her and snapped shots of the ocean, of the fishing boats, of me, and of Jared and me. Jared even coaxed the camera from her and snapped a picture of me and her.

Jared handed the camera back to my mother and pulled me off the sand, leading me out to the water.

"You can replace the one on your nightstand with the picture of us together," I said, thinking of the black and white photo beside his bed.

Jared smiled, splashing water my way. "I'll get another frame. I'm keeping the one I have of you."

I wrinkled my nose in disapproval. "Why? It's a surveillance shot, isn't it?"

Jared's eyes grew soft as he scanned my face. "I was taking some of the pictures that are now in Cynthia's safe. I snapped that one of you in the same afternoon...I wasn't sure why at the time." He grabbed my hand and pulled me through the water to him. "I took that the day I fell in love with you."

I felt a surprised grin spread across my face as my eyebrows rose. "You failed to mention that."

"You've never asked me to replace it before," he pointed out, pulling me out deeper into the water.

After another hour, Jared talked me into returning to the sand to borrow the bottle of sunscreen Cynthia had purposely left behind when returning to her cabin.

I sprawled across the lounge chair and reached for the sunscreen bottle. It instantly disappeared from my hands and Jared squirted a large white dollop into his palm.

"I don't want you to miss anything," he said, trying not to smile.

I leaned back, gesturing for Jared to proceed.

He began at the tops of my feet and massaged the lotion up one leg, and then the next. I'd had several massages before, but Jared's hands were significantly different as they pressed into and over my skin with the perfect amount of pressure. I bit my lip when he covered the skin bared by the cutout of my suit with his hands, his fingers occasionally slipping ever so slightly under my suit. He finally made his way to the rest of my body and kissed my lips when he was finished with my face.

"Front's finished," he prompted.

His head created a block to the sun that was directly above us, making his face black out and lining him in a brilliant halo of light.

I turned onto my stomach and Jared repeated the process again, this time beginning at my neck and working his way down. Once he finished with my ankles, I sat up and criss-crossed my legs. "Your turn."

"I don't need it."

"You're going to burn," I warned in a sing-song tone.

"I don't burn, Nina. Even if I did, it wouldn't hurt... the redness would go away in seconds."

I thought about that for a moment and then grimaced, looking out on the water. "Can you drown?"

He rolled his eyes, amused at my question. "I don't know. I've never tried."

"But if you did...wouldn't that kind of negate the whole you-only-die-when-I-do
theory?"

"I'm an excellent swimmer, Nina. And I seem to float easier than humans, so I'm going to say no."

"How on earth would you know that?"

He grinned proudly. "The Coast Guard guys hated me. I could out-tread any one of them by twice the time and come out of the water as fresh as when I'd gone in."

"When did you train with the Coast Guard?"

"When I was fourteen," he answered matter-of-factly.

I shook my head, thinking about him blowing away every trainee at every training facility he'd ever been at, making the recruits crazy with frustration at being outdone by a recent junior high graduate.

"They didn't object to a fourteen year old joining the ranks?"

"Gabe had more than enough connections to round out our training. Not to mention there are a few hal... Hybrids in the military and in the government. They're aware of our need to train, and that makes it easier."

I nodded as I contemplated Gabe's connections, wondering if the soldiers Jared trained beside suspected anything.

Jared rolled his eyes again, this time in real frustration. "Why do you ask me things if it bothers you to hear the answer?"

"It doesn't bother me. It's just...surreal," I said, watching the sun glistening off the lotion on my skin. "Don't you think about your life and who you are and just shake your head at how incredible it is?"

"The only thing that's surreal to me is that you're sitting here speaking to me, that I can reach over and touch you," he said, touching my face, "and that you love me. Sometimes I still can't believe it's real," he said, pulling me off the chair and carrying me to an empty hammock.

Once we were situated inside, swinging lazily back and forth in the shade, I kissed the skin just behind his earlobe. "I'm not the one who has friends mentioned in the Bible. I'm not the one who heals amazingly fast, that can do anything and do it better than everyone else in the world...I'm not the one that's practically perfection."

"You're my perfection. I'm all of those things for you," he said, shaking his head at what he considered a serious misapprehension. "I exist for you, Nina. This mortal being so precious to the Creator of the Universe that it allowed for my existence. Tell me that's not incredible."

Words failed me. The only thought I could form was to kiss him, which I did, over and over. When the kisses became more intense, he gently restrained me and I smiled to hide my frustration.

We spent our days at the beach lounging and swimming, our evenings dancing and laughing in the village, and our nights in my cabin. While Jared and I swam in the clear water on Wednesday afternoon, the clouds rolled in. The waves were soon the largest we'd seen since our arrival and when we had to dive into the water regularly to keep from getting pummeled, Jared carried me back to the shore.

When he stepped onto the sand, the rain began to fall. I looked up to the sky and smiled. The light, warm rain was a welcome change from the sharp, icy downpours of Providence. Jared and I raced to my casita—which he allowed me to win—and we parted ways to wash off the salt water in our respective huts.

Jared hadn't returned when I slipped on a pair of white canvas pants and a pink tank top, so I walked to his cabin in my bare feet. I could hear his music as I approached; I thought that he might still be in the shower, so I knocked on the wooden border of his screen door.

"Come in, Nina," Jared chuckled. "You don't have to knock."

Jared relaxed with his back against the wall, lying on top of his perfectly made bed. He was scribbling in a thick, brown book. The screen door whined as I stepped inside, and several small lights caught my attention. Monitors and electrical equipment lined one side of the room.

I raised an eyebrow. "You brought a stereo?"

He shrugged. "I take it everywhere."

"You couldn't have brought an mp3 player?"

"I can't have music blaring in my ears while I'm working."

I crawled in bed beside him and he pulled me closer. "I thought you could hear me over a stadium full of people?"

Jared wrinkled his nose. "Okay, you caught me. I don't like the way those things feel in my ears."

I bit my lip and leaned into his ear. "I thought you liked things touching your ears," I whispered, brushing my lips along the ridge of his ear. He pressed his lips firmly against mine and in the same second, I was flat on my back. His reaction seemed automatic, and I was suddenly hopeful that his weakness was my best chance at changing his mind about waiting.

Just as I settled against him, he pulled away.

"Your lips are different from a pair of hard plastic speakers. Now behave yourself," he smiled.

"Sorry," I said unconvincingly, nestling in the crook of his arm. Listening to the rain tap out a soft song on the roof, I closed my eyes and smiled. It was the first time I had ever been glad for it to rain on vacation.

The pages of the book Jared held were full of handwritten words. He had begun at the very top of the page, writing in tiny script, using every empty space available.

"What is that?"

"My journal. I thought I'd get caught up. I'm about a month behind. I didn't want to leave anything out," he said, kissing my hair.

"You keep a journal?" I asked in surprise.

"What else is there to do for the six or so hours I'm awake at night?" he smiled.

"Do you ever write about me?"

"Nina, most of this book is about you," he said, as if it should have been obvious.

I sat up. "Seriously?"

Jared grinned, amused at my reaction. "Yes. You don't believe me?"

"Of course I believe you...I just...." I looked down at the thick book, and noticed that there was only half an inch left to write in. "That's a lot of pages."

His features softened as he scanned my face. "I've been in love with you for a long time."

"You took notes on things I did?"

Jared laughed. "No. Well...sometimes. Mostly I wrote about the way the things you did made me feel, or plans I'd make, how I could get around Jack's wishes, how I would live without you, how I would make you happy. It got me through some rough nights."

"Is there anything bad?"

Jared grinned. "Would you like to read it?"

"No!" I cried. Embarrassed that he thought that was what I wanted, I felt the familiar fire burn under my cheeks. "It's your journal. It's none of my business."

"I don't keep secrets from you. You know that."

I looked down at my hands and picked at my fingernails. "It's private. I wouldn't want you to read my journal."

"You don't have a journal. I probably would have read it if you did," he said offhandedly.

I looked up at him, shocked.

"I'm kidding!" he chuckled. "There's nothing I've written that I'm ashamed of. I think it would be a good thing."

He closed the book and placed it in my lap. I was curious to know what the journal contained, but it felt wrong to read it, regardless of the permission I'd been given.

"Nina. It's okay. Read it," he said, taking a finger and flipping open the cover to the first page.

I spent the stormy afternoon with my head propped up against Jared, reading his private thoughts. Once I'd pored over the first few pages, the guilt slipped away and I found myself absorbed in every word. It was an odd sensation reading my memories from pages written at a time when I didn't know he existed.

I chewed on my thumbnail as I read through my life from the outside. Jared played with my hair; otherwise he sat motionless and silent. Half way through one of his more lengthy entries, I realized it was written the night he'd taken a bullet for me.

Claire extracted the bullet. I've been angry, but this time I was furious. I saw that bastard aim at her and I wanted to tear his head from his neck. I couldn't end his life fast enough. That's one less of Donovan's men that will go after her, but it doesn't make me feel better. I can't figure it out. I yelled at Claire to finish so I could go back to Nina. I couldn't even explain to Claire what I was so mad about, because I don't know myself. The need to get back to

362

her was ridiculous, because I knew that Dad was with her. She'd gone home by then, but I had to be near her and I was angry that I felt that way.

It's like I've been addicted to her, but I didn't know it until tonight. As if I didn't already have to be near her to protect her, now I just need to be near her. It's infuriating.

So now I'm here, watching her talk to Cynthia. I still don't know what my problem is. For the first time, I was afraid that I would fail. And not just fail — that I would fail **HER**. Claire accuses me of being a perfectionist, maybe that's what it is. Or maybe I just didn't want to let her down. But why the hell should I care? She wouldn't know either way. I don't want her to die, but that should be obvious, right? She dies, I die.

Maybe I just care. And that wouldn't be a bad thing – for me to care about her. She's a sweet girl. She's kind to others. She's intelligent. She's comically stubborn. She does that cute tuck-her-hair-behind-her-ear thing when she's nervous. She's beautiful...unbelievably beautiful. Anyone with any sense would care about her spending all this time around her, I guess it was inevitable. But this is more than just caring. If I wasn't bleeding all over myself I would have grabbed her and I don't know. What am I thinking? She can't know about me. Maybe that's what I'm angry about. Maybe I want her to know I'm protecting her. I think a part of me wants her to know. She's walking around her house and has no idea that I saved her life today. And that should bother me __WHY__? She shouldn't know. She shouldn't know that I protect her or that I care about her or that I think she's beautiful. Wouldn't that be ridiculous if I had feelings for her? Maybe that's what *it is. Maybe it's more than that. I think it's more than that.*

I think I'm in love with her.

I looked up from the pages of Jared's journal to see that he was watching for my reaction. I pulled myself up quickly and scrambled to kiss him. His mouth turned up into a smile as I pressed my lips against his, so I pulled back to look into his eyes. His expression was triumphant.

I took in a deep breath to speak, but Jared's face twisted into a frown. "Don't say 'aw'."

I shook my head quickly. "I wasn't! I was most certainly not going to say 'aw'. That was amazing, thank you."

"You should read the night of your sixteenth birthday. Or the day you graduated from high school. Or the night you went out with Philip Jacobs."

I wrinkled my nose. "I don't think I want to relive my sixteenth birthday. And I know I don't want to relive the three hours with Philip Jacobs. Yech."

Jared smiled. "I could read it to you. I'll leave out the parts you don't want to hear."

I leaned back against him, settling in to hear my life through Jared's eyes.

I was amazed at how much he loved me for so long, and how he fought the sometimes insufferable longing to speak to me. There were parts that were difficult to listen to, and parts that—if I had wanted to interrupt him, which I didn't—I wanted him to go back and read again.

He skipped to the entry he wrote the day of my high school graduation. He wrote how proud of me he was, and how beautiful I looked in my cap in gown. He spoke of how happy I felt and wondered where my college years would take us. Jared wrote a lot about being worried that once we gained distance between us and Gabe and Jack, that he would introduce himself.

His eyes clouded over as he read to me his fears that I would fall in love with someone at college, and the unknown reaction he would have watching me be with someone in that way. I learned how devastated he was at the prospect that I would never know how much he loved me, and how he dreaded the day I got married and had children with someone else. Jared's voice broke as he read the words.

When he turned to the entry on the day that my father died, tears welled up in my eyes as he described watching Gabe fade away. Jared's hand tangled in mine as he spoke of the moment he stood a few feet away from me, watching me sob on the bench. When the bus left the curb, the fight in him to stay away from me was gone. The tone of the pages changed significantly after that.

Jared smiled as he cited the joy he felt every time he ran into me, the expressions and feelings I would have, and how it felt the first time I'd said his name.

"Read what you wrote today," I smiled.

"I will later. The rain stopped," he said, shutting the book.

I looked up as I listened for the rain, but the only sounds were the intermittent dripping from the roof and the fronds of the palm trees, and the birds singing brightly just outside the cabin.

"What's the plan?" I asked, sitting up and stretching.

"Why don't you show Cynthia around the village?"

I smiled at his selfless suggestion, kissing him before I made my way to my mother's cabin. She was drying her chair with a towel, a book in her other hand.

"Hello, Dear," she said. Her sunglasses moved up with her smile.

"I was wondering if you'd like to go to the village with me. It's really eclectic. I think you'd like it," I said, resting my arms on the wooden railing.

Cynthia sat in her chair and opened her book. I knew the answer before she'd given it.

She smiled politely as she always did before she diplomatically turned down an offer. "I think I'll just relax here, Nina. Why don't you and Jared go exploring?"

"We've been almost everywhere," I shrugged. "Are you sure you don't want to go?"

Cynthia didn't look up from her book. "I'm sure. Go have fun."

I clambered up the railing and leaned far over it to land a kiss on her cheek. She simply grinned and continued reading.

Jared waited for me outside his cabin. "No dice, huh?" he said, opening his arms to hold me.

"She's never been this way. I don't understand it," I said, pressing my cheek against his chest.

"She just misses Jack," he reassured me. "What do you say we rent one of those cycles from the village and take a ride up the coast...try to find a village we haven't seen, yet?"

I smiled enthusiastically and nodded.

Jared took turn after turn, indiscriminate of dirt or paved roads. A few huts came into view, and moments later we were in more of a town than a village. It looked like it might have been one of the more populated places on the island. Jared parked the bike and we walked along a cobble stone road. The buildings were less primitive than in the village we frequented.

The sunlight began to wane when Jared squeezed my hand. "We should head back. It's going to be dark soon."

I sighed, sad that another perfect day was over. Just as we turned around, a bell began to ring. I turned my attention in the direction of the beautiful tolling and noticed a group of people standing together on a street corner a block away, staring in the same direction.

"Let's go," I said, tugging on Jared's hand. "I want to see what all the commotion is about."

Half way down the road, a bright white chapel came into view. I gasped as I watched a newly married couple walk slowly down the steep rock steps to the small crowd that cheered, chanted and sang. Soon, they all began singing the same, happy song.

The group followed the couple down the street, clapping and singing in unison. The bell tolled a few more times and, as if on purpose, rang one last time before the last of the joyful procession disappeared.

I looked back to the chapel, hypnotized by its beauty. It stood taller than the other buildings with its meager two stories.

"Do you want to look inside?" Jared asked, gently tugging on my hand.

"I don't think so. I just want to stay here."

"Okay," Jared murmured, obviously curious at my emotions.

I couldn't explain it, but I felt a bit weepy. It was as if the building had spoken to me, asking me to stay a bit longer. Jared wrapped his arms around my middle, touching his lips to my hair. I felt the sweat bead on the skin of my back that pressed against his chest.

"What is it?" Jared asked after several moments.

"It's just so beautiful," I said, my voice breaking.

"No...there's something...," he said, clearly confused by my mixed emotions.

I leaned my head back against his chest. "We're going to get married in this chapel."

"Right now?" Jared asked. I turned to scold him for mocking me, but he had a glimmer of hope in his eyes.

My grimace instantly turned into an appreciative grin. "I'd like to come back here...when the time comes."

Jared's irises glowed with the same azure blue as the sea. "I would travel to the ends of the earth to marry you."

He grazed the line of my jaw with his thumb and pressed his lips against mine. I melted against him.

Jared's grip tightened as he sensed my elation, and my imagination transformed my clothes into a white dress and Jared's khaki shorts and T-shirt into a suit.

"We'd better get back," he said, looking up at the dark clouds rolling in from the horizon.

I nodded, and he led me away from our chapel. I watched it as we walked down the block until it disappeared behind the palm trees.

Friday morning came too soon, and Jared became the authoritative personality he transformed into when organizing the progression of our things from one point to another. Once in the air, Jared put his hand on mine.

"You've been quiet all morning. You want to talk about it?" he asked.

"I wasn't ready. It went by too fast," I murmured, looking out the window of the plane.

"We'll take another vacation soon. The moment you finish your last final, I'll have Robert take us to the airport and we'll get on a plane...just you and me. Somewhere with air conditioning," Jared promised, kissing my hand.

I sighed and nodded. Even though the prospect was infinitely appealing, I couldn't rise above the morose I felt.

Jared lifted my chin to look into my eyes, appraising my mood for a moment. He seemed to deliberate something, finally pressing his lips together. "I was going to wait, but I think I should give this to you now," he said, standing up to dig inside his duffle bag.

He sat down beside me and placed a small woven box in my lap. "Open it," he smiled.

I pulled at the lid. Sitting on tiny shreds of palm fronds sat the ring I'd tried on in the village. A smile broke across my face.

"You liked that one, right?"

"I loved that one," I said.

The sadness from our departure intertwined with how touched I was that he somehow went back to the village and bought the ring without my knowledge. Tears formed rapidly in my eyes.

Jared lifted the ring and held it between his fingers. My eyes darted from his hand to his eyes; he seemed nervous about something.

"I have a request," Jared said, smiling sheepishly.

I raised an eyebrow. "A condition?"

"No, no...just a request. Once I put this on your finger, I'd like for you not to take it off until I replace it."

My pessimism all but forgotten, I didn't hesitate. "I promise."

"You don't have to promise, it's just a request," he said, heartened by my reaction.

"I promise," I insisted.

Jared beamed as he slipped the silver band on my left ring finger. It fit perfectly.

"You had it sized?" I asked.

His smile widened. "I wanted it to be perfect."

He laughed at me each time he caught me lifting up my fingers to stare at my left hand. I was still sad to say goodbye to our island, but knowing I had brought a piece of it with me made the trip home a bit easier.

Once we landed, I stepped onto the wet tarmac and pulled my coat tightly around me. The bitter cold wind swirled around me, and I was glad when Jared offered his warm arms as insulation.

"Why don't you go ahead with Cynthia? You don't have to stand in the cold with me," Jared said.

I began to argue, but I saw the clouds in his eyes. "What is it?"

Jared's brow fell inward, and I could see he didn't want to tell me. Beyond Jared's shoulder, a tall dark figure caught my eye.

"Samuel?" I asked.

"Yeah," he said through his teeth. "It must be pressing, or he wouldn't have come."

"I'll meet you in the car." I choked back the tears. We had barely touched the ground and already the harsh reality of our lives in Providence insisted we pay it attention like a spoiled child.

"If you love him, you'll have to accept that this is the way it will be," Cynthia said apathetically.

I watched Jared from inside the car. His expression was grave; it was not good news. He nodded once and walked towards the door Robert dutifully held open. Samuel was no longer there. He didn't disappear, he didn't fizzle out or his form blink from the space it occupied; he was there one moment, and then he wasn't.

Jared slid into the seat beside me. "You can go, now, Robert."

"Yes, sir," Robert said, nodding in the mirror and then looking ahead.

I watched Jared work to keep the tension from his face. I didn't need supernatural perception to know what he was feeling. He had the same look on his face when he pulled the book from the safe. He was afraid.

Chapter Fifteen
The Last Supper

Jared instructed Robert to drive us to the loft, and then take my things to Brown. I noticed that he didn't speak much on the way, but there was no point in trying to talk to him. Not with Cynthia sitting on the other side of me.

When the car slid in next to the curb, I kissed my mother goodbye. Jared led me up the stairs with one hand, his duffle bag and luggage in the other. He put a few things away, and then trotted down the stairs.

From the railing I watched him mill about. I wasn't sure when reality would finally set in. His perfection was something only seen on the silver screen or a magazine cover, and yet he casually walked around just below me. He was thumbing through his mail until he paused to look up at me.

"Everything all right?" he asked.

"I should be asking you that, shouldn't I?"

"No, not necessarily, why?" His face was too relaxed, his features intentionally at ease.

"You're not going to tell me what Samuel said?"

Jared smiled, seeming to ignore my question. "If you're worried about your things, I had Robert take them to be laundered. We'll pick them up later and swing by Andrews to get anything else you need."

"Jared...Samuel—,"

"Lillian wants to meet you," he interrupted.

"She wants to meet me? But...I've met her," I said, bewildered.

"Nina, you haven't been around her since you were a girl. She wants to be properly introduced to my girlfriend, not to mention Bex has been dying to meet you. You're sort of a celebrity at my house."

"A what?" I said dubiously.

Jared laughed. "Imagine your father guarding the king, and your big brother, whom you idolize, guards the princess. You've never met either of them....wouldn't you be excited to hear that a princess is coming to dinner? He's eleven. He's excited."

"Yes, Her Royal Highness, the Princess of Crime," I grumbled.

"Tomorrow night. She's making pot roast."

"Ugh! You're not fighting fair!"

His face contorted from playful to concern. "You don't want to meet my family?"

"Of course I want to meet your family. It's just that...being around your mother—who I desperately want to like me—and in the same room is Claire... who wishes me dead. It's going to be awkward."

Jared smiled warmly. "It will be fine. Claire will be on her best behavior, I assure you. My mother is less forgiving about Claire's attitude than I am. You don't have to worry about Lillian. She's always loved you."

I nodded, wondering what I had ever done to deserve her kind regard.

We set out on perfectly normal errands. He held me against his side while we waited for our developing film, and while walking the aisles of an antique store to find the perfect frame for our new picture. On the surface it appeared that our normal days on the island hadn't ended, but Jared had purposely made it seem that way. He was hiding something.

He seemed to have to work harder to hide his unease when he wrapped his arms around me for the night.

"You're not going to tell me, are you?"

I felt him tense. "I was hoping you'd let it go."

"Why? I thought truth was the cornerstone of our relationship? That was so important to you before Spring Break," I pointed out.

"It's still important," he sighed.

"Then what is it? Why are you keeping what Samuel said from me?"

He sighed. "Before we left you needed normal. While we were gone, we had normal. I want you to have that here, where we live. If that's what you want then you should have it. We could live like Jack and Cynthia. She didn't ask questions, he didn't divulge information, and they made it work." He pressed his lips against my hair. "Leave the details to me."

I considered that for a moment. "That's what you want?"

"I just want to make things easier on you."

I kissed his shoulder. "When do things get easier on you?"

"You're safe in my arms. I'm not outside Andrews in my SUV listening to you talk about some guy you're dating, wishing it was me. The fact that you know what I am and that we spend so much time together, my job is easier than it's ever been. This will end soon, sweetheart. I just need you to trust me."

"Sweet potato fries?" I whispered into the darkness.

Jared pulled me closer to him and kissed my neck. "Sweet potato fries."

Saturday morning I awoke to Jared standing beside the bed. He held out my buzzing cell phone and I took it, noting the unhappy look on his face.

"Hello?"

"Good mornin', sunshine. How was your trip?" Ryan said.

"It was perfect. How was yours?" I said, rubbing my eyes. I couldn't help but smile, Ryan's voice was strangely comforting.

"It was fun. You should have been there. You didn't forget about the Bio test next week, right?"

"You're calling about the test?" I asked, immediately suspicious of his ulterior motives.

"No. That's just my lame excuse. I'm calling because I haven't heard your voice in a week and I miss you."

I could tell by the tension in Jared's jaw that he could hear Ryan perfectly clear. I sighed, "Thank you. I didn't forget."

Ryan chuckled. "Good. I'll see you Sunday night?"

"What's Sunday night?"

"You're coming back to Brown Sunday night. Or did you change your mind and move in?"

I sighed. "No. I'm coming back, but not until late... I'm having dinner with Jared's family."

"Oh," Ryan dramatically exhaled, making a loud noise into the phone. "Okay, then. I'll see you Sunday night. Later, kiddo."

I hung up the phone and made a face.

"What?" Jared asked.

"He's being...weird. He's being really nice."

"I heard," Jared frowned, sitting beside me.

"He's up to something," I grimaced.

Jared watched me for a moment and smiled. "I can't say I blame him. I've been in his shoes, and I can testify that it's torture being in love with you and seeing you with someone else. I don't take a single second with you for granted."

I narrowed my eyes at him. "Okay, now you're up to something."

Jared laughed and shook his head. "Ryan is working overtime to win you over. I'm just doing everything I can to keep you. You can't begrudge me that."

"You don't have anything to worry about. I've always been yours."

Jared took my hand and kissed my new ring, content. "That's all I've ever wanted."

As the evening approached, I grew increasingly nervous. Jared reassured me that Lillian was very fond of me, but it didn't help to calm my fears.

As soon as we walked in, the wonderful smell from my childhood saturated my senses. Jared's mother greeted us in the foyer and I grinned how much Jared looked like her. She hadn't changed, only this time in a sage green apron. Her long blonde hair caressed her shoulders, and her wide, blue-grey eyes wrinkled with her broad smile. She approached me with open arms.

"Nina! Nina...it's so good to see you, honey. We've been waiting for you for a long time." She hugged me tightly, and then pulled Jared in to kiss his cheek. The plant Jared held caught her eye. "This is for me?"

"Nina insisted we bring you something. I tried to tell her the poor thing would be dead in a week."

"Oh! Jared...you're so silly," she giggled, lightly smacking his shoulder.

I could see why an angel would fall in love with her. She was a beacon of light, and love seemed to pour from her every word.

"Come in! Come and sit, dinner is almost ready," she said, carrying the small plant with her.

Bex's eyes brightened as he stood to greet me.

Jared gestured to the boy. "Nina, this is my little brother, Bex. Bex, this is Nina Grey."

"Nice to meet you," Bex said, surprising me with a hug. His blonde hair was nearly white, and his big, blue-grey eyes matched his freshly ironed shirt. Even at eleven, his muscles were already well on their way to his older brother's size, and he was almost as tall as I. Jared watched me with adoration as I hugged his brother. Bex pulled out my chair and I smiled appreciatively before taking a seat.

I caught Claire rolling her eyes and Jared cleared his throat.

"Claire? Could you help me in the kitchen for a moment?" I heard Lillian say in a slightly firmer tone than she'd had moments before. Claire stiffened and then quickly joined her mother in the kitchen.

I sat between Bex and Jared as Lillian and a significantly more affable Claire brought the dishes of food to the table.

I felt seven years old again as Lillian circled the table, scooping out side dishes to each plate. After Lillian served me, she leaned down and kissed my cheek.

"I have missed you, sweet Nina," she crooned.

When she retreated to the kitchen, Jared pulled me to him and kissed me affectionately. "I told you. She loves you."

I smiled, feeling a little overwhelmed at the outpouring of love. Apart from Jared, the only person that I felt loved me so deeply was my father. It felt as if I'd had a secret family my entire life that I wasn't aware of. They had all—but one— loved me from afar and watched me grow. Gabe's occasional proud paternal glances made more sense, now.

I looked over at Claire and wondered why they didn't regard me in the same way that she did. My family had kept Gabe away much of the time, and now I occupied the majority of Jared's and, until recently, Claire's time. I couldn't fathom the pure goodness in Lillian for loving me despite what my family had done to hers, but she sat across from me, watching me like I was a long lost daughter that had finally returned home.

I looked down to my food, the deluge of emotion threatening to bring tears to my eyes.

"Nina?" Jared whispered, gently touching my knee.

I nervously chuckled. "I'm fine," I said, looking up at him as if he'd given me the greatest gift in the world.

He was confused at first, but my overwhelming happiness prompted a wide grin across his face. We ate and laughed as Lillian and Bex told funny stories about Jared. Even Claire allowed herself to laugh a few times. Jared and I shared our time in Little Corn, and Lillian rushed over to look at my ring, kissing her son on the head in approval.

Lillian looked at her watch and smiled at her youngest son. "I'm afraid it's bedtime, Bex," she smiled.

Bex fought a look of disappointment and nodded, stopping to hug me before he retreated upstairs.

"Wow. What a great kid," I mused, watching him leave.

"He is. All of my children are exceptional," she said, watching Bex as he climbed towards the second floor.

"Yes they are," I enthusiastically agreed. We all shared a laugh at that, and Claire cleared the table of our pie plates.

Jared leaned over to kiss my forehead and Lillian beamed with joy. "You make my son the happiest I have ever seen him. You don't know how wonderful it is to see finally see him smile that way."

I looked at Jared, who scanned my face with deep adoration. He touched my cheek and I tore my eyes away from his affectionate stare, embarrassed by the intimate way we were behaving in front of his mother.

I struggled to deflect the three pairs of eyes staring at me. "So...how does that work? Bex having a bed time, I mean. Isn't he awake by midnight?" I asked.

Lillian's musical laugh filled the air. "He really has told you everything, hasn't he?" she said, winking at her son. "The younger they are, the more they sleep. They slept almost as much as other infants when they were newborns. By their first birthdays they no longer need naps, but they still slept nearly through the night. My goodness, you and I would have our work cut out for us if we had babies that only slept two hours a day!" She laughed again and I felt the blood rush to my cheeks.

Jared shifted in his seat. "We haven't really... discussed that, yet, Mom."

"Oh...I'm sorry," she smiled sweetly. "I'm notorious for wishful thinking."

I felt Jared's warm hand gently encompass mine. "Let's just take one thing at a time. We don't want to scare Nina off."

I smiled at Jared. "It would take a lot more than that to scare me off. As if that could ever happen."

Claire stiffened in her seat, and almost simultaneously Jared did the same. Lillian watched her son. She was waiting for something, but didn't seem afraid. Jared turned his head, listening intently. He reminded me of a wild animal sensing danger, on alert, ears scanning the air for movement. Suddenly Claire stood up and kicked her chair against the wall. I jumped at the noise, and then it was dark.

"Bex," Claire whispered.

Jared grabbed my arm and whisked me up the stairs, with Lillian just behind us. We rushed down a long hall, and then entered the last door to our right. He backed me into a corner and gently put his finger to my mouth. It was then that I realized something was very wrong.

I could barely make out Jared's form in the darkness as I saw him lean over Bex's bed and whisper in his brother's ear before disappearing silently from the room.

It was quiet for a long time, and I jerked when I felt Lillian's hand on my arm. My eyes darted back and forth between the door and Bex, who was lying as still as a statue in his bed.

Suddenly, a loud crash echoed from downstairs and I closed my eyes. My heart threatened to punch through my chest with every beat. Another crash came from a different area of the lower level and then two gun shots rang out. I heard scuffling, and then a male voice cried out, abruptly cutting off.

Bex remained in his bed. The room became clearer as my vision adjusted to the darkness. Unable to discern who was in the house, how many, and who was winning, I told myself that Jared was alive as long as I was.

In the next moment, a stranger dressed in black burst through the door. The bed lit up with the beam of a flashlight, and in the next moment the man charged, yanking Bex from his bed. I lunged forward when the man pressed cold metal against the boy's temple.

"NO!" I screamed. Lillian grabbed my shoulders and jerked me against her chest.

Claire appeared in the door way, targeting the intruder with her handgun. She jerked her head up once, breathing heavily. "It's been awhile, Crenshaw."

Even in the darkness I could see a smug smile on Claire's face, as if she had the upper hand. Crenshaw pressed the barrel of his gun against Bex's head.

"Claire?" Bex said, sounding as terrified as I felt.

"It's okay. Everything's going to be all right," Claire assured him.

"Just let me take her, and I'll go quietly. I'll leave the boy down the street," the man growled, true fear underlying his demand.

"You know that's not going to happen, Crenshaw. Just take your life and go," Claire said, looking down the sights of her firearm.

Crenshaw tightened his grip on his gun. "I can't go back without her—you know that. Hand Jack's kid over and I'll leave the boy," he rasped.

Bex's head tilted from the pressure of the barrel pressing harder against his skin.

Claire's expression was frightening, even in the darkness. "Do you know what I'll do to you if you leave a mark on him? Ease up on that barrel, Harry."

"I'll go!" I said, desperate to end the standoff.

Crenshaw's attention jerked toward me, then. "Nina?"

"I'll go with you. Just leave them alone," I blurted out, a tear burning down my cheek.

Claire sighed in exasperation, keeping her eyes on Crenshaw. "I'm not going to trade one brother for another, Nina. Stay where you are."

Crenshaw cocked his weapon and Claire took one hand off her gun and held it palm-out, toward Crenshaw. "Okay. Okay, Harry. I'm laying down my weapon. Easy does it," she said, moving slowly to lay her gun flat on the floor.

Lillian held her breath and her nails lightly dug into my shoulders.

"Your heart is racing, Crenshaw." Claire said, standing up slowly with both hands in front of her.

"So?"

"So they warned you about us, didn't they?"

"Yeah...so?" he sniffed.

"So, when they warned you about Jared and I, and they sent twelve of you to take on two of us, and you all came in here, guns blazing, knowing most of you wouldn't make it out...," she raised one eyebrow before getting to her point, "...did they warn you about Bex?"

Crenshaw's head darted around to each side of him, unclear what Claire meant, but he looked terrified.

A small hand slowly rose into the air. "Nice to meet you, Crenshaw. I'm Bex."

In the same second Bex's body blurred in movement, and Crenshaw's dark form bent unnaturally as he cried out. I heard bones snap as the intruder's gun fell to the floor. In the next moment, Bex stood over his assailant. In one swift jerk, Bex pulled Crenshaw's neck and a loud crack pierced the room.

Lillian exhaled as Bex stood over Crenshaw's broken body. Claire walked over to her slightly taller, younger brother and hugged him.

"I underestimated you," Claire said, smiling at the overgrown boy in her arms.

"And you said I wouldn't be able to act scared enough," he taunted.

"I admit it. I was totally wrong. There for a second I thought you were going to cry like a little girl. He didn't see you coming for a second," she said, pressing her fist against his jaw.

Bex playfully punched her in the arm and she ruffled his hair.

"Are you okay, Nina?" Bex asked, turning to me with a concerned expression.

I could only lift the corners of my mouth for a second, grateful when Claire motioned for him to follow her downstairs. I recoiled as I watched Bex step over Harry Crenshaw's body like he was a piece of furniture.

Jared came through the door moments later, and after surveying the scene, walked straight to me.

"You okay, sweetheart?" he asked, pulling me tightly into his arms.

I nodded. "Where were you?"

"I had to take care of a few things downstairs. Are you sure you're okay?" he asked again, holding my cheeks in his hands and scanning my face.

I nodded again, and then my knees buckled. Jared lifted me into his arms and carried me downstairs through the darkness.

"Should I get the lights?" Lillian asked.

"Not yet," Jared answered.

I heard Claire trot down the stairs and rummage through a cabinet in the bathroom. With a small flashlight in her mouth, she turned to look at her back in the mirror as she flattened a pink Hello Kitty Band-Aid against a deep cut on her shoulder.

Jared took me outside into the night air. "Take a few slow, deep breaths. You'll feel better soon."

I felt a blanket surround me as Lillian kissed my forehead. "I'm so sorry, Baby. We'll try again another night."

I couldn't reply. She acted as if she'd burned the pot roast, not that a group of men had broken into her home and assaulted her family to kidnap one of her guests.

"I need to take Nina home. Claire and Bex can clean up. Call me if there is a problem," Jared said.

Lillian nodded and kissed her son.

"I am so sorry," I choked, the guilt crushing me.

Jared's mother cupped my cheek in her palm and stared at me with deep sympathy. "This is not your fault, Nina. It's no one's fault. It is what it is." She shrugged with a small smile and I tried to return her expression, but I was afraid if I let the numbness escape me for even a moment, I would break down in front of everyone.

Once in the SUV, I asked Jared to take me to Andrews.

"Why?" he asked, genuinely surprised.

"I just want to go home," I said, looking out the window.

Jared traced my fingers with his. "I'd feel better if you stayed with me tonight."

"I think I...I just want to sleep in my bed," I said, stumbling over my words. I had made the decision before I got in the car.

"If that's what you want." He sighed in resignation, and then turned down a road that led to Brown.

Jared slowly pulled beside the curb and switched off the ignition. Without a word, I pulled on the handle to let myself out.

"Nina?" Jared called as he caught up with me. "I don't think this is a good idea, you're not in any condition to be alone."

"Beth is there," I said as I continued walking.

He stopped me just as I reached for the door. "You don't want to be around me tonight, do you?"

I didn't want to say it. I begged myself not to, but I had to say the words. The tears threatened to fall but I forced them back. "I can't do this, Jared."

He shifted uncomfortably from one foot to the other, shoving his hands in his pockets. "You can't do what?"

"We have to go back to the way things used to be," I said, trying to keep my voice from breaking.

I could see the clouds forming in his eyes. "What are you talking about?" he asked warily.

"I...." My lips pressed together, afraid to speak words that would be physically painful to say, "I don't think we should be together. I don't see how it can work."

Jared was instantly angry. "Don't do this. You think what happened at Lillian's tonight is your fault." He gripped my shoulders. "It's not your fault, Nina."

"They came to your mother's house, Jared. For me. If I wasn't there they wouldn't have come. Quit saying it's not my fault. It is."

Jared's eyes narrowed. "How do you think this is going to help, exactly? This isn't the first time someone has been in our home. It's not the first time Lillian has been in danger. She was married to Jack Grey's guardian angel, Nina. It sort of comes with the territory." He relaxed a bit and pulled me to him. "We can take care of ourselves, okay?"

I pulled away from him, surprised at his casual demeanor. "You brought me to meet your family and you expect me not to care what happens to them?"

Jared grabbed my hands and sighed in frustration. I could see that he was desperate for me to see reason. "Nothing happened to them. I realize you were scared, but it was completely under control. You don't think Bex has seen worse?"

"In his home? In his room? Your eleven year old brother broke a man's neck in his bedroom, Jared. That's not normal...."

"We're not normal!" He took a deep breath to keep his voice calm. "Bex just got home from training with the Marines, Nina. You're not saving him by doing this. It's who we are. What do you think you'll accomplish by pushing me away?" He shook his head and looked at me as if I'd lost my mind.

But I was resolved.

"It's going to keep them focused on me and out of your mother's house."

Jared's eyes darkened and a grave expression shadowed his face. "So we won't go back there. If that's what you want, we'll stay away from her house." Jared reached for me, but I moved away.

I shook my head. "They already know who you are. They know where your mother lives. They know about Bex, now. The damage is done, Jared."

"You're being unreasonable. This doesn't make any sense," he said in a strangled tone.

I looked to the sidewalk. "Don't make this harder —,"

"Than it already is? Original," he snapped. "How are we supposed to go about this, Nina? I'm no longer allowed to speak to you or touch you? You expect me to go through that again?"

His pointed question sent a new bolt of guilt shooting through me, and I struggled to keep his pain from overriding the guilt that I felt at Lillian's.

"I don't know what I expect, I just know this is too hard...it's too...I'm going to get your family killed! Don't you care about that?"

389

He rolled his eyes. "You're not going to get them killed. Three out of four of us are Half-breeds, Nina. Twelve well-trained humans couldn't make it out of our house alive, tonight. You don't have to do this!"

"Hybrids," I insisted. "Don't fight me on this. You know I'm right. They know they can get at one of us with the other."

"So we'll solve the problem, not run from it. I can't believe you're saying this," he seethed. "You of all people, who stood in the freezing rain for fifteen minutes because you didn't want to wait a few more days for me to appease your mother! Who sliced open your hand and nearly broke your arm because you had to talk to me! Two days ago we decided where our wedding will be, Nina! You're just going to walk away from everything we've been fighting for?"

I couldn't argue, so I simply nodded my head.

Jared grabbed my shoulders. "I don't believe you."

"You said I needed normal." I hesitated; my next words would cut him. "I can't have a normal life with you."

Jared's eyes turned a midnight blue. "Don't lie to me, Nina. You want out because you're afraid something will happen to my family if we stay together. I'm telling you, nothing's going to happen. I'm asking you to trust me."

I reached my hand up to touch his cheek; his jaws tensed under his skin. "Something will happen. I don't know what else to do, Jared. We both have to have some sort of a life."

"I can't have a life without you. I don't want a life without you." He swallowed hard. His face was locked in an agonizing expression.

I pressed my lips together, determined to make him believe the lie. "This isn't how I want to live. The fear, the guilt, the looking over my shoulder. We can't even be intimate."

Jared took my hand and pressed his lips against my knuckles, closing his eyes tight. "Please...please don't do this. I can't go back to that."

I almost gave in. I wanted to, but I stayed focused on the guilt I felt as I told Lillian goodbye. "You have to go." I placed the loft key in his palm.

"Nina...," he choked, looking down at his hand as if I had placed a hot coal there.

I reached down to pull his ring from my finger and he grabbed both of my hands. His face crumpled as if he had taken all he could stand. "Don't break your promise."

I relaxed my hands down to my sides. He was right, I had promised.

Jared pulled me into him by my shoulders and kissed me deeply—and I let him. I returned his kiss with the same sadness and fear. He held me so tightly I found it hard to breathe, but I didn't care. I let him hold me and kiss me however he wanted. It would be our last night together.

He abruptly pulled back, just a few inches, but kept me tightly in his arms. "I'll do what I have to do, Nina. If you want to go away, we'll go. If you need intimacy, I'll make love to you. I'll give you whatever you want. I'll give up everything I have. I'll give up my family. We can get in the car right now and just drive— I won't even look back. Just don't ask me to do this. I can't do it. I can't...," he choked.

I pulled away from his grip and opened the door. Jared pulled me back into his arms and kissed me again. Once I felt the tears streak down my cheeks I pushed him away, but he kept me against him. I finally had to shove him again and again, until he finally let go so that I could get through the door.

The steps to my room were endless. I stayed focused on my mission, refusing to fall apart. Jared had said it himself that he was willing to give up everything for me, including his family...and I couldn't let him do that. I couldn't let the Ryels get hurt because of me, whether it was physically or from losing Jared. I couldn't look Jared in the eye if he lost another person in his family because of the mistakes of my father.

I wiped my face and tucked my hair behind my ears before I opened the door. Beth sat at her computer.

"And she's home!" Beth said excitedly, spinning around in her desk chair. Her tone quickly changed when she saw my face. "Oh my God, Nina! What's wrong?"

"Jared and I are over," I murmured, changing into my pajamas. I wanted to sleep. It was the only thing that would alleviate the wrenching pain in my ribs.

"Didn't you meet his mother tonight? What happened?"

"All hell broke loose," I replied, scrubbing my face in the sink.

"Ugh! Why can't Hell stay where it's at? Why does it always have to break loose?" she whined.

I tried to smile at her, but my mouth wouldn't cooperate. I couldn't tell her the truth and I didn't want to lie. "It just wasn't working."

"What are you talking about? You've been talking about forever with this guy."

I looked up at the vent in the ceiling and then back to Beth. "It's the only way I know how to save him."

Beth grew quiet. "Save him from what?"

"Me."

Chapter Sixteen
The Arrangement

"Just keep walking," Beth said, coaxing me into class.

Jared stood against the wall beside the door. He didn't speak or approach me; he only watched as Beth led me in. My chest ached at the exhausted look in his eyes. He hadn't slept.

Day after day, Jared continued to wait at the doorway of any place necessary for me to enter. By the end of the week I would feel a sick feeling in my stomach anytime I was coming or going. Sometimes he watched me walk past, sometimes he kept his eyes to the ground, but he was always there.

The second week was more difficult than the first. Jared still waited for me in random places on campus, and my friends began to ask questions. Ryan guessed there was trouble and proceeded to grill me about the details. I was glad that he noticed it was too painful to discuss, and let me suffer in silence.

Jared's eyes darkened from midnight blue to black each time he saw Ryan walking happily beside me. It was unfair to let his worst fear play out in front of him, and I regretted not explaining to him the night I ended things that he would never have to suffer through that. I couldn't be with someone else knowing that I could never truly love them the way I should, least of all Ryan. He deserved someone's whole heart, and I had left mine with Jared.

Ryan knocked on my door every day, several times a day to visit or walk me to class, and I welcomed the company. It was easier to function when I was around him; he became my main distraction from all things Jared. Any obligation I felt for him had disappeared. As more time passed, I realized it wasn't just him; I didn't feel anything around anyone. I concentrated so hard on keeping Jared from sensing my grief that I felt numb most of the time.

By the second week of April, I had learned to keep my emotions in check. Kim, Beth and I passed Jared on our way into the Ratty and as usual, but I couldn't get quite past him without my eyes involuntarily glancing in his direction. When I did so, his eyes caught mine and for the first time in a month, he reached out and firmly pulled my arm, bringing me just inches from his face.

Beth and Kim stood a few feet away. They didn't protest, but they didn't leave me alone. I assumed they thought they might get an insight on the strange situation with Jared If they stuck around to eavesdrop.

I stood in front of him, obstinately silent.

Jared scanned my face in confusion. He didn't speak so I took a step toward the door. He pulled me back.

His sweet scent floated around me and my chest tightened. Feeling something other than hollow sent a wave of panic over me and I lashed out at him. "What do you want, Jared?"

He winced at my acerbic tone. "I've been patient. I've given you space. It's time we talked."

I pulled my coat from his grip. "You haven't given me space! You're everywhere."

"I thought maybe you'd break down and talk to me. This has to stop, Nina," he said, working to stay calm.

"You're right. This has to stop. You can do your job without being in my life. You've done it before."

Jared pulled up my hand, viewing his ring still firmly in place. "If you don't care about me, then why are you so adamant in keeping your promise?"

"It's still a promise...no matter who it's to," I said, pulling my hand away. My wrist ached at the remaining warmth from his grip.

"That ring will be slightly inconvenient when you get married one of these days, don't you think?"

"I can take it off if you'd like," I shrugged.

Jared's shoulders relaxed and the exhaustion set in. "Don't act like you're not hurting over this."

"I...," I should have lied to him and told him I was fine, but I couldn't. The grief in his eyes was unbearable, so I retreated to the Ratty.

Jared's hand shot out and grabbed the sleeve of my coat again, but this time I turned and jerked my arm down and away, and then yanked the door open. Beth and Kim quickly followed.

I sat between Ryan and Tucker, quietly picking at my food.

"Nina, you don't eat much anymore," Ryan said. "You look like you've lost some weight. I'm starting to worry about you."

"I'm fine," I mumbled.

He rolled his eyes and threw his French fry to his plate. "I know you're fine. You've been fine for a month."

"I'm fine!" All eyes in the room seemed to dart in my direction, looking for the source of the commotion. I stood and walked out, leaving my tray on the table.

I stormed past Jared and walked straight to my dorm, deciding to skip my afternoon class. Concentrating so hard on being void of any emotion took up so much of my energy that I tended to take naps more often than not. I rolled into a ball under my blanket and cleared my mind. Before long, I drifted off.

I awoke to a knock at the door. It was dark; I had been asleep for hours. My muscles felt heavy and congealed, so I waited for Beth to answer.

"Hey, what's up?" she asked the visitor in a hushed voice.

"Is Nina here?" Ryan asked, peering around her.

"She's sleeping," Beth whispered.

"No, I'm up. Come in, Ryan," I said.

Ryan stepped across the room, and I bounced when he plopped onto my bed. "You need to pull yourself together."

"Shut up, Ryan," I said, wiping the inevitably smeared mascara from my eyes.

He pressed his thumb gently under my eye to fix a place that I missed. "We're going out. I want you to come with us."

I shook my head. "No thank you. I don't...."

"I know you don't want to, Nina. You never want to do anything. But you need to," he said, flattening the parts of my hair that were out of place. "I know things suck right now. I know you're miserable, but maybe if he thinks you're happy he'll back off."

I looked up at him. "What?"

"I just meant that he's probably hanging around because he's worried about you. You look so unhappy. If he thought you were okay without him... maybe he'd let you live your life."

I grabbed his shoulders and pulled him tightly to me, and then scrambled across the room to pull on my jacket.

"Walk with me," I said, holding the door open.

He raised an eyebrow and stood up reluctantly. "Are you okay?"

"I'm perfect, let's go," I said, hurrying him out the door.

I pulled him along by his hand, dragging him to the parking lot. When we got to my car, Ryan paused. "We're going somewhere?"

"Just get in."

He didn't move. "You're weirding me out, Nigh."

"Please?"

"Will you tell me where we're going, first?"

"Some place we can talk. Just...trust me," I said, aware that I seemed completely insane.

"Nina, I trust you. I just think you're not yourself these days."

"If you trusted me, you would be in the car by now." I slid into the driver's seat and waited. After a few moments, Ryan opened the door and sat beside me. I smiled at him and touched his hand. "Thank you."

Ryan offered a half smile and squeezed my hand, holding it tightly the entire trip to my parents' home. When we pulled into the drive, he let go.

"Whoa," he said under his breath.

I turned off the ignition and searched each window for any sign of Cynthia, but the house was dark. Ryan followed me up the stairs to my father's office, and I closed the door behind him. He looked around, clearly nervous.

"Can we talk, now?" he asked. When I nodded, he let out a loud, frustrated sigh. "What the hell's going on with you, Nina? I'm serious...you're starting to worry me. I wish you would let me help you."

I closed my eyes in relief and whispered as quietly as I could. "There is something you can do."

Ryan leaned in, keeping his voice low like mine, "Just name it."

I kept my eyes closed, cringing at my coming request. "It's really...really selfish. It's horrible. It's the worst thing I could ask of you, but I think it's the only thing that will work. It's the only way he'll move on." I peeked up at him, already fearful of his response.

"This is about Jared?" he said.

I nodded.

"Okay, let's hear it."

"I...." Ryan's hopeful expression made me hesitate. I wasn't sure I could go through with it, even if he agreed.

"Nigh, don't be a pain in the ass. Just say it," he said, staring me down.

"I need you to date me," I breathed, barely above a whisper.

Ryan's face instantly compressed. "What? Why are you whispering?"

I ignored his last question. "I need you to date me. You know, take me on dates, to the movies, eat lunch with me, walk me to class...and hang out with me in the evenings." I forced a contrived smile. "I'll pay."

"You need me to date you," he repeated in monotone.

"Jared has it in his head that you and I belong together," I said. Ryan's face morphed into suspicion. "Just...trust me. That's what he thinks, and the only way he would ever accept that I was moving on is with you. He said once that he would step aside if I chose you. It's just for a few months—just until he gives up—and then you don't have to do it anymore," I begged.

Ryan chuckled, taking in my ludicrous idea. "I won't have to do it anymore? You know this is better than anything I could have ever hoped for, right?"

"Ryan...." Afraid he would be offended and decide not to help me, I hesitated, "I have to be honest with you...we will always be friends. I care about you, but I can't let you go into this thinking it's going to end up being something more. We'll just be pretending. I can't... I don't see myself being with anyone else. Ever," I exhaled, glad that part of the conversation was over.

Ryan rolled his eyes. "Why go through the charade? Why not just get a protective order?"

I looked down to my hands. "He's just following me around because he knows I still love him."

Ryan didn't expect my answer, and his nose wrinkled in response. "If you still love him, then why aren't you with him?"

I crossed my arms. "Are you going to help me or not?"

"Josh is going to think I'm crazy."

I shook my head. "You can't tell anyone. Not Kim, not Tucker or Josh, not your mom. If you tell anyone, even just one person, he'll find out."

"Is he FBI or something?" Ryan said, looking a bit creeped out. "What did you get yourself mixed up in, Nigh?

"Will you do it for me? I know it sounds crazy, and I know it's a lot to ask, but you're the only one that can help me," I said, tugging desperately at his shirt.

"Pretend to be your boyfriend? Lie to all my friends? Let you break my heart when it's all said and done?"

I nodded sheepishly.

"Sure," he said, smiling.

I wasn't sure if the tears came from the fact that Ryan had agreed to help me, or that my plan would work, but I grabbed him and hugged him to me as if I needed him to breathe. He hugged me back, and then pulled away, looking into my eyes.

"I'm going to regret this. I can already tell," he said, smiling softly.

We drove back to Brown, and as we walked from the parking lot, Ryan took my hand. "If we're going to do this, we should do it right, right? No one is going to believe us if we never touch."

"Right."

I struggled to keep my emotions in check as we walked down the halls of my dorm. Jared could see us and I fought against the guilt I felt for hurting him. If I was going to fool him at all, I would have to concentrate on feeling comfortable and happy with Ryan.

We stopped at my door and Ryan let go of my hand. "Are you sure you don't want to come with us tonight?"

After I nodded, Ryan leaned in and kissed the corner of my mouth. I let my feelings for him as a friend bleed through the awkwardness so Jared wouldn't be tipped off. I smiled at him as he turned to walk down the hall.

Over the next weeks, Ryan kept me busy going to the movies, meeting for lunch, and accompanying me to dinner. We spent time together every night, and shared a table at breakfast every morning. He even began to forgo plans with his friends. Soon, everyone was convinced that we were having a not–so–secret relationship.

It was uncomfortable for both of us at first, but after the first week we settled into our new roles. Ryan made a game of it, as he did everything else. We bet on how soon someone would ask us to announce our relationship, and who it would be.

Our friendship grew stronger as the days past, and I began depending on him for more than fooling Jared. Ryan anesthetized the pain, and it wasn't long before I found myself making excuses to be around him.

The day finally came that I had bet that Kim would ask what our status was. I made a show of stretching my legs across Ryan's lap.

"Cheater," Ryan whispered, too low for anyone else to hear.

"Okay. Are you guys together or not?" Kim asked.

Ryan grinned at me and I lifted all five of my fingers, reminding him that he owed me fifty bucks. Ryan shook his head at my gloating and then scanned the table. Everyone waited eagerly for the answer.

"Obviously," he said as he rubbed my leg.

A broad smile spread across Kim's face. "I knew it."

Beth and Chad exchanged glances. I didn't have to ask what was wrong because I already knew; she thought I was making a huge mistake.

"Well, that explains why you've been bailing on us every weekend," Josh said.

"Why don't we all go out Friday?" Ryan shrugged.

I shot a surprised look at him and he smiled. Jared's birthday was Sunday and the only present I could give him was to spend the weekend alone.

"I have plans with my mom this weekend," I explained.

Ryan reached out to rub my shoulder. "Not until Saturday, right, babe? We can go to the pub Friday."

I held my breath to keep from lashing out at him. I couldn't blow our cover by refusing to go to the pub or it would look suspicious. Even worse, I couldn't tear into him later because Jared would hear.

"So are you going?" Beth asked.

"It looks that way," I said, trying not to glare at Ryan.

Leaving the Ratty, I noticed something was different. I had held my breath and braced myself for Jared to be outside the door, but Jared wasn't in his usual spot. He wasn't waiting for me at all. My eyes filled with tears. I had finally hurt him enough to push him away.

"What's wrong, Nigh?" Ryan asked, touching my back.

I couldn't speak. Jared had finally given in. I had won...and I had lost.

"Nina," Beth said, bringing me under her wing like a mother hen. "Let's go home."

"Do you want me to come?" Ryan called after us.

"I've got her," Beth waved him off as we continued walking.

When Beth closed the door, her expression morphed from sympathetic to incensed.

"Okay, you are going to tell me what's going on, and you're going to tell me now...or so help me, I'm going to call Cynthia!"

While I contemplated whether I would lie or tell the truth, Beth stomped her foot.

"Nina!"

"I'm fine."

Beth narrowed her eyes. "I know you're fine. Everyone knows you're fine. But you're not fine! And what are you doing with Ryan? You look ridiculous!"

My head jerked up to meet her glare, acutely aware of the microphone in the vent. "We've been friends for months, Beth. I care about him, and he cares about me. We're just trying to see where it goes."

"Liar," she seethed, rolling her eyes. "You love Jared. I don't know why he's practically stalking you, or why you won't talk to him when it was so obvious today that you miss him...but I know that you love him. And he loves you!" she said, the pitch of her voice rising with each point.

"You don't know as much as you think you do," I grumbled.

"Jared looks miserable, Nina. Don't you care?"

I closed my eyes. "Can we please not talk about this?" I begged.

Beth sat beside me on my bed, her voice quiet. "You need to talk to someone."

"The only person I can talk to about it is Jared, and I can't talk to him."

"Says who?" she asked, wrinkling her nose in disgust.

"Me."

She rolled her eyes. "Right. Because you're saving him."

I shook my head and looked at her. "Why are you pushing this? I thought you liked Ryan."

"I do. But you belong with Jared. It's your happiness that I'm worried about, and you're not happy right now. You are the absolute opposite of happy," she said, touching my arm.

"I'm doing the right thing," I said, wiping the tears. "I am."

"How can it be the right thing when you're so sad?"

For me, the discussion was over. I walked across the room to pull a pair of pajamas from the drawer.

"Nina, no. You're not going to sleep. You sleep all the time. You've got to find another way to cope. Or just quit coping...go to him."

"Shut up, Beth."

Beth's attention was drawn to the knocking at our door. I walked over, pajamas in hand, and opened the door. Ryan's hat was pulled low over his eyes so that all I could see was his perfect white smile and his deep dimple.

He thrust a small stack of papers at me and smiled. "I brought notes," he said, pulling his hat up. "We have finals next week, you know."

"Thanks," I said, setting the papers on my desk.

"What are you up to this afternoon? You wanna go get some coffee?" he asked, his eyes fixating on the pajamas in my hand. "Oh, no. You're not going to sleep." With that, Ryan grabbed my pajamas from my hands and tossed them across the room.

"I'm tired. I didn't sleep well last night," I whined.

"You're always tired. You need to get out in the sun. It's a warm day. We could go hang out on the greens."

I shook my head, trying to push away any memories that thought created.

Ryan's eyes narrowed, and then his mouth broke into a smile. "That's it. You and I are going downtown, waste time driving around, and then I'm taking you to dinner."

"I don't think...."

"And then we're going to the pub and getting smashed. You've had that kind of day," he said, still grinning.

Beth looked up at us from her book. "She's had that kind of month. I'll call Chad. We'll meet you there."

"It's a date," Ryan said, wiping the mascara from under my eyes with both thumbs. "I'll be back in an hour. I want you dressed for a night out on the town."

I raised an eyebrow. "Is that a demand?"

"Yes. I'm a demanding boyfriend and I demand that you have a fun-filled afternoon full of slogan games, boutiques, good food and liquor. I'll even make you to get a manicure. Girls like that crap, right?"

"Oh! Can I go? I need a mani-pedi so bad!" Beth whined.

I shot her a dismayed look. "Are you serious?"

"I am so serious. Ryan and Chad can drop us off, go do boy things, and come back at dinner time. We can get polished and waxed and...I hate to say it, Nigh, but you need a makeover. I'm getting in the shower!" she said, grabbing her things.

"Be—," I began, but she was already out the door. I glowered at Ryan. "I don't feel like going out tonight."

"Please?" he pleaded. He encircled me in his arms and swayed back and forth, pressing his cheek against mine. "One last hurrah before finals week? If you don't have a good time, you can make me miserable for the rest of my life. Deal?" he asked, leaning me back until my hair touched the floor.

I had to smile. He was trying so hard to cheer me up. "Okay."

A huge grin swept Ryan's face and he righted us both. "I'll pick you up in an hour. See you soon," he said as he disappeared down the hall.

Fifty-six minutes later, the door was under attack by loud, incessant knocking. When Beth swung the door open, Chad and Ryan were still knocking on it with both fists.

"It's open!" Beth shouted over the banging.

"Don't you look awesome!" Chad said, kissing Beth sweetly on the cheek.

"Aw...you know I love it when you use the big words," she laughed, wrapping her arms around him.

Ryan stared at me.

"What?" I asked, looking down at my little black dress. "Too much?"

"No! No...it's just...I don't think I've ever seen you in a dress. It's nice."

I shrugged. "I thought it'd make me feel better to dress up."

"Did it?"

"I think so," I smiled.

Ryan rolled down the windows of his black Toyota Tundra and cranked the radio to the first rock song he turned to. The boys sang along, but I still couldn't understand the words. Beth and I giggled at the silly faces they made as they serenaded amused and sometimes bewildered pedestrians as we passed.

At the salon, Beth and I stepped out onto the sidewalk and waved as the Tundra disappeared around the corner.

"Those boys." Beth shook her head before turning to me. "C'mon!" she said, yanking me inside.

I sunk into my seat as my hands and feet were brushed, scrubbed, filed, de-cuticled, polished and lotioned. Beth prattled on to the nail techs about our plans for the night, how wonderful her boyfriend was and her upcoming apartment hunt.

"You're staying in Providence?" I asked, my eyebrows shooting upward.

She smiled. "Chad wants to get an apartment together. I didn't want to say anything before... with everything going on."

"You didn't want to upset me."

Beth bit her lip and nodded.

"You could have told me, Beth. I think it's fantastic," I said, grabbing her hand.

"You do?"

"You two are amazing together. You don't need to worry about me, I'll be fine," I said, squeezing her hand.

"Yeah...you being fine is exactly what I'm worried about," she grumbled.

Two hours later, Ryan's Tundra honked from the curb. Ryan opened the door for us and then hopped back in, turning the music down.

"Did you have a good time, babe?" he asked, kissing my cheek.

"Yeah, it was fun," I answered.

"Well, you look gorgeous. I'm afraid to take you anywhere looking like that. I might have to fight somebody," he said, winking.

"Quit it," I smiled, rolling my eyes.

We arrived at the pub, and I could hear the music thumping from the street. I knew Kim had beaten us there, because it was her crazy music filtering through the door. When we walked in, our friends were already on the dance floor, arms up, bouncing around. Ryan grabbed my hand and led me to the middle of the floor, twirling me around.

In that moment I was just like them. I was a normal college student, with my entire normal life ahead of me. I smiled, and it felt natural. I drank shots, toasted to the Big Brown Bear, and hugged my friends. It was bittersweet freedom.

The music slowed, and Ryan pulled me to him. We were both sticky from dancing, and I pulled the wet strands of my bangs away from my face.

Holding my hand up to the dim light, he smiled. "Those are some pretty nails you have there."

"My boyfriend forced me to go to the spa today. He made me spend the afternoon with one of my girlfriends," I teased.

"Really? He sounds like a great guy. If I were you, I'd hang on to him...sounds like a keeper."

I watched his face for a moment and then rested my cheek on his shoulder. Ryan wrapped his arms tighter around me and pressed his face into my hair.

"It wouldn't be so bad, would it?" he whispered in my ear. "If we stopped pretending?"

I shut my eyes and remained silent.

We returned to the bar for another round of shots when I saw Kim heading outside, a cigarette already between her lips. I stumbled out behind her and raked my matted hair from my forehead as she flicked her lighter.

"Can I have one?" I asked, breathless and weaving.

"You want a cigarette?" she asked in disbelief.

I nodded and Kim shrugged, pulling a stubby white stick from the small box she was holding.

I put the cigarette between my lips flicked the lighter. Just as it sparked, Jared appeared in front of me with a disgusted look on his face.

"What are you doing?" He pulled the cigarette from my mouth, broke it in half, and threw it to the ground. "You don't smoke." He frowned in disapproval, and I shrunk back into Kim.

"You're drunk, Ryan's drunk, I'm taking you home," he said in a father-like tone.

I turned to open the door to the pub, but Jared grabbed my wrist. "Then let me call you a cab," his voice lost its authority and I winced at the pain in his voice.

Jared's hand was the same warm blanket I remembered. After the number of drinks I'd had, I couldn't hide my feelings. Jared's eyes became animated in reaction.

He looked down to my hand and caressed my skin with his thumb. He had sensed the pensive feeling I'd had at his touch.

I pulled away. "You need to go."

"I can't let you go with him when he's been drinking."

"Ryan already—," I began.

"Jared," Ryan said, bursting out of the bar. He nodded once at Jared and then looked at me and smiled. "Hey, babe," he said, jerking me against him and planting his mouth on mine.

My eyes widened and then I clinched them shut, trying to cover the fact that I was taken off-guard. After a few seconds, he pulled away, looked into my eyes and then cupped my cheeks, kissing me again. I could tell by the way he held me that it was no longer for show. He had forgotten about our audience as he parted his lips, lightly touching his tongue to mine.

I pulled away and immediately watched for Jared's reaction; his expression frightened me. I slowly moved to stand in front of Ryan.

"Jared...." I warned.

Jared's breathing was uneven, and his eyes were raging storms. "Move out of the way, Nina."

"She's made her choice, Jared. It's time you found someone else to...."

Jared lunged forward and then jerked back, held by two small hands.

"It's time to go," Claire said as her brother froze under her touch.

"Hey, Claire!" Ryan smiled, unaware of how close he was to another trip to the hospital.

Claire glanced at him with an uncomfortable expression, keeping firm hands on her brother. She seemed surprised that Ryan had acknowledged her.

The cab slowed to a stop beside us and honked. I backed up against Ryan, turning to push him to safety. Jared walked toward me and for the first time I felt safer knowing Claire was near.

"Nina?" Ryan called from inside the cab.

Jared stood just a few inches from me. "Don't go home with him," he begged, his face compressing inward. "You don't have to do this. I'll stay away; you won't even know I exist. Don't do something we'll all regret just to push me away."

Ryan poked his head out of the open door. "Who says she hasn't already?" he asked, gripping my inner thigh.

Jared didn't get far when he charged Ryan for the second time. Claire had kept her grip on him.

I wanted to tell Jared the truth: that he was the only one I'd ever wanted in that way, and he would always be the only one. But I couldn't. He had just told me he would move on, and I had to let him.

"Come on, Jared. She's not worth it," Claire said, tugging on him.

Jared puffed as if the wind had been knocked out of him. "She's worth it. She's worth this a thousand times," his eyes glossed over then, and he finally tore his stare away from mine to follow his sister.

I slid in next to Ryan and he reached across me to shut the door. The cab ride seemed to take an eternity. I could hear Ryan chattering, but the look on Jared's face had me spiraling into devastation so deep that it grew difficult for me to breathe. I rolled down the window and rested my head against the door, letting the icy wind burn my face.

"Hey? You okay?" Ryan asked.

I couldn't answer. My heart was breaking; a real, physical pain radiated from my chest and throughout my entire body. Ryan put a gentle hand on my shoulder and pulled me against him. I expected to feel the comfort I always felt with him, but it only made me feel worse.

When we pulled into Brown, Ryan reached up to pay the driver and then stumbled from the cab. He twirled me a few times as we walked to Andrews, and when we reached the door, he pulled me to him.

"Goodnight," he said, kissing my cheek. His lips brushed against my skin as he tightened his grip around me and took a few steps, prompting a slow, silent dance in the middle of the sidewalk.

"I should go in," I whispered.

Ryan's lips grazed my cheek and skimmed across my mouth. He sighed as he made his way to my other cheek, and then kissed me again.

He took a few steps backward and grinned. "I'll call you tomorrow," he said, turning to disappear into the darkness.

With each step to my room I tried to figure out where everything had gone so horribly wrong. I hadn't set out to hurt anyone, yet every decision I made seemed to cause others pain. I pushed open the door and collapsed onto my bed.

Through the whiskey fog I searched my past, trying to remember the exact moment that I'd made a mistake, where I could have made a better choice. If I had chosen to stay with Jared, no matter how sure he was, his family would be in danger. My choice to end things had left both of us in agony that didn't seem to be subsiding. Persuading Ryan to engage in a fake relationship with me had only accomplished Ryan having false hope, and if it were even possible, I hurt Jared worse than I already had.

Beth's key rattled the door knob. She walked in to our dark room, throwing her purse onto the bedside table.

"Nina?" she whispered. "Are you awake?"

"I thought you went to Chad's," I said, turning to face her.

She sat on my bed and placed her hand gently on my leg. "I wanted to make sure you were all right."

"Why wouldn't I be?" The liquor helped to keep my voice even.

Beth was irritated with my calm demeanor. "We all saw what happened. Is Ryan insane?"

"He was just trying to make a point."

Beth shot a disgusted glance at me. "What point would that be? That he has suicidal tendencies? Jared could have wadded him up like a piece of paper, and considering his state of mind...that was just really, really stupid."

"I'm going to sleep. I have a lot to do tomorrow," I said, settling against my pillow.

"Why are you so calm about this? I don't understand you anymore, Nina. It doesn't seem like you're thinking clearly."

I smiled, my eyes closed. "I'm not thinking clearly. I've had a lot to drink."

Beth shook her head. "You're not acting like yourself. It's like you left the best part of you behind when you left Jared."

"Thanks," I snapped, turning my back to her.

"That's not what I meant, I just meant...." Beth sighed and then left without saying goodbye.

Sunday morning I woke up to the sound of the rain pelting against the window. I peered out, seeing Jared's Escalade just down the street. My chest ached, knowing how hard it must have been for him to be alone on his birthday. I fantasized about bringing him a present, or simply running out to hug him, but I could do neither. When I shut the door behind me from returning from the shower, there was a knock at the door.

"Just a minute!" I called, rushing to throw some clothes on.

I opened the door to Ryan's smiling face, his hair dripping wet. "I was wondering if you wanted to take a drive?"

"Your truck is at the pub, Ryan."

He smiled, wiping away the water that ran down his forehead from his hairline. "Josh took me to get it earlier. You wanna go?"

I shook my head. "It's pouring outside."

"So...," he stalled, shoving his hands in his pockets, "you wanna hang out here?"

I smiled apologetically. "I have a huge test tomorrow, first thing in the morning. I need to cram."

Ryan shrugged again. "I can help you."

"I have to do it by myself. You know how I am," I said dismissively.

"Yeah, I just...," he sighed, "I can't quit thinking about that kiss."

"Oh."

Ryan walked past me into my room. "I know what you said. But...don't you have any feelings for me at all? Can't we stop pretending long enough to find out if I could make you happy? I could, you know...make you happy."

Ryan's mention of our arrangement caused me to glance up at the vent, but it didn't matter. Jared saw right through me from the very beginning.

"You do make me happy. I just don't have anything left to...," I shook my head. "I can't talk about this right now. I have to study," I said, opening the door.

"Do you have plans for dinner?" he asked.

I hugged him. "No. I'll talk to you tomorrow."

It would be the beginning of the end for us. Jared had agreed to stay away, and Ryan knew that our time was limited. He nodded and left my room, disappointed.

Studying was nothing less than impossible, knowing Jared was outside. I peered out the rain-streaked window again to see that Jared hadn't moved. The urge to go to him became unmanageable, so I grabbed my keys and set out to take a coffee break off campus.

I drove just a few blocks to the nearest coffee shop and went in, ordering my usual. I took my time, lingering in the booth, watching different faces come and go. Fantasies of surprising Jared with a gift kept creeping into my thoughts, and I finally resorted to returning to my dorm.

As soon as I walked outside, I noticed Jared in my peripheral. His shirt was wet from standing in the rain, and I held my breath as I passed him. The circles under his eyes were dark, and his face appeared paler than his natural golden tone.

My feet refused to take another step. No matter what I had said, I still loved him. I couldn't make him feel like a ghost on his birthday. I closed my eyes, knowing I would go against everything I had worked for in the last six weeks. I was at a crossroad, and I was about to deliberately take the wrong turn.

I turned on my heels and walked straight up to him. Jared watched me with wary eyes, obviously unsure of what to expect.

Although I had made strangers of us over the last weeks, it felt right be close to him again. I felt no awkwardness or tension, and I could see beyond his cautious expression that he felt the same.

I took a deep breath. "Happy Birth—,"

Before I could finish, Jared grabbed my shoulders and pulled me against him into a deep kiss. My lips melted against the familiar heat of his mouth, and as I breathed in his amazing scent, I felt a bit lightheaded. When Jared realized I wouldn't pull away, he wrapped his arms around me and held me tightly against him, shamelessly taking advantage of the moment. Minutes passed and I could hear the giggling of children and teenage girls as they walked by. When his lips finally left mine, he hugged me tightly and buried his face in my neck, taking in a deep breath through his nose. He caressed his cheek against mine for a few moments more, and then finally released me.

He scanned my face for some sort of reaction. I wasn't sure what expression was on my face, but Jared looked cautiously pleased.

"Day," I finished, breathlessly.

His eyes were a few shades lighter than I'd seen them in weeks. I waited for a moment, and allowed my lips to form a tiny smile before returning to my car.

"Nina?" Jared called.

I turned around and a tired smile touched his face. "That's all I wanted today."

My heart sank at his words, and I wished the world would leave us alone so I could stay with him. The memory of Harry Crenshaw pressing a gun to Bex's temple flashed in my mind, and I stiffened.

"Goodbye, Jared."

Chapter Seventeen
Absolution

Finals week arrived. The little sleep I'd gotten before became nonexistent with the amount of studying and cramming I had to do. I studied with the group at the Rock every night, only to return to my room to read and memorize in solitude.

Ryan continued to pretend, walking me to lunch, to classes, and back and forth from my room. He was the perfect boyfriend; he opened doors, brought late night brain food, and he even rubbed my shoulders while quizzing me on study guides. A part of me wondered if he was trying so hard because he knew the end of the week meant the end of pretending, and he hoped I would change my mind.

Beth and Chad found an apartment, and some of her things were already packed in boxes. A sad air befell the room when we were both in it, surrounded by cardboard. The walls looked empty and clinical without her teddy bears and tiaras displayed on the walls and ribbons dripping from the shelves.

Thursday night, occasional cracks of thunder rattled the windows. The rain beat against the window in a heavy gust, and Beth sighed at her carefully highlighted textbook. I slammed my book shut and put a CD in the stereo, twisting the volume knob as high as it would go.

"What are you doing?" Beth yelled over the music.

I jumped up and down, holding my hands out to her. "It's our last night as roomies, roomie! We're sending you out in style!"

Beth giggled and stood up, grabbing my hands and shaking her hair to the beat as we bounced together. After a few songs, a loud banging resounded from the door. I shimmied over to open it, laughing when I saw Kim's smiling face.

"Sounds like a party!" she yelled, holding up two six packs of cheap beer. "I come bearing gifts!"

"Woo!" Beth squealed. Her hair flapped about as she danced in her bare feet.

Before I'd finished my first can, another knock on the door revealed a rather wet and confused Ryan, who cringed at the volume of the stereo.

"What are you doing?" Ryan yelled. A wide grin stretched across his face as he watched us bounce.

"It's our impromptu going away party for Beth!" I yelled back.

"Cool! I'll make phone calls!" Ryan exclaimed, pulling out his cell phone.

Within twenty minutes, our room was shoulder to shoulder with our entire study group, plus a few girls from down the hall that had wandered in out of curiosity. Kim and Tucker were jumping on Beth's bed, and the rest of us were dancing and laughing.

By midnight, everyone except Beth, Chad, and Ryan had cleared out to study. Beth grabbed her purse and hugged me.

"Thank you so much! I needed that. It's been so sad around here!"

"You're welcome. I'm going to miss you terribly," I said, jutting out my bottom lip.

Beth squeezed me until it was hard to breathe. "I'm going to miss you, too. But we'll still see each other, right?"

"Of course we will." I smiled.

I waved goodbye to her and Chad, and then sat on my bed, exhausted. As usual, any normal, content feelings I had left with the moment.

Ryan turned to see the look on my face. "What is it, babe?"

I smiled. "No one's here, Ryan. You don't have to call me that."

"I don't do it for other people," he said, an amused grin spanning his face.

"Ryan...," I began. Knocking at the door provided a perfect excuse to postpone the inevitable. "Beth must have forgotten her keys." I opened the door and gasped.

She wouldn't have come unless something was horribly wrong. The adrenaline exploded through my bloodstream as I braced myself for what she might say.

"I need to talk to you," she said.

"What are you doing here, Claire? Is it Jared

She looked at Ryan and then back at me, and for the first time she didn't have a murderous expression on her face. "Alone."

"I'm not leaving," Ryan said, standing in front of me.

She rolled her eyes. "If I wanted to hurt her, Ryan, you standing there with your hands in your pockets wouldn't do much in the way of a deterrent," she said, looking back to me. "It's important, Nina."

I could feel my heart thudding against my chest wall. "What? He's okay, right?"

"He's at home. He finally agreed to get some sleep."

421

"Oh." The numbness came like second nature, and automatically an emotional wall surrounded me.

Claire frowned at my generic answer. "Oh? I can't stand to see him like this anymore, and you're the only one that can fix it. He's been a mess since his birthday. He's been a mess for weeks, but he's been really bad since Sunday." She looked to the floor, clearly disturbed by whatever image was in her head. "I think it's finally hit him that you're not going to change your mind."

I found my focus again, grateful to Claire for the reminder. "He's right."

Claire looked at Ryan and then at me in disgust. "You two aren't fooling anyone. Jared knows exactly what's going on. It was a stupid idea, Nina. You're putting him through hell for nothing. I could understand if you didn't feel the same, but I know you do."

I shook my head, the consequences to his family coming to the forefront of my mind. "I can't."

Claire's face twisted into a heartbreaking expression, and I was taken aback when I saw her eyes gloss over.

"I've never seen him like this, Nina. Not even when Dad died. I was hoping he would snap out of it, that after a while he would get over it, but he hasn't. He won't sleep, he can't eat, he's forced to watch you ignore him every day...it's torture," she said, stubbornly wiping a rogue tear from her cheek.

"Stop it. I don't want to hear anymore," I said, closing my eyes.

Claire blinked the tears away and glared at me. "Well, that's too bad. He has to live it, the least you can do is listen to it," she said, pulling my arm toward her. Ryan took his hand out of his pockets and moved toward Claire. She pressed one hand against his chest and effortlessly pushed him against the door, holding him there. Ryan leaned forward, but he was helpless against her angel's strength.

"Don't hurt her," Ryan said, glowering at Claire.

Claire took her eyes from me and glanced at Ryan, taking her hand from his chest. "I'm not going to hurt her. Stay out of it, Ryan."

Ryan stood in place against the door and looked at me. "Nina?"

"It's okay," I assured him. "You have to go, Claire. Please, just go."

"He's broken, Nina," she pleaded. "Don't you see it? Don't you care? The pain he's going through is enough, but he has to feel your pain, too. Can you imagine the pain you feel missing him, being without him, wanting him...doubled? He kept saying that you just needed space...that you would come around, but after Sunday, after you told him goodbye...it broke him."

My resolve waivered, but I fought my weakness for Jared, knowing I was at another crossroad. I had to make the right decision.

She took a deep breath. "I know you think you're atoning for Jack's sins. But what you're doing, Nina? It's killing Jared. Nothing can be worse than watching him die a little more every day."

I closed my eyes and the tears finally overflowed.

Claire looked down at her hands, her next words not coming easily. "It's not your fault we lost our father, Nina."

I pursed my lips and then sucked in a deep breath. "I couldn't look him in the eye if it happened again."

"Keeping my family safe isn't your job. It's Jared's, and it's mine. And I'm very, very good at my job. You can't keep making him suffer because you're afraid to repeat Jack's mistakes." Her eyebrows pulled in. "It's not a good enough reason to break his heart."

Ryan watched both of us, confused by the exchange.

"Time will make it easier," I whispered.

"Time will make it worse!" she snapped, disgusted at my suggestion. "You're his Taleh, Nina...the other half of his soul. He's never going to get over you. And no matter how much you hope that you will... you'll never get over him. You're going to wake up one day and realize what you've done, and you're going to regret the time you wasted apart from him for the rest of your life." A tear careened down her perfect cherubic cheek and she left it there, too intent on convincing me to save her brother.

I felt my face crumple. I knew she was right.

Ryan's hand lightly touched my back. I looked at him, and although his eyes were full of hurt, he smiled.

"Go," he said.

I smiled at him and began to speak, but he simply shook his head, hugged me tightly, and walked out the door.

I wiped my eyes and took a deep breath.

"You're coming with me?" she asked.

I nodded, and for the first time I saw Claire's face light up. She threw her arms around me, hugging me a little too tight.

"Come on!" She pulled me by the hand down the hall, unable to contain her triumphant smile. I had to jog keep up with her.

I squinted, recoiling from the remnant rain of the departing thunderstorm. The Lotus chirped when she clicked the keyless entry, and I slid in beside her, wiping the water from my arms.

"What about Ryan?" I asked.

"Bex is home," Claire smiled. She slammed the gear shift into place and we peeled away from the curb, the engine growling as she soared toward Jared's loft.

We didn't speak; I fumbled with my ring and tried to imagine Jared's reaction when I showed up unannounced.

Claire pulled beside the curb behind the Escalade. I took a deep breath and opened my door with shaking fingers.

Jared was already standing in front of the loft under the light of a street lamp, looking exhausted and confused. He tore his eyes away from mine for just a moment to look at Claire, who stood with her door open on the other side of the car.

"Is she okay?" he asked Claire.

Claire only offered a smug smile.

He looked back at me with concern. "Did Claire force you to come here?" he asked, wary.

I shook my head, afraid to speak. His wasn't the reaction I expected.

"I don't understand," he said, his eyes darting back and forth between me and Claire. "What are you doing here? Did something happen?"

Claire smiled. "Don't make her beg, Jared. Just take her back." With that she ducked into her car and pulled away.

Jared's face darted back to mine. "W...What?"

"I'm so sorry," I whispered.

Jared stared at me, his light blue T-shirt transparent from the rain.

I realized that Claire had a point to what she'd said to her brother. "I'll beg," I nodded, taking a step toward him. "I don't deserve forgiveness, I know, but I was hoping...." I sighed and shook my head. Nothing I could say would be enough.

"You came here to beg me back?" Jared asked, bewildered.

"Or humiliate myself by babbling incoherent nonsense in the rain...." I laughed nervously. Thunder rolled in the distance and I pulled my arms around me, chilled by wet clothes.

Jared took a few steps toward me and stopped. He watched me for a moment, though I wasn't sure what he was searching for.

"This was a bad idea. I should have called." I fidgeted, feeling more embarrassed by the second.

"You came here to apologize?" Jared asked again, taking a few more steps.

The humiliation boiled the blood under my cheeks. "I made a mistake. A huge, horrible mistake and I wouldn't blame you if you hated me."

He stared at me in disbelief and I shifted nervously, worrying that I had hurt him beyond forgiveness.

I took another step. "You were right. I was afraid they would hurt your family trying to get to me. But to save them, I hurt you. I don't expect you to trust me again, but I am so, so sorry. I love you, Jared, and if I've learned anything over the past weeks, it's that no matter what happens...I'll love you the rest of my life."

Jared watched me prattle on with an indiscernible expression on his face.

I bit my lip; the suspense of his answer was insufferable. "Please say something."

Jared took a few more steps until he was only inches from me. The rain dripped off his chin and nose as he looked down at me. "I'm going to kiss you, now," he said, cupping my cheeks in his hands as if he was holding his most precious possession. "And I don't know if I'll ever stop."

He didn't waste a second longer. He pressed his lips against mine, and I wrapped my arms tightly around his neck. My feet left the ground and the rain disappeared as Jared whisked me into the loft and up the stairs, his feet barely touching the steps.

In seconds his mattress was beneath me. Caution was nonexistent; Jared's mouth begged mine to open as his lips worked impatiently against mine. My lips parted as my knees did, and Jared's hand grabbed my thigh and pressed upwards, taking my skirt as he went. He reached back to lift his shirt over his head, and I dug my fingers into the lean muscles of his back.

Jared rocked against me, sending adrenaline racing through my body. His lips found their way to my waist, and his kisses ran up the midline of my stomach as he pushed my tank top up and over my head. His breathing grew uneven as he hovered above me, watching me slowly pull the straps of my bra from my shoulders. I arched my back to unsnap the clasps behind me and he tenderly kissed my lips as he pulled the straps from my arms and tossed the lacey fabric to the floor.

He clenched the hem of my skirt and panties, pulling them down until they were lost somewhere in the mangled sheets. I sighed as he pressed his bare chest against mine, kissing my neck while I reached down to pull his belt from the loops. Jared moaned as I ripped open the top button of his jeans and shoved them down over his hips. He used his feet to push them passed his ankles, and I heard them drop to the floor at the end of the bed.

Jared paused to look into my eyes for a long moment, and his fingers glided down my face and neck.

"I guess no one is going to interrupt tonight," I said.

The corners of his mouth turned up and he slowly shook his head.

The grin faded to a serious, focused expression and he leaned down to kiss my lips. Jared took a deep breath in through his nose and his body tensed as he pressed himself inside me. I clinched my eyes shut and involuntarily turned my head away, feeling pain and pleasure at the same time. My insides blazed as his lips brushed against the skin just in front of my ear.

"Are you okay?" he whispered, breathless.

I nodded and pulled his mouth to mine; we were finally close enough. My hands slid down his neck to his shoulders and I dug my fingers into his flesh at the intense pleasure searing through my body. A quiet groan escaped his lips as he tensed again. I felt his hands encapsulate my calves and slide down to my ankles, pulling my legs up and around, crossing my legs behind his back.

His tongue tasted the inside of my mouth as he pressed himself gently inside me, and I tensed with unadulterated bliss at every movement he made. My senses were overwhelmed to the point where I couldn't think straight, so I couldn't imagine what he must have felt. With his scorching chest against mine and his hips pressing over and over into my thighs, I couldn't help but sigh his name. He groaned in response as his lips eagerly searched my skin from lips to collar bone. The hours passed as minutes, and the minutes as hours. I had no concept of time; I had no need for it. That moment was all I'd ever wanted, and I never wanted it to end.

I awoke on my stomach, sprawled across Jared's bed with nothing on but the sheets tangled around my waist. I peeked over at Jared, who was on his side, watching me with a sweet expression.

"Good morning," he crooned.

"Did you get any sleep? I asked.

Jared chuckled. "Five hours. The longest I've slept since I was a kid."

I smiled and leaned over to kiss his lips. My body felt stiff and relaxed at the same time, and my muscles ached in a wonderful way.

He touched my face. "You were sleeping so soundly I didn't want to wake you, but your last final is in ninety minutes."

"Oh!" I scrambled off the bed with Jared's sheet twisted around me and I held it to my chest as I shuffled to the bathroom. I stopped in my tracks, flipped around and returned to the bed, planting a ridiculously long kiss on his lips.

"I love you!" I called back as I ran to the bathroom to get in the shower.

Everything felt different; the water, the soap, my skin. I couldn't stop smiling as I recalled the events of the night before. My fingers were starting to prune when I heard a soft knock on the door.

"Better get a move on, sweetheart."

I shut off the water and rushed through my morning routine.

"Claire brought my clothes this morning?" I guessed, trotting down the stairs.

Jared smiled, standing by the door with my coffee. "She dropped them off at the door."

I kissed his lips as I passed, and he followed me to the Escalade.

I made it to my desk just as the professor began passing out tests. It was difficult to concentrate; my mind wandered to Jared's lips—and other parts of his body—and the fact that we had the entire summer to make up for lost time.

I was the last person to finish, and when I handed in my paper, the professor added it to the thick pile, nodding politely.

"Enjoy your summer, Miss Grey."

"Oh, I will," I said, smiling when I saw Jared standing in the doorway.

When we pulled to the curb in front of the loft, he turned off the key and sat in his seat, keeping my hand in his.

"I feel like I should apologize to you for last night," he said, kissing my fingers.

"Why?" I asked.

Jared shifted in his seat. "It wasn't exactly planned. I feel like I ambushed you."

"That's the kind of ambush I don't mind," I smiled, leaning over to kiss him. "I've never wanted anything more."

Jared cautiously smiled. "You're okay, then?"

"I'm better than okay. I'm looking forward to the next ambush, actually." I leaned over to kiss his neck, making my way to his ear.

Jared chuckled. "We might not leave the loft for the rest of the summer with you behaving like that."

"That wouldn't be so bad, would it?" I whispered, grazing my tongue along the edge of his ear.

"When do you plan to move your things from Andrews? Your mother is expecting you home this weekend. I have quite a bit of work to do, taking down the tech from your room, the hall...," he trailed off, distracted by my mouth on his ear.

I pulled back and stared at him for a moment. Before I could verbalize the ingenious idea that popped into my head, a broad smile spread across my face.

"What?" he asked, smiling as well.

"Since we're moving my things...why don't we just bring them here?" I said, searching his eyes for a reaction.

Jared's eyebrows shot up in shock. "You want to move into the loft?"

I shrugged, unsure what his reaction meant. I wasn't exactly confident that the offer was still open. "If it's okay."

"If it's okay? Do you know how happy you just made me?" he said, scanning my face with unconditional devotion in his eyes.

"So that's a yes?"

Jared laughed out loud, shook his head, and then kissed me enthusiastically. "That is a definite, without a doubt, absolutely yes."

I giggled with excitement as Jared pulled me over to his lap, kissing me with every bit the joy that I felt. In the course of just twelve hours, the last six weeks dissolved as if they'd never happened. Before the nightmare had ended, we'd gotten our miracle. It had turned out that it was up to us all along.

We spent the rest of the weekend moving boxes and small pieces of furniture. Jared insisted on doing most of the lifting, and I hummed along with the stereo as I unpacked my things. We seemed to only get a few boxes unpacked at a time before we were celebrating my homecoming upstairs, only to come downstairs, unpack a few boxes and start the process over again.

After a heated weekend inside, Jared decided that we should get some fresh air. Monday morning I walked outside to perfect weather. The air smelled of freshly cut grass and sunshine. I lifted my head towards the cloudless sky, closing my eyes and smiling as the sun filtered through my eyelids.

Jared climbed onto his Vulcan and smiled. "Lillian wanted me to ask you to dinner. Before you say anything," he hedged, seeing my shocked expression, "she suggested we meet in a restaurant. She doesn't want you to feel obligated, but she would like to see you again. She misses you."

I sighed. "How can she miss me? I assumed the undeserved partial treatment would end after she heard what happened."

Jared tucked my hair affectionately behind my ear. "She knows what you're going through, and you're the only one that knows what she went through. You have a lot in common."

"We don't have to go to a restaurant. She can come to our place or we can go over there. I'm not afraid."

Jared's eyes poured over my face, wearing a perfectly content expression.

I raised an eyebrow. "What?"

His eyes turned soft. "Our place."

He started the engine and I slipped on my sunglasses, climbing on behind him. The summer air whipped around us as Jared flew down the streets, and I pressed my cheek against his back, feeling happier than I ever had.

We came to a stoplight and Jared rested his hand on my knee. "We can get the rest of your things from Cynthia's in the morning. And if you want to get some paint, we can do that, too," he said, trying too hard to sound casual.

I peered around to see his face. "And why do we need paint?"

Jared shrugged. "The loft doesn't exactly scream cohabitation. If you want to make it your own, we can get you what you need."

"Aw!" I lilted, making Jared cringe and shake his head.

I tightened my grip and then rested my forehead on his back. He stiffened and I raised my head to see what had caused him to tense. Samuel stood in front of us, massive and dark as night. His arms were crossed over his chest, making him seem even more ominous. I cowered behind Jared, my heartbeat instantly pounding in my chest.

"Hello, Nina," Samuel spoke. His expression seemed to soften but his features were so severe it wasn't as comforting as he might have meant for it to be.

"You must have news," Jared said.

"I do," Samuel said, breaking his stare from me. "Shax has received information that Jack had the book secured in a bank that you and Nina alone have access to."

"This is bad," Jared said in a low, portentous tone.

"They also know that Nina's ring has a code embedded in it that they need. There is talk, Jared. They'll be coming for her soon."

Jared sat for a moment, lost in thought. His head jerked up to look at Samuel. "Not if we give it to them."

"Jared!" I cried.

He turned to me and touched my face. "Nina, I don't know why Jack has the book. But it's not worth your life."

"You're assuming Shax will stop once he has the book," Samuel said, his voice matching his frightening features.

"How did they come into this knowledge?" Jared growled.

"How else?" Samuel narrowed his eyes. "Humans."

I began to ask Samuel what he meant, but just as before, the space he occupied lost any memory of him.

Jared revved the engine and flew to the loft. He dismounted and pulled me off the seat, barely letting my feet touch the ground before pulling me up the stairs.

He kicked the door shut and held my shoulders. "I'm going to figure this out, Nina. No one's in danger. I'm going to end this, okay?" His words were so fast they blurred together, and his eyes were stormy and tense.

"Okay," I said, wrapping my arms around him and kissing his lips.

He watched me warily when I pulled away. "Okay?" he asked.

I touched his face lightly with my fingertips. "I couldn't stay away from you even when I thought I had to. I'm not going anywhere. I promise."

Jared's eyes turned soft, and he lifted my hand with his ring still in place. "And you keep your promises."

Chapter Eighteen
Shax

The next morning I awoke in the same state I had the five days before: tangled in sheets, muscles aching, eyes tired, stomach hungry, and everything else in an utter state of bliss.

Jared tightened his arms around me as I stretched. "Why don't you go back to sleep?" he said, kissing my neck.

I slid my bare leg over his hip. "Why would I want to waste time sleeping when you're awake?"

He grinned as he ran his hand up my thigh. "Because you're human, and you need more than two hours of sleep a night. Not that I'm complaining, I just need to quit being so selfish and make sure you get to sleep earlier than six A.M."

"Don't you dare," I yawned.

"You're hungry. I'll make breakfast," he said, pushing himself off the bed.

After a long shower, I dressed and trotted down the stairs. I grabbed the newspaper and sat at the table with my coffee, freezing mid-sip as I saw the headline.

Local Banker Found Dead, Mutilated

"Jared?"

"Yeah, sweetheart?" he replied, distracted by the pan of eggs in front of him.

"Have you seen this morning's paper?"

"Not yet, what's up?" He turned when he felt my fear as I read over the article.

I swallowed nervously before meeting Jared's eyes. "James Stevens from the bank...the man that let us into the vault...he was found dead yesterday."

I handed the paper to him and watched his eyes scan over the words.

"What does it mean, Jared?"

Jared's irises were clear and his features smooth. "He must have been one of the humans Samuel was referring to. I would have to see the body to be sure if it was Grahm or...."

I nodded, realizing where he was getting at.

"Oh, no," Jared said.

"What?"

Jared handed the paper back to me, pointing to what he'd read.

Local Jeweler Robbed, Assaulted
Police Say String of Crimes
Coincidence

"Vincent!" I said, looking up at Jared. "Do you think he's okay?"

Jared's eyes darkened a shade. "It just says assaulted, so I'm assuming he's alive," he said, sitting in the chair beside me.

I fidgeted. "What do we do?"

Jared shook his head, sliding his fingers in between mine. "You and I will get the book, and then I'm going to return it to Shax."

"You mean we're going to return it to Shax," I said, squeezing his fingers between mine.

Jared shook his head. "I'm sorry, Nina, it's too dangerous."

"Jared...." The fear choked off my objections.

Pulling me into his lap, Jared shrugged his arms around me. "Nina, I'm going to take care of this. Claire will stay here with you. I promise you'll be safe."

I pressed my cheek against his and closed my eyes. "What about you? Isn't that like walking behind enemy lines?"

"I have something he wants. As long as you're here, safe, I'll be fine. Trust me?" he said, holding me at arm's length to search my eyes.

"I do. Just...be careful."

"Oh, I'll be careful. I've got plans for you." He pressed his forehead against mine. "Your eggs are getting cold. I'm going to call Claire...get this over with."

Claire walked through the door less than an hour later, her casual expression matching Jared's. She also seemed significantly more relaxed around me, even smacking me on the backside when she walked by.

"We're going to have fun, Nina. I brought movies."

My face slowly morphed to disgust. "Movies? You think I'm going to be able to watch a movie while Jared is in a room full of demons?"

Claire rolled her eyes and a smirk sharpened her features. "Don't you know what Jared is capable of? I'm not worried. You shouldn't be, either."

Jared's mouth turned up a bit, shoving a handgun in the back of his jeans. "You're overdoing it, Claire."

Claire shot an expression of chagrin at her brother, and they traded glances.

"She doesn't want me to freak out and leave again," I said. I looked at the floor and then back at her. "You're stuck with me, Claire."

She pulled one side of her mouth into an appreciative smile. "Good. Because I'd just track you down and bring your butt back here."

Jared walked toward me and kissed my forehead first, and then my lips. "You ready?"

My fingers involuntarily gripped his jacket. "What if they're waiting for us at the bank?"

"Then I'll protect you. Claire is coming with us...if anyone should be afraid it's Grahm and his men."

My body felt rigid from the moment we stepped out of the door into the alley. Jared kept my hand in his until we pulled up to the front entrance of the bank. Claire on one side of me, Jared on the other, we walked inside and across the lobby. An older gentleman in a dark suit and tie approached us.

"Can I help you?"

"Yes, we will be retrieving our effects from the vault downstairs," Jared said.

"Er...c-can I have your name, sir?" he stuttered, anxiously tapping the ends of his fingers against each other.

"Jared Ryel. Is there a problem?"

"No...no sir, there's no problem. I'd be glad to help you."

Jared's eyes swept the room, and I noticed Claire was on alert, as well. They kept close, both of them in contact with my arms as we walked. Just before the elevator opened to the sub-floor, I noticed a break in

Claire's breathing. It was completely silent for a fraction of a second until the doors slid open to a large, empty room.

Claire quietly exhaled and Jared gripped my arm, cautiously pulling me forward. We went through the tedious procedure to gain access to the vault while Claire nonchalantly glanced around the perimeter. Her ice blue eyes would miss nothing.

"You put the paper in the safe, Jared," I whispered. "We don't know the combination."

"I know it," he said, shoving the key into the lock.

I looked over at Claire, whose eyes focused on the closing vault. Once it closed, she looked up and slowly scanned the ceiling.

"What is it, Claire?" I asked.

"I don't know," she murmured. "Something."

Jared kept the book under his arm on the return trip to the loft. He escorted me to the end of the alley and then leaned down to kiss me goodbye. Before our lips touched, he looked up as if he sensed something around us.

"I should go. It's already attracting them."

I clenched his jacket. "I don't want you to go alone."

"Claire needs to stay here with you. I can't leave you unprotected."

"What about Bex? Can't he stay here with me?" I asked, searching his face as my mind raced to find an alternative.

"Bex is with Lillian," he said. I immediately understood his indicative reply; he was covering all the bases.

"Jared...." I said, tightening my grip.

He pulled me to him. "If we wait much longer, they'll come to us, and we don't want that. This is our only option."

I leaned back and closed my eyes, shaking my head. "There has to be another way. There has to be —,"

Jared cupped my jaw and his thumb brushed my cheek. "As long as your heart is beating, so is mine."

I tried to forge a brave expression on my face. "I love you."

Jared's eyes grew soft and the corners of his mouth moved upward. "I love you. I'll see you soon."

Claire gently rested her warm hands on my shoulders as we watched him pull from the curb and then disappear around a corner down the street.

I felt my insides wrench. "Tell me he's going to be all right."

Claire turned me to face her and grinned. "I wasn't overdoing it, earlier. He will come back. And if they piss him off, he'll come back with a few demon notches in his belt. Jared doesn't know how to fail."

We walked upstairs and I sat on the couch, trying to relax so Jared wouldn't be distracted by my fear.

Claire sat beside me, fidgeting.

"You want to watch a movie?" she asked.

I slowly turned my head toward her in disbelief.

"You want to watch TV?" she asked, leaning over to grab the remote from the coffee table.

"No," I snapped.

Claire blew her bangs from her face and sat quietly beside me for a while. After a long, awkward silence, she took in a deep breath of air.

"I was a daddy's girl," she mused. "When we used to go on vacations, tagging along with your family, of course, I'd get so jealous when my dad would compliment you or even mention your name. When he would be away, with Jack, I would get so angry that you were spending time with him instead of me. My mom would try to explain, but...to a little girl that would rather be with her dad than at an amusement park, I refused to even try to understand."

Claire's eyes darkened. "When Jack died...I hated him," she swallowed. "When my father started feeling weak just an hour later...I hated you. My Dad was an Archangel. I never thought I would lose him. He was lying there, fading away, and all I could think about was that I had all of this strength, this speed, the intelligence...I was built to be a savior and I couldn't save my own father.

"As hard as it was for me, Jared took it harder. When Dad took his last breath, I thought Jared was going to die with him," she closed her eyes and a tear fell down her cheek.

"I was angry with him at first. I felt betrayed that he went to you. Now I see that he didn't have a choice. You were the only hope he had left...you were the only one that could make sense of his purpose for existing, and he needed you. He needed to know that our lives were worth something. I can see that now, and I'm glad you have each other."

I didn't realize my mouth was open until she looked at me with wet eyes and chuckled.

She scooted closer. "I shouldn't have hated you. My father loved you like family and it was just as important to him to keep you safe as it was any of us.

It didn't mean he loved me any less, I know that now. I'm sorry for the way I've treated you."

I wanted to hug her, but thought better of it. To my surprise she clasped my hand between hers.

I shook my head. "I owe you for so much—for the time away from your father, for my life...for Jared. You don't owe me anything."

A warm smile spread across Claire's face and she squeezed my hand. "So we'll start over."

I started to speak but her eyes widened, and in the same second she stood with her back to me. I peeked around her to see the door slowly open, and for one fleeting moment I expected Jared to walk in.

But it wasn't Jared.

A man in a charcoal-grey suit and tie strolled in through the door, looking around as if he were appraising the loft. When he smiled at me, Claire's hands balled into fists at her sides, and her knuckles turned white under the pressure of her grip.

He was extraordinarily handsome, teeth gleaming white, black hair perfectly trimmed and slicked back. At first glance he seemed benign, but I recoiled when his black eyes bored into mine.

"How wonderful to see you, Claire," he spoke, a low hissing sound underlying his voice.

Claire reached down and gripped my shirt in her fist, slowly pulling me up behind her. "You just missed Jared, Shax." Claire said.

My blood ran cold. A Duke of Hell was standing just feet from me in my home. I gripped Claire's arm and she reached around to pull me against her back, slowly sidestepping until we were standing exactly between the kitchen and the front door. Shax watched us shift with his shark's eyes, as if he were alert to our every breath.

"Jared is looking for me?" he said, dropping his chin to look straight at Claire. "How interesting."

The iron stairs clanged with heavy footsteps, and five men encroached upon the doorway. Shax took a few casual steps forward as the men positioned themselves in a half-circle behind him. I dug my fingers into Claire's arm when I saw a familiar pair of eyes. It was Grahm.

"Nina," he nodded with a smug smile.

"You take one step near her and you're a dead man," Claire seethed.

A wicked smirk twisted Shax's mouth. "Now, now, Claire. That's no way for a young lady doing His work to behave."

"What do you want, Shax?" Claire snapped.

The demon looked down, and then his eyes shot up to target me from under his thick, black eyebrows. "I think we all know what I want, Claire. Nina's father took something from me," he tilted his head and stretched his long neck, "it's quite an embarrassment for a thief to be stolen from—especially the greatest thief that's ever lived."

Claire laughed without humor. "You've never lived, Shax. It's nice to see that you've developed some humility."

"I want the ring, Claire," he hissed.

"You don't need the ring. Jared has your stupid book."

Shax's beady eyes narrowed. "Where is he?"

444

Claire shrugged, slowly pushed me back as she took a half-step forward. "He took it to you. I'm sure he's in your building as we speak."

"Why would he do that?"

"He didn't want a filthy demon for a house guest," Claire growled.

Shax eyed me with curiosity. "Or was he trying to avoid us coming near his Taleh? I understand he's fallen in love with her. How precious."

"You can leave, now," Claire said, more of a demand than an offer.

Shax's crooked mouth pulled up into a half-smile. "Thank you, Claire. We were just on our way out, and we'll be taking Nina with us. Jack owes me that."

"And I owe Jared one," Grahm said with a smirk.

"I'll rip out your throat before I'll let you touch her!" Claire snarled. The guttural sound that came from her throat when she spoke was frightening.

Grahm signaled his men, and they walked cautiously past Shax. Claire gestured behind her for me to stand back as she crouched slightly, set to defend me. One of the men lunged at her, and so quickly that I missed some of her movements, she incapacitated him without effort. The second man tried to swing at her, but she jerked to the side just as two other men rushed from the side. I took a few more steps back as I watched her head butt one of the men, blood spattering in the air, and then strike another in the throat with her fist. The man made a horrific gurgling noise before falling to the ground.

Just as Claire turned to face Shax, Grahm pulled out a gun and held it to Claire's forehead. She froze.

"I was just going to take Nina, but I think it would better settle the score if he came home to see your sweet face blown away and a little note to let him know we're violating his girlfriend in a hundred different ways before we kill her."

I felt my legs disappear, and I reached back to steady myself against the table as Grahm gave me a lewd once-over with his eyes.

Claire smirked. "You'll fit right in where Jared's going to send you, Grahm."

Grahm cocked his weapon, and I felt a solitary tear seep from my eye and trickle down my cheek. Time passed in slow motion as I looked at Grahm's arrogant expression and then back to Claire. The scene was surreal: Full grown men sprawled on the floor in pools of their own blood, and tiny Claire, a fair-haired teenaged-girl moments away from execution. I held my breath as I watched her slowly close her eyes and wait for the bullet to leave its chamber.

In the same second that Grahm's finger pressed against the trigger, Claire's body blurred. The bullet from his gun whirred past me and into the tile above the stove, and Claire rammed her elbow in Grahm's face, sending blood exploding from his nose. The blow sent him flying through the air, landing at Shax's feet. Grahm sat up on his knees, teeth gnashing in pain. The blood pooled in his palms and dripped through his fingers onto the floor.

"Enough!" Shax commanded.

Claire immediately backed up against me. She turned her head slightly, still keeping her eyes on

Shax. "I'm going to hold him off, Nina...you're going to have to run. Jared will find you," she whispered.

"You think you can hold me, Claire? You're nearly human."

Claire smiled. "Maybe so, Shax, but my angel side can still kick your ass."

Shax wasn't amused. He crouched in preparation to attack, and a strange snarl emanated from his chest. Inside his throat, a screech and an animalistic growl intertwined. It was the most terrifying sound my ears had ever experienced. The demon's black irises bled into the whites of his eyes, and I braced for impact.

As if I had blinked and missed a second of time, a dark massive figure stood between us and Shax. Claire's body relaxed and she maneuvered us around him, bringing Shax back into view.

Jared stood in the doorway, glowering at Shax with a lethal expression. Sensing my fear and relief, his attention broke to me and instantly he was at my side, pulling me from Claire's grip to the safety of his arms.

Shax was cautious in the Archangel's presence. "The book is mine, Samuel!" His sinister eyes were wild and shifted between each of us like a cornered animal.

Samuel tossed the book at the demon's feet, just beside Grahm. "Take your blasphemous book and leave from here. In the name of the Most High, I will end your existence if you come near this family again, foul beast!" Samuel bellowed, his voice shaking the walls.

Shax recoiled from the command of the Cimmerian and backed slowly out the door, hissing at his injured minions to follow.

Grahm smiled at me with bloodstained teeth. "I'm going to see you again soon, baby doll."

Jared lunged at him, but Samuel held his hand to Jared's chest. "Let them go," he ordered.

Jared watched Grahm, reluctantly allowing him to retreat with his wounded partners. Claire stood at the entryway and made sure they were gone before she closed the door.

"Has anyone told you that you have excellent timing?" Claire asked, smiling at her brother.

"Once or twice," Jared said.

Claire ran towards Samuel at full speed, leaping up to wrap her arms around him, her legs dangling two feet from the ground. I jumped at the sudden movement, but when Samuel hugged her and a wide smile flashed across his face, I sighed in relief.

"I think you missed your calling, little girl. You were meant to be Cimmerian," he chuckled.

Claire giggled and squeezed his neck. "I'm half human so it evens up the odds, Sam. If I were Cimmerian, you'd be out of a job."

Samuel bellowed a laugh and shook his head. "And you accuse Shax of lacking humility!"

Jared turned to me. "Are you all right?"

I didn't want to lie, so I remained silent.

Jared pulled me into his chest and kissed my hair. "It's over."

"Not according to Grahm," Claire said after Samuel set her on her feet.

"It's over," Jared said in a firm voice.

448

Claire wiped the blood from the floor and straightened the furniture. She skipped about, the confrontation and victory making her a tad giddy. I watched her as she hummed an indistinct tune while she cleaned.

An hour later, Claire said her goodbyes to drive to Ryan's hometown as the sky outside faded to deep blue. The loft was as before, the furniture in place, the broken glass hidden in the trash, the blood mopped up and the red stained rags thrown away.

"Are you hungry?" Jared asked, poking his finger through the bullet hole above the stove. I shook my head and Jared turned to face me. "No?"

I shook my head again.

"Nina," he chided. "You've barely said a word since I've been back. Are you sure you're okay?"

I closed my eyes. "I'm fine."

"It's normal to be afraid. Talk to me."

"Just...don't leave me again. Okay? Claire was prepared to defend me with her life, but I was so scared, Jared. I was so afraid they were going to kill me and you would die."

He walked across the room and held my cheeks gently in his hands, raising my eyes to his. "You were afraid to die only because I would?"

I smiled, but my face crumpled around it. "I'm so weak, Jared. I'm just a stupid, weak, human, and that makes you so vulnerable. It's not fair."

Jared chuckled in amazement and shook his head. "Nina...," he breathed out a small laugh, rendered speechless. He leaned down and kissed my lips, his mouth conveying what he couldn't say.

Chapter Nineteen
Saving Grace

Over the next weeks life had returned to normal. Jared and I spent our time painting and rearranging the furniture, and the space metamorphosed from Jared's dark loft to our bright and cheerful home.

I wouldn't have thought to change a thing, but Jared insisted I add a feminine touch. I hung up self-portraits we'd taken of ourselves, bought a new floral comforter, and even picked out new china. Jared regarded the transformation with wholehearted gratitude. There were times that I thought Jared wanted me make the changes so that he had tangible proof that I was, in fact, living there.

A month after I had officially moved in, Jared wanted to celebrate with an evening out. I put on a strapless black dress with red pumps and Jared made the effort of putting on a tie. We walked out to the curb and Jared straddled his Vulcan. I raised an eyebrow, pointedly looked down at my short skirt and then back at him.

Jared laughed out loud and dismounted. "Just kidding."

He walked over to the Escalade and opened the door.

"So, where are we going?" I asked.

"Somewhere new. You'll like it," he said before closing my door.

We pulled up to a dark, brick building. He helped me to the curb and held open a glass door, kissing my cheek as I passed. A small Asian woman greeted us, and Jared grabbed my hand, leading me to a table bearing a beautiful arrangement of pink and white tulips. We were the only patrons in the small eatery and I smiled at Jared as he sat in front of me. The woman walked halfway across the room to a waiter's station to fill our water glasses, and I leaned against the table.

"Are they getting ready to close?" I whispered.

Jared chuckled. "No...I arranged for us to have the place to ourselves."

"Oh," I said, watching the woman bring our water and menus.

Jared uttered something in Japanese to the woman and she nodded, leaving us alone.

"Have I told you how exceptionally beautiful you look tonight?" Jared asked.

"Only four or five times," I smiled. "Thank you."

The woman returned, chattering something I didn't understand. Jared looked to me and then back at her. "No, I think we'll need a few more minutes."

"Are we meeting your mother here or something?" I asked.

"No. Why?"

"I was just wondering...why all the effort? The tie, the flowers, the empty restaurant...the secrecy."

Jared raised an eyebrow. "What secrecy?"

"You were sneaking around the loft earlier. I may be human, but I'm not blind."

Jared's laughter filled the room. "I can sneak past trained assassins, but I can't get anything by you."

"That's because they're not around you every second of the day," I qualified.

Jared smiled, pressing his lips together. "We're celebrating."

"A month of cohabitation. You mentioned that."

"Exactly," he smiled, an edge of nervousness to his voice.

I narrowed my eyes and pursed my lips at his evasive answer, but I let it go. He was obviously having fun keeping it from me.

I chose a dish from the menu that seemed close to my usual. When the waitress returned, Jared ordered in perfect Japanese.

I tapped my finger on the table.

Jared watched me fidget with an amused expression. "Do you have somewhere to be?"

"No, I'm just waiting for the explanation."

He leaned forward. "You're very impatient this evening."

I sighed and leaned back against my chair. "I'm sorry. I just feel a surprise coming on."

"Do you, now?" he teased. "And why is that?"

"C'mon, Jared. I know something's up."

He smiled at the waitress as she brought our plates of food, and I sighed.

Jared led us into conversation about other things as we ate. He had made plans for us to have dinner at Lillian's that weekend. Ryan had returned to spend a few days with Josh, so Claire was in town. I discussed my fall schedule, and we talked about the changes living off-campus would pose. We also decided to call Beth and Chad and invite them to our place for dinner as soon as possible.

"I've always liked Beth," Jared mused.

"Me, too!" I teased, feigning surprise.

"She's always been a good friend to you, but I particularly appreciate the talks she gave you in my favor. She's a smart girl, that Beth," he said, nodding with a smug smile.

I spun the noodles around my fork as I spoke. "There were moments I thought you had her on the payroll. She was very persistent."

"That's why I like her," he smiled. "She knows what's good for you."

"She knew better than I did that we would end up together."

"You didn't think we'd end up together?" Jared asked, looking a bit surprised.

"Well...I wanted to. At the time I didn't think we should," I explained, stabbing my fork into some type of meat.

"I'm glad you got over that," he said, deep in thought. "I don't know what I'd do if...," he looked at me with deep affection. "You make me so happy, Nina."

"You make me happy, honey," I cooed.

Jared raised his brow at my uncharacteristic use of an endearing term and smiled, but his expression changed as his thoughts did. "I know things have happened fairly quickly between us," he grimaced. "Most people would say too quickly, but we're not most people."

"Definitely not," I said. I rolled the broccoli to one side of my plate and noticed Jared's expression twisting to chagrin.

"I should have ordered that without broccoli, I'm sorry."

I giggled. "It's fine, Jared. I can separate the broccoli from my food."

"I just want tonight to be perfect...I'm forgetting things," he said, glowering at the broccoli on the rim of my plate as if it had insulted him.

That one phrase caught my attention. "Why does it have to be perfect?"

Jared shifted uncomfortably in his chair and sighed with relief when the waitress came to refill our water glasses.

"Where was I?" he asked after the waitress left.

I blotted my lips with a napkin. "We're moving too fast?"

"No...I mean yes, that's where I was at, but no, I don't think we're moving too fast," he paused for a moment and then looked warily at me. "You don't think we are, do you?"

I giggled and shook my head. "No." My eyebrows moved in as I watched him get increasingly nervous. "Are you okay?"

"I'm good. I'm perfect. You okay?"

"Yeah...you're kinda freaking me out, though," I turned my head to the side slightly as I eyed him with suspicion.

Jared closed his eyes and then took a deep, relaxing breath. "I'm sorry. I'm just a little keyed up."

"Relax. It's just dinner," I said, reaching across the table to his hand.

"Huh...yeah," Jared said, laughing once at my suggestion, and then looking down at his plate.

"I was thinking St. Lucia for our vacation. They have air conditioners, there," I smiled.

"I'll make the calls tomorrow," he said, distracted.

I pondered that for a moment and then narrowed my eyes. "My mother must pay you well."

"Very well," he nodded.

I rolled another piece of broccoli to the side of my plate. "Well, technically, I pay you well."

"What?" Jared said, freezing in the middle of a bite.

I shrugged. "Well, when Jack died—his estate, his assets, everything...it's mine."

"What? I thought your mother...." Jared shook his head, taken off-guard.

"Oh, she can live there, she can deal with the bills and the taxes and the rest of it until I graduate. I can't deal with it all right now."

"So...you pay me?" Jared asked, grimacing. He didn't seem happy at the idea.

"Why? Do you want a raise?" I smiled.

Jared laughed. "As much as I love my job, maybe I should be paying you." I smiled at his words, and he worked to relax his expression. "So, it's been a month since you moved in. Are you comfortable? Does it feel like home, yet?"

I sighed, looking into his breathtaking blue-grey eyes. "It felt like home before I moved in. You're my home, Jared."

He beamed at my words and reached down into the inside pocket of his jacket. "Nina, there's something I...."

The waitress approached the table and Jared slumped against his chair, looking slightly disappointed. She took our plates and left us alone with the dessert menu.

"Angel Food cake is on the menu," he smiled.

"I'm definitely going to have a slice of that."

I watched Jared scroll over the list of pies, cakes and ice cream. While he searched, I noticed a small, glowing red dot appear over his shoulder and then slowly make its way across the table. I lowered my menu as I watched it hit the edge of the table, and then travel up the bodice of my dress, settling over my heart.

"Huh," I said in a higher, bewildered pitch.

"What, sweetheart?" Jared asked, still looking over the menu.

"There must be someone else in here. They're playing with one of those laser-pointer thingies," I said, still watching it quiver on my chest.

My body jerked, and I felt the world spin in slow motion. The sounds of war impeded the air around me and I struggled to gain my bearings. Glass crashed to the floor, and high-pitched buzzing noises accompanied the staccato of gunfire. My arms and legs felt constricted and heavy, but at the same time weightless; flying through the air, higher and higher. I closed my eyes and tried to sift through the confusion.

Jared's voice called to me from far away, and as his voice grew closer, so did the buzzing and tapping noises.

"Nina!" Jared yelled.

Sitting on the ground with my back to the inside of the waiter's station, time sped up and the noises blurred together. Jared reached above me, and I heard a ripping noise. With one hand he placed a large board behind my back, leaning me against it. He ducked once and called my name again.

"Nina!"

My mind abruptly caught up with the present. Jared had reached across the table the second he'd noticed the red dot, and we flew together under a slew of gunfire to the middle of the room. He quickly righted me and ripped the marble countertop off above us, placing it behind me as a shield.

A hail of bullets soared around us again, and I could hear the waitress screaming from the back in Japanese. Jared yelled something back to her and then turned to me.

The red table cloth had made the journey with us, and I was tangled in it. I covered my head as the next barrage of bullets surged through the restaurant. When I looked up, I noticed a red stain on Jared's shirt that grew larger with every passing second.

"Jared!"

He looked at me with confusion and then followed my line of sight to his shoulder.

"It's fine," he said, shaking his head dismissively. "Are you okay?" he yelled over the breaking glass and gunfire, ducking as he spoke.

I nodded, watching Jared's confused expression turn to concern. He looked down at his thigh and touched his pants.

"Did you get hit in the leg, too?" I asked, ducking with another onslaught of gunfire.

"No...I...," he said, looking back at me. Suddenly his eyes widened and he looked down to my lap, pulling at the tablecloth twisted around me. Finally freeing me from the fabric, he yanked up the skirt of my dress, seeing a bloody mess on my thigh.

"Oh my God, Nina, you're hit."

We exchanged fearful expressions just as the next barrage of bullets ricocheted through the room. My brain registered the pain the moment I saw the wound, and a searing sensation immediately radiated from the bullet hole in all directions.

"You're going to be okay!" Jared yelled over the breaking glass, his face tightening.

The restaurant was being torn apart by bullets. The walls and tables were splintered, the floor covered in glass shards. He pulled the tie from his neck and looped it around my upper thigh, yanking it tight, and then he wadded up the table cloth and pressed it against my leg. The sting intensified as it shot throughout my body, and I cried out in pain.

Jared's face tensed and he lifted his hand from the table cloth, both dark red with my blood. He put more pressure on it and I cried out again.

He shook his head. "I've got to get you out of here."

He kept his hand on my leg as he backed up to the station beside me, and then slowly leaned his head out. He immediately jerked back, narrowly dodging dozens of shots aimed directly at him. Whoever was outside only had to keep us pinned down until I bled to death, and they would succeed in killing us both.

Jared's eyes searched the room in desperation. He scanned the ceiling and walls, and attempted to see what was in the back, ducking at another set of bullets. When more firing resounded, I noticed that those shots sounded different, closer.

I pulled his hand from my leg and pressed my hand on the tablecloth, wincing. "Go, Jared. Find a way out."

"I won't leave you," he said, desperate.

I took in a deep breath, trying to focus beyond the pain. "If you don't, we're both going to die."

Jared clinched his eyes shut and pressed his lips together, the clash of priorities sending him into anguish. He turned to me, his eyes midnight blue.

"I'm going to go straight down the hall to see if there's another way out, and then I'm coming back, okay? I'm going to get us out of here," he promised.

I smiled and nodded, my eyes glossing over. "I know."

He grabbed each side of my face and kissed me on the lips first, and then on the forehead.

More bullets cascaded through the building, and the different pitch of gunfire was just behind us. Jared pulled me close and I flinched at our impending end.

Jared laughed and I looked up, seeing Claire ten feet away, her back against a concrete pillar.

"Thought I'd come join the party!" Claire called to us, throwing a gun to Jared and then situating herself with her rifle.

"I love you, baby sister!" Jared cried.

Claire winked at him. "I told you that you'd figure that out one of these days!" She cocked her gun and then looked up, took a deep breath, and then twisted her body, taking several shots before turning back around to escape the return fire.

She turned to Jared, then. "You've got four in the upper floors of the North building, two behind the dumpster, four each on both roofs, and three on the ground, on your ten, twelve and two. I'll stay here with Nina. You go clean house."

Jared smiled and turned to me. "Hang on, honey. I'll be back in a sec."

"Have a good day at work," I smiled.

Claire tossed him a few more clips of ammunition, and then he leaned into me, his lips pressing hard against mine. "Promise me you'll stay awake."

"I promise," I whispered, and then he disappeared.

Claire was beside me in the next moment, and she immediately pressed down on the table cloth.

"Agh!" I screamed.

"You've got to keep pressure on that, dummy, or you're going to bleed out before we get you to the hospital," she barked, taking a few shots behind us with her rifle.

I closed my eyes and shook my head. "Bitch," I said, laughing when Claire did.

"Open your eyes, Nina! You have to stay awake!" she yelled, patting my cheek.

I widened my eyes and blinked a few times. "I feel nauseous," I said, swallowing.

She looked down at my hand on my thigh, both covered in scarlet. "It's because you're losing so much blood. I've got to cover Jared, but you stay awake!"

Claire pulled a hand gun from the holster on her back and shot several rounds, simultaneously whipping a rifle over her head and stabilized it on top of the remaining wood of our makeshift fort. Staring down her sights, her tiny frame jerked back with each shot as large brass casings flipped out and over, landing all around me.

"Your SIX, Jared!" Claire screamed as she took more shots with her rifle with one hand, and intermittently straightened her head to use her hand gun with the other.

The bullets no longer showered the restaurant as they seemed to be mostly out in the street. Claire repacked her guns on her person and grabbed the back of my dress, pulling me across the floor. She sidestepped down the hall to the kitchen in a crouched position, and I swallowed back the nausea as I noticed the thick trail of blood along the white tile behind us.

She propped me against a cabinet and appraised my condition. "Yikes, you're really pale," she said, leaning back quickly to look down the hall and then righting herself to reload her firearm.

"I feel pale, thanks," I mumbled, my eyes feeling heavy.

"Hurry up, Jared," she muttered, wiping my bangs from my eyes. I noticed, then, that I was sweating, my wet hair matting against my brow.

The gunshots were quieting down outside, with only sporadic shots fired every minute or so. I began to shiver and Claire frowned, concerned with my diminishing state.

The waitress was curled up in a corner across from us. She looked at me with wide, terrified eyes, noticing my leg.

"It's getting quiet," I mumbled.

"That's because Jared has taken care of most of the people shooting at us," Claire said with a contrived smile.

"Where is Jared? Why isn't he back, yet?" I struggled for breath.

"He's coming. Just hang on, Nina," she said, distracted as she checked the hall again.

I needed a more specific time frame. Worried about how much longer I would have to fight to hang on, the question fell short. I looked around the room and it began to blur and spin.

"You're losing too much blood. We have to move," Claire said, pulling me to the doorway. She peered out quickly before leaning back to speak to the waitress, asking her something in Japanese. The woman pointed and nodded, whimpering back an answer.

Claire smiled at me. "There's a back door. We'll pick Jared up on the way...let's go."

"I'll be right behind you," I deadpanned.

With her rifle in one hand, she tossed me over her shoulder with the other. As if I weighed nothing, she carried me down the hall, took a turn, and then stopped for less than a second before issuing a damaging blow with her foot to a heavy steel door.

I could feel the night air cooling the warm blood on my leg, and I breathed a sigh of relief that we had finally escaped into the alley. We had almost made it to the street when Claire froze and lowered me to the ground.

"Rookie mistake, Claire Bear," Grahm said, pointing his gun. His nose was still taped from where she'd shattered it with her elbow.

"Awfully brave of you to come alone," she smiled.

I had seen Claire's smug expression before, but this time it was different. She had an edge of fear in her eyes. She knew that I was running out of time.

Grahm turned to me. "I told you I'd see you soon, Nina. Looks like I'm not even going to have to waste a bullet...you're knockin' on death's door. Such a waste, too," he said, clicking his tongue in disapproval. "I was looking forward to spending some time with you."

I held myself up with my hands, but my arms were quivering from exhaustion. I struggled to keep my eyes focused, and my lungs were having a hard time feeling satisfied with each shallow breath. Grahm was right, but I would fight it; I had to keep my heart beating to save Jared.

"If she dies, Grahm, I won't kill you quickly," Claire said through her teeth, her voice quivering with anger. "You will suffer...for days. Maybe even weeks...Hell will be a sweet relief compared to what I will do to you."

Grahm laughed, pointing his shotgun at me. "I could end her life right now, but I think I like watching you squirm while we watch her die."

I coughed and fell to my elbows, my palms flat on the damp pavement of the alley. The nausea became more of a promise than a threat, and the sweat dripped from my hairline into my eyes. Grahm planned to hold us at gunpoint until my heart stopped beating, and Jared would soon become sick and die. The rage welled up inside me and I gritted my teeth in anger.

I looked up at the barrel of the gun. "I wish I could watch what she does to you, Grahm, you sorry sack of—,"

"Now, now..." he laughed. "Do you kiss your mother with that mouth?"

"Do you even have a mother, Grahm? Or did you just come straight from the bowels of Hell?" I gasped, feeling my life slipping away.

Grahm cocked his gun. "You're sassy, Nina. I like that. Maybe I will show a little mercy...not really my style, but I'll make an exception for Jack's daughter."

I shut my eyes tight and waited, but the end never came. When I looked up, Grahm stood with his back arched, his eyes wide and bulging, staring straight ahead. A string of drool fell from his mouth as he fell forward. Jared stood in his place with a bloody fist.

"Nice," Claire said, lifting my limp body from the ground.

"I ran out of bullets," Jared quipped, taking me from Claire's arms. We surged forward, taking off so fast I thought he had finally sprouted wings.

I tried to focus as he lifted me into the backseat of his Escalade, cradling me in his arms. Claire jumped into the driver seat. "Rhode Island Hospital is closer, right?"

"Yes!" Jared cried. "Go, Claire, Go!"

"I'm going to bleed on the seat," I mumbled.

Jared laughed nervously. "I don't care about the seat...you just stay with me."

"I'm cold," I whispered. My body shivered uncontrollably even against his warm body.

"Claire," Jared warned, holding me tightly against him.

"Two minutes," she said as the SUV jerked with a sharp turn.

"She doesn't have two minutes," Jared groaned.

"Jared?" I called into the dark.

I felt his warm hand on my cheek. "I'm here."

"Jared?" I cried. I was so tired, and I was afraid. I didn't know if I was strong enough to keep us both alive.

"I'm here, Nina. You stay with me, do you hear me?" I heard his voice break. "I've got plans for you."

I felt the Escalade screech to a halt and the door flew open. Jared scrambled from the back, holding me tightly in his arms.

Jared yelled for help, and then a large group of people surrounded me.

"Sir, I need you to put her on the gurney," I heard a woman say.

I felt Jared's warm lips on my forehead and his grip tightened.

"Sir!"

"You promised me," Jared choked. "Keep your promise, Nina."

Jared lowered me onto a hard mattress and his hand squeezed mine before he let go. "I'll see you soon."

I searched for Jared's face with my unfocused eyes as the doctor's and nurses' voices blurred above me.

"Jared?" I called to him.

"You need to leave the room, sir. Sir? You'll have to leave!" I heard as I reached out for his hand with the last bit of strength I had left.

When I rose to the surface again, the early morning sun was peeking through the blinds. I looked over to my right hand that was tangled in Jared's large, warm fingers. His head rested on the hospital bed beside me, his face still and peaceful. It was such an extraordinary sight to see him sleeping, so I let him be. I sat completely still, keeping my breaths even, watching the shadows dance down the wall with the rising sun.

When the sun lit up the room, Jared stirred. His eyes blinked and he lifted his head, looking up at me.

"Good morning," I smiled, running my fingers through his tousled hair.

"You kept your promise."

"I always keep my promises," I said, arching my back against the bed, wincing with the pain that ensued.

His face tensed. "You had me worried there for a while. We lost you a few times."

"Really? I feel cheated. I don't remember a single white light. My life didn't even flash before my eyes."

He pressed his lips together. "Leave it to you to joke about dying."

"Are you okay? When that happens and they bring me back...that doesn't hurt you at all, does it?"

"Don't worry about me, I'm fine," he shook his head both in answer and in disapproval at my question.

"How's your shoulder?"

"Good as new," he said, making a show of patting the point where the bullet had entered.

"Yeah...I think my leg is going to take longer than your shoulder to heal." I looked down, seeing the thick layers of gauze wrapped around it.

He nodded, but his face was pained.

I touched his cheek with my fingers. "What is it?"

Jared shook his head, trying to keep the corners of his mouth up. His smile faded to a compressed frown and his eyes glossed over.

"Jared," I said, trying to think of something comforting to say. I couldn't imagine what he had gone through, letting someone else try to save my life.

He sucked in a breath and held my hand against his cheek. "I thought I lost you...," he cried, his eyes closed, "...I thought I lost you." His voice was agonized, and he groaned as he buried his face into my stomach.

I rested my hand on his head, unsure of what to say. He sucked in another quick breath and wrapped his arms around my hips, pulling me gently to him.

He kept his face hidden against me. "I didn't know what I was going to do...I begged Gabriel to take me at the same time. I didn't want to live a single second without you."

He lifted his face to meet mine, his eyes moist and red.

"I'm fine," I smiled, sweeping his cheek with the back of my fingers.

Jared wiped his eyes and sighed. "This isn't how I wanted to do this, but it will do."

I watched him with confusion as he leaned down to pick something off the floor. He sat up and placed a petite box on my lap.

It was a takeout box from Blaze on Thayer.

I giggled. "Sweet potato fries?"

Jared smiled. "Sweet potato fries."

"For breakfast?" I asked, lifting the lid. It was empty except for a small black box. I looked at Jared, and felt my eyebrows shoot up. He lifted the box and held it in front of me.

"Open it," Jared whispered, wiping his eyes again.

I carefully lifted the lid, revealing a golden band. A large diamond sparkled in the center.

I gasped and looked at Jared.

"I exist for you. And I live for you. And I live to love you," he paused. "Marry me, Nina."

I looked back at the ring, and a broad smile stretched across my face.

Jared watched me as I stared at the glittering diamond. "Will you marry me?"

I looked at him, tears overflowing my eyes. I nodded emphatically and laughed. "Yes."

Jared's smile matched mine, and he took the ring from the box and lifted my hand, pulling the silver band from Corn Island off, and slipping the delicate gold band onto my finger.

He stared at it for a moment in awe, and then leaned forward, touching his lips to mine. I wrapped my arms around his neck, crying tears of pure joy.

Jared smiled, triumphant. "We didn't have to get through the nightmare to get our miracle. You, Nina....you're my miracle. It's always been you."

Epilogue

I subdued my laughter while Jared washed the paint from his hair in the kitchen sink. He'd just finished rendering the bullet hole above the stove invisible; it was the last item on his list of things to remove, replace or repair since Shax's visit just two months before.

Jared was covered in ivory specks, and I found it amusing that he was so graceful and agile; yet he couldn't seem to pick up a paint brush without half the bucket inexplicably appearing all over him.

"What?" he asked, smiling as he scrubbed his hair with a towel.

"You look good in Honeysuckle Beige. I think it's your color," I giggled.

Jared tossed the towel onto the counter and walked to the couch where I rested. "How's the leg? Need anything for the pain?" he asked, crouching beside me.

"It's okay. How's the shoulder?"

Jared grinned at me for a moment and then intertwined his fingers in mine. "Did something happen to my shoulder?"

"Is that like the tree falling in the woods making a sound question?" I asked, watching the large diamond glitter on my finger.

Jared's bellowing laughter filled the room. "Yeah, something like that. Claire will be here soon with Mom. They're bringing over some magazines, catalogs, things like that."

I smiled and ran my fingers through his wet hair. "You keep me fairly entertained."

"They're bringing wedding stuff. Lillian has resorted to harassment to get me to let her come here. I made her wait until you were a little stronger before she ascended the loft with swaths and centerpiece options. I'm afraid it's just given her time to collect more supplies."

"You didn't tell them about the island, did you?" I accused.

Jared squint one eye. "I think I'm going to need back up for that."

"You're letting them come over here thinking we're planning a big wedding? Jared!"

He cringed at my reaction. "It's okay! We'll explain it together."

I rolled my eyes and nervously twisted my engagement ring around my finger. "If I can tell Cynthia I'm getting married before I graduate college, you can tell your mom we're going simple."

Jared looked down and smiled. "You used to do that with Jack's ring. It's funny to think this time last year I would smile when I'd see you fidgeting with the Peridot. Now you're twisting your engagement ring around when you're nervous. It's very....surreal," he mused.

"Tell me about it," I grumbled.

Jared nodded once. "Cranky when planning weddings...check."

I pressed my lips together, trying not to smile.

Jared pulled my hand to his lips and kissed my fingers tenderly. "It will be fine. I promise."

The sheer white curtains swayed lazily back and forth with the summer breeze. The walls of the loft were now in beiges and whites, and when the sun filtered through the windows, everything seemed to glow. Light seemed to engulf Jared, and I smiled at the halo it created around him. His eyes were a soft blue-grey, cloud free since he'd brought me home from the hospital.

Seconds later there was a knock at the door. Claire, Lillian and Bex walked through, arms full of sacks and thick catalogs.

Jared smiled at the sight of his family, and then laughed when he turned to see my overwhelmed expression.

"Be brave, sweetheart. Show no fear," he whispered into my ear before affectionately greeting his mother.

"Nina!" Lillian gushed. "You look so much better, honey. You had us so worried!"

Claire set white sacks on top of a hot pink duffle bag while Lillian straightened a stack of bridal magazines on the coffee table.

Lillian smiled as she looked around the room. "Oh... Oh! I just love what you've done in here! It's so light and peaceful! I've been telling Jared for years to brighten this place up and you manage to talk him into it within weeks!" She winked. "That a glrl, Nina."

"He practically forced me to choose a new color palette and shop for new décor. He was sure I didn't like it before." I smiled warmly at Jared who watched me with a soft expression.

"New color palette and décor?" Bex snorted.

Jared lunged at him and wrestled him to the floor, putting him in a headlock and rubbing his knuckles against Bex's head.

"You'll understand one of these days, punk," Jared said, laughing.

Laughter filled the loft as we watched them wrestle on the floor. Bex made an impressive effort, but he was unsuccessful in escaping Jared's grip. Jared finally stood up, bringing Bex with him by the collar. Jared hooked Bex's neck with the crook of his arm and squeezed, and Bex threw his arm up and over his big brother's shoulder.

"Have you seen this one, Nina?" Lillian asked, grabbing a magazine from the top of the stack. She licked her thumb and flipped to an earmarked page.

The picture was of a woman standing on a beach, the bright blue sky and azure waters behind her, looking quite bored and desperately in need of a meal. She wore a bright white V-neck dress, clinging to the edges of her shoulders. The bodice was gathered from shoulder to the silver beaded empire waist. The chiffon and silk dropped straight down into a flowing A-line skirt.

"It's perfect," I said, sighing over its beauty.

Jared peered over from the end of the couch and Claire covered his eyes with her hand. "You can't look!"

"Well, you're going to be easy to shop for!" Lillian giggled. "Does your mother have any favorites?"

"Cynthia doesn't...do weddings," I said with a smirk.

Jared pulled his sister's hand from his eyes and smiled at me. "You like that one?"

"Well, I'd have to try it on."

"Oh my, you will look so beautiful in that dress, Nina." Lillian said as she hugged me to her, kissing the top of my head.

"Does it go with a small white chapel on a tiny island off Nicaragua?" Jared asked.

I looked up at him, trying to keep the corners of my mouth from turning up. "I think so."

"What?" Lillian asked, looking at Jared with a confused half-smile.

"When we went to Little Corn during Spring Break, we found a little chapel on the island. That's where the ceremony—the very small ceremony—will be. It only seats about fifty...possibly less."

Lillian looked at me with surprise.

Claire gasped and then laughed, her mouth formed into an 'O'. "You are so dead, Jared!"

"A Nicaraguan island?" Lillian said softly. "Okay... we'll make it work," she said with a sweet smile.

"You have to take a boat to get there, Mom," Jared added.

Lillian looked at Jared and then at me, trying to find words. "Wedding guests taking a plane to Nicaragua, and then a boat to a tiny island with huts for accommodations," she thought aloud.

I shut the magazine as Jared walked over to his mother, patting her shoulder. "It gives us a good excuse to keep the guest list to a minimum."

Lillian's eyes brightened. "There's always the reception," she chirped, thumbing through another magazine.

Jared laughed at his mother's unfailing optimism.

473

Lillian hugged me again and stood up, hooking her arm around the shoulders of her youngest son. "Bex has an early training session in the morning. Let me know if you need anything, Nina. I love you both," she smiled.

Claire shook her head at her mother with amused affection and then looked at me. "She lives for this stuff."

"Don't think you're going to get away with anything like this, young lady," Lillian called to Claire. "Plan on a ridiculously lavish church wedding, now."

Claire waved to her mother, and I could see her expression turn to unease as I looked down to flip through more pages of the magazine.

"What is it, Claire?" Jared asked.

"We left a few loose ends at the restaurant. Those men are loyal to Grahm, Jared."

After several moments of silence, I looked up. Jared's expression was impatient. "This could have waited."

"I disagree," Claire said in a concerned tone. "Bex will be watching Ryan for me. I won't let them come after Nina again." She looked at me with a maternal softness.

"What do you plan to do?" I asked, feeling a twinge in my chest.

"I'm going to find every person involved, every enemy of Jack's, every cop that is willing to avenge Grahm's death...and I'm going to eliminate the threat." She looked at Jared. "It's what Dad would have done."

Jared looked at his baby sister with an appreciative smile. "When?"

Claire walked over to the table and unzipped the hot pink duffle bag. Within seconds, she molded a rifle from several pieces and then clicked on the scope, swinging the thick black strap over her shoulder.

"When are you coming back?" I asked, leaning forward in reaction to her apparent departure.

"When the job's done," she smiled, loading her holsters. She lifted her foot to the table and twirled a large knife around her finger, shoving it into a case in her thick, black boot.

Jared rested his hands gently on her shoulders, kissing her forehead. "Watch your six," he said, joining me on the couch.

"Claire...." I said, feeling my eyes gloss over.

She laughed. "Don't be ridiculous. I never miss." Her eyes became unfocused and her expression turned menacing. "They ended their lives when they aimed at my sister."

She pulled her sunglasses over her eyes, and her straight, platinum bangs fell over the top of the rims. Walking to the door, she gripped the strap of her rifle with one hand, and twisted the knob with the other.

"Gotta go to work," Claire smiled wickedly, and then shut the door.

Acknowledgements

Thank you is not enough to say to my amazing mother Brenda, for a lifetime of love and encouragement, and to my daughter Eden and Hailey for hugs, kisses, and patience when Mommy was on a roll;

My best friend/sister/cheerleader Beth for inspiration, endless enthusiasm, support, and encouragement, and for being–without fail–overly confident that good things would come;

My friend Lisa for swinging her pompoms after every chapter, and without whom this book might not have been finished;

My editor Ginger Hunter, who spent an entire summer turning the pages of Providence with a red pen so that it would be a novel instead of a good try;

To Trisha Johnson of Shutter Full of Dreams Photography for working pro bono on a tight schedule, and for answering without so much as a dramatic pause;

To Dr. Ross Vanhooser, whose knowledge, trust, and support has been invaluable;

Last, but certainly not least to Wanda Bookout, Chad Petrie, Jimmy Dean Hartzell, Kyra Bright, Erin Androulakis, Gregg Burlison, Shelly Stutchman, Jimmy Rivera, Larry Harris, Orlin and Terry Harms, and Jeff and Bobbi Washburn for their selflessness so that I might succeed.

Jamie Mc Guire graduated from Northern

Oklahoma College with a degree in Applied Science in Radiography, and lives with her two young daughters in Oklahoma. Her website is www.jamiemcguire.com. She is now a full-time, independent writer, currently working on the third and final installment of the Providence trilogy, Eden. She has also written Requiem, book two of the Providence series, and best-selling contemporary romance novel Beautiful Disaster.

Made in the USA
Lexington, KY
04 January 2013